TORN VEIL

TORN VEIL

SHARI T. MITCHELL

Dedication

For Finnegan and Pip, my ever-loyal international dogs of mystery. I love you to the moon and back x 3.

Gramma Bea, I've left a copy open on my desk for you to read when you're ready to come for a visit.

Prologue

...but sometimes you have to swim through the darkness to get to the light.

-CHAPTER ONE-

Monday, December 7th

Meandering footprints marred the snowy path leading to a quaint chapel in St. Michael's Cemetery. The chapel was covered with straggling and decayed reminders of last summer's lush and vibrant ivy. The harsh, clanging echo of a shovel striking frozen earth broke the silence of the early morning calm.

The Collective, a group of six men and seven women, clustered around the wielder of the shovel, watching his progress. His every breath huffed with the labor of trying to break the frozen ground. He steamed white puffs into the cold winter's air as he exhaled. He drew in a sharp breath of relief as the shovel finally broke through the hardened earth. Each slice of the shovel into the ice-encrusted ground reminded him of the sound of a knife blade going through skin and hitting bone. He grimaced at the thought and pushed his flashbacks of war to the back of his mind. He clenched his cold hands around the handle of the shovel and continued his work like any good soldier would do.

He had doubts about whether this was the correct thing to do, but they had taken him into their sanctuary when he'd arrived in Creekwood. They had fed him, given him clothes and counseled him. They had prayed for him and with him. They gave to him when so many others had taken away. He could finally help them, and so he did; digging a hole in the frozen earth so that their work could begin seemed such a small price to pay for their kindness. Hushed voices broke the quiet of the winter's dawn. He heard plotting and scheming in the hissing voices around him. The tone of the conversation dripped with acid, and he quietly prayed for them and the souls against which they plotted and schemed.

When the hole was three feet deep and three feet in diameter, The Collective moved closer and peered into the hole. A small, round woman with cropped red hair, a sour face and a prominent birthmark over her left eye pulled a small cloth sack from her enormous handbag. Alice opened the sack and took out pictures of Carl Parkins and Marnie Reilly. She placed the pictures into the hole. Next, she removed two vulture feathers from the sack and placed them atop the pictures. She sprinkled some of the frozen earth over the top and then dried leaves of water hemlock and a scattering of rock salt. Last, she added a dead rat with six black feathers from a crow piercing its chest. Alice stepped back and motioned for the other members of The Collective to complete their tasks. One by one, they picked up handfuls of dirt and, in turn, threw their dirt into the hole. When the hole was filled, Alice stepped forward and jabbed a sprig of holly wound with a sprig of mistletoe and a sprig of water hemlock into the earth. Alice stood back and looked at the first step of the ritual that they were creating. The final step in the ritual is always a chant, and so it began:

"The divine power of The Collective, gathered in glorious quest,
Emblazons power on hallowed ground and scavenging pest.
Your duty is to abolish those we distrust!
Accept your burden, and make it just!
We beseech the Holy Spirit for absolution;
Protect our souls as we deliver retribution.
So it shall be!"

The Collective held hands in a circle around the small grave, chanting as the sun peeked over the hill of St Michael's Cemetery.

Alice tied her scarf around her red, chubby face and flashed a satisfied smile. "Well, then, by Christmas we won't have to worry about Carl and Marnie damaging our reputations anymore. God will protect us. He will keep us safe."

The man who had just dug the hole moved to the inner edge of the gathering. He turned slowly and watched the expressions on the faces of the members of The Collective. He stopped when he reached Alice and anxiously said, "Ma'am, I d-d-don't understand w-w-why you w-w-want to hurt these p-p-people. Carl was kind to me, and I thought you all liked him. Didn't h-h-he help you, too? Didn't he help y-y-your c-c-clients?"

Alice shook her head dismissively.

"We don't want to hurt them, Patrick. We want God to teach them a lesson. Carl has left our group to work with Marnie. She mocks us, calls us names and steals our customers – well, our clients. She has spread horrible rumors about us over the years."

Alice paused and looked up into Patrick's face, searching for his understanding and acceptance.

After a few minutes, she continued, "We helped her, Patrick, just as we helped you. She has taken our love and kindness and thrown disdain and disrespect at us in return. She has taken Carl away from us, too. Carl was a very important part of our team. His work brought money to The Collective. He helped us pay our bills. He helped us take care of people like you. We need to find another source of income now to continue our good work. We want to help people like you and others who are tormented by pain and spiritual hunger. We need a new energy healer to ensure that money flows and that we, The Collective, prosper."

Alice stepped back and turned to the others for confirmation.

As they all stood beneath the rising sun, nodding in agreement with Alice, a crow flew overhead and cawed at them. Patrick looked toward the crow, flinched and shook his head fretfully.

"That's a b-b-bad omen. What you have d-d-done h-h-here is wrong. You should n-n-not have d-d-done this." Patrick nervously searched the faces of the people in the group – eyes darting from person to person. He wrung the hem of his camo jacket in his hands, and he leaned into the group and whispered, "God will p-p-punish y-y-you for this." As he searched the faces and saw no remorse, his voice grew louder and stronger and he shouted, "G-g-god will p-p-punish you. God will punish you. God *will* punish you!"

Patrick stood with defiance in the center of the group. The dull expressions on the faces that looked back at him told him it was futile to believe that anyone in The Collective would regret their actions. He crushed the hem of his jacket with trembling hands and anxiously retreated a few steps.

"I have seen evil and hatred in my life. I have seen people killed and maimed and destroyed out of hatred. So much evil, b-b-but n-n-nothing that compares to the evil I-I-I see in front of me. Your souls are empty… d-d-dark… sick – all of you. Empty and d-d-dark and sick," Patrick lamented, turning slowly and purposefully to address everyone in the group.

"Hang on just one minute, Patrick, and you listen to me," Alice chided, anger reddening her face under her twisted brow.

"No!" shouted Patrick as he turned quickly and ran down the path, covering his ears as the crow flew over again and cawed.

Alice turned to the group and ordered, "Someone run along and get Patrick. Who knows what that idiot will do. That boy's behavior, well, we never know when he might explode, PTSD and all." Alice rolled her eyes.

A tallish, skinny man with a sallow complexion and beady brown eyes hidden behind huge eyeglasses, Allen patted Alice's chubby shoulder reassuringly. He bent close to her ear and spoke quietly. "Don't worry. Patrick is a harmless soul. He won't do anything to hurt any of us. He has his mental exercises; Carl made sure of that. We've taken care of him. He's as loyal as a Labrador. Of that, I am certain."

Alice scowled and shrugged away from Allen's reassuring pat. "That boy isn't harmless. He's a train wreck waiting to happen and we're sitting on the railroad crossing with no gas," she replied sharply.

Allen turned to watch Patrick running away. He touched his bicep lightly and truly wished that he'd put a nicotine patch on this morning. It was going to be a long day.

"Alice, let the boy go. He'll be back in time for lunch. He never misses a meal. He's just like a Labrador. He'll be back," Allen assured her.

Alice watched Patrick disappear down the snowy path and knew that Allen was probably right, even though she'd had a nagging feeling since she woke up that morning – about what, she didn't know. It was just there, nagging at her. It was true. Patrick never missed an opportunity to eat. She let that thought settle for a moment, and a small smile came to her lips. She gave a slight nod. He would be home for lunch, and the doubt crept back in, replacing her smile with a pained grimace.

~~~~~~~~~~~~~~~~~~~~~~~~~~

Patrick halted sharply, glanced quickly up the road to see if anyone was chasing him and looked up to the sky. He saw the huge crow soaring toward him and land softly on a long granite tombstone. Patrick stepped off the path and studied the crow as he preened his glossy feathers with his yellow beak under the rising sun. The crow turned his head and peered directly at Patrick. Patrick eased forward gingerly to read the stone.

"Colin Reilly and Sophia Reilly
Loving Parents of Marnie and Sam"

He continued reading the poem that followed.

The woods are lovely, dark and deep,
But I have promises to keep,
And miles to go before I sleep,
And miles to go before I sleep.
-Robert Frost

He studied the tombstone and crinkled his forehead. He took a small step back and murmured to the crow, "Marnie? Marnie Reilly? This is a sign, right? You've given me a sign, haven't you?"

The crow ruffled his feathers, cawed, spread his wings, and flew away. A northern wind swept through the cemetery and whistled through the tall pines and the bare, leafless branches of the trees.

Patrick shivered and pulled his gloves out of his coat pockets. His hands were cold, his ears hurt, his eyes were teary, his feet were numb and his nose was running. He stomped his feet to get some feeling back, shoved his gloves onto his hands, wiped his nose on the back of a glove, turned toward the path and ran as if the devil himself was following him. He had to get to Creekwood. He had to find Marnie Reilly and Carl Parkins. He had to warn them – of what, he wasn't sure.

-CHAPTER TWO-

"Come on, Tater. Get a move on!" Marnie Reilly gave Tater's lead a light tug. Her rough-coat black-and-white Border Collie, Tater shot her a quick, distracted glance and continued snuffling through the powdery snow. Sniff, sniff, sniff and then head up, still and watchful. Ears perked up, listening, alert.

"Tater, it's 6:15. It's cold. It's dark, and I need to get to the office. Come on, buddy. Move it!" Marnie scolded softly.

Tater turned and walked slowly to Marnie's side. He sat, looked up at her and patted her leg with his paw. Marnie bent and unclipped Tater's lead so that he could run off some energy on the last leg of their morning jog.

"You are a cheeky brat, Tater. Let's go get breakfast."

Marnie and Tater jogged through the moonlit woods and headed to the cabin as light snow fell around them. The woods and its creatures were just waking up to a fresh dusting of snow. A doe stood stock-still on the path ahead, and a rabbit snowshoed out of the undergrowth and into the clearing. Tater turned his head sharply, but he continued trotting at Marnie's side along the path to the cabin.

There was something about this time of year. Thanksgiving was just over; holiday parties were in full swing, and Christmas was on the way. Marnie's brain raced with the myriad of things that she had to do over the coming weeks, and her thoughts drifted to another topic entirely – a tall, intelligent distraction. He annoyed her. Detective Daniel Gregg was the most infuriating man whom she had ever met, and truth be told, she kind of liked that about him. He challenged her.

She stopped running when she saw Danny; he was shoveling a small bit of the driveway just outside the big garage door. He was a bit of a neat freak about shoveling the snow into even piles on either side of the garage. Danny was also pedantic, and that was another thing that she actually liked about him. It annoyed her, but it certainly wasn't a deal breaker.

Danny was an oddly handsome man. His dimpled smile didn't quite go with the rugged face that wore well laugh lines and the slight crinkle of crow's feet. His thick, sandy brown hair was often slightly messy from running his fingers through it when thinking or stressed. He was a tall man, solidly built and some would say a force to be reckoned with when angered or protecting the innocent. His sharp wit and astute sixth sense about people made him a great cop. A steely blue gaze is the second thing that most people notice about Danny. The first is his badge; he wears his gold shield with great pride.

A widower, Danny lost his late wife Sarah several years back to suicide. No matter how Danny tried to forgive himself, just under the surface loomed guilt for not saving Sarah from her deep dive into depression. He lost his mother Carol to depression and suicide, too. He still carried a great deal of guilt because he couldn't save the two women whom he loved dearly. Danny typically steered clear of relationships. Investing emotionally in love was low on his list of priorities – until now. Danny met Marnie while investigating the murder of her ex-lover, Ken Wilder. She annoyed the hell out of Danny, and he had found her to be the most irritating woman whom he had ever met. Her kindness, independent nature, warmth, wisdom, sassiness and beauty won him over, yet she still frustrated him beyond belief.

"What do you think, Tater? Is he a keeper?" Marnie glanced down and tugged gently on one of Tater's ears.

Tater glanced up at Marnie, barked twice, smiled a big Border Collie smile and then ran full speed ahead to Danny.

"You're a traitor, Tater!" Marnie giggled to herself. She called out quietly to the birds and trees, "The canine vote is in, ladies and gentlemen! Tater thinks that he's a keeper, but for the lady… well, folks, the votes have yet to be counted! Tune in next week for the final tally!"

Danny's head shot up when he heard Tater's bark. He clapped his hands and called to Tater. "Come on, boy. It's time for breakfast," he said.

Tater skidded to a stop on the icy path at Danny's feet. Danny stooped to ruff up Tater's fur, all the while watching Marnie walk the rest of the way up the path.

Danny smiled and commented, "Tater seems to be in good spirits this morning. He seems okay today."

Marnie pushed snow around the path with the toe of one running shoe and replied, "His energy seems to be back. At least he's smiling again. It seems to come and go. I could punch my brother in the face for what he's done."

Danny nodded somberly, remembering. Marnie looked out into the forest, folded her arms around herself and shivered as the last few weeks played out in her head.

Marnie's abusive and wealthy ex-lover had been found murdered in the shed in her backyard. She was set up to take the fall for his death. At first, Marnie had believed that The Collective had tried to frame her for Ken's murder. As it turned out, her best girlfriend, Kate Parish, and her brother Sam, whom she had believed was dead, were responsible. Making matters more treacherous, they had tried to kill her when plans hadn't worked out the way that they had wanted. The collateral damage had been two dead police officers, two wounded officers and the loss of her home. Well, the house wasn't lost; she just couldn't bear the thought of living there with the memory of all that spilled blood and death on her doorstep – spilled blood for personal gain. Marnie was thankful that Danny had given her and Tater a place to call home while she searched for a new house.

Kate's involvement had been a hard pill to swallow. Marnie and she had been friends since grade school. They had seen one another through good times and bad. Kate's betrayal was almost worse than her brother's treachery. Marnie and Sam weren't close. The sibling rivalry created by Sam years earlier left Marnie marginally unsurprised by *his* actions, but Kate was different. The bond that they shared had been strong – some would say sisterly. Marnie had believed that Kate always had her back – until now.

Marnie stood motionless on the path – thinking. She was a clairvoyant – a reluctant clairvoyant, but a clairvoyant nonetheless. She had tapped into her gift when the situation had become dire. She needed answers, and with a bit of divine guidance, she had received helpful information from her mother and father who had passed away years earlier. They were on the other side of the veil – the veil between this life and the hereafter. A veil that Marnie protected every day. A veil that she considered sacred. The veil *is* sacred and should never, ever be torn down for personal gain.

The Collective was a group of charlatans. Marnie had spent some time with them years earlier when she had escaped her abusive relationship with Ken. Her friend Carl Parkins, a once brilliant psychotherapist, had introduced her to the group, thinking that she might like to socialize with people who were also spiritual. Marnie soon learned that The Collective had no regard for right and wrong. Everything that they did was for money or favor. They didn't care about the poor souls that they duped. The Collective pulled threads out of the veil every day, fraying its edges with their lies and trickery. They sold hope to people who were searching for answers – people who needed professional help, not a tarot reading or a potion. Marnie left the group and spent her time discrediting them. A successful psychologist, Marnie reached out a hand to The Collective's victims. She did everything that she could, in a spiritual sense, to weave the threads back into the veil and help the souls damaged by The Collective.

Marnie shook her head, clearing away the memory, and said, "Right! Time to move. We need to get breakfast, and I need to get to the office. There's a lot to do."

Marnie, Danny and Tater climbed the steps to Danny's cabin. Once inside, Danny disappeared into the kitchen to make a pot of coffee for himself and a pot of tea for Marnie. Marnie went upstairs to get ready for the day, and Tater scooted under the pool table and chewed contentedly on a bone.

As Danny made coffee and tea, his mind drifted to Marnie; it did that quite often these last few weeks. He shook his head and grinned. Marnie came into his life a month ago when he was investigating the murder of Ken Wilder. He walked into her house on Creek Road on November 9. From the moment that he laid eyes on Marnie Reilly, he knew that everything was about to change – he knew it in his gut.

Marnie Reilly is compassionate, ethical, quirky and loyal – qualities that actually irk some people. She is a force of nature for sure. Tall and athletically built, Marnie's style is casual – she opts for jeans and boots over skirts and heels. Her job calls for skirts and heels – her home life the former. Her straight blonde hair, with hints of strawberry shining through the long layers, falls just below her shoulders. She normally wears it in a ponytail, but Danny loves it when she lets it fall loose around her shoulders.

Marnie is incredibly independent and guarded. People who know her well attribute this to the tragic and untimely death of her mother and, just a few years later, her father. She believes that she can take care of herself. She hates asking for help, and she doesn't let people in easily, but when she does, she expects them to be kind, considerate and honest. She's had her fair share of bad relationships. The worst, or the absolute worst, had been Ken Wilder; he was a cruel and abusive cheater – not a good guy.

The first thing that most people notice about Marnie is her eyes – aquamarine and haunted. Aquamarine is the color; haunted is her gift of clairvoyance revealing itself. The second thing that people notice about her is her undying devotion to her Border Collie Tater. They're a package deal.

Marnie dedicates her life to fixing things – mainly people and stray dogs. She's a psychologist, but she refers to herself most often as a counselor. Marnie is often so busy fixing things for others that she forgets to take care of herself. Does she really forget, or is there just so much to fix that she focuses on other things? Danny isn't sure, but he plans to stick around to find out.

~~~~~~~~~~~~~~~~~~~~~~~~

Marnie crunched through the snow on the way to her office. She glanced up at the sky, thinking to herself that a white Christmas was likely. She could hear the church bells ringing in the distance. Snow fell softly on her face as she walked through town. She stopped for a moment, closed her eyes and breathed in the smells of the season – balsam, wood fires and the aroma of cinnamon and ginger wafting from the bakery. Her cheeks and nose were pink from her walk through the cold of the morning. The falling snow kissed her gently with each falling crystal. Tater stood quietly on his lead next to her, watching with intelligent eyes.

"Ah, Tater," cooed Marnie. She reached down and tugged gently on his ear. "The season of miracles is upon us, buddy. I need to have faith that the heavens will guide us. We just need to listen. Divine guidance is there if we listen with our hearts."

Tater smiled up at her and wagged his tail happily. Marnie patted his head, and they crunched through the snow the remaining few blocks to her office.

-CHAPTER THREE-

Marnie sat at her desk with her eyes closed, her hands resting gently on the papers in front of her. When the outer door opened and the bell rang, she didn't move. She heard them moving through the outer office, their presence comforting. Then she felt them standing in her doorway. She didn't look up. She knew they were there. She could smell their aftershave – both earthy with citrus undertones – the scents complemented one another. These were the scents of the two men whom she trusted most. She sat quietly and reflected.

Detectives Tom Keller and Daniel Gregg watched her for a moment, looked at one another and shrugged.

"She must be meditating," Danny whispered.

"Maybe she's trying to pick something up – you know, energy, from the papers on her desk," Tom said quietly, nodding in Marnie's direction.

"Maybe she's talking to someone," Danny whispered and pointed up with a mischievous grin. "You know, a long distance call."

Tom looked uncomfortably around the room and tried to hide a shiver. He was Marnie's best friend from childhood, and he was always unstrung by her powers.

Danny laughed quietly and backed out of the room, pulling Tom with him when he heard the bell above the door ring once more.

Carl Parkins came through the door, loaded up with packages. He placed the bundles on the floor and smiled at Tom and Danny.

"Good morning, gentlemen. How are we today?" Carl crossed the room and put his hand out to Danny.

Danny shook his hand, but narrowed his eyes at Carl. "Whatcha doin' here, Carl?"

Carl turned to shake Tom's hand. He glanced over his shoulder at Danny and replied, "I've got a meeting with Marnie. We've got a few things to discuss, and I'm dropping off these packages for Toys for Tots. Marnie wants to make sure that the balls stay in the air. Now that Ken's dead, she's decided to ramp things up a bit with the drive."

"Yeah, we know about that, but what do *you* have to do with that?" Danny asked, narrowing his eyes once again.

Carl shifted uncomfortably and nodded toward Marnie's office. "Like I said, I have a meeting with Marnie."

Before Danny could respond, Marnie walked out of her office. She looked around the room and grumbled, "Play nicely, boys. The smell of testosterone is drifting into my office."

Marnie crossed the reception area to the kitchenette, poured herself a glass of water from the dispenser and started going through a drawer in the kitchenette. She frowned and turned to her assistant's desk to find it empty.

"Has anyone seen Andrea?" Marnie asked.

Danny shook his head. "Nope. She wasn't here when we arrived."

Carl nodded and added, "She's at the bakery. I passed her on my way here. She said that you're in a shitty mood and maybe some sugar would sweeten you up." He laughed and poured himself a cup of coffee from the pot in the kitchenette.

Marnie's face clouded. Glancing sideways at Carl, she shot back, "I'm not in a shitty mood. There's a lot to do, and I'm just, um, focused. I'm focused on getting things organized, and I have a full schedule. I'm not in a shitty mood. I'm focused." She wheeled about and stomped back into her office with her water.

"Whoa... that was quick. She's still not coping, is she?" Tom asked, looking from Danny to Carl.

Carl shook his head and replied, "Nope. Then again, I think she's coping more than most people would be. How would you be handling everything that's gone on the past few weeks?"

~~~~~~~~~~~~~~~~~~~~~~~~

Marnie slumped in her chair, contemplating the last few weeks once again. So many lives damaged and all that blood. Marnie shivered and refocused her attention to the papers on her desk and to Tater, who was under her desk.

Tater was quietly chewing on a marrow bone given to him this morning by Danny's grandmother. Gram had stopped in on her way back to her diner from her early morning visit to the butcher. Tater looked up for a minute and went back to chewing his bone. Marnie was worried about him. He hadn't been the same since her brother Sam had tried to choke the life out him a few weeks ago. He wasn't smiling as often, and he was unusually quiet. He typically ran out to greet people when the bell rang over the office door, but here he was chewing quietly under her desk. He wasn't obeying her, and he was distracted on their morning runs.

Marnie picked up the phone to call the vet's office, but was distracted by Danny's presence in her doorway. Her frown from earlier disappeared as she looked up and smiled. He was tall and broad, and his face was the perfect combination of craggy and handsome. When he smiled back, two big dimples lit up his face and melted her heart.

"What can I do for you, Detective?" Marnie teased.

"Well, to start, I was wondering where Tater is? He didn't run out to greet us." Danny tipped his head to the side, scowling slightly.

"Under here chewing a bone your grandmother dropped in for him this morning. He's still not himself. He was fine for a few days, and he seemed okay for a few minutes this morning, but it's like he remembers what happened. I'm worried about him, Danny. I was just getting ready to call his vet." Marnie scooted her chair back, looked under the desk and glanced back up at Danny.

Danny walked around Marnie's desk and peeked under. Tater looked up for a second and went right back to chewing on his bone.

Danny puckered his brow and turned to Marnie. "He didn't smile. Let me get Tom. He always smiles at Tom."

A few minutes later, Tom walked around Marnie's desk, got down on his hands and knees and stuck his head under the desk.

"Hey, Tater Tot," Tom called calmly. "Whatcha doin'? Come on out and see your Uncle Tom."

Tater let out a low warning growl. Surprised by Tater's reaction, Tom withdrew, knocking his head on the underside of the desk. He shot a look of concern to Danny and Marnie.

"Somethin' ain't right there. Tater doesn't growl at me. Never has, even when he's eating. Have you called Ellie?" Tom stood and turned to Marnie.

"I was just about to do that. He's not himself at all," Marnie said wincing. She picked up her phone to call the vet.

Danny and Tom left Marnie to her phone call and went back out to the main office. They heard the bell ring again as Andrea walked in carrying two boxes from the bakery.

"Good morning!" Andrea chimed cheerfully, nodding to Tom and Danny. "Donut, officers?" she teased with a wide grin and put the donuts on the small table in the kitchenette.

Danny acknowledged Andrea with a slight nod of his head and a smile. "Mornin', Andrea. You got a jelly donut in one of those boxes?"

"Yes, of course. Would I get donuts and not have at least one jelly donut for the man who almost always puts a smile on my boss's face? Get in there, and find out what the hell is going on with her. She's been crabby all friggin' morning," Andrea retorted and held out the box to Danny.

"She's worried about Tater," Danny advised. He helped himself to a jelly donut and nodded toward Marnie's office. "She's calling the vet right now."

Tom leaned on the sink in the kitchenette with a bear claw in his hand. Between bites, he said, "I just stuck my head under Marnie's desk, and Tater growled at me. Somethin's not right."

Andrea walked past Tom, gave his cheek a light slap and teased, "If I were cornered under a desk and saw that mug coming at me, I'd growl, too."

She smiled sweetly, turned, winked at Danny and walked to her desk.

"That's like the third or fourth time in the past few weeks that you have intimated that I am a very unattractive man," Tom complained, looking at Andrea blankly.

"You're not unattractive, Tom. I just like messin' with you." Andrea smiled and wrinkled her nose at him.

"Andrea, stop flirting with Detective Keller," Marnie said dryly as she walked out of her office, pulling on her coat clumsily as she went. Tater was following slowly with his head down. "Can you please move my 11:30 and 12:30? I'm taking Tater to the vet right now. He just growled at me, and that's not okay."

Danny helped Marnie into her coat and looked down at Tater. "What's up, pal?" Tater looked up at Danny with mournful eyes and put his head down again.

"I gotta go. Sorry, everyone. Carl? Can we catch up after hours?" Marnie glanced in Carl's direction.

Carl nodded his head and replied, "Yeah. Sure. I'll be around most of the day. We can chat around 5:00."

"Detectives, did you need me for something?" Marnie asked, turning to Danny and then to Tom.

"We'll catch up later. Just need to finalize a few things regarding Sam and Kate. You can have your car back, too. The forensics team just released it this morning," Danny advised.

He took Tater's lead off the coatrack and handed it to Marnie.

"Thanks. We'll talk in a bit." Marnie bent to clip Tater's lead onto his collar. She stood straight, nodded to the room and then left.

Danny turned to Tom with worry written all of over his face. "Tater's out of sorts. She's out of sorts. They're both up at night sitting by the fire, not sleeping. Marnie's barely eating, and she's working crazy hours. They're going out for a run every morning and evening, but they're not settling in. I think that we need an intervention. We need to do something about this. They were both fine on Thanksgiving, and now, well, they're not okay. Everything has sunk in, and they are not okay."

Tom winked at Andrea and Carl and turned to Danny. "You know, there is a solution. Move her out of the spare room and into *your* room, and things might change. All that sexual tension can't be good for anyone."

Danny glared at Tom and shook his head, "Sex? You think this is about sex?! You're an idiot, Tommy. What happens between me and Marnie is between me and Marnie."

Danny's phone began ringing before he could say more.

He answered it curtly, "Detective Gregg."

He listened intently, his annoyance with Tom gone for the moment.

"Yes, sir. We're on our way," he responded.

Danny grabbed his gloves out of his pockets and reached for the door.

Over his shoulder, he scolded, "I've got work to do, and so do you, Detective Keller. We've got a body on the tracks."

Danny yanked the door open, and the little bell rang violently. He looked up and shook his head.

Tom shrugged as he zipped his jacket and headed out the door with a small salute.

Left alone, Carl turned to Andrea. "So, Marnie said you needed my help getting another consult room set up. What can I do?"

Andrea let out a long sigh and nodded to a door at the back of the office. When she spoke, her tone clearly revealed that she was not pleased with Carl's presence in Marnie's life or counseling practice. Carl's previous ties to and involvement with The Collective made Andrea wary of his intentions. Marnie could often be too forgiving; Andrea wasn't. She would make it her personal and professional mission to ensure that Carl didn't have an opportunity to hurt Marnie or her practice.

"Right through that door, Carl. Set it up however you like. I ordered the stuff that Marnie asked me to order, and it's all still in boxes. The desk is old, but it's in good shape. We have a new chair arriving sometime today," advised Andrea, obviously not intending to help him with the setup.

Carl smiled awkwardly and walked toward the door. He stopped abruptly and turned back to Andrea. The situation weighed on him heavily. He knew that there was suspicion – a sense of intrusion with Andrea that he could not understand.

Trying to cut the tension, he offered, "Hey, I'm not here to cause problems. I'm here to help and to get my life back. I don't know or care much what you think you know, but Marnie offered me help and I accepted. Do you think maybe you and I could get along?"

Andrea narrowed her eyes at Carl and threatened, "You do anything to damage her reputation or anything that brings that loony group in here, and I swear to God that I will stomp on you like a bug."

"Oh, so that's it. Andrea, I am not planning to get in touch with The Collective or anyone in The Collective. I've had enough of that life. This is where I want to be. I want to fix my reputation and start doing *good* work again. That part of my life is over," Carl assured and gave a resolute nod of his head. He turned on his heel, walked into the room that would be his office and closed the door softly.

For a moment, Andrea was stunned by his candor and wondered why she might just be starting to trust him. She shook her head and got back to work.

Carl sat on the corner of his desk, contemplating Andrea's distaste for his presence in Marnie's life. He wasn't sure how to win her over. He laughed quietly to himself. Winning people over was typically not a problem for him. Carl was tall and academia attractive. His short russet hair with graying temples and his perfectly groomed silver-specked russet beard and mustache added to his professor-like appearance – things most people found comforting. He'd been told that his deep brown eyes held warmth, empathy, wisdom and a spark of mischief. *Maybe I need to change my look?* Carl looked down at his clothes. Chinos, button-down shirt and suede driving shoes. *Hmm... Nothing sinister about that.*

Carl took his pipe and a satchel of cherry tobacco out of his shirt pocket; he opened the satchel and fiddled tobacco into his pipe. He set the pipe between his teeth for comfort. He wouldn't light it here in the office; he would wait until he went out for a walk at lunchtime. Carl looked around, assessing his work space. He lifted a box of office supplies off the floor, set it on top of the credenza and went to work setting up his new office.

-CHAPTER FOUR-

Marnie and Tater walked down the street to Ellie's office. Tater's steps were slow, soundless. He didn't sniff or lift his leg on anything along the way. He hung his head, barely keeping at Marnie's pace. She stopped several times and looked down at him, but he didn't look up and smile.

When they arrived at the vet's office, Dr. Ellie Nikol was chatting with an elderly man who was holding a cat carrier. The cat looked out from behind the small screen of his carrier and hissed at Tater. Tater stepped back, flattened his ears to his head and ducked behind Marnie, putting his nose between Marnie's legs to peek out.

Marnie reached down, patted Tater's back reassuringly and cooed, "It's okay, boy. The cat can't get you. It's locked up."

Just like they are – Sam and Kate. Both are locked up now, waiting for justice to be done. No reassurance helps me, Marnie reflected. She shook her head and smiled absently at Ellie.

What a lovely friend she had in Ellie. Ellie loved animals and had the most beautiful nature. She was tough but kind, and her kindness showed in her cute face. She was medium height, athletic in frame. Her short brown hair had streaks of ash blonde running through it, and her light hazel eyes twinkled.

Marnie loved spending time with Ellie. They always laughed when they were together, and no one could pull her into line better than Ellie.

As the old man and his hissing cat left, Ellie shut the door, gave Marnie a quick hug and looked down at Tater.

"How are you, Tater Tot? I hear you've had a rough few days. Let's take a walk back to my office and see if we can figure it out." Ellie took the lead from Marnie and gave Tater's back a firm stroke.

Marnie followed and sat on a chair in Ellie's office. Ellie sat in her desk chair, put on her reading glasses and opened Tater's file.

"Okay, from everything you told me on the phone, poor Tater here, in my humble opinion, has had a shock and is adjusting to a whole lot of change." Ellie looked at Marnie over the top of her reading glasses.

"Uh, yes. I would say that's about right." Marnie nodded.

"You told me earlier that you're not staying at your house. Right?" Ellie asked.

"Right. We're staying with Danny Gregg at the moment. He knows that I don't want to be at the house after everything that happened, and he's letting me use one of his spare rooms," Marnie replied, shifting in her chair.

"You could've called me. We would have made room for you at our place," Ellie said, giving Marnie a sideways glance.

"No. You and Julie have enough on your plates with her kids and your practice. It wouldn't have been fair. Besides, we're comfortable at Danny's. It's a nice big cabin in the woods right off Lake Road. It's lovely." Marnie looked down at Tater and asked, "Isn't it, buddy?"

Tater flopped down on the tiled floor and looked up at her with sad eyes.

"He's not happy, Marnie. Look at him. He's miserable. You've taken a pack animal who has had Beta status for years and knocked him down to Gamma. His routine has been disrupted, and he's sharing you with a man. Plus, your brother tried to choke the life out of him a few weeks ago," Ellie commented matter-of-factly and wheeled her chair over to the exam table.

The exam table was low to the ground – perfect for dogs like Tater. Ellie knew that dogs could be intimidated by so many things in a vet's office, and she wanted her furry patients to be relaxed for exams. The dog's comfort was paramount in her practice.

Ellie slapped her hand on the table and called to Tater as she gave his lead a gentle tug. "C'mon, mister. Step up, and let's have a look." Slowly, Tater eyed the table, leapt up easily and sat down.

Marnie shook her head and responded, "He's not sharing me with a man. It's not like that. We're – um – Danny and me – we are trying to figure out the relationship thing, and Tater and I are only staying there until I can find a new place. It's only been three weeks, and nothing has happened – not that I wouldn't like something to happen – but we're being logical about it. It would be stupid to jump into a full-on relationship while living under the same roof after such a tragic event. It would be stupid."

Marnie realized that she was rambling and stopped.

Ellie stared at Marnie over the top of her glasses again and, with a hint of sarcasm, replied, "Yeah, it would be stupid to meet a gorgeous man and have a relationship with him. Poor you."

Ellie tipped her head at Marnie as she felt around Tater's rib cage and lower abdomen. The dog shifted just once at Ellie's probing hands.

"Well, you need to concern yourself with Tater's diet. The poor boy is constipated. What have you been feeding him?"

"Tater? Constipated? No way! He's eating what he normally eats – kibble and fish. Sardines, tuna, you know the usual," Marnie responded sharply.

"You mentioned to me when you called that he was chewing a bone. What kind of bone?" Ellie asked.

"Uh, a *bone* bone. A marrow bone. Danny's grandmother brings him one most days," Marnie answered.

"Right. Well, has it occurred to you that Tater has never been a beef eater? He's always eaten fish, chicken and vegetables. Suddenly, beef has been introduced into his diet. He can't digest it the same. This happens with a lot of Border Collies. Stop giving him beef bones, make him feel important and he'll be fine. Give him some yogurt and half a can of pumpkin tonight, and take him out for a long walk. It will take care of itself in a couple of days," Ellie prescribed, giving Tater's head a pat.

"That's it?" Marnie asked as she roughed Tater's fur and kissed his head.

"That's it." Ellie nodded. "Now, let's talk about you and Detective Daniel Gregg, shall we?"

"No. We're not having that conversation today. Tater and I are heading back to the office. I have work to do."

Marnie curled her lip at Ellie and put Tater's lead on him. Tater jumped gently off the exam table and stood there looking between his mistress and his doctor.

"Marnie, sit down," Ellie said sternly with raised eyebrows. She pointed to the side chair next to her desk.

"Sit *down*, Marnie. We are going to have this conversation. You need to talk to somebody who isn't Tom Keller or Carl Parkins." Both Marnie and Tater sat, both reluctantly.

Marnie shrugged her shoulders and sheepishly asked, "What?"

"Don't 'what' me. You know what. Take a chance, Marnie. How often do gorgeous, kind men walk through your door? Hmm? C'mon, Marn. Stop protecting yourself and let him in."

Ellie put her hand on Marnie's arm and looked intently at her friend.

Eyes on Tater, Marnie responded, "Who says I'm not letting him in? I am. Slowly, but I am. I think I'm doin' pretty well for a woman who's had relationship train wrecks most of my life."

Marnie scratched Tater's ears and looked down at the ground.

"Marnie, you need to stop protecting yourself. All guys are not Ken Wilder. All guys are not going to treat you like a punching bag, and all guys are not going to try to string you up with piano wire," Ellie responded with less sympathy than she had intended.

Marnie's hand instinctively went to her neck. She felt the scar left a few years earlier when Ken had wrapped piano wire around her neck. The memory rushed back, and she had to count to 10 in her head to push through the panic attack that she felt coming on.

Ellie stood up and walked to a cupboard. She took a small treat out of a bottle and gave it to Tater.

"Doggy laxative. I can't handle that sad face any longer. Take a long walk through the park on the way back to the office. Trust me." Ellie laughed and handed Marnie a plastic bag.

Marnie nodded and confessed, "Look, I know that Danny is nothing like Ken. I get that, but I really just want to take things slow with him. He's a lovely man, and I don't want to screw things up."

Marnie stood and put her hand on the doorknob.

Ellie threw her head back and feigned a growl of exasperation. "Really? Marnie, just sleep with the man. Have some fun. Relax. Let your hair down, literally. Get rid of the ponytail. Let your hair down, girl. Seriously, you are wound tighter than a clock. Poor Tater here is absorbing your stress. I was at the cabin on Thanksgiving. The sexual tension between the two of you hung in the air like... like, well, I don't know like what, but it was there. You two are perfect for each other. Take it to the next level, Marnie."

Ellie patted Tater gently on the rump and slapped Marnie on the backside.

"Get out of here, and don't come back until you've done as you're told," Ellie scolded.

"Don't slap me on the ass. You know how much I hate that!" Marnie gritted teeth and clenched hands.

"Get over it. Go back to work, walk through the park and think about it." Ellie pushed Marnie and Tater out the exam room door.

"I'll call you later and let you know how the little man here is doin'," called Marnie over her shoulder.

Marnie and Tater walked through the outer office to the street and headed to the park.

Even though she knew that she was talking to the door, Ellie quickly shot back, "More importantly, let me know how you and the big man are doin'."

-CHAPTER FIVE-

Detectives Gregg and Keller stood somberly to the side of the railroad tracks leading out of town. They were standing at a section of the track just outside of a nearly collapsed tunnel. This set of tracks hadn't been used in over a year, and according to a recent budget report, it wasn't scheduled to be repaired for a long time.

The man was lying face down in snow-covered gravel. He wore jeans, a belt, a plaid flannel shirt and socks. He had neither a coat nor shoes – no wallet, no identification of any sort. The only things that had been found by the forensics team were a coin and a business card.

The forensic tech handed the evidence bag with the coin in it to Danny and passed the bag with the business card in it to Tom.

The coin was just a bit bigger than an inch around – maybe pewter or nickel, dull and heavy. Wings unfurled, an angel kneeling in prayer adorned one side. Danny flipped it over to find a verse on the reverse of the coin. Squinting, he read aloud:

> *Guardian Angel, protect us all,*
> *Giving strength when we might fall,*
> *Watching, guiding, lighting the way,*
> *Through the night*
> *And every day.*

Danny frowned, turned the bag over a few times and glanced at Tom. "What have you got?" Danny asked Tom.

"You first," Tom replied, dropping his hand with the business card in it to his side.

"Just a coin. A guardian angel coin to be exact," Danny said. "Your turn. What are you hiding there?"

Tom shifted from one foot to the other. He closed his eyes briefly and held out the evidence bag to Danny.

"Shit!" Danny shouted.

The quiet of the crime scene was broken by Danny's shouted expletive, which traveled down the tunnel, echoed and made the patrolmen and forensics team jump.

Danny turned, paced away a few steps and studied the scene from different angles. He walked around the perimeter a few times, looking at the card again with each turn. *Shit*, he muttered to himself.

Tom stood quietly next to him, staring up the tracks to the tunnel. Tom did a double-take; he was certain that he'd just seen something move inside the tunnel. Just a flash of movement. Something gray or red – or both. He shook his head and returned his attention to Danny, who was still turning in circles trying to put the pieces together.

"Hey, guys!" Rick Price, head of forensics, called out to Danny and Tom, "Something here you might want to see."

Rick had rolled the body over thinking cause of death might be an overdose, and he had rolled up the sleeves looking for signs of track marks. Danny and Tom approached and saw several tattoos on the man's arms. Each arm had three tattoos – symbols. All were charcoal tattoos – no color. Danny took photos and stood back to examine the pictures. Tom knelt down and examined the man's arms.

"Is that it? Are there others?" Danny asked.

"None that I can see without undressing our victim here, which is not terribly respectful," Rick replied, looking over the top of his glasses at Danny.

"Yeah. I guess so, but can you check his chest?" Danny asked.

Rick bent over the body and undid a few buttons of the flannel shirt, revealing a large tattoo of the All Seeing Eye.

Danny nodded. "Can you send me pictures of anything else that you find?" Danny requested.

"Sure. We'll get him out of here shortly. We've got three ahead of him, but Dr. Markson should have those finished by the time we get back," Rick replied.

"What are the other three?" asked Danny.

"One's an overdose, one's a drowning and the other appeared to be a heart attack," Rick answered.

"Any of them suspicious? Any tattoos?" Danny asked.

"Not as far as I know. We'll see what Dr. Markson's reports have to say," Rick replied.

Danny turned to leave and caught a glimpse of movement near the tunnel. Something gray or red – or both. He watched the tunnel for a moment and saw that Tom was studying the same area. He saw nothing further, touched Tom's arm, nodded toward the car and walked away with Tom following, muttering to himself.

-CHAPTER SIX-

Patrick needed to find Marnie Reilly. He'd asked around, and when no one could or *would* tell him anything, he went back to The Collective's house and snuck quietly through the back door.

Patrick knew that they'd have information somewhere, and of course, he found it easily in the files in the cellar. The file on Marnie was intriguing. He decided that he wasn't going to leave it with them. He stuck it under his shirt and down the front of his pants, tucked his shirt in and zipped his jacket.

Patrick went back to his room, gathered his things and then walked out the front door. No one was there to stop him. He knew that they were all at Station Hall preparing for tonight's event. He wondered if Marnie would turn up tonight to keep them honest. He hoped not. After what he witnessed today, she was in enough trouble with them.

Patrick thought about making himself a sandwich to satisfy the rumbling in his stomach, but he left, more eager to be away from here.

He wandered into Creekwood Square. The bus out of Creekwood would take him to the top of Creek Road. He looked at the bus – nearly empty; no one would bother him. He gazed up the road. Too long a walk – yes, the bus would do. He thought that Marnie's house should be easy to find. There wasn't much out there.

Patrick boarded the bus, found a seat near a window close to the back of the bus and closed his eyes for a moment. The bus was quiet midmorning. There were only two other people traveling with him, not including the bus driver. In the second seat, there was a young girl of about 10 years old. She had long, thick, brown braids with thick bangs to frame her round freckled face. She wore a purple puffy jacket, red ski pants and purple boots. She was fiddling with her phone and didn't appear to even notice him. Further back, a lump, covered head to ankles under a gray wool blanket, appeared to be a man, considering the boots sticking out into the aisle, but Patrick couldn't be sure. He seemed to be sleeping. Patrick passed both to take a seat near the rear.

Patrick studied the road signs at each stop. He didn't want to miss Creek Road. When the bus slowed down at the fifth stop – his stop – Patrick jumped up, hurried up the aisle, muttered his thanks to the driver and hopped down the steps to the shoulder of the road. The door squeaked shut, and Patrick turned slowly, taking in his surroundings.

Creek Road loomed ahead of him. It was a tree-covered lane, really. There were pines, firs, cedars, spruce, leafless maples, birch, ash and a few others that Patrick didn't know. He walked slowly up Creek Road, stopping every few yards to take in the smells and sights of the forest. He knew that there was water close by; he could smell it. An icy north wind blew up the drive. He shivered, pulled his collar up and continued walking. Patrick stopped at the top of a big driveway and let out a sigh of relief.

There it is. Marnie's house, Patrick thought to himself. *It's the same house in the picture that The Collective has on file. It's beautiful.*

Marnie's house was a large Cape Cod with a sprawling driveway. The forest surrounded the house, and there was a bridle trail to left that looked like it might lead down to a creek or a lake. He stood at the top of the driveway, admiring the house and land, and wandered down the driveway.

It looks like home. It looks like a place that I could call home, Patrick thought, as he walked up onto the veranda and rang the doorbell. He looked around as he waited. He noticed yellow tape flicking in the breeze and walked over to inspect it. It was crime scene tape. Then he remembered the news of the last few weeks.

This is where the two officers were murdered and where Ken Wilder's body was dumped. Alice was talking about this just a few days ago; she was talking about Marnie staying with a friend. He remembered Alice had gestured quotes every time she said "friend." *I think Alice mentioned something about the situation being shameful. Alice sure gossips a lot. She says a lot of bad stuff about people. I can't be around her or anyone in The Collective anymore. I need to get away from them forever. The Collective is trouble. They're all trouble with a capital "T."*

He turned the situation over in his head several times, thought about the rights and wrongs of it and decided his next step. Marnie's house was empty, and it would make a good home base for a short while.

He reached and opened the storm door and turned the knob on the big oak door. *Locked.* He released the storm door slowly, soundlessly. He went around the side and peered through the windows. *It looked cozy and warm.* He tried the side window, and it gave. He pushed hard, and the window creaked in its frame. As he scrambled through the window, he listened closely for an alarm. Nothing. He fell into the living room, stood up and assessed the room. He nodded his head with approval. *This will do for now.*

He went into the kitchen and opened the fridge. There wasn't much in it. No milk, a few eggs, some cheese, pickles, mayonnaise, a few withered vegetables, apples, wine and beer. He looked in the pantry. Bingo. It was fully stocked. There were coffee, tea, canned goods and cans of evaporated milk. He opened a large chest freezer. It was fully stocked, too.

He wandered around the house searching for the cellar door. He needed wood for a fire. A house this size would surely have a wood room and a cold storage room with more food. He settled himself into Marnie's house.

-CHAPTER SEVEN-

Marnie and Tater walked slowly through the park. As they walked past Station Hall, Marnie heard the irritating drone of Alice's voice barking directions at the other members of The Collective. She was fussing about something, walking back and forth, taking things out of the trunk of a car and stacking cartons on the sidewalk as she glowered at the others. Marnie frowned and kept walking.

Alice glanced up, saw Marnie walking nearby and toward them and yelled, "Marnie, get out of here. You've caused enough trouble for us. You are no longer welcome. Leave us alone!"

Marnie rolled her eyes, threw a dismissive toss of her arm and walked on with Tater. Alice picked up a handful of snow, made a snowball and threw it as hard as she could at Marnie. It wasn't a very good snowball or a very accurate throw, but it managed to hit Marnie lightly on the arm. Marnie stopped and shook her head at Alice. *Sad, sad little woman*, the gesture said.

Not getting the response that she wanted, Alice made another snowball and threw it with all of her might. This time, the snowball missed Marnie and hit Tater squarely on the back. Tater shook the snow away and growled. Marnie shot an icy glare at Alice. She walked quickly across the path and stood tall in front of Alice, reining in Tater's lead.

A scattering of The Collective's members watched in silence and gathered closely together on the sidewalk outside of Station Hall to await the heated exchange that would surely ensue. They mumbled quietly to one another and waited for the action to start. They were not disappointed.

"What the hell is your problem, you stupid, stupid woman?! How dare you throw snow at Tater!" Marnie shouted, her eyes wild with anger.

Marnie stood a foot taller than Alice, and confronted, Alice shrank back against her car, pulling her scarf up around her face.

Marnie continued. "I'm going to call the SPCA and report you for cruelty to animals. They'll make your life uncomfortable for a while!"

"Marnie, calm down," soothed Allen. He saw that Alice was losing face with the crowd.

He pushed his way between Marnie and Alice.

"I'm sure that Alice didn't mean to hit Tater. I'm sure that snowball was meant to hit you." Some in the crowd tittered behind gloved mits.

"No shit, Allen. You know what? I'm just going to call the police station right now and have a chat with Detectives Gregg and Keller. I'll file a complaint and make sure that they come and arrest Alice just when she's going up on stage tonight. How would that look to your fans, you little troll?" Marnie threatened and edged closer to Alice.

Alice was now covering her face with her pudgy hands.

Allen reached out and put his hand on Marnie's shoulder, both to ease her back and calm her anger.

"C'mon, Marnie. There's been enough torment. Step back and leave Alice alone. She's still upset with you and your friends for kicking us out of your office a few weeks ago."

Marnie slapped Allen's hand off her shoulder.

"Don't touch me!" Marnie warned.

A low growl started again in Tater's throat. Marnie looked down and saw a snarl forming around his muzzle. She pulled his lead gently.

"C'mon, Tater. Let's go," Marnie said soothingly to Tater and turned to walk away.

No longer threatened by her proximity, Alice shouted, "You're going straight to Hell, Marnie Reilly! Straight to Hell! Living in sin with that detective and threatening people. You're going straight to Hell. The Lord is coming for you, Marnie. He's coming for you!"

Marnie turned around and glared at Alice for a few seconds, then her face softened in pity. Marnie dug deep for her counselor-brain to take over – for just a second – but then it was gone. She took a deep breath. Her voice changed from anger to softness and steadiness, and her eyes lifted so to seem condescending.

"I feel sorry for you, Alice. You need help. You ooze hatred. You have a big black hole in your soul, Alice, and you know what? I'm quite certain that the Lord isn't judging my choices the way you are. You have no right to judge me, Alice, and I have no right to judge you. Why are you so filled with hatred? That's the question that you should be asking yourself. What is it about you, Alice, that makes you hate me so much? What is it about *you*?"

Marnie turned sharply and walked away, leaving a shocked Alice searching for words. Her crowd, uneasy, drifted back and murmured amongst themselves.

Allen placed a hand on Alice's shoulder to calm her down.

"Alice, why do you have to instigate. Why can't you just leave well enough alone?" Allen asked.

Alice shook her head and mumbled, "Marnie Reilly is going to straight to Hell, and I am going to do whatever I can to help her along."

"Alice, you are making things worse for yourself and for the rest of us. Let it go. Let. It. Go," Allen scolded. "I'm heading home for a few minutes to get some lunch and a nicotine patch. Your behavior, Alice, does nothing to help my anxiety. I want a cigarette so bad right now, I... I... I don't know what. Stop looking for trouble, Alice, where there isn't any."

~~~~~~~~~~~~~~~~~~~~~~~

As Marnie walked past the police station, she looked up and considered whether she should report Alice. She shrugged her shoulders and walked up the steps. Sergeant Beaumont was sitting at the duty desk, talking on the phone. When he saw her, he smiled and waved her up the stairs to the squad room. Marnie smiled, waved, pushed through the doors and went upstairs. Sergeant Beaumont had been so kind to her in recent weeks. She and Tater stood at the entrance of the squad room and searched for Tom and Danny. Both were on the phone, so she waited.

Captain Sterling, the commander of their unit, walked out of his office and stared for a moment in her direction. Marnie smiled and stayed where she was. She knew that she wasn't one of his favorite people and was surprised when he waved to her and walked over. Captain Sterling didn't dislike Marnie, but he didn't *like* her, either. He was a bit wary of her gift. He was a nonbeliever and felt that anyone who believed in psychism or the paranormal was a bit daft. Captain Sterling wasn't entirely comfortable with the influence that Marnie had on his two best detectives, either. Both adored her, and it concerned him that she used her "feminine wiles" as a distraction.

Captain Sterling was a barrel of man with a big face, bristly white hair, bear-paw hands and fingers that looked like thick sausages. He carried himself with the confidence of a man much taller than he was, and he had an annoying air of authority – *excessive authority*.

"Ms. Reilly, what can we do for you today? It's always good to see you and Tater. Detectives Keller and Gregg are returning phone calls. Can I get someone else to help you?" Sterling asked.

He stood with his chest out, and he twiddled a pen back and forth between his sausage-fingers.

"No, sir," Marnie replied with a shake of her head.

Marnie hoped that one of them might see her soon. She wasn't comfortable with Captain Sterling. He didn't necessarily make her nervous, but his bluster and officiousness made her the tiniest bit edgy.

"I just stopped in for a moment. I thought perhaps Danny and Tom might like to get some lunch."

Tom glanced up at hearing her voice. He smiled, waved, kicked Danny's chair and nodded in Marnie's direction. Danny looked up, smiled two big dimples in her direction, held up his index finger and mouthed "one minute." Marnie nodded.

Captain Sterling saw the exchange and dryly commented, "Well, it looks like they're nearly done. Have a nice day, Ms. Reilly."

Sterling turned and headed back to his office before she could respond. Marnie watched him disappear into his office and shrugged. This wasn't new. Captain Sterling was always just a bit dismissive of her. Maybe that was it. Maybe that was what bugged her about Captain Sterling.

Tom finished first and walked across the squad room to greet Marnie. Tom's tall lanky frame always made Marnie laugh just a little. He was built like a distance runner, he had short black hair, he sported chiseled features and his eyes were so blue that they were almost violet. He would be handsome if he wasn't Tom. He was cute, though. Marnie knew him too well, and while most women swooned over him, she would always remember him as he was when they were kids. She loved him just the same.

Tom bent down, gave Tater a scratch and asked, "What was Ellie's prognosis? Tater okay?"

"Yeah. Apparently he's not coping with all of the change, and he's a bit constipated from all of the bones," Marnie replied.

She bent down and patted Tater's head.

"I have to watch his diet for a few days and get him back on track. I really need to find a new house, too. I guess that I can start looking this weekend. Wanna go house shopping with me?" Marnie asked.

"Aren't you going to stay with Danny through Christmas and the new year?" Tom asked, raising his eyebrows.

He glanced over his shoulder at Danny, who was just hanging up the phone.

"I'm not sure that's a good idea, Tom. Let's talk about it later, okay?" Marnie replied.

Marnie furrowed her brow and watched Danny pull his jacket off the back of his chair and walk toward them.

Tom put a finger to his lips, nodded his head and went back to his chair to grab his jacket.

"Let's go get some lunch, Ms. Reilly. Hungry?" Danny came to a halt in front of her, stooped to pat Tater and then tugged Marnie's hand gently. Suddenly, Ellie's words and the sting of the butt slap sent a chill through Marnie, and she wished that she had not stopped, the confrontation with Alice no longer with her.

"I could eat, but I really need to get back to the office. I've got client appointments this afternoon and an appointment with a financial advisor. I've got to figure out what to do with the inheritance from Ken, and I need to work through the Toys for Tots thing, too. There's a lot to do," Marnie replied.

"Look, we need to talk to you about something altogether different, but you do know that you don't have to try to do everything by yourself. Tom, Carl, Andrea and I are all here for you, and I think that Ellie would really like to help, too, if you'd let her. You've got a whole squad room of guys who will help get toys sorted out, and I'm sure that we can find some people to do the wrapping. Let's go to lunch, talk about the case we're working and break everything down – make a list and plan. We can get it all done. Don't worry," Danny reassured.

Marnie loved and hated this about him. She knew that he would help and that he would get others to pitch in, too. The biggest challenge for her was to give in and let him. Easier said than done. But there was so much; maybe she could use some help.

"Okay. Let's get some lunch, then I have to get back," Marnie relented with a nod.

"C'mon, Tommy. Let's take this lady out for lunch." Danny grinned, pushed the door open and motioned out the door with his head.

"Danny, before we go to lunch, maybe we should show Marnie what we want to speak to her about. Might be better before lunch rather than during lunch? I know that I don't want my appetite ruined," Tom suggested. Marnie raised her eyebrows in curiosity.

Danny stood with his hand in the middle of Marnie's back, nodded and gave Marnie a small nudge toward an interview room.

Tom, Marnie and Tater walked into the first available interview room while Danny went back to the squad room to get the case files. Tater trotted into the room, circled the table three times and then curled up under the small, gray metal interview table.

"What's going on?" Marnie asked.

"We've got a suspicious death down on the railroad tracks – you know, the tracks that are no longer in use near the old tunnel that's about to cave in," Tom answered.

Marnie gave Tom a long sideways glance.

"Yeah, and what does that have to do with me?" she asked slowly.

"Well, the victim…"

Tom started to respond, but Danny came back into the room with the files.

"Marnie, we need to ask you a few questions about a case we're working on," Danny said matter-of-factly.

"Uh huh. The last time that you had to ask me a few questions, Detective Gregg, you thought I'd killed someone. Let's just not play games, okay? What the hell is going on?!" Marnie demanded.

Tater heard Marnie's voice rise and peeked out from under the table, ears perked and mouth closed tightly.

"It's nothing like that, Marnie. It's just that we found your business card in the victim's pocket. We don't think that you had anything to do with it, but we're just hoping that you can identify him," Danny assured.

"My business card?" Marnie asked. Her eyebrows shot up, and her shoulders stiffened.

She reached a hand out and rubbed one of Tater's ears. Her voice had softened, so the dog sank back and sighed.

"Yup. See here. This is the card that was in his pocket. It doesn't look like the cards that you use now – you know, today – so I thought that it might be an old design." Danny handed Marnie the evidence bag.

Marnie sat down in one of the uncomfortable chairs and studied the business card. Tater stood and rested his head in Marnie's lap.

"I haven't used this card in years. I was certified as a counselor at that time and had just completed my master's, and I wasn't a practicing psychologist yet." Marnie examined the card closely.

"You're a psychologist?" Danny asked.

"Yeah." Marnie turned to Danny and frowned.

"You always say you're a counselor. You never say psychologist," Danny responded.

"You sometimes say you're a cop and not a detective," Marnie challenged. "Potato, potahto!"

Danny's and Marnie's eyes locked as each leaned on the table. Danny clenched his jaw, and Marnie squared her shoulders. Tom rolled his eyes, opened the case file and put a photo of the victim on the table in front of

36

Marnie.

"Okay, Sherlock and Frau Freud, do you think that we can get back on topic, please, or do you want to stand around and talk about your credentials a bit longer?" Tom asked sarcastically. He pushed the photo across the table and closer to Marnie.

Marnie shot a glare between the two detectives and finally studied the photo. Her face lost all color and expression. She reached out and touched the man's face lightly with her fingers. She closed her eyes briefly, and when she opened them, tears spilled silently down her cheeks and onto the table in front of her.

Tom sat on the table next to her and studied her face. Danny pulled a chair out and sat opposite her.

"Marnie, who is it?" Tom asked, placing a hand gently on her shoulder.

Marnie searched for words, but couldn't speak. When she opened her mouth, no words came – just heart-wrenching, sorrowful sobs. Danny moved quickly around the table to comfort her, but he was too late. Tom put his arms protectively around Marnie, and she wrapped her arms around Tom's neck as she clung tightly to her best friend.

Danny stood helpless – not knowing what to do – so he stroked Marnie's arm gently and remained quiet. Tom was murmuring something to her, but Danny couldn't hear. Marnie's sobbing drowned out Tom's words.

Between sobs, Marnie gasped for air and finally croaked out, "It's William, Tom. You must remember William?"

Tom's face blanched. He hugged Marnie tighter as he turned to check the picture and whispered, "I do. I remember William, Marnie. I remember William."

Tater sat at Marnie's feet, gently put a paw on her leg and whined. Marnie drew back from Tom, bent and hugged Tater tight and then held his face in her hands. Tater searched Marnie's face with his intelligent gaze and bumped her gently with his nose.

"Okay. Right now, I really don't want to be this guy – the irritating detective who is trying to solve a case – but who is William?" Danny asked.

"William was a friend. He was a foster kid my folks took in when we were in middle school. He stayed with us until he was 16, then he just disappeared. My parents searched for him everywhere; we all searched for him – Mom, Dad, Tom, me, Kate…" Marnie replied, wiping her nose with a tissue that Tom had handed her.

"Sam? Did Sam help you look for William?" Danny asked.

"Probably. You know, I don't really remember. Not sure Sam was around much then. He would have been away at college." Marnie frowned, searched her memory and looked to Tom to confirm.

Tom shrugged and added, "I don't remember, either. It was a long time ago. I do remember the three of us – Marnie, Kate and me – searching all of our favorite spots. To be honest, William wasn't around all that much when he was here. He was involved in a lot of sports, and he helped Mr. Garver at the grocery store after school and on weekends, you know, when he wasn't playing football, basketball or baseball. He was closest to Marnie, but he wasn't an easy guy to know."

"He was a year older than us. He was fun. He would fish with me and take me out on the boat. We talked a lot. He had a tough time – his mother was involved in drugs, to what extent, I really don't know – and his dad was in prison. He killed someone. That's how he came to live with us, and Tom is right. He was always busy once we were in our teens. I had a huge crush on him, but he was always interested in Kate. Most boys were interested in Kate. You were, weren't you, Tom?" Marnie said.

Tom rolled his eyes and blushed a bit. "Not really. She was a bit of a princess most of the time. She stopped being fun when we were around... what? 12 or 13?"

Marnie nodded and added, "Yup. That's about the time she got boobs and decided being pretty was better than fishing and playing tag."

"Anyway!" Danny interrupted, "Kate really isn't the topic here."

"Anyway! I was William's buddy. The one who helped him sneak in if he missed curfew." Marnie shrugged and glanced back down briefly at the picture on the table.

Danny shook his head at her.

"Anyway, do you two have a last name for William?" Danny asked.

Tom and Marnie responded in unison, "Williams."

Danny looked at them doubtfully.

"What? Really?" he asked.

Marnie replied, "Yeah, and guess what his middle name is."

"Let me guess. William?" Danny replied with sarcasm.

"Nope. It's Billy." Marnie rested her chin in her hand.

"Seriously?" Danny asked.

"Yup. William Billy Williams," Marnie replied.

Danny shook his head in disbelief. "Well, that's definitely different, but it gives us something to work with. I'll be back in a minute. I'll get someone onto finding out what William Billy Williams has been up to since he disappeared." Danny put his hand on the doorknob to the interview room door. "Tom, can you show Marnie those symbols – you know, the tattoos? Maybe the Good Witch of the North here can tell us what they mean."

Danny walked out into the squad room while Tom spread more photos out onto the table.

Tom smirked. "Good Witch of the North? That's a new name. I kind of like that one. I was hoping to hear him call you darling or sweetheart, but Good Witch of the North works. It brings a bit of lightness to this dark and somber day."

"Shut up, Tom." Marnie scowled. "A friend is dead and you… you… well, you know better."

Tom stood straight, dropped his chin to his chest and pointed to the photos. "Marn, have a look at these. I'm sorry for the content, but we really need to understand what these symbols mean. Danny thinks this one is a devil symbol. What can you tell me?"

"What? A devil symbol?" Marnie asked and put her attention to the photos. "This one here? This is a pentacle, also called a pentagram. That *is not* a devil symbol. This is a five-point star. It's a pagan symbol of protection. It represents five elements – earth, air, fire, water and spirit. Danny's thinking of a hexagram. Now, a hexagram is a different story. A hexagram, well, that is a devil symbol. It has six points and six sides."

"You mean like 666?" Tom asked with an uneasy tone.

"Yeah. Like 666," Marnie replied with a curt nod, "You don't want to mess with that one, but the pentacle, it's all about protecting yourself. Are all of these tattoos on William's arms?"

"Yes. We took pictures at the scene." Tom shivered, remembering the morbid scene.

"Holy crap! Something had him scared. All of these symbols – every single one – these are for protection. That's a lot of ink. He was protecting himself from something or someone." Marnie turned the photographs over and trembled.

Sitting back in her chair, Marnie felt under the table for Tater. His nose bumped her hand, and he nuzzled her palm. She scratched his ears and turned her attention back to the symbols.

Danny returned to the interview room with three coffees.

"Sorry, Tater. I don't have anything for you, buddy," Danny said.

He held out his full hands so that Tom would take a coffee. He handed one to Marnie and pointed down to photos.

"What do you think? Devil worshipping?" he asked.

Marnie shook her head, flipped the photos over and spread them out. She pointed to the tattoos in the photos.

"No, not at all. As I was just telling Tom, this is a pentacle or pentagram. It's a five-point star, and it's for protection. You're thinking of a six-point star – that's for the devil. See this one here? This seven-point star? This is a septagram – a faerie star or elven star. It represents heaven, the seven chakras and the seven directions – north, south, east, west, above, below and within. The septagram is for protection and harmony," Marnie said, pulling her chair closer to the table.

Danny sat down in the chair next to her. Tater dropped his head into Danny's lap, and Danny scratched his ears. Tom stood over their shoulders with his hands on the backs of their chairs.

"What about this one? This weird stickman," Tom asked.

Marnie glanced up at him and shook her head. "That's not a stickman, Tom. That's an ankh. It's also for protection. The Latin phrase for this is 'crux ansata.' Translated – cross with handle. It's also the Egyptian symbol of life. I'm pretty certain that Wiccans use this symbol to represent life. Um… I'll have to double-check, but I'm pretty sure that it's a symbol of eternal life and, I think, the sun and, as I mentioned, protection."

Danny pointed to one of the symbols. "This one here. This is a Celtic symbol, isn't it?"

Marnie nodded. "Yes. It's a Celtic knot. This particular one is a shield, or it represents a shield – no matter which way you turn it, it's always the same. It's endless – unbroken. It represents the four elements of earth, fire, water and air – also for protection. People often wear a Celtic knot to ward off negative energy."

Marnie tilted her head back to see Tom. He was truly enthralled with the symbols and their meaning. Digging into the details of a case always held Tom's attention; he couldn't get enough detail, and he would investigate endlessly to find answers.

Danny touched Marnie's arm and pointed to another tattoo.

"What about this one, Marnie?" Danny asked.

Marnie rubbed her eyes, dabbed her nose again with the tissue and then shifted her attention back to the photos and the tattoo to which Danny pointed on William's forearm.

"This is actually quite interesting." Marnie picked up two of the photographs and held them up. "If you look at these two, the Eye of Horus and the Eye of Ra – same-same really, but they're not – but they are. Sorry.

Some say Horus and Ra are the same being. Some say they are not. The Eye of Horus is for protection and healing. The Eye of Ra is for protection. Both are Egyptian. Horus is the Sky God, and Ra is the Sun God. Horus's eye was injured, then it healed. Um… I think that there were connections to power, good health, healing, redemption and transformation related to the Eye of Horus. I'll have to look it up to be sure. The Eye of Ra, um… I'll have to look that up, too. I know that there is a connection to power and authority with both, but it's been a long time since I studied these. The key thing to remember is that both are for protection. I think that's the tie-in."

When Marnie finished speaking, Tom slid the photo of William's chest in front of Marnie. Marnie tipped her head and rested the side of her face in one hand as she studied the image. She furrowed her brow as she focused on the symbol.

"Well, what I do know is that William was scared absolutely shitless of *someone* or *something*. You don't have all of these symbols of protection tattooed on your forearms and chest for the fun of it," Marnie speculated.

"Some people just like tattoos, Marnie. We all know that. There are a lot of people out there who cover their bodies with art," Danny said.

Marnie turned slowly toward Danny. "Danny, this tattoo on his chest is the All Seeing Eye or the Eye of Providence. It's associated with Freemasonry, the Illuminati, Christianity, Egyptian gods. Note the triangle around the eye. That triangle – the three sides – represents the Trinity. I do remember that William remained devout throughout his time with us. He never missed Mass on Sunday, he never ate without bowing his head in prayer and crossing himself and he never ate meat on Friday – not just the Lenten observance – I mean, never meat on Friday. Never. I can go on and on. William was devout. The Eye of Providence tattooed on his chest absolutely convinces me that he was afraid. I'm taking a shot in the dark, but I'm guessing that he thought that, if the other symbols didn't work, this one sure as hell would. If you look up 'providence' in the dictionary, you're going to find that it loosely means '*the protective care of God or the higher power you believe in.*'"

Marnie pushed back from the table and patted her knees to call Tater to her. Tater stood slowly, his back end up in the air as he stretched and yawned. He trotted to Marnie and placed his head in her lap for an ear scratch.

Danny studied the photographs and symbols silently while Marnie and Tater played a game of fetch with a crumpled-up piece of paper from the wastebasket. Tom stood staring off into space, contemplating their next move, and he broke the silence in typical Tom-fashion.

"I'm hungry. Let's get out of here," Tom announced, as his stomach growled in protest of the lack of sustenance this late into the afternoon.

-CHAPTER EIGHT-

Alice, Allen and other members in The Collective stood around the stage at Station Hall discussing their lineup for the evening. Bookings had all been made online, and no tickets would be sold at the door. They had a system. They collected information that would help them obtain valuable information about their attendees – first name, middle name, last name, personal E-mail address, phone number (preferably a cell number), address and date of birth. Sometimes, people were too willing to share information when spiritual guidance was on tap. The Collective had a system that worked.

The Collective's designated "researcher" was reviewing the list of people who had booked the event tonight. This researcher, a young techy named Justin, was backstage furiously tapping away on his laptop, gathering background information on the attendees. Those presenting would only take questions from people from whom they could gather data and who might be helpful to them in gaining some credibility. The loads of data that a researcher as deft as Justin could pull down from the Internet made their job of recruiting followers a lot easier. People were careless. Their social media pages did not always have high privacy settings. People laid their lives out online for all of the world to see, and The Collective profited from their carelessness. Of course, profile pictures of their attendees made the whole process so much easier. They would have a face to put with the name.

The Collective would choose exactly 10 people from the bookings and focus their attention on this small group. These would be the people who had provided them with the best data from which to work.

"Hey, here's a lady whose husband just left her. She's got photos of him up here, too. We can describe him to her – no problem. Here's his page. He's got pics of his new girlfriend up here. I'll follow it around and see what else that I can get. Here's a guy who has a blog about his treatment. He's quite sick, and he's got quite a few pics and info about his family, too. He's an engineer. He's got a wife and four kids. I'll have information sheets and photos for everyone in about two hours. Tonight should be easy. Good for us that people overshare." Justin smirked and went back to tapping on his keyboard.

Alice moved to the front of the stage and motioned for Allen to follow her. She spoke sharply in a harsh whisper. "We need an energy healer, a Reiki Master or an empath. We need to replace Carl now. We cannot get by without a replacement for him. He was our moneymaker."

Alice peered nervously over her shoulder at the rest of the group and then up at Allen. She could see his mind working as he nodded in agreement.

Allen placed a hand on Alice's shoulder and leaned down to speak. "What if we use Patrick? He worked with Carl for months. He could do it. He's a bit weird, but that's good. He honestly wants to help people. If he thinks that he's helping, he'll do it. If nothing else, he can talk from experience and offer advice. We can tell him to do what Carl did for him. He knows better than anyone what Carl's treatment plan is, and more importantly, Patrick feels a sense of duty."

Alice nodded in approval and turned to look for Patrick. He was nowhere to be seen. He should be here at this hour of the day. Patrick was never late; then again, he was quite upset the last time that they saw him at the cemetery that morning.

Alice called out, "Has anyone seen Patrick? He ran off this morning, but he usually comes back. Anyone seen him?"

The people standing on the stage looked at each other and either shrugged or shook their heads.

Alice patted Allen's arm and urged, "Go see if you can find him. He can't be far. Maybe he's at the house. Check there first."

Allen nodded. "I have to stop at the pharmacy first. These nicotine patches aren't working. I'm going to need a stronger patch or maybe some gum. I want a cigarette more now than I did this morning."

Grabbing his coat, Allen walked offstage. He strode through the arena and, once at the doors, pushed out onto the street. Just as he turned toward the pharmacy, he saw Marnie walking with Tater as well as Detectives Keller and Gregg. Quickly, he turned up his collar and pulled his hat low. He wheeled about and stretched out his hand to grab the door, but it was too late. They had seen him. Allen pushed his glasses up and straightened his shoulders. He smiled nervously at their approaching figures.

"Good afternoon, Marnie." Allen's tone was syrupy sweet.

His beady eyes were just a bit close together, and the pupils always looked like pinpoints – his glasses magnified the teeny tiny pupils. It always gave Marnie a bit of a shiver to look Allen in the eyes.

Marnie narrowed her eyes and gave one curt nod. "Allen. I trust that you have Alice under control?"

Allen stepped back against the door as Detectives Keller and Gregg moved closer to him, surrounding him, and they all stopped on the sidewalk outside of Station Hall.

Allen cleared his throat nervously and stammered, "Yes. Yes. Yes. I've spoken with her. She knows that she was in the wrong. You know Alice. She's just so passionate about what we do that she gets carried away sometimes."

Allen shifted uncomfortably and looked from the detectives to Marnie nervously. He tried to smile, but didn't quite get there. His upturned mouth looked more like a ghoulish grin than a smile. Detectives Keller and Gregg were both big men, and they made him uneasy. Marnie was intimidating enough without the two detectives standing with her.

"Hmm... passionate? I think that the word is greedy, Allen. The word you should have used is greedy... and contemptible. Contemptible is another good word to describe Alice," Marnie commented and turned to the detectives. "She threw a snowball earlier and hit Tater. Can you believe that? She assaulted a dog. I really should press charges. Don't you think, Detectives?"

Both Tom and Danny could see the sparkle of playful mischief in Marnie's eyes. Allen didn't.

"Come now, Marnie," Allen sputtered. "She wasn't trying to hit Tater at all. You know that snowball was meant for you – not Tater. Alice wouldn't throw a snowball at Tater. It was meant for you."

Danny and Tom both took a step closer to Allen.

Danny looked down and used his height to intimidate Allen. "Are you tellin' me that Alice meant to hit Marnie with a snowball? She meant to assault Ms. Reilly? Is that what you're tellin' us? Is that okay with you, Allen? Is it okay that your friend and colleague assaulted someone?"

Allen was leaning against the door, glancing from one detective to the other and then at Marnie.

"Just a little misunderstanding. Alice was upset about her last meeting with Marnie when you, Detective Gregg, yelled at her," Allen said, trying to regain his composure.

Danny poked his index finger into Allen's face. "Then you tell Alice to throw a snowball at me. You tell her to take her anger out on me. Ms. Reilly did nothing to her. That was me. You tell her that, and you tell her that I'm watching her. I'm watching all of you. One wrong step, and I will be on all of you so fast that you won't know what hit you."

Allen laughed nervously. "You're a homicide detective. You don't have jurisdiction over what we do."

Danny laughed and shook his head. "I'm a cop. You mess with Ms. Reilly or anyone else in Creekwood, and I will investigate."

Danny stepped back and slapped Allen on the shoulder with the palm of his hand. The slap wasn't hard, but it was hard enough for Allen to know that Alice had picked a fight with the wrong person.

"We clear, Allen? We understand each other?" Danny raised an eyebrow, challenging Allen.

"Yes. Yes, we... I understand," Allen stammered again. He watched as Marnie, Tater and Detectives Keller and Gregg turned from him and walked away.

He leaned back against the door, puffed out his cheeks, exhaled sharply and shook his head.

"Alice, what were you thinking? We can't have the police watching us. Not now. We just can't," Allen whispered.

Allen pushed himself off the door and headed to the pharmacy. Next, he would find Patrick. A familiar face rounded the corner, stopping Allen dead in his tracks. The pharmacy and Patrick would have to wait. Yes, they needed Patrick to complete their circle. Yes, Patrick was their only hope to keep the money rolling into The Collective. Yes, if things went wrong, they would have someone to blame, but this familiar face couldn't and wouldn't wait. He pulled out his phone, dialing Alice. He didn't want this person to get away.

-CHAPTER NINE-

The diner was quiet at this hour of the afternoon. Ryan's Diner had been busy for the lunch rush, but it was well past that now. Gram smiled widely when she saw her grandson and his friends enter.

"Hello! My favorite people. Come in! Your table is free," Gram welcomed them in her Irish brogue. She rushed to the door and led them to a booth at the back of the diner.

Margaret "Gram" Ryan is Irish/American. She moved to the United States with her now late husband, Daniel Ryan, when they were in their late twenties. They purchased the diner, which back in their day had been an Irish pub, just a few years after immigrating. Gram changed the name to Ryan's Diner after her husband passed away because she worried it wasn't ladylike for a woman to own a pub, albeit she still has her license and regularly pulls a pint or two. Margaret and Daniel Ryan had three children – a daughter, Carol, and two sons, Fionn and Liam. Detective Danny Gregg's late mother, Carol was the eldest. Fionn and Liam both emigrated to Ireland as college students and remain there to this day.

Gram has maintained her Irish brogue all of these years. She speaks with friends and family back in Ireland often, and she visits when able. Her sons visit her from time to time, too. She is a huge fan of Irish television programs and watches them regularly; thus, her accent has barely faded. Gram is average height and, some would say, amply built and fit. She wears her thick, wavy white hair short, and her blue eyes dance when she smiles.

Gram fully embraces her keen sixth sense – she, like Marnie, is a talented clairvoyant. Gram's finely honed gift has made her a bit of a legend in Creekwood. She knows everything and everyone and where all of the skeletons of Creekwood are hidden. No one knows if the rumors about Gram's gift are true; people just trust that Margaret Ryan is, indeed, a powerhouse.

Tom bent to kiss Gram's cheek. Danny gave her a warm hug and a kiss on the top of the head; and Marnie smiled, hugged her and kissed her warmly on the cheek. Gram bent down, gave Tater a pat on the head and then pulled on his ears.

"Do you want a treat, Tater?" Gram asked, smiling down at him.

His ears twitched, he tipped his head to the side and he lay down at her feet.

"What's wrong with Tater?" Gram's concerned gaze met Marnie's.

"He's not feeling too good. His vet says that he can't have any more beef bones." Marnie sighed and looked down at Tater's sad face.

Gram nodded sympathetically. "Okay, well what about a tiny bit of something else then?"

"How about veggies? Maybe squash?" Marnie asked.

"I should have something in the kitchen. Let me check." Gram nodded briskly. "Now, what can I get for all of you?"

Marnie breathed in the aroma of the diner's menu. "Soup. You have clam chowder, right?"

"I do, but you need more than soup, lass. How about a salad, too? A nice house salad and some sourdough bread?" Gram fussed, put the salt and pepper shakers to the back of the table and rearranged the mustard and ketchup bottles too.

"That would be lovely. Thanks, Gram," Marnie responded with a smile.

"I'll have a steak sandwich and fries please," Tom said, as he played with a sugar packet.

"Danny boy, what can I get you, son?" Gram asked her grandson.

"Ahh... I don't know what I want today, Gram. Surprise me," Danny answered, leaning over and hugging his grandmother around her waist.

Gram nodded and headed off to the kitchen. A waitress, Dorie, brought them water, silverware and napkins.

"Is everyone ready for Christmas? All of your shopping done, Marnie?" Dorie placed glasses of water on the table in front of each of them.

Marnie glanced up at her and shook her head tiredly. "Haven't even started, Dorie. You? Are you ready for Christmas?"

"I'm picking my tree up tonight. We'll decorate it this weekend, and my shopping has been done for months. I just need to wrap." Dorie grinned cheerfully. "I better get back to the other customers." Dorie waved and went along to the next table.

Danny nudged Marnie's hand with his and looked at her across the table.

"Let's get a tree tomorrow night. What do you say? Tom can help, too," Danny suggested, trying to lighten Marnie's mood.

"It may put me in the holiday spirit. I kinda thought that I might try to find a place to live before the holidays, though. Tater and I are going to overstay our welcome. Are you sure that you want us around through the holidays?" Marnie turned to Danny, studying his face carefully.

Danny didn't hesitate in responding. "Of course. Of course, I want you and Tater to stay through the holidays. It gets lonely up there this time of year. Having you two at the cabin makes it feel homey. Besides, I've gotten used to the furry little freak waking me up every morning."

Danny nodded and nudged Marnie's hand again and coaxed. "C'mon. What do you say?"

Marnie glanced down at Tater, then back up at Danny and nodded. "Okay. We'll do it. Tree, we can stop at my house and get some of my decorations and then I need to put together a Christmas shopping list. Tom, are you in?"

Tom stretched, leaned on the wall and casually responded, "Yeah. I got nothin' better to do with my time these days. My personal life has been a bit on the dry side. I can live vicariously through you two basking in the holiday spirit."

Marnie gave him a small shove and teased, "We could invite Andrea to come along. Would that cheer you up?"

Tom sat up straight and replied sharply, "No. Andrea? Why would you invite Andrea? She digs at me every time that I see her. Besides, she's not my type. She's too... too... well, she's just not my type."

"Just because she doesn't swoon over you, Thomas Keller, does not make her not your type. Get over yourself, would you please? She's lovely and stable and cute. C'mon, Tom. You know that you want to say yes," Marnie teased again with a little grin on her face.

"No, Marnie, I really don't. Don't try to fix me up with anyone. Seriously, Marn, don't!" Tom's tone was a bit harsher than he intended. He turned his attention back to the sugar packet and went quiet.

Marnie grinned at Danny and shrugged. He shrugged back and turned to Tom.

"Tommy, you gotta get out of your rut, man. C'mon. We'll have a tree trimming party and invite a few friends. Andrea, Ellie and Julie, Rick, Tony, Jalnack, Gram and a few others. Okay?" Danny suggested with a nod of his head.

Tom shrugged and conceded, "Yeah. Okay, but I'm not in a rut. I just haven't been out there a lot lately. Work has been busy, and may I remind you, I've been recovering from a concussion. I'll be fine, and I don't need help finding a date. I can find my own, thanks."

Danny grabbed the sugar packet away from Tom and threw it at him. Danny thought about how lucky they were that Tom was sitting here right now. Sam Reilly and Kate Parish had attacked him on the bridle trail near Marnie's house. Danny and Marnie had gone searching for him and found him lying unconscious in the snow – he'd been struck on the head with a large rock. Danny pulled himself from his thoughts and back to the conversation.

"Great. Christmas tree shopping shall commence tomorrow night at 6:00 sharp. All of us," Danny chimed.

Marnie shifted forward in the booth, energized, and she tapped the table and asked, "Okay, who has some paper? We need to make a list of things for the party. Friday night good for everyone? We'll need to stop at my house tonight or tomorrow night to pick up some things, and we need to get a list together for Toys for Tots, too. I would really appreciate it if you two could give me a hand with a few things. I've got most of it organized, but there's still a lot to do. We need to get some people together to help us deliver on the 22nd or the 23rd. Oh, and the Mayor called. He thought it might be fun to get some of the kids involved in Santa's parade next week. What do you think?"

"Whoa, now. Marnie, you're rambling again. You're overtired, and you've been pushing yourself. You need to get some sleep tonight. You know that, don't you?" Danny placed a hand on top of Marnie's. She pulled her hand back, and her face darkened. Then she shrugged and nodded, peered out the window and turned to see Gram and Dorie bringing their lunch to them.

Gram set Tom's steak sandwich down in front of him. It was huge, and the side of fries was a golden mountain spilling over the plate. Marnie reached over and grabbed a French fry.

Tom rolled his eyes. "Eating lunch with women; they always steal your food. If you wanted fries, you should have ordered fries, Marnie."

Marnie grinned at him and said, "I only wanted one."

Danny slid his plate across to Marnie and offered, "Here you go, kiddo. Help yourself. More than enough to share."

Marnie scowled at Tom. "See. Danny knows how to share."

Tom shook his head again and took a big bite out his sandwich. When he was nearly finished chewing, he looked up at Marnie, held out his sandwich and, with a full mouth, said, "Want a bite?"

"No, thank you. I wouldn't want to deprive you of food." Marnie tossed her head dramatically. She wrinkled her nose up at Tom and helped herself to one of Danny's fries, then she looked out the window again.

Danny had produced a notepad and was busy writing a list while nibbling on his fries. He glanced up and noticed that Marnie wasn't eating her lunch. Her focus was out the window. He waved his hand in front of her face.

"Hey, Marnie? You gonna eat? Where are you? You were staring off into space again. Is there someone having a chat with you who we can't see?" Danny asked, half kidding and half serious.

Marnie turned to Danny and, with a shrug of her shoulders, replied as casually as she could muster, "I was just watching Kate walk down the street with Harry Carnegie."

Both Tom and Danny stood quickly and gawked out the window. They watched as Kate Parish got into Harry's car. Harry was the best defense attorney in the area. As soon as they saw Kate with Harry, they all knew what that meant. Kate had just cut a deal and was free.

"You okay, Marn?" Tom asked, turning from the window to check Marnie's reaction.

Marnie nodded stiffly. She looked down at her salad and started eating. She glanced up, straightened her shoulders and, between bites, replied, "We were expecting this to happen. We knew when she started blurting out everything that had happened that they would cut her a deal. I'm surprised that it took her this long to get out of jail. She knows how to play men and the system. She's a lawyer – not a very good lawyer – but she knows how to get what she wants. She always has. First thing that I'm going to do tomorrow morning is have a restraining order put on her. She was conspiring with my brother to kill me. Facts are facts. She admitted to it." Marnie stabbed a tomato and went back to eating her salad.

Tom and Danny exchanged glances and peered out the window again. Harry got into his car and drove off toward the center of town with Kate in the passenger seat.

"Sit down and eat guys," Marnie said, motioning to their food with her fork. "There's nothing that we can do right now. I just want to make sure that she can't turn up on my doorstep or at my office. She'll get all teary and beg me to forgive her yet again. I've got nothing left where she's concerned – nothing left at all."

Tom and Danny sat down, and they all discussed the "things to do" list while they finished eating. Marnie checked on Tater while they talked, ate and planned. He was lying quietly next to their table. He didn't ask for food, and he didn't bump her with his nose. He just wasn't himself.

Gram rushed out of the kitchen and directly to their table with a big bowl filled with mashed vegetables.

"This is for Tater. I've mashed together some leftover squash, broccoli and cauliflower for him. Can he have it now?" Gram asked, turning to Marnie.

Marnie smiled up at Gram and said, "Thank you so much. This is lovely. He'll love it, and yes, he can have it now."

Marnie took the bowl from Gram and set it on the floor next to Tater. Tater sniffed the bowl, stood up and gobbled up the mashed vegetables quickly. When he was finished, he looked up at Gram and smiled.

"There you go, little fella. I hope that makes you feel better. Lovely, lovely boy," Gram cooed and patted Tater's head. "Can I get you anything else to eat? Do you want coffee or tea? Maybe a piece of cake or pie?"

"Thanks, but no, Gram. We need to get Marnie back to work, and we have a lot of detecting to do. Do you want to have dinner with us on Friday night?" Danny asked. "We're having a tree trimming party."

Danny stood and hugged his grandmother.

Gram smiled up at him and clapped her hands together cheerfully. "Oh, Danny boy, that sounds like magic. What can I bring?"

"We'll let you know, Gram. We're still writing a list. I'll stop in tomorrow morning for breakfast, and we can have a nice long chat."

Danny hugged Gram again and headed for the door with Marnie, Tater and Tom following behind.

Tom and Marnie stopped on the way past the counter and stuffed some bills into the tip jar. Gram wouldn't let them pay for lunch, so they contributed to the tip jar every time that they ate at the diner. Gram always scolded them, but they did it anyway.

"Why do the two of you do that? Every single time. You put money in the tip jar. When you come here, you're my guests. I don't give you money when I come to your houses for dinner, do I?"

Gram shook her finger at Tom and Marnie, and they both laughed. Marnie hugged Gram at the door, and Tom bent down and kissed Gram on the cheek.

Tom added, "It's the holiday season, Gram. Everyone can use a bit of extra cash during the holidays."

Gram shooed them toward the door.

"Off with all of you. Be safe and stay warm."

Danny pulled the door open, the bell above it dinged, and they all looked up and smiled, remembering that, every time a bell rings, an angel gets its wings. Gram had installed the bell with the very thought of contributing to the number.

Out on the street, snow was falling lightly, and there was a Santa on the corner ringing a bell, collecting donations. Off in the distance, the bells of St Michael's were chiming "The First Noel." It certainly looked and sounded like the holidays, but something about this year was nagging at Marnie. She just couldn't get into the spirit.

Danny and Tom said their goodbyes to Marnie, and as Marnie and a much more spirited Tater headed back to her office, she heard her name shouted from across the street. She turned.

"Hey, Marnie!" the voice called again. "Over here!"

Marnie stopped and waved to Erin Matthews, the bubbly sales clerk from Drake's Drugs. Erin was tall and willowy – drop-dead gorgeous with a face like a pixie and burgundy hair to match. Erin's pronounced Southern drawl added to her charm. Her smile was mischievous, and her green eyes glinted with delight as she gazed up at the falling snow.

"Hey, Erin!" Marnie called back.

Erin sashayed easily across the street, stopping traffic along the way. She smiled and waved at drivers who braked and beeped at her. Erin was oblivious to the traffic jam that she was creating.

"Marnie, I wanted to see if ya need any help with the Toys for Tots thingy. I heard a rumor about ya helpin' with the parade. You're organizin' a float with kids singin' carols, or so some are sayin'. Is it true, or is it just the rumor mill weavin' another delicious tale?" Erin giggled.

"Ah, the rumor mill is indeed weaving a tale. I said that I would help organize some of the Toys for Tots recipients for a float, but a float full of caroling children was never discussed," Marnie replied with a shake of her head.

Erin tossed her head and gave a small shrug. "Well, that's the rumor mill for ya. Commit ya to a task that no one else wants to do, and it's too late to back out when ya find out. That's how it goes here in good ole Creekwood, Marn."

"That's about right. Um, let me guess… It was Irene Hazelton, Carol Chadwick and Susanne Connor? They were having coffee at Drake's lunch counter right there next to the pharmacy; you overhead them chatting about everyone and everything; and my name popped up?" Marnie raised one eyebrow and shot Erin a knowing look.

Erin laughed and replied, "Ya forgot about Corinne Hooper. She was fillin' their coffee mugs, and I believe that she's the one who added in the float and carols bit. Swear to God, Marn, they sound like a bunch of monkeys chatterin' every day. Every mornin' at 8:00 AM, they gather to drink coffee, eat scones and gossip. They love to gossip. Mr. Drake tells them to stop. They keep right on a-goin', but he doesn't help much. He's a bit of an old gossip himself."

"That's Creekwood. You never know what you've been up to until the coffee counter klatch delivers the news like a trashy tabloid." Marnie grinned, tugged Tater's ear and shivered.

Erin touched Marnie's arm lightly. "Hey, I'm sorry to hear about your brother, Marn. Really horrible business, it is. I can't believe that you went through all of that, but hey, you've got two dishy detectives watchin' over you. That has to be a small blessin', eh?"

"Dishy detectives? You mean Detective Gregg and Tom?" asked Marnie, a delicious thought flickering in her head.

"Uh, yeah! Don't ya think they're dishy? Tom Keller has always has been a bit of a cutie… a bit annoying sometimes, but that's part of his charm. Detective Gregg? Wow! He looks all gruff and businesslike, then he smiles. A handsome man. Don't ya think, Marn?" Erin replied, eyebrows raised in anticipation of Marnie's response.

The delightful notion in Marnie's head grew brighter.

"Erin, what are you doing Friday night?"

The words rushed out of Marnie's mouth faster than gossip spread around Creekwood. Marnie's question rushed out so fast that Erin took a step back.

"Uh, no plans. I'm workin' Friday, but I should be done around 6:30. Why?" Erin asked.

"Well, we're having a tree trimming party at Danny's, uh, Detective Gregg's, cabin on Friday night. Just a few friends – nothing fancy. Thought you might like to come along. Tom will be there," Marnie said with a twinkle in her eye.

"Sure. Sounds like it could be fun." Erin nodded enthusiastically.

"Excellent! I'll text the address to you." Marnie cheered internally.

"What can I bring?" asked Erin.

"Gosh, I haven't really thought that far ahead, Erin." Marnie tipped her head in thought.

"I can pick up some wine or beer on the way," Erin suggested.

"That would be great! I'll put you down for a bottle of wine and some beer. Thanks, Erin." Marnie smiled appreciatively.

"Not a problem. I'll get a twelve-pack, a bottle of white and a bottle of red," Erin confirmed.

"Thank you so much! I'm pretty certain that Gram… Mrs. Ryan…

Danny's grandmother will make something delicious, and Danny and I will organize some drinks and food, too. My brilliant assistant Andrea is coming along, too, and so are a few of Danny's and Tom's friends and colleagues." Marnie pulled her list and a pen out of her bag and made a note.

"What about that Carl guy you work with?" asked Erin.

"Uh, yeah, sure. I'll invite Carl. I didn't realize that you knew him," Marnie replied.

"Oh, well, I've seen you two walking and talking through town once or twice. I've heard a few interesting rumors about that one, let me tell you. Sounds like he's got a bit of a dark side to him." Erin raised one eyebrow.

Marnie's face reddened. She didn't like where this conversation was headed, and she was looking for an easy out.

"Yeah, well, you know the rumor mill. They turn a molehill into a mountain. Besides, don't we all have a dark side lurking in the corners of our crazy and twisted minds?" Marnie beamed a mischievous grin, followed by a knowing nod.

"Ha ha ha! Yes! Yes, I suppose we do." Erin agreed with a nod.

Marnie checked her watch. "Goodness! Look at the time! I have to get back to the office."

"Yes, and I need to get back to the pharmacy. I just came to grab a bit of takeout on my way to the evening shift," Erin nodded toward the diner.

"I'll text you Danny's address. See you Friday night!" Marnie called over her shoulder as she made her way to the office with Tater in tow.

"You will!" Erin yelled back. "I can't wait to see where the dishy detective lives," she said quietly.

Erin smiled to herself as she watched Marnie walk away and turned to head back to the pharmacy.

-CHAPTER TEN-

"We need to discredit her!" A tallish woman with silver hair that was swept into a soft bun waved her arms dramatically to enunciate her point. She wore a knee-length, dark gray woolen cape with red piping and a red button at the throat over her black skirt and sweater. Her leather gloves and calf-length boots were the color of holly berries. Her stark blue eyes darkened with anger as she continued. "We need to make sure that she never, ever causes problems for us again. That little display at the cemetery this morning won't stop Marnie Reilly. She will continue her interference until there is nothing left. She will chip away at The Collective until, bit by bit, we are destroyed."

The caped woman stood in the alleyway behind Station Hall, speaking with Allen, Alice and a man of about 30. Allen had spotted the woman minutes earlier and convened a quick meeting. They all nodded in agreement with the woman's statement until Alice, her mind not quite made up, raised her hand slightly to silence the woman.

"Now, just wait a minute. The ritual at the cemetery *will* work. It just needs a few days. I have been reading up on this type of thing, and this should work. I know that it's more or less white magic, but it will work. Besides, we have God on our side. Marnie doesn't. She's living with the detective. God will strike her down for that. We're just helping a bit – moving things along," Alice commented with conviction.

The caped woman looked down on Alice with a distasteful grin and chastised her in a mocking, condescending tone. "Alice, you are a silly, daft woman. You don't know the first thing about white or black magic. I've been told that you added salt to that little spell you did. Do you know what salt does, you ninny? It protects and purifies. You reversed the spell as soon as you added the salt!"

Alice's eyes widened with shock. Could there really be a spy among them? Who would have informed this woman of what was buried at the cemetery?

The woman sneered, waved her gloved hand in front of Alice's face and continued, "Abracadabra! Marnie is dead. For the love of God, Alice, do you really think that's the way this will work? Do you really believe that you have the power to vanquish Marnie Reilly and Carl Parkins? After all that we have done, do you honestly believe God will help us? You are an idiot if you believe that!"

Alice started to speak, but was cut off abruptly. The woman in the cape wasn't finished yet.

"Alice, we need help from other sources – darker forces, the likes of whom you wouldn't know how to contact. You certainly wouldn't know how to speak to them if you did reach out to them. No. You need me. You need my help. I'm the only one capable of doing what needs to be done. I've learned things over the last few years that would impress you."

The caped woman threw back her silver head and issued an unsettling and wicked laugh as she wheeled about and disappeared down the alley with the thirtysomething man following closely behind her.

Alice and Allen watched them go down the alley, both feeling a slight bit of dread about what was to come for Marnie Reilly and Carl Parkins.

-CHAPTER ELEVEN-

Patrick trudged back up Creek Road. This time, he was heading into town. He loved watching the snowflakes fall. He loved the cushiony sound that the snow created around him. He felt like he was walking in a winter wonderland, just like the song. He watched cardinals sitting aloft pines and ash branches and squirrels playing chase up and down an old maple tree. He thought about Marnie's house and how warm and cozy it felt being in a home like that. He gazed up at the sky and saw a crow flying toward him, and in that moment, he felt cold and lonely. He wished that he had a friend whom he could trust. He had thought that Carl Parkins was his friend, but now, he wasn't so sure.

The crow flew past him, swooped around and then landed on a fence post just up ahead. Patrick kept his eyes on the crow. As he drew nearer, the crow cawed and flew off toward town.

Patrick was going into Creekwood to find Marnie and Carl. He had searched Marnie's house for information about where she worked. He'd found mail on her desk in the home office. He wanted to see if Marnie looked like the pictures that he had seen. He wanted to see if Carl was trustworthy. He wanted to feel safe. Right now, he just didn't know whom to trust.

The crow circled back around and landed again. Patrick was certain that it was the same crow that he had seen at the cemetery that morning. He watched it closely. As he approached the crow, it appeared to be looking right at him. He stopped on the road and glanced back at the crow.

"I know. I know. I have to tell Marnie and Carl about this morning. I'm going there now. Want to come along?" Patrick asked.

The crow tipped its head to the side like it understood what he was saying and took flight once again. Patrick watched it disappear into the snow-lit sky. He trudged to the end of Creek Road and waited for a bus. A few minutes later, he was sitting in the furthest front-right seat near the bus driver. He watched the road silently as they drove into Creekwood. The bus smelled like diesel, wet wool and fried food. He turned around to see a man eating something out of a grease-stained brown bag. The man looked back and nodded a hello. Patrick nodded back, turned in his seat and resumed watching out the big front window of the bus. To his delight, he saw that the crow was up ahead on another fence post. It flew off as the bus drove past.

Patrick began to watch the side of the road, reading the signposts, waiting for his bus stop. He wanted to get off at Town Square near Marnie's office. As the bus drove into Creekwood, Patrick turned his face to the sky, searching for the crow. It was nowhere to be found. Patrick shrugged.

Stepping off the bus, Patrick looked around at the festive sights of Creekwood. There was a massive Christmas tree in the square. It was lit up with colorful lights and baubles. He smiled up at the tree and tried to remember back to a time when Christmas had been a happy occasion for him. He closed his eyes and thought about his mother, his father, his two brothers, grandparents, aunts, uncles and cousins – all gathered around a tree singing Christmas carols. He was five years old again, and it was Christmas Eve. They had all just come home from church. He loved church on Christmas Eve. He got to light a little candle from the Nativity candle, stand on the pew between his father and mother and hold the candle up high while singing "Silent Night." His smile dimmed, then turned to a frown rather quickly. Memories, even the happiest ones, could become painful this time of year.

Patrick shook off his bitterness and looked about, spotting Marnie's office on the other side of the square. He saw a woman putting Christmas lights in the window, and he saw Carl holding the ladder for her. He knew that wasn't Marnie. The woman had brownish hair. He'd seen a picture of Marnie, but he hadn't seen her up close. Still, he knew Marnie's hair was blondish. People always look different in pictures, though. Pictures could never capture a person's soul quite right. He set off across the square and shivered at the cold wind blustering through the center of town. He glanced up and saw the crow sitting on a granite statue of Henry Hudson. The crow peered down at Patrick, cawed and then flew away. Patrick waved and returned his attention to the couple in the window at Marnie's office.

"Patrick!" a voice called out. Patrick winced. It was Allen's voice, but Patrick could not see him.

"Patrick!" Allen yelled out again and waved to Patrick.

Patrick's eyes scanned the crowd of people bustling about with shopping bags, briefcases and takeout coffee cups. When he spotted Allen, he wanted to run, but he just stood still and waited. Allen waved again and ran through the crowd. He was out of breath when he reached Patrick.

Allen bent over and tried to catch his breath. "I have been looking for you everywhere, son."

"Why? Why are you l-l-looking for m-m-me, Allen?" Patrick squinted as sun broke through the snow-filled clouds.

Allen held out his hands, cocked his head and managed a shocked expression. "Why, Patrick, we need your help tonight. We need you to be our energy healer. Don't you know that you are the perfect person? We know that you are gifted, and we want you to work with us."

Allen patted Patrick on the shoulder and smiled closely into his face. Patrick took a step back.

"I d-d-don't think I c-c-can help you. I don't think I c-c-can stay with you anymore. What you d-d-did this morning was... was... was evil. It was horrible, and I don't w-w-want to b-b-be with p-p-people like that," Patrick replied, fear hanging in his voice. Then his eyes were drawn beyond Allen, and he saw Alice walking toward them.

"I c-c-can't h-h-help you. I d-d-don't want that witch anywhere n-n-near me," Patrick shouted, pointing to Alice.

When Allen turned to look in the direction Patrick was pointing, Patrick ran into a crowd of people and disappeared.

Allen turned in circles looking for him. Alice hurried to his side, grabbed Allen's sleeve and pointed across the square to Patrick pushing open the door to Marnie's office. Both stood with their mouths agape, their panic-stricken faces slack.

"No! He can't be going in there! Allen, why didn't you stop him?" Alice's voice was loud and harsh.

She was staring up into Allen's face with fear written all over her own. Her face was red, and her eyes filled with dread. She suddenly grabbed at her chest and sat quickly on a bench near the bus stop.

"He just ran away. I couldn't stop him. He's fast. Alice, are you okay?" Allen reached a hand out to Alice.

He sank down on the bench next to Alice, her face scarlet as she gasped for air.

"You need to calm down. Are you having an asthma attack?" Allen rested a hand gently on her shoulder.

Alice nodded and reached in her pocket for her inhaler. She deftly lifted it to her mouth and gave it two quick puffs. She caught her breath, calmly inhaled through her nose and exhaled through her mouth.

Clutching Allen's arm, Alice spoke shakily, "We need to get to the cemetery and remove the pieces of the spell from the ground. If Marnie and Carl find it, we will be implicated. Patrick will tell them. He will tell them!"

Allen peered over his shoulder directly at Marnie's office and nodded. He stood and helped Alice to her feet.

"I'll take you back to the hall, go to the pharmacy and then go to the cemetery. He may tell them, but they won't get there before me. It's going to be fine, Alice. Don't worry yourself. I'll take care of everything." Allen patted her arm gently.

Allen and Alice slowly walked back toward the hall.

~~~~~~~~~~~~~~~~~~~~~~~~

Patrick stood inside the door of Marnie's office, taking in the Christmas decorations. Carl and the brownish-haired woman whom he had seen through the window were standing in the kitchenette filling their coffee cups. Carl turned to see who had come in the door and smiled when he saw Patrick.

Carl walked across the office in three long strides and held out his hand to Patrick. "Patrick. It's good to see you. How are you? Ahh... this is Marnie's assistant Andrea."

Andrea nodded to Patrick. He nodded back.

Patrick studied the office nervously and didn't know what to say. He had a lot to say, but he didn't know how to say it. He looked from Carl to Andrea and back to Carl. He hesitated and slowly said, "I'm okay, Mr. P-P-Parkins. I'm a b-b-bit worried about you, and I'm w-w-worried about Marnie R-R-Reilly, too. Is she here?" Patrick glanced around the office, searching for Marnie.

Carl frowned and observed Patrick intently.

"What's up, Patrick? What's got you worried?" asked Carl.

"Um... I... um... th-th-there's a th-th-thing at the cemetery. There's a thing that Alice d-d-did that scares me," Patrick replied, licking his lips and swallowing hard. He always found it hard to tell people bad things. It made him remember the past, and he didn't like remembering the past. It hurt.

"Okay, Patrick. How 'bout you and I go into my office and sit for a minute. I'll get you some water. and we'll talk. Does that work?" Carl said over his shoulder, as he slowly and methodically got a glass of water from the dispenser. Carl gave Andrea a dismissive shake of his head, and she took the hint as she stepped out of earshot.

Patrick nodded and followed Carl. He walked slowly and carefully, glancing from side to side searching for Marnie. Carl walked into his office and sat behind his desk. Patrick followed and sat in a visitor's chair.

"Patrick, can you tell me what's happening? What's got you so upset?" Carl asked.

Carl slowly placed his hands on top of his desk and waited.

"Uh... well, Alice d-d-did something to you and M-M-Marnie. She did it this morning... at the cemetery. She and A-A-Allen and the others."

Patrick took a drink of water and considered the room.

"Okay. Keep going. What did Alice do?" Carl waited.

"Um... uh... she b-b-buried you. She threw d-d-dirt on you, and she put a c-c-curse on you," Patrick said, speaking quickly, his eyes scanning every detail of the room as he spoke. He appeared frightened and nervous. He was twisting the hem of his jacket as he spoke.

"She w-w-wants you to h-h-hurt. She wants Marnie Reilly to hurt. She wants to k-k-kill your Christmas. She wants to m-m-make y-y-you hurt. She wants to m-m-make M-M-Marnie hurt. She wants you dead!" Patrick blurted out the last four words sharply.

"Okay. Okay. Slow down, Patrick. Did you see her do this thing? Were you there?" Carl waited.

"I d-d-didn't want to be. I was t-t-trying to help b-b-because she took me in. I wanted t-t-to help b-b-because they g-g-gave me food. I didn't mean to hurt you. I d-d-don't want M-M-Marnie Reilly to b-b-be hurt. I w-w-want all of this to stop n-n-now! Stop now!"

Patrick covered his ears with his hands and put his head down. He was crying and shaking.

Carl stood slowly and walked around the corner of the desk. He heard light footfalls and glanced up in time to see Marnie peek in the door. Carl held his hand up to her, and she stopped. But Tater rushed passed Marnie and nudged Patrick with his nose. Patrick took his hands off his ears and looked down at Tater. Tater was smiling up at him. Patrick patted the top of Tater's head and spoke quietly, snuffling his nose.

"Who are you? You're beautiful. Do you have a name? Do you have a family?" Patrick asked.

Tater barked and put his paw on Patrick's knee. Patrick smiled down at Tater and scratched his ears. Carl motioned for Marnie to come into the office.

"Marnie, come meet my friend Patrick. He came here to talk to us," Carl said and shot Marnie a knowing look. Marnie understood.

Marnie walked in, smiled warmly and held out her hand to Patrick.

"Hi, Patrick. It's lovely to meet you. My dog's name is Tater. Thank you for saying he's beautiful."

Patrick stood up and shook Marnie's hand. His tear-stained face turned red, and he turned away when he spoke.

"P-P-Pleased to m-m-meet you, ma'am," said Patrick with a small bow.

"Marnie, Patrick came to warn us about Alice and her friends. Apparently, they are up to a bit of mischief," Carl said with a nod in the direction of the phone.

Marnie nodded, excused herself and left the room for a minute. Marnie whispered loudly, "Psst! Andrea!"

Andrea glanced up from her desk and asked, "What?"

"Call Danny or Tom or both. Get one of them here. Now. Please."

Marnie ducked back into Carl's office after Andrea reached for her phone and was heard to be punching in numbers. Patrick was rambling when Marnie returned.

"You h-h-have to go to the c-c-cemetery. The one where Marnie's p-p-parents are. You have to g-g-go now. I can show you. I can help. I'm s-s-sorry for what's happened. I didn't m-m-mean to h-h-hurt you. I would n-n-never hurt you. I would never h-h-hurt you. I would never hurt you. P-P-Please come with me. Please let me. Please."

Patrick was out of breath and gulped another drink of water. His hands were shaking. Carl raised an eyebrow and turned to Marnie with concern.

Patrick stood up quickly and started for Carl's door.

"We need to go now. We have to g-g-go now. Come with me, p-p-please. Please, come with m-m-me," Patrick pleaded with Marnie and Carl. He grabbed Marnie's sleeve.

As he tried to leave Carl's office, Marnie put her hand on his arm and comforted him back into his chair.

The bell over the office door rang out, and Andrea saw that it was Tom who walked into the office.

Andrea looked up and said, "You're quick."

"Music to every man's ears," Tom quipped. "Where's Marnie? She signed on the dotted line, and her car is free from the forensics lab. I was on my way here with her car keys when you called."

Tom jiggled the car keys as he walked through the office. Andrea shook her head, smiled and pointed to Carl's office.

"She's in with Captain Crystals and his little friend."

Tom laughed and walked through to Carl's office. He stopped outside the door when he heard Patrick's rambling.

"We n-n-need to go n-n-now. We have to go. We have to go. If we don't go now, it will be b-b-bad. It w-w-will b-b-be bad. Bad. We have to go now," Patrick pleaded, looking back and forth quickly between Carl and Marnie.

Tom pushed the door open, stuck his head in the office and said, "Hey, Marnie. Everything okay?"

"Look. It's Tom. Tom's here," Marnie said awkwardly. She gave Tom a funny look and pulled his arm so that he would come into the office. "Come in and meet Patrick. Patrick, this is my friend Tom. He's a detective. Detective Tom Keller. Tom, this is Patrick. He's a friend of Carl's."

Patrick jumped up from the chair, looked Tom up and down and held his hand out to shake Tom's hand. Tom looked at Patrick in a way that good detectives do. He was sizing him up.

Tom saw a man of medium height with the build of a wrestler. He had short brown hair, hazel eyes and a broad face with high cheekbones and a crooked nose. He looked like he'd been through a war. He had a scar across his forehead that, at first glance, could have been a very long wrinkle, but Patrick wasn't old enough for that. Patrick's left ear was horribly scarred, and his left hand was, too. The scars appeared to be from burns. Serious burns. He was wearing a well-worn camouflage jacket; a blue flannel shirt; faded, worn jeans; and work boots. He was clean and tidy, but definitely didn't spend money on his clothes. There was something in his eyes. He'd lived a lot of years in a very short time.

Tom shook Patrick's hand and continued to observe him closely.

"Hi, Patrick. What's goin' on? You sound upset. Wanna tell me about it," Tom urged gently.

Patrick gave Tom another quick once over, scanning him head to toe. He looked down at Tom's shoes and shook his head in disapproval.

Patrick commented, "You need to p-p-polish your shoes, D-D-Detective. Your shoes are scuffed. Give'em to me, and I'll p-p-polish them up for you."

Tom looked down at his shoes and back at Patrick. "Yeah, well, I've been walkin' around all day. My shoes have seen a lot of snow, mud and salt. I'll take care of them when I get home tonight, but thanks for the offer, Patrick. I appreciate it."

Patrick replied, "No problem, s-s-sir. It's real important to t-t-take care of your shoes, you know. You have to t-t-take care of your shoes and k-k-keep your feet dry. It's real important to keep your f-f-feet dry."

Tom went along, nodded at Patrick and leaned on the file cabinet in the corner of Carl's office.

"Yeah. I'll keep that in mind. Hey, how 'bout you tell me where you want Marnie and Carl to go with you?"

Patrick frowned, dropped his gaze down at the floor and then looked back up to Tom.

"The cemetery. We n-n-need to go the cemetery. The cemetery. Alice d-d-did some things this morning, and I helped her. Something that c-c-could hurt people." Patrick looked around nervously and rushed his words as he continued. "I need to fix it. I need to fix it. I need to fix it."

A panicked Patrick looked quickly between Tom, Marnie and Carl. He put his hands over his ears, bent over and whispered quickly.

Over and over again he said, "I need to fix it. I need to fix it. I need to fix it."

Tom shot a dubious look to Carl and motioned with his head toward Patrick and frowned.

Carl came around his desk again and put his hand on Patrick's back. Patrick stood up quickly and stared up at Carl.

Carl spoke softly and firmly. "Patrick, can you sit down for me? We can help you. I know you mean well. Okay?"

Patrick sank back down into the chair and put his head in his hands.

"Patrick, what cemetery do you want us to go to?" Tom asked.

Patrick lifted his head and said, "Where Marnie's p-p-parents are."

Tom nodded and calmly said, "Okay. Let me call my partner, and we'll go."

Tom stepped out of Carl's office and called Danny.

"Hey, man. I'm at Marnie's office. Where are you?" Tom whispered.

"About 2 minutes away. What's up? Why are you whispering?" answered Danny.

"There's a guy here, uh, Patrick. He says that The Collective is trying to hurt Marnie. Uh... and Carl. I'm not so worried about him, but Marnie, well, you know," Tom's tone still hushed.

Tom leaned back and peeked into Carl's office.

Danny clenched his jaw and, through gritted teeth, responded, "Yeah. Give me a sec. Just parking. Be right there."

Tom walked back into Carl's office and said, "Okay Patrick, let's go to the cemetery. My partner's here, and we'll help. Okay?"

Patrick jumped up, nodded and quickly agreed, "Okay. We n-n-need to hurry. We need to fix it. We need to fix it. F-F-Fix it."

"Okay. Come on," Tom said.

Carl and Marnie stared at Tom.

"You two stay here. We'll be back soon," Tom ordered, turned and walked to the door as Danny walked into the main office.

Carl, Marnie and Tater followed when they heard the bell over the door ring.

Danny stood by the door. His jaw was clenched. He gave a brief wave to Carl, a nod to Andrea and then a small smile in Marnie's direction. Tater walked over and put his paw on Danny's leg.

Danny bent over to scratch Tater's ears and turned to Tom.

"C'mon. Let's get moving," Danny said.

Tom nodded, moved toward the door, turned back and looked at Patrick. Patrick hesitated. He was nervously assessing Danny.

"Patrick, this is my partner, Detective Gregg. C'mon. We'll take you to the cemetery." Tom looked expectantly at Patrick.

"He tried to hurt Alice," Patrick accused, pointing to Danny.

"No, Patrick. That's not true," Tom reassured. Tom turned to Carl to provide reassurance. "Carl, tell Patrick that's not true," Tom coaxed.

Carl turned to Patrick and explained, "Patrick, Detective Gregg didn't try to hurt Alice. That's not true. I can assure you that Detective Gregg is one of the good guys. He doesn't hurt people. He protects them. Just like you, Patrick. Detective Gregg protects people."

Carl walked over to Patrick, put his hand on Patrick's shoulder and nudged him toward the door.

"Go with the detectives, Patrick. They'll help you."

Patrick nodded hesitantly at Carl. He walked across the office and stood next to Tom. "Okay. Let's go."

"Okay," Tom replied with a grin.

Tom opened the door, and Patrick followed. Danny gave a small wave and turned back to Marnie.

"Marn, I'll be back soon to pick you up. I'd feel better if I followed you back to the cabin. Okay?" Danny asked.

Marnie nodded her acceptance – a bit reluctantly. She wasn't thrilled with the thought that someone felt that they needed to take care of her, look after her and protect her, but still, there was something comforting about knowing that someone wanted to do so. Besides, she could stay here with Carl, and he could fill her in on Patrick's history. Perhaps they could help him.

-CHAPTER TWELVE-

Street lights were coming on as they drove through town to St Michael's Cemetery. Patrick sat in the back. He peered out the side windows at the Christmas lights on the streets. He turned away from the window and focused on happy thoughts. Carl explained to him that, when he gets anxious, it is important to think happy thoughts. He remembered Carl telling him, *"We're retraining your brain, Patrick. If we work together, your PTSD will get better. You won't forget things, but we can retrain your brain to react in a better way."* Carl was helping Patrick work through his past trauma, and Carl was always honest with him. Patrick believed now that he could trust Carl.

Danny and Tom spoke quietly in the front seat.

"So, what's the story?" asked Danny, motioning to the back seat with his head.

Tom checked on Patrick in the vanity mirror on the passenger seat's visor.

"Apparently, Alice and company were up to no good at the cemetery this morning. Not sure. Just following Ms. Reilly's direction on this one." Tom shrugged and reached to turn his seat warmer down.

He glanced back at Patrick again. Eyes closed, Patrick seemed more relaxed than he had been at the office.

"You know, I'm not so keen about going to the cemetery under normal circumstances. Going at night when it's dark? Well, let's just say it's not makin' me feel all warm and fuzzy. Know what I mean?" Tom said with a shiver.

"Yep. You're a bit skittish for a detective." Danny laughed quietly.

"Hey, I just don't want a ghoul sneaking up behind me. That's all. I watch TV. I've seen those ghost shows where people get scratched and shit. Not me. Not gonna happen to me. That's all that I'm sayin'," Tom replied with a wave of his hands and a knowing sideways glance.

"Marnie's right. You are a bit of a scaredy cat." Danny laughed again and glanced into the rearview mirror.

"Yup. Happy to admit it," Tom replied candidly.

"Hey, Tom, can you call in to see who the forensic team is tonight? I think that we should have them ready."

Tom raised an eyebrow. "You really think that we're going to need them? Seriously? This is probably nothin'."

"Call it a gut feeling, Tommy. I really do think that we're going to need them – not sure why, but something feels off about this. I don't like the vibe, so to speak," Danny answered.

"No worries," Tom said, pulling his phone out of his pocket to make the call.

They drove in silence the rest of the way. When Danny pulled into the driveway of the cemetery, Patrick opened his eyes, sat up straight and peered out the windows.

"Where to, Patrick?" Danny stopped the Jeep and turned in his seat to face Patrick.

"Straight ahead, and turn left at the chapel," Patrick instructed, leaning over the center console between Danny and Tom to watch the road ahead. "Right there. See that wreath? Right there near the statue of St Michael. Stop here. Stop here. Stop here."

Patrick undid his seatbelt, slid across the seat to the door behind Danny and jumped out as soon as they stopped. Tom and Danny quickly followed as Patrick ran across the path and stood next to the statue.

"Right here. Right here. Right here." Patrick bounced on his toes with awkward excitement and pointed down to the freshly dug earth with the holly, hemlock and mistletoe sticking out. He moved quickly from foot to foot waiting for Tom and Danny.

"Okay, Patrick. What's this about?" Danny glanced down at the messy pile of disturbed earth and stood next to Patrick. Searching Patrick's face for some sign of ulterior motive or devious scheming, Danny came up empty. The guy seemed to be legit.

Patrick knelt down, pulled a pair of work gloves out of his pocket and reached out to start digging. Danny quickly pulled his hands back, much to Patrick's surprise.

"Hang on, Patrick. We need to get a photo of this site before you dig. Step back, please! Don't touch anything." Danny reached out a hand to help Patrick stand back up. Patrick assessed Danny's gesture for just a moment and accepted Danny's hand and assistance.

Their heads shot up when they heard a car coming up the driveway. As the car drew closer, Patrick recognized the car to be Alice's and the driver to be Allen.

Danny took his phone out his pocket. He took pictures of the site, their surroundings and the car idling in the driveway. He snapped that picture of the car on a hunch. Tom pulled out his phone to get several more angles of the scene. He, too, snapped a picture of the idling car.

Allen stopped his car but stayed put… watching. Patrick ignored him. Tom and Danny turned their attention to the idling car and tried to get a look at the driver. There was something familiar about the driver. Tom squinted to get a better look. Danny glanced down at Patrick.

"Here! Look! This i-i-is what Alice did." Patrick pulled on Tom's pant leg and pointed to the ground.

"Okay. We need to take it slow. We need to dig carefully, Patrick," Danny said calmly.

Danny reached into his pocket and took out a pair of Nitrile gloves. He knelt down next to Patrick; bagged the holly, hemlock and mistletoe; and then started pushing and scooping the disturbed earth very carefully.

Patrick mimicked what Danny was doing, and they quickly scooped the earth to the side, setting it in neat piles so that forensics could sift through it later.

"There, there, there. Look! It's the r-r-rat Alice p-p-put in the g-g-grave. There! The leaves and the s-s-salt and the f-f-feathers and the pictures. Look at the p-p-pictures!" Patrick pulled on Danny's arm and turned and looked up at Tom.

Tom and Danny peered into the shallow grave. They saw a dead rat with six black feathers piercing its chest, vulture feathers, dried leaves, rock salt and the photographs. Tom knelt down. He and Danny looked closer, and they recognized the faces in the photographs. Tom grabbed his phone out of his pocket and started taking pictures. Danny told Patrick not to touch anything. When Tom finished taking pictures, Danny placed all of the items into evidence bags.

Tom glanced up at the car. It was still idling at the top of the driveway. He grabbed a flashlight out of Danny's Jeep and started walking up the driveway to the car. *Hmm… that looks like Alice's goon Allen behind the wheel.* It was the outdated frames of his glasses. The frames were unusually large and made him look like a demented owl.

As Tom got closer, Allen nudged the car forward bit by bit. He wasn't concerned. These people weren't going to get in The Collective's way. He figured that he could just rev the engine, and the detective would move out of the way. He felt strange – invincible. He saw that Tom continued walking toward him. It was dark, and the headlights weren't very bright as they were covered with salt, dust and mud. Allen knew that there was an exit on the other side of the cemetery. A straight line is the quickest way, so he gunned it. He pushed his foot down hard on the gas. Tires spun on the snow-covered path, the car fishtailed and then it corrected and sped straight at Tom.

At the sound of the revving engine, Danny jumped up and ran to the road. He saw the car barreling toward Tom. He leaped, tackling Tom and driving them both onto the snow-covered lawn. The car careened onward toward the exit.

Patrick stood up and ran onto the driveway. He saw the dim headlights coming right at him. Danny and Tom jumped up, ran across the path and both shoved Patrick off the road to safety. The car sped off, kicking back snow and dirt as it flew through the exit gate.

"What the hell!" Tom stood up and brushed the snow and dirt off his pants and jacket.

"Patrick, you okay, buddy?" Danny stood and held out his hand to Patrick.

Patrick lay on the ground, legs splayed in front of him. He looked up at Danny, shakily took his hand and stood up unsteadily.

Patrick shrieked, "That was Allen. That was Allen. That was Allen! He tried to h-h-hurt me. He told m-m-me that he would n-n-never h-h-hurt me. He t-t-told me that he w-w-was a friend. H-H-He..."

Patrick put his hands over his ears, bent over and rocked from side to side.

Tom and Danny gave each other a sideways glance and turned back to Patrick.

"C'mon, Patrick. Let's get our police work done, okay?" Danny patted Patrick on the shoulder gently. "You've been a big help to us. We can make sure that Marnie and Carl are safe because you helped us. Okay?"

Patrick stood up straight. He looked from Danny to Tom and down at the ground. "Okay, if you say so. I was so scared." Patrick's voice trailed off. He brushed the snow from his pants and nodded slowly at Danny. "I'm okay now. I can help. But I n-n-need to talk to St. Michael over there, just for a m-m-minute."

Tom and Danny watched Patrick approach the large monument. They turned and finished gathering the evidence, bagging up the dirt that they'd removed from the site and packing everything into the back of Danny's Jeep. Then they placed a tarp over the hole, securing it with tent spikes. When they finished, they turned to look for Patrick and saw him standing calmly with his head bowed in front of the statue of St Michael. The light over the chapel shone brightly on the snow and made a halo effect around Patrick.

Danny walked across the path, stood next to Patrick and bowed his head, too. Tom stood on the road, his eyes darted from grave to grave uncomfortably.

Danny gazed up at St Michael, patted Patrick's shoulder to get his attention and motioned to the car with his head. Patrick nodded, turned back to St Michael, smiled up to the saint's face and then followed Danny to the car.

"Where are we going?" Patrick asked as he climbed into the back seat.

"We're taking you back to Marnie and Carl, then Tom and I have some work to do," Danny responded.

He watched Patrick in the rearview mirror for a second and turned his attention back to the road.

Patrick nodded. Murmuring to himself, he buckled his seatbelt and settled back into the seat.

"That was definitely Allen back there, wasn't it, Patrick?" Tom turned in this seat to see Patrick's reaction to his question.

"Yes. Yes, sir, it was. That's Alice's car, but that was d-d-definitely Allen. That was Allen. That was Allen. That was Allen," Patrick said as he nodded his head and shivered. He rocked in the seat for a minute, comforting himself. Then he peered out the window in silence.

"Well, we know where Allen will be tonight... and Alice," Tom said a bit too loudly, with a glance in Danny's direction. "We've got an eyewitness who saw everything, including that little ritual that we dug up back there."

Tom motioned to the back seat with his thumb.

Danny checked the rearview mirror and met Patrick's hazel eyes looking back at him.

"Yeah. We need to ask Carl about the stability of the informant. Know what I mean? Nut job or plausible witness? If it's the latter, I reckon a field trip to Station Hall may be in order." Danny shifted in his seat so that he could meet Tom's eyes.

"Yup. I was thinkin' the same thing," Tom replied. He sat back, watched the side of the road and wondered about what was coming next.

-CHAPTER THIRTEEN-

Marnie and Carl sat at the conference table with notepads open, pens raised and spread sheets in front of them. They were working through the practice and how they would move forward when Danny and Tom returned with Patrick.

Marnie heard a knock on the outer door and went out to the main office. Tom waved through the glass and pointed to the lock. Marnie nodded, crossed the office and unlocked the door.

Tom walked in and headed for the coffee machine, followed by Danny and Patrick. Danny embraced Marnie quickly and gave her a small kiss on the cheek. She smiled up at him. Patrick stood in the middle of the room, awkwardly assessing the situation.

"Everything okay?" Marnie scanned Danny's and Tom's faces for confirmation.

"Where's Carl?" Danny asked.

Marnie gave him a small frown and motioned to the conference room. Danny nodded and walked through.

Tom followed with a cup of coffee in his hand, but paused in the doorway.

"Hey, Marn? Can you please get Patrick a drink while we chat with Carl?"

"Uh. Yeah. Sure," Marnie replied. She glanced at Patrick and then at Tom's and Danny's backs as they disappeared into the conference room. "Um, Patrick, let's go see what your options might be."

Patrick shyly smiled at Marnie and followed her into the kitchenette.

Carl had heard the detectives arrive, but didn't glance up as the detectives walked into the conference room. He was writing notes on a spreadsheet as Tom and Danny each pulled out a chair and sat. Silently.

Carl finished his notes and looked up. "What's up?" An expression of concern shadowed his face.

Danny picked up a pen and started twirling it around his fingers.

"What can you tell us about Patrick?"

Carl thought carefully about his response and cleared his throat. "Uh. Well, he's a special person. Um... he's had a rough life. He always means well. He feels a duty to serve people. He suffers." Carl put his pen down and pushed his chair back. "You know, I'm not saying anything else. Doctor-patient confidentiality."

"Is he your patient? I mean, legally. Is he legally your patient?" Danny swiveled his chair impatiently.

"Well, I helped him when I was with The Collective, so yes. He is my patient," Carl replied.

"Have you got a case file on him, notes, things like that?" Danny pulled his chair closer and leaned his elbows on the table.

"No," Carl replied.

"Did you have your license while you were working with him?" Danny raised an eyebrow.

"Well, no, but that doesn't change anything. He was under my care," Carl shot back.

"Carl, doctor-patient confidentiality is one thing. Attempted murder is another."

Carl cut Danny off. "He tried to murder someone?" Carl asked suspiciously.

"Well, he helped at the cemetery this morning, and even though he came forward, what we found points to attempted murder or menacing behavior. We're looking at our options on this one. It's strange." Danny turned to Tom for confirmation.

Tom nodded in agreement. "Yeah. What we found implicates several people. I've got a call into the DA. We should hear back from her soon."

"So, Carl, tell us about Patrick, since he wasn't technically under your care," Danny said.

Carl hesitated. He stared down at his hands and lifted his gaze to Danny. "Why should I tell you anything?" Carl clenched his jaw and challenged the detectives.

Tom shot back, "'Cause we're askin', Carl. The guy has a screw loose, and we're tryin' to figure out if he's bein' straight with us. You want to help this guy? Tell us what you can."

Carl stood, and he stared down at Tom. Carl's anger was obvious by the tinge of red rising in his face. "He's got a screw loose? Christ, Tom. The guy's a vet. He's been to Afghanistan for two tours. He mustered into the Army when he was 18. He's been through a war, and you want to tell me he has a screw loose? He suffers from post-traumatic stress disorder. Do you know what that does to a person?"

Tom shrugged sheepishly. "No, I don't. Sorry. I had no idea. I just know how he's behaved since I came in here earlier. I'm sorry. I didn't mean to offend anyone."

Danny glanced down at the table and nodded. "I know what it does to people. My father... well, I know. I know it's serious, and I know that most people don't get the help that they need for it. I know all about it. Well, maybe not the way you do, Carl, but I know some things."

Carl sat back down and met their eyes across the table again."Give the guy a break. He just got out about six months ago. Honorably discharged, I might add. He came back here because it's where his family used to live."

Carl leaned forward and continued softly, calmly. "Look, guys, his folks were killed in a fire when Patrick was just a kid. That guy out there was pulled out of the fire by the fire department, then he ran back into the fire to save his parents. He ran *into* the fire. A little kid ran into the fire. Do you get it?"

Danny and Tom both nodded somberly.

"He was in foster home after foster home until he ran away when he was 16. He's been running from life his entire life. He's back here, and I'm trying to help him. I don't know everything yet. He shares bits and pieces here and there. He's got no one. When his folks died, none of the family wanted him. He's very high energy – not ADHD. He is incredibly focused. He's brilliant, actually. He's highly emotional and unusually strategic in his thinking. He thinks in terms of, well, he always thinks about the outcome of actions. So, uh... essentially, every action that he sees – that another person does or, in fact, that he does – he thinks about the outcome rather than what's happening in the moment. He is five steps ahead of the average person. It's how he's wired. I can't explain it. I've never seen anyone like him before."

Danny and Tom nodded slowly. Carl realized that he wasn't making himself clear.

"Okay. Say he was sitting here right now. Danny, you picked up a pen when you sat down, right?" Carl asked.

Danny nodded.

"Okay. We – meaning me and Tom – weren't thinking about what you were going to do with the pen. We just know that you picked it up. Then again, we may not have paid attention to the fact that you picked up the pen. On the other hand, Patrick would already have a scenario running through his brain about what you were doing with the pen; how that would affect him, you, Tom and me; and how he can or should react to the fact that you just picked up a pen. He's already five steps ahead of us. We just know that you picked up a pen. We're not actually thinking about what you're going to do with it. Honestly, we don't care. Patrick does. He wants the whole story about that one action right now. This happens to him with every action. When I meet with him, I sit in my chair and use a tape recorder. I don't write. I don't move because I want his attention on thinking about himself and talking, not on what I may do next if I scratch my nose."

Tom stood up, peeked out the door and closed it again. "Holy shit! The guy must be exhausted."

Carl nodded and agreed. "Yes. He needs help.

Danny put the pen down on the table and considered his next question. "Is he truthful? Is he competent?" Danny thought for a moment and continued, "As in a competent witness? Is he a competent witness?"

Carl nodded and replied, "Yes, of course he is. He's troubled, but he is honest and competent. He knows right from wrong and will always do the right thing, even if it will be bad for him. He will always do the right thing."

Danny watched Carl's face carefully and leaned forward again. "Is he medicated? Is he a risk to himself or to others?"

Carl shook his head and responded, "No. He's not medicated. He refuses medication, and he is not a risk to anyone else. Absolutely not! He *would* put himself in harm's way to protect someone, though."

Danny tapped the table with his knuckle. "Okay. Keep him here with you and Marnie. We'll be back soon. We need to call our SPCA guy and go to Station Hall."

"The SPCA? Why?" Tom wrinkled his forehead.

"I've got an evidence bag in the back of my Jeep. That evidence bag has a dead rat in it with six black feathers stuck through its chest. Something about that image makes me think cruelty to animals. What about you?" Danny raised his eyebrow and cocked his head in Tom's direction.

Tom nodded his agreement. "Yeah. I can see your point. I get that." Tom stuck out his bottom lip and considered Danny's thought process. His mind ticked through the list of things that they now had to sort out about The Collective once and for all.

Carl interrupted, "Six black feathers?"

"Yup. That gets Allen and Alice off the street for at least 24 hours. A holding cell should do them both some good," Danny said decisively.

Carl pulled a confused face and asked, "Just Allen and Alice? What about the rest of them? Fill me in."

"Let's see," Danny replied, holding up his hands and counted off. "One, Alice threw a snowball at Marnie this morning, missed and hit Tater. Two, Alice or someone shoved six black feathers through the chest of a rat. Three, Allen turned up at the cemetery, tried to run Tom over, kept going and nearly took out Patrick. Four, Alice and company did a little ritual at the cemetery with the intent to kill and/or harm you and Marnie. Five, we get a chance to walk into Station Hall and wreck their night. Six, we can get a warrant to search their house and discover whatever dirt that they've got hidden. We may get lucky and get the rest of them, too, but for now, let's focus on the two who we know that we can collar."

Carl nodded. "Fair enough. You should take Marnie with you, though. She'll be able to help you calm down the attendees when you pull Allen and Alice out of the building. You're going to need her there to keep things on an even keel, and hell, she'll probably get some good people the help that they need if she gets a chance to speak to them. From what Patrick tells me, it was everyone from The Collective this morning. They were all there conspiring to kill or cause harm. Just sayin'. You know?"

"Good point." Danny nodded and considered Carl's suggestion. "Can you give me a list of their names? I'll confirm it with Patrick."

"No problem." Carl picked up his pen and started writing names on a pad of paper.

"Marnie, can you come here?" Danny stuck his head out the door and scanned the outer office for Marnie.

"What's up?" asked Marnie, emerging from the kitchenette and poking her head into the conference room.

"We need your help." Danny sat on the edge of the table.

"Tell me." Marnie pushed a box over and sat on the credenza.

Danny replied, "We're going after The Collective at Station Hall tonight."

He finished telling Marnie about the plan, tipped his head to the side and asked, "You in?"

Marnie smiled and said with a laugh, "You had me at 'We're going after The Collective.' I am in!"

-CHAPTER FOURTEEN-

Danny, Tom, Marnie and Eric Harland from the SPCA stood outside Station Hall. They stood back, observing the latecomers filtering into the building. Alice's car was parked behind the building in a loading zone. With no one in sight, Tom made a call and arranged to have the car towed to the forensics lab.

Danny paced back and forth on the sidewalk around the corner from Station Hall. They were waiting for two paddy wagons to arrive. He had given Captain Sterling the heads-up about what was about to happen, and in turn, Captain Sterling had given his full support to move the plan forward.

Danny pulled everyone into a huddle on the side street, away from the main doors of Station Hall. "Okay, Eric, you'll take care of charging Alice with cruelty to animals. You know, Tater and the rat. I don't expect it to go too far, but let's do it anyway. We're also charging Alice, Allen and the other people who attended this morning with menacing in the third degree. We can also charge Allen with assault on police officers with intent to do grievous bodily harm."

A search warrant had been prepared for The Collective's house, Station Hall and Alice's car. Officers were at the house now conducting the search. Carl had provided details about what they should be looking for, and all items had been clearly listed on the warrant. Danny didn't want any mistakes. He'd spoken with the District Attorney and found a judge who was more than happy to sign the paperwork. There were quite a few people in Creekwood who would rather enjoy the disbandment of The Collective.

The number of people whom The Collective had duped over the years was well known in Creekwood. They preyed on the elderly, people with mental illness, mourners wishing to speak to their dearly departed and those in poor physical health. People could buy hope at $150 a pop. Their network of customers expanded outside of the area because most people in Creekwood weren't fooled by them anymore. Some still were, and this was the chance for justice to be done for the good people of Creekwood. The Collective needed to be stopped, and this was the perfect opportunity.

Four patrol cars and two paddy wagons pulled up in front of Station Hall. Two officers stepped out of each vehicle. Danny, Tom and the officers gathered in a small circle. Danny briefed them on how the plan would go down. Danny told them that there were six exits – the front door, two side doors (one on each side of the building), one rear exit and two fire escapes near each of the two side exits. Two officers would guard the front exit, two would cover the back exit, two would guard each of the side exits (including the fire escapes) and four would come inside with him. They all nodded and followed Danny to the door.

Danny turned to Marnie. "You ready?"

Marnie nodded. "Yup. Ready to go."

Danny placed a hand on Marnie's arm and locked his eyes on hers. "You stay behind me, and stay close. Any sign of trouble, any guns, any weapons of any sort, you get down. Do you understand?"

Marnie nodded.

"Of course. I'll stay out of the way," she replied.

Danny leaned in close, his lips almost touching Marnie's ear. "Stay safe. I meant stay safe. You're never in the way. Just be safe. Don't take any silly chances. Okay"?

Marnie locked her eyes onto Danny's and nodded her agreement and understanding. He nodded back and gently pushed her behind him.

"Okay. Let's do it!" Danny said as he pushed open the doors to the foyer.

Danny, Marnie, Tom, Eric and the four officers entered the foyer.

The thirtysomething man from the alley was standing in the foyer and closing the doors to the auditorium as they approached.

"Sorry. Tickets aren't available at the door – only online. You'll have to check the Web site for the next event. This one is sold out," he advised. Then he looked at Marnie. He instantly recognized her.

He held up a hand. "Hang on. What are you doing here? This event is not open to speakers outside of The Collective. You can't be here." He took a step toward them to stop them from approaching the doors.

Danny held up his badge and the warrant and advised, "I'm afraid we can be here. We're here for Alice Wells and Allen Schofield." Danny stood firmly between Marnie and the man. "What's your name, pal?"

"Why? What does my name have to do with anything?" the man responded tersely.

Danny narrowed the space between him and the man. The man backed up quickly and shrunk under the towering frame of Detective Daniel Gregg.

Danny was calm, authoritative and just on the edge of condescending. "Well, pal, it isn't for my Christmas card list. Your name may or may not have anything to do with it, but I'm asking your name, and I am expecting an answer. Now!"

The man backed up and stared up into Danny's face, meeting Danny's steely stare with discomfort.

"Uh... my name is Reuben," he stammered.

"Reuben what? What's your last name, Reuben?" Danny leaned closer.

Reuben tried to back up again, but the door stopped him. He replied with a stammer. "Uh... Wilmot. Reuben Wilmot. My last name is Wilmot."

"Thank you, Mr. Wilmot. Please step away from doors, and wait here with the officer." Danny waved his hand toward one of the officers.

Reuben narrowed his eyes at Danny. "What's this about? I have a right to ask what this is about."

"No, you really don't," Danny growled.

He pushed past Reuben and opened the doors to Station Hall with Marnie, Tom, Eric and three officers following him.

Marnie grabbed Tom's arm and whispered, "Reuben Wilmot is Grace Wilmot's son. Remember Grace?"

Tom stopped short and nodded his head. Of course he remembered. He patted Marnie's hand and gave her a quick hug. Grace Wilmot was a charlatan of the worst kind. She had witnessed a murder, withheld evidence and strung the police along for months as she built up her business. She had watched the murder of Henry Jackson, a well-known restaurateur, and fed the police only bits and pieces of information at a time. She made it look like her psychic abilities were hard at work helping the police, which in turn found her client list growing by the day. In the end, the devious game found Grace in Witness Protection because the man who had murdered Henry was part of a violent gang. Her testimony and cooperation were traded for her freedom, but at least she was alive and not in jail for interfering with a murder inquiry. Her son was just a young teen and would have been placed in protection at the time as well. Tom wondered what had brought him back to Creekwood. Why was he using his real name, and where is his mother?

~~~~~~~~~~~~~~~~~~~~~~~~~~~~~

Detectives Daniel Gregg and Thomas Keller stood at the back of the auditorium waiting for an opportunity to pounce. Eric Harland and three policemen flanked them. Marnie tucked in behind Danny and Tom, positioning herself so that she could see the action in a small space between Danny's and Tom's shoulders.

As the audience settled in and the lights began to dim, Allen walked out of the wings, cordless microphone in hand. He took center stage.

"Welcome, dear friends. We are honored that you have chosen to spend the evening with us. We are very excited to be here to help you along your journey," Allen held out his arms in a welcoming gesture and bowed to the audience as their applause began.

Marnie frowned and poked Danny in the side to get his attention.

Danny turned to her. "What's wrong?"

"Something's weird, Danny. Allen never does the introduction. He hates talking in front of people. He's a nervous Nellie. He gets sick just thinking about talking to a group larger than two. Look at him up there. He looks like he's about to break out in song and dance."

Danny observed Allen's overtly comfortable demeanor while speaking with the audience.

He shrugged. "Maybe he's gotten comfortable speaking to large groups. Maybe he had a few drinks. I don't know. He looks just fine to me."

Marnie scowled. "No. You don't get it. This guy would literally vomit if he thought he had to speak to people, and that was just a few years ago. You saw him today. He was nervous speaking with just us outside, and there were only three of us."

Danny nodded and shrugged again. "Yeah, but he had Tom and me breathing down his neck. He was scared. He felt outnumbered – threatened. Tom and I are each twice his size."

Marnie rolled her eyes and muttered, "Okay, don't trust me. I'm just an expert on human behavior. Something isn't right here."

"What's that?" Danny asked, leaning closer to hear her over the crowd's applause.

"Nothing," replied Marnie curtly.

Danny's face deadpanned, he shook his head and then he turned to the others. "Hit it!"

With a nod of his head to the others, Danny, Tom, Eric and one officer walked up the center aisle. Two officers stood at the back doors blocking the exits. Marnie hung back by the doors – staying out of the way.

The lights shining on the stage didn't allow Allen to see who or what was coming up the aisle, and he continued his preamble to the evening.

"We have some great spiritual talent here for you tonight; to ensure that no one is interrupted and that psychic energy isn't fogged, I ask everyone to please turn off your phones and put away recording devices, cameras and the like. If you would like a DVD of tonight's activities, we will have these available for sale on our Web site in just a few days."

Marnie cringed with anger and frustration and couldn't help but shout out, "Selling hope again are you, Allen?"

Recognizing her voice and hearing Marnie's taunt, Allen stepped to the front of the stage and peered down at what and who was coming. He set his feet and puffed out his chest, and with all of the bravado in the world, he bowed to the figures approaching, believing it to be Marnie.

"Good evening, Ms. Reilly. So nice of you and your friends to join us."

Danny turned and shook his head in Marnie's direction. He ran a hand across his throat telling her to cut it out.

Marnie strode forward up the aisle to Danny and hissed, "I'm sorry. I just... These people are... These people make me sick. Look at Allen. He's not one bit nervous. He's not one bit scared. Look at him, Danny. Look at him!"

Danny nodded, patted her arm and then proceeded quickly to the steps at the side of the stage. He took the steps three at a time, crossed the stage in five huge strides and stopped at center stage, ready for a showdown with Allen.

Allen turned to Danny and said, "Tell me, Detective Gregg, what I can do for you on this fine evening. Did you and your friends find anything interesting at the cemetery?"

Danny frowned and thought: *This guy is taunting me. He's taunting a detective. What the hell is wrong with him? He normally quivers and shakes. He doesn't taunt me. He doesn't challenge me.*

The audience sat with their mouths open in stunned silence at the spectacle unfolding before them.

Danny put a hand up to block the spotlight from his eyes and studied Allen closely. His pupils were huge, and it wasn't his glasses magnifying his eyes. Allen's eyes were dilated. The guy looked high on something.

Allen took a few steps forward and stood toe to toe with Danny. Danny put his hand out and nudged Allen back a few steps to put distance between them. Allen took a few steps forward again. Danny put his hand up on Allen's shoulder and held him back.

"What are you on, Allen?" Danny asked quietly.

"On? What do you mean 'on?' I'm high on life, detective," Allen replied with a haughty laugh and a flourish of his hands.

Danny studied Allen and proceeded to take the microphone from Allen. Allen held tight and kicked out at Danny, catching him on the shin. Tom slowly walked up the steps and positioned himself to step up if needed.

Danny snatched the microphone out of Allen's hand, tucked it inside his jacket to muffle the sound and said, "Allen, step over there to my partner. See Detective Keller standing right over there. I want you to walk slowly over to him, and I want you to do it now."

Allen scowled at Danny. He reached out to grab back the microphone. Danny held him back with his forearm while Allen started swinging wildly at him. Tom's lanky frame flew across the stage and grabbed Allen from behind. He twisted Allen's arms behind him and cuffed him. Allen twisted around and glared at Tom. Tom put a hand on his shoulder and pushed him toward stage left.

Danny pulled the microphone from his jacket and addressed the crowd.

"Good evening. I do apologize for the disruption. It would be appreciated it if you could all please stay in your seats. Our officers and our colleague, Ms. Reilly, will get your names, and we will help if we can to ensure that everyone gets a refund for this evening."

Alice darted clumsily from the wings and wobbled onto the stage. As she approached center stage, she began to wheeze, and between wheezes, she pointed her finger and threatened, "Marnie... Reilly, you... get... out... of... here."

Alice wheezed and caught her breath, and her rant continued. "The Collective... has booked... the... hall for... the evening. We... have... done... nothing... wrong. I... want... you to... leave... now."

Alice's face reddened, her breathing labored. She doubled over and fell to the stage. Marnie ran up the steps to Alice's side.

Danny called for an ambulance and knelt down next to Marnie. Marnie pulled her coat off, and Danny folded it and placed it under Alice's head.

"Alice, where's your inhaler? Alice, is it in your pocket?" Marnie asked, remembering Alice's asthma from the short time that she had spent with the group. Marnie patted Alice's pockets, searching for the inhaler.

Alice shook her head and fought to take a breath. She gripped Marnie's hand tightly and choked out her words in a raspy whisper.

"It's in... my coat... pocket. Please..."

Marnie jumped up quickly and ran backstage. People scattered. No one wanted to get involved. The police were here. Marnie Reilly was here. They all knew that shit was about to get real.

Tom grabbed the microphone from Danny's hand and addressed the crowd. "Everyone, please stay in your seats! We need to keep the aisles clear for the emergency medical team. Everyone, please stay in your seats! Officers, please stand by at the doors for the emergency medical team." Tom handed the microphone back to Danny, jumped off the stage and moved through the audience, asking people to remain seated.

Marnie shouted, "Where is Alice's coat? Can someone tell me where Alice left her coat?"

No one responded. They all backed into the wings, regarding Marnie with anger and fear.

"You! You, Justin! That's your name, right? Where is Alice's coat?" Marnie demanded.

"I... I... don't know!" Justin shouted back.

Justin grabbed his laptop off a table and ran for an exit.

"What is wrong with you people? Alice needs help. Someone help me find her coat! I know it's pink and puffy. Where is it?" Marnie shouted, as she searched the faces standing in the wings.

She saw another familiar face – a woman wearing a gray cape with red piping and red buttons – and when Marnie realized who she had seen and turned to confirm her suspicion, the woman was gone.

Marnie scanned the room. A grouping of chairs lined the back wall, and Alice's pink coat rested on the back of a chair. She raced over and grabbed it up. When she did, a bag fell out of the pocket with a light thud, and an inhaler mouthpiece popped out on the floor next to it. Marnie grabbed the bag, opened it and pulled out a box containing a small canister. She snapped the canister into the mouthpiece and ran back to the stage.

Marnie handed the inhaler to Alice, who shook it and took two quick puffs. Alice's face flushed pink, and Marnie reached out to take her hand once again. Alice closed her eyes; drew in a constricted, jagged breath; and grasped Marnie's fingers tightly. Her head lolled to the side, her grip relaxed on Marnie's fingers, and Alice Wells died on the stage at Station Hall in front of a stunned audience who were there to buy hope. Marnie picked up Alice's hand and spoke calmly, coaxing her back.

"Alice? Alice? We're right here. There's an ambulance on the way. Please, Alice, stay with us," Marnie said, gently stroking Alice's hand.

"Marnie! Marnie! We have to give her CPR. Do you know how?" Danny said, rousting Marnie from her daze.

Marnie nodded, and just as she and Danny were set to administer CPR, the emergency medical technicians were at their sides, gently pushing them aside.

84

"She had an asthma attack. We found her inhaler, she took two quick puffs and then she... she...," Marnie said, rambling her words together.

Danny wrapped his arms around her and led her to the wings so that the emergency team could help Alice.

~~~~~~~~~~~~~~~~~~~~~~~~~~~~

Allen sat in the back of a patrol car, gnawing on his bottom lip. When the officer had put him into the car, he had kicked the back door so hard that he was sure that he felt something crack. His foot was now beginning to ache. However, the ache in his foot was nothing compared to his craving for a cigarette.

Allen had smoked 30 or more nonfilter cigarettes most days since he was a teenager. He rolled his own and always had papers and tobacco on the ready. Quitting the habit was just about the hardest thing that he'd ever done. He knew that, if he could just reach into his back pocket, he could get one of his patches. He twisted his hands and contorted himself just enough to pull a patch from his pocket. He fumbled with the package and finally tore it open. He pulled the plastic tabs off and realized that he couldn't reach his shoulder, so he improvised and stuck the patch on the back of his hand. He sat forward for a moment and watched an ambulance arrive. A man and a woman took a stretcher from the back of the ambulance and carried it into Station Hall. Allen closed his eyes, settled back into the seat and relaxed. His mind drifted to his teens, when life was easy and he didn't have a care in the world.

Allen was peacefully hallucinating, drifting on an inner tube in the middle of a lake in the bright sunshine of summer, and in reality, he was drifting out the world at the exact moment that Alice was drawing her last breath.

-CHAPTER FIFTEEN-

As the emergency team left, Reuben saw his opportunity. He quickly slipped past the officers and entered the auditorium. The people in the audience were all standing by their seats and into the aisle, and this made it easy for Reuben to sneak down the aisle and disappear into the darkness of the wings.

Danny and one of the officers worked to ensure that the attendees took their seats once again, while Tom and another officer corralled the members of The Collective from the wings and into the auditorium.

Danny remembered that Tom had given him back the microphone and shouted into it, "Can someone turn on the lights in the auditorium? We need some lights on in here. Now!" The squawky feedback made the attendees cringe.

Marnie had backed into the wings so that she could search for the caped lady whom she had spotted earlier, but she couldn't find her anywhere.

Laptop in hand, Justin headed for the nearest exit, but found it flanked by officers. As the exits were all most likely blocked, Justin considered the available options. He chose up – reluctantly. He quietly climbed the circular stairs to the crow's nest and ducked down behind several rolls of backdrops that were carelessly leaning against the metal cage and a vertical beam. The catwalk over the stage was certainly an option, if one wasn't prone to vertigo, which Justin was. He held tight to the laptop and made a mental call to suck it up and risk the catwalk. The catwalk had waist-high handrails. It should be safe enough. He reminded himself to look straight ahead – *don't look down.* Justin stepped out onto the catwalk and looked down. His heart pounded in his ears – the sensation of rushing waves and the buzzing of a strange white noise surrounded him. The aural sensation wasn't real; he knew that it wasn't. It didn't change the overall effect that it was having on him. His stomach started to churn, he felt dizzy and he froze with fear. His sweaty hands struggled to grip the precious laptop.

Reuben climbed the circular staircase to the crow's nest so that he could get a bird's-eye view of the commotion below. Once at the top, he saw a man's back. Grasping one of the handrails, the man was swaying slightly. It appeared to Reuben that the man was holding something in his other hand; it looked like he held that *something* tightly to his chest.

"Hey, man. You okay?"" Reuben asked quietly.

Justin heard a voice through the static and crashing waves. He was terrified – he couldn't move. The voice came closer.

"Justin? Is that you, man?" Reuben took a step onto the catwalk.

Justin nodded his head, but didn't turn around.

"Reuben? Uh… I'm… uh... I'm… afraid… uh… of… um… heights," Justin said shakily.

"Yeah, it's me," Reuben responded.

"Uh… I came out here to get… uh… away. The doors… uh… the doors are blocked." Justin trembled.

"Yeah. The roof is the only way out of here," Reuben advised.

Justin swallowed hard. "The roof? No… no… I can't."

"You don't have to go to the roof. You can stay here and take your chances. Those cops are gonna be crawling all over this place soon. I'm heading to the roof, and that means that I have to get past you." Reuben took another step onto the catwalk.

-CHAPTER SIXTEEN-

Officer Connor, the cop who had placed Allen in the back of the patrol car, opened the back door and leaned into the car.

"Allen? Mr. Schofield? Hey!"

Officer Connor reached out a hand and gave Allen's shoulder a slight nudge, then a pinch. Allen tipped slightly. His mouth was agape – his body lifeless.

"Shit!" shouted the officer, as he slammed the door and ran to the ambulance.

He grabbed the arm of an EMT and said, "Can you have a look at the guy I've got in the back of my squad car? He's unresponsive."

The EMT grabbed his bag and ran to the squad car.

Over his shoulder, he said, "What's his name?"

"Schofield. Allen Schofield," Officer Connor replied.

Officer Connor opened the door, and the EMT leaned in across the seat. He checked Allen's vitals, shone a light into his eyes and pulled NARCAN out of his pack.

The EMT pushed Officer Connor back from the car.

"I'm gonna need some room."

Officer Connor stepped up onto the sidewalk and watched.

The EMT sprayed the NARCAN up Allen's nose and stepped back quickly as Allen inhaled sharply, sat bolt upright and jerked wildly, hitting the metal cage of the squad car with his head. He was gasping and flailing, struggling to get loose.

The EMT turned to Officer Connor and advised, "He's gonna have to ride along with me to the hospital. He overdosed, and we need to get him into care."

The EMT motioned for his crew to come retrieve Allen from the back of the squad car.

Watching the ambulance crew approach with a stretcher and restraints, Officer Connor said, "Yeah, sure. I'll just let Detective Gregg know and follow you to the hospital."

The EMT shook his head, pointed to the ambulance and said, "I'll see you at the hospital. We've gotta get her to the hospital ASAP – suspected asthmatic coma – she's critical. I can't wait for you, and we don't have another ambulance available. We've got two, and we're both out on a call."

Officer Connor nodded and said, "Yeah. Okay. You do what you gotta do. I'll be right behind you, but the guy – uh, Mr. Schofield – he tried to run over a couple of cops tonight."

"I get that, but her health and his health are my job, and I have to go now!" the EMT replied.

"Need an assist, Connor?" a voice asked.

Officer Connor turned around and saw Officer Sam Jalnack standing at the curb next to the open back door of the squad car.

"Yeah! Can you let Detective Gregg know that I'm heading to the hospital with Allen Schofield?"

Jalnack said, "Sure. I'll let Danny know. What's up with Schofield?"

"Overdose," responded Officer Connor.

"What?" Jalnack blurted, eyes wide with disbelief. "That guy? He wouldn't take anything stronger than a Tic Tac."

Officer Connor shrugged, got into his squad car and left for the hospital.

-CHAPTER SEVENTEEN-

Onstage and still searching for the caped woman, Marnie heard a noise from above, glanced up and saw two men on the catwalk. She wasn't sure, but she thought that one of the men was Reuben Wilmot. She looked about for Tom and Danny, but saw neither.

Marnie ducked backstage and quickly located the winding stairs. She gingerly climbed the steps.

When Marnie reached the top, she waited for her eyes to adjust to the darkness. She took a step closer to the catwalk, and when she did, her shin hit something dark and heavy, dislodging it with a loud clang.

Startled by the noise, the men on the catwalk turned to see Marnie standing in the shadows. One of the men skulked along the catwalk to see who was spying on them.

Marnie squinted and peered into the darkness. She could only make out shapes – silhouettes. One was moving toward her slowly – skulking.

"Marnie!" Danny called out from the auditorium below.

Marnie turned to Danny's call. She never had a chance to answer him. As she turned back to the shadows, a fist appeared out of the darkness, struck the side of her head and drove her into a wall. A second hit took her to the floor and into a vortex of blackness that shoved her violently into a place that she visited often in her nightmares.

~~~~~~~~~~~~~~~~~~~~~~~~

Officer Sam Jalnack found Danny and filled him in on both Allen Schofield's trip to the hospital and Officer Connor following him in a patrol car. Danny asked Sam if to stay out front and ensure that no one entered or exited the hall until he gave the okay. Sam obliged.

"Hey, Tommy! Have you seen Marnie?" Danny called to the other side of the auditorium.

Tom shrugged and replied, "Not in the last few minutes. She was on the stage – what – 10 minutes ago."

A patrolman walked from the wings and headed straight toward Danny.

"Detective Gregg, Ms. Reilly said to tell you that she's heading to her office to check on her dog. Said she'd be back in a few minutes."

Danny tipped his head and scowled. "Who the hell are you?"

"Ah… sorry. I'm Johnson from Hudson Division. We got a call that you might need help," the patrolman answered.

"Johnson, huh? Never heard of you. Who called you?" Danny pressed.

"Uh… well, honestly, I was just heading home for the day, and I heard the call on the radio. Drove over here because – well, I don't really fit in over at Hudson. I've been looking for an opportunity…"

Danny held up his hand. "Stop! Okay. We hear it a lot. Hudson is a tough division – not easy to make friends."

"Sorry if I've caused trouble, Detective Gregg. I, well, I just wanted to help," said Johnson.

"It's okay. We could use some help. How 'bout you go over there and help Connor get witness statements. Can you do that?"

"Yes, sir. No problem," Johnson replied.

"Okay. Good. I would appreciate it," Danny said.

"Why is it so dark?"
"Where am I?"
"Why can't I feel my toes?"
"Why are my fingers numb?"
"Why can't I breathe?"
"Where's Tater?"
"I'm dreaming. It's just a dream. It's only a dream. I'll wake up in a minute."

Witness statements finished and evidence gathered, Danny, Tom and the officers agreed to meet back at the station at 7:30 the next morning. It was late, everyone was tired and Danny needed to swing by Marnie's office to pick up her and Tater.

Tom stood at the front door of Station Hall, chatting with Patrolman Johnson.

"Hey, Tommy, can you make sure that everything gets back to the station? I need to pick up Marnie and Tater at her office and head home," Danny asked.

"Yeah, sure. I didn't even realize Marnie left earlier. It's not like her to not stick around, and it's definitely not like her to *not* stick her nose into police business." Tom laughed.

Danny furrowed his brow – shoved his fingers through his hair and turned to Johnson.

"Where was Marnie when she told you she was leaving? You said that she went to check on her dog. Marnie would never say that. She would say…"

"Tater. Marnie would say Tater!" Tom said loudly, snapping his fingers.

Danny turned to Tom and nodded. "She would. She would say 'Tater' – not 'her dog.'"

"Where's Ms. Reilly, Johnson?" Danny leaned threateningly close to Johnson.

"Look, guys, I don't know who Tater is, and the only thing that I know about Ms. Reilly is that a guy backstage asked me to tell Detective Gregg that Ms. Reilly was going to check on her dog and that she would be back soon. He seemed really friendly and all. I thought that he was one of your tech guys. He had a laptop and was up on the catwalk with another guy," said Johnson.

Johnson stepped a few feet away from Danny and Tom and shrugged.

"Really. That's all that I know," said Johnson, hands out, palms to the sky.

Danny slammed his hand on the door. It banged open so violently that Johnson stepped back a few feet further.

"Dammit! Dammit! I've got a bad feeling about this!"

"Yeah. Marnie wouldn't have left without telling one of us. She *wouldn't* have. She would've come to one of us." Tom rubbed the back of his neck.

"Yeah. Like I don't know that," Danny replied angrily.

Tom studied the length of the aisle in the darkened theater, shivered slightly and quietly replied, "Hindsight."

Danny pulled his phone out of his pocket and dialed Marnie. Her phone went directly to voice mail. He called Carl Parkins's number.

-CHAPTER EIGHTEEN-

Marnie Reilly had few fears. Spiders, snakes and creepy-crawly insects didn't scare her. She wasn't afraid of ghosts – that was certain. She'd been seeing ghosts her whole life. Unlike some of her friends and clients, she really didn't fear being alone. She was used to being alone. She liked her own company.

What Marnie Reilly did fear was dying in a fire or drowning, and she feared losing those whom she loved. She didn't fear any of those things as much as she feared closed spaces. Marnie could break into a cold sweat just thinking about confinement in tight quarters. Closed spaces made her skin crawl. The one sure thing to send Marnie Reilly into an all-out panic attack was being trapped – confined – bound, gagged and shut into a dark, cramped space, which was where she was now. Marnie Reilly was trapped in a prophetic, recurring nightmare that she had experienced throughout her life. Sometimes, months would go by without the dream, then the dream would come night after night after night. In her dream, her father would come to her side, shake her gently awake and tell her that everything would be fine.

Marnie closed her eyes and willed herself awake. Her head hurt, and she struggled to clear her vision. The difference this time was that she *knew* that she was awake. She was trapped for real, and no one was coming to shake her gently awake.

Marnie's eyes stung with tears. She could barely breathe. The tape covering her mouth was covering her nose partially, too. Her hands were bound behind her back. Her ankles were bound together, and she was on her side. She couldn't roll over onto her back – the space was too small. One shoulder touched the top of her tomb and the other, the floor. Her legs were cramped – she couldn't kick. It was dark. She couldn't see. She could smell, though. She could smell lavender, sage, frankincense and dragon's blood, and she suddenly knew exactly where she was. She was in one of The Collective's prop boxes. She tried desperately to draw in a deep breath through her nose. She tried to make a noise – any noise. Only a muffled, mournful moan would come out. She couldn't flail or tap or make any sounds other than her futile attempts to cry out; she put her head down, and it clunked to the floor of her leather-bound prison.

Then she remembered her shoes. Her shoes had heels. Three-inch heels. If she could somehow jiggle her shoes off... Well, that would give her about three inches of space, and with that three inches of space, she could make one hell of a noise.

~~~~~~~~~~~~~~~~~~~~~~~~~~~~~

Carl and Patrick sat quietly perusing menus in a booth at the back of Ryan's Diner. Tater was seated on the window side of a bench seat next to Patrick.

"What would you like to eat, Patrick? Anything look good?" Carl asked.

"Hmm... Everything looks good. Do you have a favorite?" Patrick replied.

Tater rested his chin on the table and glanced back and forth between Carl and Patrick. Carl reached across the table and gently scratched the top of Tater's head. Patrick jerked sideways at Carl's reach – startled – but then settled back.

"What would you like, Tater?" Carl asked with amusement.

Tater popped his head up and smiled. Carl turned to see who had Tater's attention and saw Gram bustling across the diner toward their table.

"Evenin', Carl. What can and I get you and your friend?" Gram asked.

"Hi, Mrs. Ryan. I would love a glass of iced tea. I'll have the meatloaf with mashed potatoes and green peas, thanks," Carl said.

"All right, and for your friend?" Gram asked.

"M-M-My name is Patrick, Mrs. Ryan," said Patrick.

"Good to meet you, Patrick. Do you know what you'd like?" Gram smiled.

"I would like the h-h-hot t-t-turkey sandwich on sourdough, please," Patrick said.

"Do you want a side of fries and somethin' to drink?" Gram asked.

"Y-Y-Yes, please. F-f-fries and water, p-p-please," Patrick replied.

"What about Tater? Are you watchin' him for Marnie? Has he had his dinner?" Gram asked.

Carl nodded and replied, "Yes, Marnie is with Danny and Tom. Tater had a bit of tuna at the office, but I'm sure that he would probably eat something else. It wasn't a very big can."

"How about some beans and carrots? I know Marnie is watchin' his diet, you know," said Gram.

"Yes, ma'am. That would be great, Mrs. Ryan. Thanks." Carl nodded and smiled.

Carl's phone rang. He looked down to see who was calling. The screen said "Detective Dickhead," and he reached to cover it up quickly. He glanced up to see if Gram had seen, but she was already bustling away with their order.

Carl answered, "Detective Gregg?"

"Carl, it's Danny. Is Marnie with you?" Danny asked.

"Marnie? No. I thought that she was with you?" Carl replied.

"Dammit!" Danny exploded.

Carl pulled the phone away from his ear.

"We've got Tater here with us at your grandmother's diner. Patrick is with me. It got late, and we came here. We thought that Marnie was with you. I left her a message about 20 minutes ago to let her know where we were headed." Carl glanced down at his watch.

He could hear Danny's footfalls as he paced back and forth. Danny drew in a deep breath and exhaled loudly.

"Carl, do you know if Marnie's car was still at the office when you left there?" Danny asked.

"Uh… yeah. It was out back," Carl replied.

"Okay, Carl, I need you to do something for me," Danny said.

"What do you need?" asked Carl.

"Can you come to Station Hall with Tater, please?" requested Danny.

"Uh… sure," Carl responded and added, "Danny, what's going on?"

"Marnie is missing. She was here, then she wasn't. Someone told one of the officers here that she left to go back to her office to check on her dog," Danny said.

"Well, she never returned to the office. Her car is still at the office, so she couldn't have gone too far. Do you think she went to her house?" Carl said.

"Not without Tater. Not without her car and not without personally telling Tom, me or you where she was going. She would have picked Tater up first," Danny answered.

Carl scratched his chin, looked down at his watch again and glanced out the window. It was starting to snow.

"Carl? You there?" Danny asked.

"Yeah. I'm just thinking. I'll get the food to go and be right there. I don't think Patrick has eaten all day."

"Okay. We'll see you soon," Danny replied.

~~~~~~~~~~~~~~~~~~~~~~~~~~~~~

Danny surveyed the room. He ran a hand over his tired face, rubbed his tensed jaw, narrowed his eyes, scanned the theater and finally set his focus on the stage. Tom paced through the rows of the now-empty theater. He raised his hands in frustration to Danny. From across the theater, Officer Johnson joined them.

"Okay. We need to think like Marnie. Where could she have gotten to? When did we actually see her last? Where was she in the theater?" Danny turned to face the stage.

Tom's gaze followed Danny's to the stage. He ran the last few hours through his head, putting the timeline together like a jigsaw puzzle. One piece here, another piece there – the borders and center falling into place.

"Last time that I saw her, she was on stage. I think you were asking her a question," Tom said to Danny.

"I remember calling out to her at one point, but she didn't answer, then someone interrupted me. Jalnack, maybe. I moved on to other things, and I can't even remember what I was going to ask her." Danny took a few steps toward the stage and stopped. He knew that Marnie wouldn't just leave. She would know that he and Tom would worry.

"Maybe she locked herself into a room. You know, maybe she was snooping and accidentally locked herself in somewhere," Tom suggested.

"If you want me to start searching the ground floor, I can help with that," volunteered Johnson.

Danny considered the limited manpower available and nodded in agreement. "Yes, thanks. If you could take the left side of the building, I'll take the right side. Any locked doors, jimmy them open."

"I'll stay here and wait for Carl *and* for Marnie just in case she does return. Who knows, maybe she did go out. Maybe she got Carl's message and is heading to the diner right now," Tom said hopefully.

Danny jerked his head in a tight nod and set off down the aisle to the right side of the theater where signage indicated that's where offices, dressing rooms and a green room were located.

Johnson turned and walked off to the left where signs indicated the location of the prop, wardrobe and facilities rooms.

Tom wandered through the theater again, checking behind acoustic curtains and in the depths of dark alcoves to see if they had missed anything. A soft thump drew his attention to the stage.

"Hello?" Tom said.

Silence.

Tom called out again. "Hello!"

Thump!

Tom turned to see the theater door swing open abruptly and realized that the thumps were most likely Carl and Patrick arriving at the theater. Carl and

Patrick walked through the door, both carrying food and drinks. When they had asked for their food to go, Gram had bustled about making extra for Tom and Danny, too. She sent them quickly on their way with hot coffee and hot chocolate thrown in for comfort.

Tater trotted to Tom's side and gently placed his paw on Tom's leg.

"Hey, Tater Tot." Tom bent to give Tater a scratch behind his ears.

Carl and Patrick walked to the stage, placed the food and drinks down on the stage and turned questioningly to Tom.

Carl asked, "Anything? Have you heard from Marnie?"

Tom shook his head.

"I just tried to call her again. It went to voice mail after about four rings," Carl said.

"Danny and I have both tried to call her, too. Went to voice mail every time," Tom replied.

~~~~~~~~~~~~~~~~~~~~~~~~~~~~

Marnie could hear her phone ringing, but she couldn't answer it. Her phone was in her coat pocket, and she couldn't reach it. She mustered another kick and jiggled from side to side as best as she could. She was having difficulty breathing; not only was the tape partially covering her nose, but the overwhelming smell of incense and her perception of a depleted air supply were sending her into the same panic that she experienced in her nightmares. She closed her eyes and focused on her breaths. One, two, three – calm. Four, five, six – breathe. Seven, eight, nine – calm. Ten, eleven, twelve – breathe. With that breath, Marnie drew her knees up as far as she could and kicked again with all of her might.

-CHAPTER NINETEEN-

"Dammit! The pair of them – Alice and Allen. What have they done?" The woman in the gray cape snapped at Reuben.

Her tone shifted, and she smiled conspiratorially at him. She praised him. "Well done, sneaking out of there with the laptop. How did you get it away from Justin?" she asked.

Reuben leaned against the cold exterior of the brick wall of the old, abandoned railway depot near the collapsing tunnel. He wanted to stand tall and proud to entertain her praise, but he was freezing and just wanted to get somewhere warm.

"Yes, I did what you asked. I got the laptop. You know, every time you called, the cops looked at me suspiciously. I had to tell them that it was my girlfriend giving me a hard time," said Reuben.

The caped lady tossed her head and waved her hand in the air, which told Reuben that his discomfort wasn't important. He scowled at being so easily dismissed.

"How did you get out of the lobby? I was surprised when you called and said that you were on the way."

Reuben rolled his eyes.

"As soon as the EMTs arrived, I snuck in behind them when the cops' backs were turned. I went around back and found Justin up on the catwalk."

"Well?" she asked "Where is it? What have you done with it?"

Reuben shook his head with annoyance. "You know, a little gratitude would be nice."

The caped woman clenched her gloved hands into fists. "I don't have time to pat you on the head right now, Reuben. Where is the damn computer?"

Reuben glared at her and tautly replied, "It's back at my apartment. I popped up one of the floorboards under my bed and hid it there. No one will find it."

The caped lady exhaled loudly, exasperated with Reuben's response. "You'd better hope that they don't find it. Did Marnie Reilly recognize you? Did anyone recognize you?"

"They know my name, if that's what you mean," Reuben responded with a hint of sarcasm.

"Jesus, Reuben! What were you thinking? Do you have a brain in that head of yours?" The woman knocked hard on Reuben's head with red-gloved knuckles.

Reuben shoved her gloved hand away, his face red with anger. "You know what? A cop surrounded by other cops asks my name, there is no way I'm gonna lie. If one of them knew who I was and I made some shit up, I would have been screwed. There is a strong possibility that someone would know my name after the long history of crap that you've pulled."

"You listen to me, you little shit. If you screw this up, or if that laptop gets found, the cops will be the least of your worries. You'll have me to answer to, and that, my dear, is not a threat," the woman warned. "They've got your name. Don't you think that they might just wonder where you are? Don't you think the cops might go looking for you at home? Did you think about that, Einstein?"

Reuben dug his cold hands into the pockets of his corduroys and shrugged with resignation.

"I'll head over to my apartment now. I'll scope out the area. I'll see if any cops are hanging around, and if not, I'll grab the laptop. Any suggestion on where you want me to take it?"

The caped woman thought for a moment. When she responded, Reuben simply nodded his understanding and disappeared from view.

As Reuben walked away and when he had no fear of receiving a backhand to the face, he called out over his shoulder, "I'm getting sick of your bullshit! A 'thank you' would be nice from time to time!" Under his breath, he muttered, *"Witch!"*

~~~~~~~~~~~~~~~~~~~~~~~~~~~

Reuben was happy to get away from her. He didn't have the nerve to tell her that he and Justin had knocked Marnie out and tossed her into a prop box. Reuben still couldn't believe that it had happened. Fear had driven him. He had placed the laptop quickly into his backpack, told Justin to get a message to Detective Gregg that Marnie left the hall to pick up her dog and then raced to the roof; he'd jumped onto the roof of the garage next door, slid down a drain pipe, hopped onto a fire escape and rushed to his apartment. He didn't even remember running through the back alleys of Creekwood; he didn't know if anyone had seen him or if Justin had gotten out of the theater unnoticed. He did know that, if Marnie Reilly wasn't found soon, she would suffocate. That did weigh on him. He wasn't a murderer. He didn't hurt people – that was his mother's job. Now, she had pulled him into her dreary world of deceit, darkness and death.

-CHAPTER TWENTY-

"How many people will pay for Allen's and Alice's stupidity?" The caped woman spoke aloud to herself as she swept along the path toward the dilapidated tunnel.

"The ritual at the cemetery and that Patrick character running off were the last straw! I had to take control. The Collective must never be dissolved. It must continue!" she shouted, then looked about to see if anyone was nearby. She was alone, but shaking with anger and frustration. "It *must* continue," she cried, her voice echoing in the night.

Turning, she purposefully strode forward and soon found herself just a few steps from the tunnel. She tapped a red-gloved finger on her chin and looked off down the tracks into the darkness of the tunnel. It was still.

She muttered to herself, "I am so sick of cleaning up other people's messes. Why is everyone so stupid? Why do I surround myself with stupid, stupid people? Alice can't even get a spell right. Salt? Really, Alice! Let's just reverse the entire spell with a pinch of salt. What was she thinking?"

The gray-caped lady turned on her heel and walked up the platform toward an old storage silo. The silo hadn't been used in years. At one time, this had been a very busy station.

Farmers used to bring their wheat and corn here for weighing, payment and storage. The wheat and corn were then transferred into railcars and delivered to the mill at Spires Corner, 50 miles up the line. This section of the line was closed 30 years ago when a new line had been built, bypassing Creekwood altogether. The engineers on the ground simply switched the tracks to the new route and never switched them back. Old handcarts used to run up and down this line from Hudson Hollow to Creekwood every few months for maintenance. The Creekwood line had been maintained in case of emergency, but was rarely used. Then the tunnel started to collapse last year, and that was that.

The caped woman pushed open a small hatched door on the side of the silo. She stepped carefully through the door and turned and locked it. She glanced around the cavernous space inside the silo. It was the perfect place to hide. No one would look here. She had been preparing for her comeback for the past two years. Under the cover of night, she had smuggled in furniture, floor coverings, appliances and food. She had a generator for electricity. She had kerosene heaters and lamps scattered throughout the space. She had an electric blanket for the cold winter nights. Reuben and Allen had helped her get the bigger items through the large door on the rail-side of the silo. They had used an old handcart to transport heavy items from the last stop at Hudson Hollow to the final stop at Creekwood.

The space still had an old, stale silage smell to it, but candles and essential oils covered the smell sufficiently. The woman dropped her cape from her shoulders onto an ottoman, removed her red leather gloves and walked across the room to light a kerosene lamp. As she struck the match, she saw someone move in the shadows. It startled her, and she dropped the lit match onto the floor. Stomping her foot on the floor to extinguish the match, she cursed.

"Dammit! Who's there? Reuben? Who is it, dammit?"

She picked up the box of matches and struck another on the side of the box. This time, she connected the flame of the match to the wick of the lamp and another lamp and another. The three lamps lit up the cavernous space. It was an eerie light that cast long shadows on the curved walls.

A petite woman stepped from the shadows. She was dressed in a pair of dark navy jeans; long black boots; and a chunky, cable-knit, dove gray, turtle necked sweater. A wool wrap, gloves and a beret all perfectly coordinated in robin's egg blue complemented tonight's casual style. Beneath the beret, her raven hair was long and sleek. Her features were stunning, and her eyes – indigo – were sharp and cunning.

"Who are you? What do you want, and how did you get in here?" the caped woman demanded.

"My name is Kate Parish, Ms. Wilmot. A friend and I have been watching you these last few months. We've watched you, Allen and Reuben set up this charming little hovel. I've been told tales of your alleged prowess in the dark arts – black magic, if you will. I could use someone like you – someone with skills like yours," Kate said casually.

"Just why should I help you, Kate Parish?" Grace Wilmot asked in a menacing tone.

Kate crossed the room, positioned a chintz throw cushion on the back of the couch and sat down. She leaned back, crossed her legs and flashed a smile as sinister as the devil's himself.

"Ah, Ms. Wilmot, like you, I have a bone to pick with Marnie Reilly."

Kate Parish's laugh ran a chill through Grace Wilmot's bones.

-CHAPTER TWENTY-ONE-

Danny returned to the auditorium to find Tom, Carl, Patrick and Tater standing near the stage, drinking coffee and eating.

"Hey! Why didn't you call me to let me know that Carl was here with Tater?" Danny yelled from the wings to Tom.

"Danny, I just took a sip of this coffee and was taking my phone out to call you," Tom snapped.

Danny held his hands up and apologized.

"Okay. Sorry. I'm worried. This isn't like Marnie." Danny ran a hand over his tired eyes.

"Where's Johnson?" Danny asked.

Tom shrugged and said, "He hasn't come back."

Danny clenched his jaw and stared up the aisle.

"Okay, we're not waiting for him." Danny knelt down and motioned Tater to come. Head down and tail between his legs, Tater loped across the floor and tucked himself under a seat. He put his head between his paws.

"What's the matter, Tater?" Danny asked.

Carl answered, "That hand gesture you just did is what Marnie calls 'the naughty puppy' command. She used it when Tater was a little pup and wouldn't settle down. That gesture is telling him to settle down and get in his crate."

Danny frowned. "Tater doesn't have a crate."

"Not anymore, but he did until recently," Tom said.

Danny held out his arms. "Come here, Tater. Come see me, buddy."

Tater picked up his head, jumped up and trotted over to Danny. Danny scratched Tater's ears and gave him a hug.

Danny tugged one of Tater's ears gently. "You're not in trouble, buddy. Good boy! Let's find your mom."

Tater's ears shot up, he bounced forward and then he sat.

Tom gave a command that Tater would understand. "Tater, where's your mom? Go find your mom! Scootchem!"

Tater shot forward with a fury – barking, smelling the floor, looking up and down aisles, stopping every few seconds and perking up his ears. He ran up onto the stage, sat and barked at Tom, Danny, Carl and Patrick.

"I think that he wants us to follow him. Good boy, Tater." Tom praised him.

Tom, Danny, Carl and Patrick climbed the stairs and awaited Tater's instruction. Tater stood, turned, ran backstage, ran up the spiral stairs and sat at the top.

Tom, Danny, Carl and Patrick followed Tater up the stairs.

Tater perked up his ears, tipped his head and slowly belly-crawled his way across the floor. He stopped, stood, sat and listened, then he made a beeline for the prop trunk. He circled the prop trunk three times, jumped on the lid and started pawing at it – barking frantically. He jumped off the box, ran to Tom, grabbed his pant leg in his teeth and pulled him to the trunk.

"Okay, Tater. Calm down. Is your mom in there?" Tom patted Tater's head. Tater snuffled the floor at the front of the trunk.

Danny ran the few steps to the trunk and pulled at the clasp. It was locked. Tater jumped on the lid, lifted his head and let out a loud, deep, mournful "a-rooh!"

Danny knelt next to the box. He rapped firmly on the lid. "Marnie, it's Danny! We're right here. The trunk is locked, and we're looking for a way to break the lock. We're right here, Marnie. We're going to get you out! Talk to me, Marnie! Can you hear me?" He turned to the others. "C'mon, guys, find a crowbar or something to break this lock."

Danny stepped away from the trunk, turned in a circle and ran a hand through his hair.

"If she is in there, she's not answering." Danny's face paled.

"She's got swimmer's and runner's lungs, Danny. She's gonna be fine," Tom said, not sounding all that convincing.

"She's terrified of closed spaces. Closed spaces... She's... Marnie is a chronic claustrophobe. We've got to get her out of there. Now!" Carl shouted.

Tom, Danny and Carl raced through the upper level of the theater, searching for anything that would break the lock open. Patrick calmly searched through a toolbox that lay open on the floor near some scaffolding and found a screwdriver. Danny found a prop sword leaning in the corner in its sheath. He ran to the box, pulled the sword from the sheath and wedged it between the locked clasp and the box. Tater was atop the box, desperately trying to dig through the leather-bound lid.

"Stay calm, everyone. We'll get Marnie out of there. She's going to be okay. We can get her out," said Patrick. He walked calmly to the back side of the trunk with the screwdriver and started removing screws from the hinges. Tater stopped digging at the leather and sat on his haunches, panting with his efforts.

Patrick reached up and patted Marnie's dog. "I'll get her out – don't worry. Now, you get down, please." Patrick snapped his fingers and pointed down. Tater easily hopped down and sat next to Patrick, but lifted a paw for Patrick to shake. Patrick grinned.

Danny groaned aloud as he pried with the sword, but the latch wouldn't budge. The sword was a flimsy prop and not strong enough to break open the trunk. Danny threw it in frustration and rummaged through the mess of props, searching for something to get Marnie out or to puncture the trunk to let air in.

"Argh! Of all the days to leave my Leatherman at home! It's right there – on my dresser," Danny growled.

"I've got a tiny knife on my key ring, but it isn't going to do us any good," Tom groaned.

Tom and Carl had disappeared into storage areas, also searching for a crowbar or something else to break open Marnie's locked, leather-bound prison.

Patrick ignored the others and methodically, calmly removed all of the screws, placed the screwdriver between the lid and base and pried the top up. He got his fingers into the gap and forced the lid off the trunk.

Marnie was curled up on her side in the bottom of the trunk. The smell of lavender, sage, frankincense and dragon's blood drifted from the box. Marnie's tearstained eyes were closed. The duct tape covering her mouth and most of her nose was still in place. Tater placed his paws on the side of the trunk, dropped his head down to Marnie, licked her face, put his nose under her chin and nudged. Marnie did not respond.

Patrick called out, "Marnie!" Danny, Tom and Carl raced back and watched Tater nosing Marnie's still form.

Patrick leaned down, scooped Marnie out of the trunk, lay her gently on the floor and felt for a pulse. Tater lay down next to Marnie, placed his nose under her hand and bumped her hand up. Marnie was still. Patrick gently removed the tape and bindings, then he turned to Tom, Carl and Danny. They were all drained of color.

Danny raced over, knelt next to Marnie and took her hand. Tater barked sharply and nudged Danny under the arm. Danny held tight to Marnie and ruffled Tater's fur. "It's okay, buddy. It's okay. We're gonna take good care of your mom."

"Detective Keller, please call 911. Carl, please comfort Tater so that Detective Gregg can help me give her CPR," Patrick directed calmly and firmly.

"911. What is your emergency?"

"This is Detective Thomas Keller of Creekwood PD. We've got an unresponsive woman, Marnie Reilly, at Station Hall on 1612 Station Road, Creekwood. We need assistance immediately. We don't have a pulse. Officers are administering CPR."

"We have a unit on the way, Detective Keller. Please stay on the phone until they arrive."

"One. Two. Three. Four. Five. Six. Seven. Eight. Nine. Ten. Eleven," Patrick said.

When Patrick counted to thirty, Danny administered two breaths.

"It's okay, Tater," Carl said softly.

Carl held Tater's collar tightly while he scratched his neck and ears. Tater struggled to get to Marnie's side.

"One. Two. Three. Four. Five. Six. Seven. Eight. Nine. Ten," Patrick said.

"Detective Keller, is Marnie responding to CPR?" asked the 911 attendant.

Tom shook his head.

"Twenty-five. Twenty-six. Twenty-seven. Twenty-eight. Twenty-nine. Thirty," Patrick counted.

"Detective Keller?"

"No! She's not responding. How much longer for the ambulance?" Tom asked.

Danny administered two breaths.

Tater couldn't stand another second. He squiggled away from Carl and ran to Marnie. He sat next to her feet and began to howl.

"One. Two. Three. Four. Five. Six. Seven. Eight. Nine. Ten." Patrick's voice was like brass.

Sirens could be heard in the distance.

Tater continued to howl in unison with the approaching ambulance.

Tom ran down stairs and up the aisle to open the door for the EMTs.

Twenty-eight. Twenty-nine. Thirty," Patrick counted.

Danny administered two breaths.

Tater darted forward, leaping onto Marnie's chest and licking her face. Her body startled, and she gave a gasp.

"One. Two. Three," Patrick said.

Marnie's eyelids flickered. She lifted her arm ever so slightly.

Patrick sat back.

Danny grabbed her hand and kissed it gently.

Tater licked her face.

Marnie coughed, squinted her eyes open and turned her head. Tater snuggled his nose into her neck.

A slight grin appeared on Marnie's pale lips, and she hoarsely muttered, "Tater."

-CHAPTER TWENTY-TWO-

Erin Matthews sashayed into Ryan's Diner. She had been so excited after she'd spoken to Marnie earlier in the day about attending a party that she hadn't picked up her lunch. She was starving.

"Evenin', Mrs. Ryan! I'm so sorry that I forgot to pick up my lunch earlier today. I ran into Marnie along the way, she invited me to a party and I was so excited."

"Never mind, Erin. It happens all of the time." Gram smiled. "What can I get for you, lass?"

"Do you have any pot pies left? Turkey?"

"I just finished making a new batch. I figured that we would have a rush on the diner before the end of the evening, and my turkey pot pies are always a favorite," Gram said.

"Excellent! Do you think that I might get that with a pint of something frothy?" Erin asked with a wink.

"Of course, darlin'! Dark, light or half and half?" Gram picked up a pint glass and set it on the counter.

"Oh, half and half would be great, thank you." Erin turned to see who else was in the diner and sat on a stool at the counter.

Gram put in Erin's order and bustled back to the counter where Erin had settled to pull her a draft.

"Now, what time was it that you ran into Marnie? You said before you were meant to pick up your lunch?" Gram asked.

"Yes, ma'am. We were having a chat, and she invited me to Detective Gregg's place on Friday night," Erin replied.

Gram stared off into the diner. There were only a few customers at the moment as well as her cook and waitstaff. Dawn and Simone could handle any rush. Kelly was cooking. Margie was bussing the tables and doing the dishes. Gram dearly wanted to be anywhere but here. She couldn't stop thinking about Marnie. Where could she have gotten to? Gram had a sixth sense about most things, but there was a fog around Marnie's well-being. She searched desperately for a sign that everything was just fine, but no signs came. She worried so about Danny – he'd lost his wife so young. If something were to happen to Marnie, she didn't know how her grandson would pull through another tragedy.

"Mrs. Ryan? Are you okay?" Erin asked.

"Yes, I'm fine, dear. It's just this time of year. So much to do." Gram set the pint down in front of Erin.

The phone on the diner wall rang. Gram nearly jumped out of her skin.

"I'll get it! I've got it." Gram rushed to the phone.

"Hello!" Gram practically shouted down the phone line.

Erin sat at the counter, doing everything that she could to hear the voice at the other end of the phone. Gram was cradling the phone so closely to her ear, and she walked a few steps away, so Erin couldn't hear the other side of the conversation.

"Yes. Yes! Oh, glory be to the angels around us! Thank you! Thank you, Danny boy. Do you need anything?" Gram asked. "Yes, yes, of course.

Gram nodded and turned back to Erin, who could see Gram's eyes flooded with tears.

"On the heels of the wind and the wings of the angels," Gram replied. She pulled off her apron and tossed it on the counter.

Before Erin could ask her what had happened, Gram hung up the phone and called out, "I'll be back. I'll be back when I'm back. I'm… I'm… If you need me, call Danny. I'll be with Danny." Up the back stairs she flew, leaving a flummoxed Erin with her pint.

Gram scuttled up to her apartment above the diner; grabbed her coat, scarf, gloves and car keys; and hurried down the back stairs to the garage. There sat her 1959 Hampton Green Cadillac Eldorado Biarritz. It gleamed with polish, and the interior smelled of Aqua Velva aftershave. Gram never took this car out in the winter, but something told her to drive it tonight. It was her late husband's car, and she needed him with her tonight.

~~~~~~~~~~~~~~~~~~~~~~~~

Erin sat stunned for a minute, then she spun around on her stool and turned to Dawn, Margie and Simone, who were busy with customers and tidying tables.

"Well, what do you suppose that was about?" Erin asked, her eyes wide with curiosity.

The girls exchanged knowing glances.

"We learned a long time ago not to ask Mrs. Ryan questions about her personal life. She'll share if she wants to, and she won't if she doesn't," replied Margie a bit gruffly.

"But she just raced out of here like the devil was chasin' her," Erin said.

"Well, then, may God help the devil!" Dawn snickered.

"The devil himself wouldn't have a chance against Margaret Ryan. She would take him down in a rain of holy water and thunderbolts." Margie giggled.

Margie, Simone, Dawn and the customers in the diner shared a good laugh at the thought.

Erin turned her stool back to the counter and snuck a sideways glance at them all. Kelly emerged from the kitchen with Erin's meal and asked her if she would like a drink.

Erin downed the remains of her pint and pushed it across the counter to Kelly. "Another pint, please."

Kelly obliged and slipped back into the kitchen.

Erin hadn't been in Creekwood all that long and didn't know all of the local lore. She now had the feeling that there was much more to Margaret Ryan than being the kind old Irishwoman who owned the local diner. She added "getting to know Mrs. Ryan" to her list of things to do.

-CHAPTER TWENTY-THREE-

Grace Wilmot frowned deeply at Kate Parish. Kate smiled mischievously from the depth of the overstuffed chair and bounced her leg up and down, waiting for Grace Wilmot to speak.

"What is it that you think that I can help you with, Kate Parish?" Grace Wilmot pointed a gnarled finger at Kate.

Kate stretched out her arms and admired her expertly polished fingernails. She dropped her right arm into her lap, and extended her left hand toward Grace. She wiggled the fingers, as though putting forth vibes. The hand was deformed, maligned.

"Anything missing?" Kate asked, a derisive tone to her question; she raised her eyebrows and held her left hand up to Grace for inspection.

"Well, the obvious answer is that your ring finger is missing. Is that what you mean?" Grace asked and took one cautious step back.

"Mmm… Yes, it is. How observant of you," Kate replied, her tone condescending.

Kate stood quickly, which made Grace Wilmot take another step back. Grace was now standing between the light and the shadows, the darkness hiding her face. Grace was not typically fearful of people, but Kate Parish had her spooked. There was something about her that unnerved Grace.

Grace read the news. She heard the rumors. She knew that Kate Parish and Sam Reilly, Marnie's brother, had been involved in the murder of Ken Wilder. They had dumped his body in Marnie's garden shed, trying to frame Marnie for the murder. Ken was Marnie's abusive ex-boyfriend who had nearly killed her a few years earlier. As the story unfolded in the newspaper, it was discovered that Kate had been a mostly unwilling accomplice to her lover Sam. Their plan was to kill Ken for his money. Kate seduced Ken, married him and then set the scene for Sam to kill him. When Kate and Sam had finally located Ken's will after murdering him and dumping his body in Marnie's garden shed, they learned that Ken had never changed his will. Marnie was still a major beneficiary, so they plotted to kill her, too, but it all went wrong.

During the murder investigation, Officers Webb and Weaver had been brutally murdered. Officer Jalnack had been shot, but had recovered. Tom Keller had been knocked unconscious in the woods on the bridle trail behind

Marnie's house. If not for Kate's feelings of guilt about Sam killing a childhood friend and Detective Danny Gregg and Marnie searching the woods for Tom, he would be dead now, too. Grace had also overhead a conversation that Kate had lost a finger during a struggle with Sam over a strand of piano wire – Sam's murder weapon of choice. Grace knew some of the story, but she also knew that the rumor mill and newspapers only revealed so much.

Grace Wilmot was familiar with Sam. They'd had occasion to speak in the past, but Kate had always been in the background. They had never conversed or met in person. Now, she was face to face with a very damaged person – one with much more damage than one missing finger.

"What could you possibly need from me, Kate Parish?" Grace asked.

Kate crossed the space between them like a cat stalking a mouse; she gracefully slunk across the room soundlessly until she stood nose to nose with Grace Wilmot. Grace stared into Kate's deep blue eyes. What Grace saw made her shiver. This woman wasn't an unwilling accomplice. She was a murderous seductress, and she wasn't finished yet.

Grace arched her back slightly to put some distance between her and Kate. She didn't dare take another step back. Kate would know that she was terrified. Grace reached out and pulled a long dark strand of Kate's hair from her sweater. Kate swatted her hand away, flipped her long dark hair over her shoulders and then launched into a rant about Marnie.

"Marnie Reilly has been a thorn in my side since – well, since we were teenagers. She's always been deviously pathetic. She's the faux damsel in distress who every man wants to save. Personally, women like that are hateful! She always has to do the right thing. She never crosses the line between good and evil – bad, perhaps, but never evil. Marnie Reilly wouldn't cross that line if her life depended on it. She's a fucking Goody Two-shoes, and it has become tiresome. Actually, it became tiresome when we were in high school. She expects everyone around her to be perfect! She expects everyone around her to pander to her mindless whims. She goes on and on and on about The Collective and how they do such terrible things." Kate whirled about in fury. "The Collective are charlatans! They're fakes! They're phony! They're this! They're that! It's infuriating how sanctimonious Marnie Reilly is! She's boring! She's boring! She's so fucking boring!"

Kate stopped abruptly at the faint sound of a cackle – a subdued, witchy cackle. She turned to Grace, who was smirking ever so lightly.

"You just said that she is deviously pathetic. Doesn't that mean that she's cunning? Isn't that a quality that you find interesting? Even admire a little bit?" Grace commented with a snigger.

"Shut up! You! Shut! Up!" Kate shouted in a roar that echoed fiendishly through the cavernous silo. She pointed a finger into Grace's face and glared. "Don't you ever be condescending toward me. Don't you ever mock me!" Kate spat her words out with such vitriol that Grace took two steps back.

Grace was now completely in the shadows. She was closer to her comfort zone. Masked in the shadows, she crept ever so softly to a small oak cupboard that housed her armory. Kate could just barely make out Grace's shape skulking through the darkness. She heard a slight click and stepped a bit closer.

Then Kate heard mumbling – no, it was a chant. She peered into the shadows, and she screamed in terror. A horrible pain burned in the middle of her forehead. Grabbing her head in her hands and praying for the pain to stop, Kate dropped neatly to the floor of the old silo. She closed her eyes and drifted into terrifying dreams of monsters, demons, Sam and, of course, Ken Wilder coming back from the dead to avenge his death. It was a restless sleep, as Grace hoped it would be.

Grace stepped from the shadows holding a totem – a voodoo doll. The single strand of Kate's hair that Grace had plucked from her sweater was wrapped around the head of the doll, and a pearl-topped pin pierced its forehead.

"That, Kate Parish, you murderous bitch, is how people like me handle people like you." Grace tilted her head back, and the cackle that followed was chilling… and apt.

-CHAPTER TWENTY-FOUR-

"I just want to go home with you and Tater. I don't need to go to the hospital," Marnie argued.

Marnie stood her ground, even if it felt a little shaky under her feet. Her head was swimming, and her right shoulder ached. She had no recollection of what had happened before she was put in the trunk. It was taking every ounce of energy to stay upright.

"Marnie, you need to go the hospital. They need to make sure that you're okay. Stop arguing," Danny scolded.

The EMTs stood patiently listening to the debate, giving knowing glances to one another and betting who would win this argument.

"Marnie, if one of your clients had just been through what you've been through, you would be telling them to go to the hospital," Carl gently challenged.

"Marn, whoever dropped you into that box took a swing or two at you. You do know that you have two big bumps on your head, right?" Tom reached a hand out to touch one of the contusions.

"What? What are you talking about? I don't have a bump." Marnie scowled and swatted Tom's hand away.

Marnie lifted her hand and touched her head. She knew that she had a bump; she just didn't want them to know that she knew that she had a bump. Of course, she could feel the swelling in her temple and the nausea rising in her stomach. She just wanted to go home.

"Look! I made it all of the way down the stairs by myself and have been standing here on the stage for at least 20 minutes. I'm fine. I want to go home!" Marnie shouted.

Everyone turned as the auditorium doors flew open and Gram appeared, waving her hands and running as fast as she could manage to the stage.

"Oh, goodness me! What have they done to you, dear?" Gram wrapped Marnie in a hug.

Rolling her eyes, Marnie returned the hug. "I'm fine, Gram. I just want to go home."

"You'll do no such thing! You'll go the hospital and have that head checked. Don't be stubborn, Marnie Reilly! You could have a concussion."

"Gram…" Marnie started to argue, but Gram cut her off.

"Marnie, if you don't want to go in the ambulance, I will drive you myself, but you *are* going to the hospital. No two ways about it, lass. You are going to the hospital." Gram's stern expression won the argument.

Marnie threw her hands up in the air and rolled her eyes with exasperation.

"Fine! I'll go to the damn hospital, but I'm walking to the car. I'm not an invalid. I don't need an ambulance or a stretcher to take me to the hospital," Marnie replied haughtily. *As tough as that sounded, I sure hope that they are buying this…* she thought.

Marnie took one step forward, and the wooziness overtook her. She faltered and swayed, and Danny caught her just before her knees buckled.

"Well, Ms. Reilly, that's not exactly how I had intended on sweeping you off your feet, but this'll do." Danny chuckled and scooped Marnie up into his arms. He carried her down the steps into the auditorium. Marnie didn't argue. She put her head on his shoulder and fought the queasiness.

With Marnie in his arms, Danny turned and did a final scan of the auditorium and stage.

"Anyone seen Johnson?" Danny asked.

Tom, Patrick and Carl all shook their heads.

"Didn't think so," Danny replied.

"What's up? What are you thinkin'?" Tom asked, eyebrow raised.

"I'd bet my cabin that he isn't from Hudson," Danny replied.

"Who is he then?" Tom asked.

"That's what we're gonna find out in the morning," Danny replied.

-CHAPTER TWENTY-FIVE-

Reuben Wilmot approached his apartment building from the rear. He thought that his chances of getting inside without being noticed were better if he went up the fire escape and through his apartment window rather than going through the front door. He left the window unlocked in case of an emergency. This was Creekwood. Nobody was going to break in and steal the few measly belongings scattered throughout the apartment. Anything of value was well-hidden under the floorboards.

Reuben wished that he had a pair of gloves. It was a frigid night, it was snowing lightly and the metal rungs of the fire escape ladder were piercingly cold on his bare hands. When he reached the top, he peered over the edge to the street to see if anyone was watching. It was a quiet night in Creekwood – not a soul on the street. He turned back to the window and pushed it up, then he swung in onto the drab, beige, carpeted floor.

A table lamp switched on, and Reuben spun around to see Justin sitting in his favorite chair – laptop in hand.

"Never con a con artist, Reuben."

Reuben crossed the room and tried to pull the laptop from Justin's grasp. Justin stood to get a better hold on the computer and spun it away from Reuben's reach. Reuben let go, threw up his hands and backed across the room.

"How did you get in here? It certainly wasn't through that window! You're terrified of heights. You were frozen on that catwalk. If I hadn't helped you, you would still be on the catwalk," Reuben said.

Justin laughed and shook his head.

"I am afraid of heights, so chances are that I didn't come through the window. I walked through the front door of the building, came up the stairs and jimmied the lock." Justin smirked and settled back into Reuben's chair.

"You jimmied the lock?" Reuben replied.

Justin twisted his smirk and shrugged his shoulders. "I'm a thief. It's what I do. I steal information, money, identities, police uniforms – anything, really."

Reuben's eyes grew wide with disbelief. "You what?! You stole a police uniform?"

"Ya gotta do what ya gotta do to survive, man," Justin responded smugly.

Reuben shook his head and rested a hand on the back of the ladder-back chair. "Why would you steal a police uniform? You know, impersonating an officer is against the law!"

"*Against the law*? You're talking to me about *against the law*? Your mother is the infamous Grace Wilmot – the grand dame of thieving charlatans. The grand mistress of misdeeds. *You* knocked Marnie Reilly out cold. Twice! *You* put her in a trunk. *You* stole my laptop, and you're talkin' to me about *against the law*?! Really?!"

Reuben placed both hands on the back of the chair, trying desperately to compose himself. Stomach acid was rising at an alarming rate, and he just couldn't be sick in front of Justin. His mother had dragged him back to Creekwood, and he felt himself sinking into her world – her dark, putrid world. Reuben took a deep breath and let it out slowly. He calmly put his hand out for the laptop.

"Give me the laptop, Justin. Grace wants the laptop." Reuben did his best to summon up a stern glare. It didn't work. His big eyes were Cocker Spaniel – not Doberman Pinscher.

Justin rolled his eyes and smirked. "Fuck off, Reuben! I'm not giving you the laptop. Your mother sent me here to get it away from you! How do you think that I knew that it was under the floorboards? Huh? What's that? You don't know? Pfft… Your mother told me. That's how!"

"Wha…What?" Reuben stammered.

"Wha…What?" Justin mocked.

"She doesn't trust you, Reuben. No one does. Poor Reuben. His momma doesn't approve of him. Poor, poor Reuben," Justin taunted, pulling his face into an over-exaggerated pout.

"Get out, Justin. Leave now," Reuben hissed through clenched teeth.

"Oh, I'm outta here! You're a loser, Reuben. Your mother thinks so. I think so. Everyone in The Collective thinks so. I can tell you that, if Detective Gregg finds out that you're the guy who put Marnie Reilly in that box, you're as a good as dead."

Reuben sucked in a breath. Calmed himself. Exhaled. "Get out. I'll take care of Detective Gregg."

"What the fuck is that supposed to mean? You'll take care of Detective Gregg? What the fuck? You wouldn't kill a cop," Justin challenged.

"You don't know what I'll do, Justin. You just don't know what a person is capable of until he is pushed too far." Reuben's glare came short of Doberman Pinscher, but he gave it a good effort.

"Yeah. Well, whatever! Fuck off, and do whatever you need to do." Justin sauntered to the door and walked out, pulling the door shut with a resounding slam.

From the window, Reuben watched as Justin walked out of Reuben's apartment building with the laptop. Reuben turned quickly and checked under the floorboards to see if Justin had taken anything else that he had in his stash. Reuben unlocked a lockbox in which he kept his cash and was relieved to see that Justin hadn't taken that. All of his cash was still there. Reuben opened his phone and double-checked that the backups from the laptop were still in the cloud. He'd backed up the entire contents of the laptop to three separate cloud accounts before stashing it under the floorboards.

"You never know when you might need insurance." Reuben smiled and wondered whether Justin would turn him in for placing Marnie in the box. He shook his head. *Nah. He'll implicate himself if he does.* The thought brought him some comfort – not much, but a bit.

-CHAPTER TWENTY-SIX-

Tom sat in the hospital reception area while filling out Marnie's paperwork. Head throbbing and stomach churning, Marnie sat between Gram and Danny on a long hospital-blue banquette with an ice pack from the EMTs on her temple. Tater curled up under the banquette at her feet. Gram stroked her hand, and Danny stroked her back. It took every ounce of strength that Marnie had not to vomit right there in the waiting area of the emergency room.

Danny excused himself, feigning a "police business" call, but called Marnie's godfather instead. Dr. Giles Markson was Creekwood's resident coroner and one of the few people whom Marnie Reilly trusted implicitly.

"Detective Gregg? What can I do for you this evening? Do we have a body?" Dr. Markson asked dryly.

"No, sir. I just wanted to let you know that I'm here at the hospital with Marnie. She's got a bit of a bump on her head, and I thought that you should know. I didn't want you to hear about it in the cafeteria tomorrow morning." Danny turned to see if Marnie was okay. Her eyes were closed, her pallor tinged with a hint of green.

"Oh, dear. Thank you for calling, detective. Has she seen the doctor yet?" Dr. Markson asked.

"Not yet. We've just arrived," Danny responded.

"Well, I'll be there in a few minutes. You and I both know that my goddaughter can be a handful when she sets her mind to it. I'm sure that they'll want her to spend the night with a head injury, and you and I also know that she won't want to do that," Dr. Markson said.

"No, sir, she won't. She didn't even want to come get checked out. My grandmother had to be called in as backup to get her here," Danny replied with a brief laugh.

"I'm on my way, detective."

"Thanks, Dr. Markson. I greatly appreciate the assist." Danny hung up.

His next call was to Captain Sterling's office voice mail. He needed to provide Captain Sterling with an update and didn't have the patience to actually speak to the man tonight. He knew that it was the easy way out, but he was tired and just wanted to get Marnie taken care of and settled into a room.

As Danny returned to the waiting room, a nurse approached Marnie and Gram.

"I'm sorry, but you'll have to take that dog out of the hospital," the nurse advised.

"He's a service dog. There shouldn't be a problem." Marnie frowned and her eyes grew stormy.

"He's not wearing a vest. I'm sorry. You'll have to remove him immediately." The nurse pointed to the door.

"He doesn't need to wear a vest. That's not a law in New York State," Marnie argued.

"Well, it's a law of this hospital. Please remove the dog." The nurse placed her hands on her hips and glared at Marnie.

Before Marnie could erupt and start an all-out war, Danny stepped into the fray.

"Excuse me. I'm Detective Gregg of Creekwood PD. Ms. Reilly has a head injury, and I would rather that you not upset her. Tater is a service dog. I can assure you. He accompanies Ms. Reilly into the police station quite often." Danny smiled warmly.

The nurse raised an eyebrow and narrowed her eyes. "I don't care where *Tater* goes as long as he's not in my waiting room. I've had enough of people claiming that their pets are service pets. Emotional support pigs. Emotional support iguanas. What will it be next?"

His voice getting louder with every word, Danny responded, "Okay. You must be new to Creekwood. People here are a bit kinder than that, especially in the emergency room where people need all of the support that they can get."

Sensing that Danny was about to explode, Tom quickly decided to try a different approach.

"I'm sorry. I'm Detective Keller. You look like a nice lady. I'm sure that you can find it within yourself to let this slide. Our friend has been injured, and we're just waiting for an exam room. We'll be out of here in no time. Tater will stay right here with me." Tom bent and scratched Tater's head.

The nurse pursed her lips, readying her response, when Gram threw up her hands.

"Okay, boys. Have a seat. Let me handle this." Gram stood and moved to stand between Danny and Tom. She placed a hand on one of Danny's arms and the other on one of Tom's.

"Allow me to introduce myself. My name is Margaret Ryan. and you are…" Gram said before Marnie cut her off.

"Nurse Ratched, I presume?" Marnie giggled.

As the nurse spun around and glared at Marnie, Dr. Giles Markson walked through the emergency room and scanned his badge at that very moment.

"Marnie, what happened to your head?" asked Dr. Markson, crossing the reception area.

"You *know* these people?" the nurse asked gruffly.

"Why, yes, they are my goddaughter and her friends."

"She was just telling us that we need to take Tater out of the hospital," Danny said.

"Why would you do that? Tater is a service dog and is most certainly welcome to stay," Dr. Markson said.

"They called me Nurse Ratched."

"Not before you got all up in our faces about taking Tater outside," Danny snarled. Tater dropped his head between his paws and looked up with sad eyes.

The nurse stood with her hands on her hips, chewing the inside of her cheek.

"You're new to Creekwood Memorial, aren't you? I've seen you in the cafeteria once or twice. I've been here 30 years and know everybody. You, I don't really know." Dr. Markson pushed his glasses up with his index finger and furrowed his brow in thought.

"I've been here a little over two weeks. I moved here from Los Angeles," the nurse replied.

"Well, there you have it. Different hospitals. Different rules. Never mind. Have a good night." Dr. Markson dismissed her with a smile and a nod. Never giving her name, the nurse huffed in annoyance, turned on her heel and marched off.

Once the nurse had disappeared down the corridor, Dr. Markson turned to the group.

"Okay, which one of you called her Nurse Ratched? Don't deny it. Tom Keller, I've known you since you were a boy. You can't help yourself," Dr. Markson scolded.

"It was me, Uncle Giles. Sorry. She was being, you know, all Nurse Ratchedy," Marnie replied.

Dr. Markson peered at Marnie over the top of his glasses, the slightest of grins lifting at the corners of his mouth.

"We'll move on. Marnie, let me have a look at that bump on your noggin." Dr. Markson pushed his glasses up again as he approached his goddaughter to inspect her injuries.

"It's nothing, really, Uncle Giles. Just a bump." Marnie rolled her eyes.

Dr. Markson gently took Marnie's chin in his hand and turned her head to the side. "Hmm… Are you feeling queasy? Have you vomited?"

"A little queasy, but I think that's just adrenalin. I was locked in a trunk." Eyes wide, Marnie tilted her head up to connect with Dr. Markson's gaze.

"Locked in a trunk? Whoever would do that?" Looking for answers, Dr. Markson turned to Tom and Danny.

A steely voice interrupted the interrogation. "Ms. Reilly, if you would come with me, we have a room ready for you now." The scowling nurse from earlier stood waiting for Marnie to follow her.

"You want me to come with you?" Tom asked.

"No, thanks, Tom. I'm okay." Marnie shook her head and gently squeezed Tom's arm as she walked past.

As soon as Marnie had disappeared down the hall, Danny pulled Dr. Markson aside.

"Doc, is there some way that you can convince Marnie's doctor to keep her overnight?" Danny asked.

"Well, the doctor will most likely do that anyway, Danny. That bump on her head is fairly serious, and she is feeling queasy. Concussion is not something that will be taken lightly. They'll want to run tests, of course." Dr. Markson pushed out his bottom lip and thought about Marnie's injuries.

Tom had edged his way into the conversation. "Doc, do you think it may be possible for the doc to recommend medical leave for a few weeks?"

"A few weeks? My goodness, she hasn't been examined yet." Dr. Markson's eyes narrowed. "Why do you ask that, Tom? Is something going on with Marnie other than the bump on her head?"

"I don't want to tell tales out of school, but… Well, she's been zoning out a lot lately. She's not eating, she's not sleeping, she's snappy. She won't admit it, but we think she's internalizing a lot of what happened with Ken, Kate and Sam," Tom replied.

Gram sidled up, nodding her head in agreement with Tom.

Dr. Markson turned to Danny. "Do you think this, too, Danny?"

"Yes, sir, I do." Danny nodded.

Dr. Markson raised an eyebrow. "Well, have you asked Carl about her behavior?"

"Carl? Carl Parkins? Are you serious?" Danny asked, his voice rising with utter disbelief.

"Well, yes. Carl is an excellent practitioner. All that nonsense with The Collective. Well, a desperate man will do what he needs to do to make ends meet. I'm not saying that better choices could have been made, but Carl's reputation had been destroyed by a disgruntled client – a client who fell in love with him. When Carl didn't reciprocate that love, well, let's just say that a high-powered, pathological, scorned woman is not someone who you would want stalking you?" Dr. Giles waited solemnly for the small group to consider this.

"What? Carl had a stalker? I didn't know about this. Marnie never said anything," Tom said.

"She wouldn't, of course. That's not her information to share." Dr. Markson lifted a shoulder and frowned.

Tom, Danny and Gram all stared at Dr. Markson with astonishment.

Dr. Markson shook his head tightly and sighed. "It's not my information to share, either, but I've had just about enough of the secrets. Carl Parkins is a good man. He did nothing wrong, and I respect him."

Danny twisted his mouth. "How do you know, Doc?"

"Carl and I have spoken," Dr. Markson responded.

"That's it? That's all that you can say?" Tom pulled a face.

"It is," replied Dr. Markson.

Danny, Tom and Gram considered Dr. Markson's answer for a moment.

"Do you think that Carl could get Marnie to slow down? Take some time off?" Tom asked.

Dr. Markson tipped his head in thought for just a moment.

"I do." Dr. Markson gave a curt nod.

Tom and Danny exchanged glances. Gram, who was standing between Tom and Danny, looked up at the two men and gave Tom a little nudge.

"Go get him, Tom. Go get Carl. Take Tater with you for the drive." Gram nudged Tom again.

"It's late! Carl is probably home in bed by now. I'm not going to drive all that way for nothing," Tom replied, an indignant smirk on his face.

"Call him, then." Gram pushed.

Tom looked at Danny. Danny shrugged. "You can call. It won't hurt." Danny shrugged again.

"Well, then, you call him." Tom frowned.

"Gram asked you to call." Danny grinned.

Tom rolled his eyes, pulled out his phone and reluctantly called Carl.

Carl answered on the first ring. "Hello! Tom? Is everything okay? How's Marnie?"

"Hi, Carl. Yeah, it's Tom. Sorry to bother you so late. Marnie is in the exam room right now. We don't know anything yet."

"Oh, okay. I assumed that you were calling me with an update. Patrick and I were sitting, waiting, hoping to hear." Carl sounded anxious.

"Look, Carl, we're wondering if you could come to the hospital. We want to talk to you about Marnie – you know, Marnie's behavior. Her general behavior lately. You know." Tom struggled to find the words to ask Carl for help.

"Marnie needs my help? Wait, you want me to help Marnie?" Carl asked incredulously.

"Well, Marnie's godfather thought that you could help," Tom replied.

"Ahh… Giles is there with you? Let me speak to him, please," Carl said.

"Hang on." Tom rolled his eyes and held out his phone. "Dr. Markson, he'd like to speak to you."

Dr. Markson took the phone from Tom and stepped a few paces across the waiting room for a bit of privacy. Gram and Danny went to the cafeteria for coffee, and Tom and Tater sat in reception waiting for Dr. Markson to complete his call.

"Carl, how are you? Of course, that's a rhetorical question. Someone calls you in the middle of the night… Well, how *you* are really isn't the point, is it? It's about how *Marnie* is," Dr. Markson said.

"Giles, can you please tell me what this is about?" Carl asked, exasperation edging into his voice.

"Yes. Yes, of course. I'll get to the point. The boys believe that Marnie needs to take some R and R. They believe that she's internalizing grief, anger, the whole gambit. Tom told me that she's zoning out, whatever 'zoning out' means," Dr. Markson advised.

"I wouldn't disagree with the boys' observations. I was waiting for Marnie to figure it out. You and I both know that diagnosing Marnie with anxiety or PTSD without her asking for a diagnosis could be detrimental to my health," Carl said matter-of-factly.

"I don't disagree with you, Carl. Do you think that's what it is? Is that your diagnosis?"

Carl was silent for a brief moment while he considered his answer. "Well, she's not my patient at the moment, so no doctor-patient confidentiality exists, nor does a proper diagnosis. As her friend, have I observed behavior that could point in that direction? Absolutely. Do I think that she needs to slow down? Yes. Do I think that she needs to take some time off? Yes. Do I think that she will do it? No."

Dr. Markson glanced up, thinking about Carl's response. "Carl, do you think you could try talking some sense into her? Marnie does respect you. She and I both believe that you are an exceptional practitioner. We trust your analysis of human behavior."

"Yes. I can try. I'll be there within the hour, and just between you and me, all that you had to say was that Marnie needs help. I would have been there in a heartbeat."

"Yes, I did pour it on a bit thick. Nonetheless, I do trust you, and some of that was for Tom to overhear," Dr. Markson replied. "I'll let the others know that you are on the way."

"Yeah. I just need to get a houseguest organized, and I'll be right there," Carl replied.

-CHAPTER TWENTY-SEVEN-

Kate awoke with a banging headache, a dry mouth and a woozy stomach. She was no longer on the floor of Grace's silo, but on the couch in her own apartment near the center of town. She reached clumsily for a table lamp and tipped something over in her overreach to push the switch on the lamp. She heard a clatter and jumped up. The sudden movement made her dizzy, and she sat down awkwardly on the couch.

Kate noticed a book lying upside down on the floor. It wasn't one of her books. The leather binding was old, and it looked just a bit moldy. Kate rolled her nose with disdain. She stood, steadied herself and reached out to pick up the book. She raised her eyebrows and smiled as she turned the book over to read the title: *Mysteries and Methods of Black Magic: A Beginner's Guide.*

"Thank you, Grace Wilmot." A sinister grin broke across Kate's face.

Kate's phone buzzed. She frowned and turned to face the clock on the mantle. It was after midnight. She reached into her pocket and peered at her phone's screen – "Hudson Correctional" glared back at her. She felt a wave of dread sneak up her spine to her throbbing head. She steeled her nerves and straightened her spine.

"Hello, Sam," Kate purred.

"What the fuck were you thinking?!" Sam Reilly shouted down the line.

Kate jerked the phone away from her ear for a second and took a deep breath. "Sam, darling, what did you want me to do? Do you want all of our work to go waste? Do you want me behind bars, too? Surely, you don't want that for me, Sam. Surely, you don't," Kate purred again, this time with a lilt.

"Kate, you told them everything! You told them enough for them to lock me up for life! Did you or did you not cut a deal?" Sam shouted.

"Well, of course I made a deal, Sam, darling," Kate replied, this time with a bit of an exasperated edge. "What would you have me do? Don't you want me to be safe, Sam? Don't you? Really, Sam, you did kill two police officers. You wouldn't want me to be implicated as an accomplice to that, would you? Who would you have on the outside fighting to get you out of prison if I were behind bars, too? Truly, Sam, think these things through, darling."

"I didn't kill those cops by myself, and you know it! You are as guilty as I am! Kate, I could wring your neck!"

"It's such a pretty neck, Sam, darling. Why would you want to do that? Sam, dear, how did you get a phone at this hour of the night?"

"You don't need to worry your pretty little neck about that, Kate. I have connections. Remember that, Kate. I have connections, and if you keep fucking with me..."

"Sam, darling, I must go. I've had a long and trying day with my lawyer. I need to rest up so that I can work on your release. First thing tomorrow, I'll start working on that, darling." Kate sighed.

"Kate, don't fuck with me! I'm warning you!"

"Night-night, darling. Shall we chat tomorrow or perhaps the day after?" Kate disconnected and turned off her phone. She caught a glimpse of herself in the mirror, and she stretched out her neck. *Yes, it is a pretty neck...*

Sam Reilly clenched his jaw and narrowed his eyes at the prison guard who had eagerly allowed Sam to make a call to Kate.

"She doesn't know who she's fucking dealing with! I will kill her! I will fucking kill her!" Sam sneered.

-CHAPTER TWENTY-EIGHT-

Marnie's hospital room was stuffy – the air filled with antiseptic odors. She was cranky and uncomfortable in the rough cotton hospital gown instead of her own pajamas. She was muttering to herself about being stuck in the hospital overnight when the door burst open and Tater bounded into the room, dragging Gram along on the other end of his lead. They were followed by Tom, Danny, Carl and, finally, Dr. Markson, who brought up the rear.

"What was that, dear?" Gram asked.

"Nothing," Marnie replied through gritted teeth.

Tater ran around to the side of the bed, sat down, put one paw up on the side and smiled at Marnie. Marnie patted the bed. Tater jumped up, licked Marnie's face, turned in three circles and then settled at her feet.

"Good news, Marnie! The doctor said that you can go home tomorrow afternoon," Dr. Markson advised cheerfully.

"I know when I can go home." Marnie frowned.

Clearly exasperated with his childhood friend's stubbornness, Tom rolled his eyes. "Marn, you have a concussion. You couldn't think that they were going to let you go home tonight, did you? Really?"

"I'm fine, Tom," Marnie shot back, but when she raised her voice, she winced and raised her hand to her forehead.

Tom rolled his eyes again and fired back with sarcasm. "Yeah, you keep sayin' that. Keep sayin' it, and you might actually start convincing us."

Danny gave Tom a little nudge with his shoulder, scowled at him and shook his head lightly.

"Tater and I will pick you up tomorrow at 2:00," Danny said gently.

"What do you mean you *and* Tater? Tater can't stay here with me tonight?" Marnie replied, her eyes starting to fill with tears.

"What if he has to go out in the middle of the night? He'll have to go out first thing in the morning, and you won't be able to take him. That wouldn't be fair to Tater, now would it?" Dr. Markson's gentle reasoning tone softened Marnie's face. She relented, but she turned her eyes away from them and reached for a tissue.

"I would like it if everyone would just leave. Please go, and leave me alone." Marnie slunk down in the bed, turned away from them and pulled the covers up to her chin. Tater jumped up and tried to snuggle with her, but

Marnie shrugged away from him. Tater put a paw out and patted her arm. Marnie shrugged away from him again. Tater dropped, lay his head on Marnie's hip and whimpered. Marnie stuck one hand out from under the covers and scratched him behind one of his ears.

"C'mon, Tater. Let's go home. We'll come back to get your mom tomorrow," Danny said.

Tater stood on the bed and looked between Danny and Marnie.

Tom stood at the door and snapped his fingers. "Tater, come!"

Tater hopped down off the bed, gave Marnie a backward glance and then trotted to Tom's side.

"Good night, Marnie. I'll see you tomorrow." Tom backed out the door with Tater.

"Good night, lass. I hope you sleep restfully, child." Gram gently patted Marnie's leg and followed Tom and Tater to the corridor.

"I'll stop in and see you first thing in the morning, Marnie." Dr. Markson followed the others out into the hall.

Danny walked to the side of the bed and kissed the top of Marnie's head. "Night, Marnie. I hope that you're feeling better in the morning. Call me if you need anything. Anything at all."

Danny turned to Carl. Carl placed a finger up to his lips, sat back into a chair, crossed his legs and settled in for what he was certain would be a long night. Danny nodded and left.

~~~~~~~~~~~~~~~~~~~~~~

As soon as the door closed, Marnie started to sniffle, she burst into tears and then heart-wrenching sobs poured out.

Carl sat quietly in the chair. When Marnie sat up to look for a tissue, she was startled and annoyed that someone had been present for her weak moment. Carl said nothing; he just continued to sit there quietly.

"Why are you still here?" Marnie angrily pulled her blanket up harder than she had meant and punched herself in the face. Frustrated, embarrassed and angry, Marnie covered her face with her pillow and burst into tears, blubbering uncontrollably.

Carl went to the side of her bed, wrapped his arms around her and held her tight. Marnie's tears flowed freely for the better part of an hour. Carl's shirt was drenched by the end of it, and Marnie was thirsty.

Carl went into the bathroom, filled a cup with water and handed it to Marnie. He went back into the bathroom and came out with a cold washcloth.

He washed her face, handed her the wet washcloth and sat on the edge of the bed.

"Ready to talk?" Carl asked.

Marnie nodded tightly and burst into tears again.

Carl put his hand on Marnie's shoulder. "Marnie, you've been through a lot. You haven't given yourself time to process everything, and you never do. I've been your advisor, your therapist and your nemesis, but through all of it – even when I was your alleged nemesis –I have been your friend, and you have been my friend. Let me help you, Marnie. This is what you and I do – we counsel each other. We're here for each other because, deep down in our less-than-normal relationship, we find commonality, and we love each other – dearly."

Marnie threw her arms around Carl's neck and hugged him tightly. Though muffled and tearfully spoken, Carl understood every word that Marnie said.

"I'm a mess, Carl. I don't want anyone to know how messed up I really am, and I don't know how to fix it. I don't know how to fix what's broken. I don't know how to accept help graciously, and I need help. I know that I need help. It's killing me right now that I'm staying at Danny's because I'm terrified to stay in my own home. I'm terrified that Sam is going to get out of prison and kill everyone who I love. I miss my parents. I never got to say goodbye to either one of them. I never got to hug them goodbye. I wasn't there to help them when they needed me. I'm terrified that I allowed someone like Ken into my life *and* Kate. What the hell is wrong with me, Carl? Why couldn't I see that they are terrible and toxic people when they come through the door? I'm college educated in human behavior. I'm a freaking clairvoyant – an empath. What the hell is wrong with me? What if I allow someone equally as bad into my life – someone who could hurt all of you? I have so many wonderful people in my life – Tom, you, Danny, Gram, Andrea, Ellie, Uncle Giles, Erin – but what if you're all toxic, too, and I just can't see it because I am so utterly fucked up?"

Marnie pulled away from the hug, took a huge breath and tried to fold the tissue she had been clinging to, but it was shredded and soggy. She tossed it into the taped bag on her tray and stared down at the covers on her hospital bed. Her snuffles were interrupted by an occasional hiccough.

"Marnie, all of those people who you just named – Tom, Danny, Gram, Andrea, Ellie, Giles, me – and who was the last? Erin? Well, I don't know Erin, but the rest of us, Marn, we all love you very much. We're here for you – good or grumpy. Marnie, I want you to remember something. You have a beautiful gift. You see the best in people. You're a clairvoyant, and that allows you to see a person's potential, but potential isn't about you. It's about the other person and whether or not they want to reach their potential. You have no control over that. You can't repair them so that they reach that potential. They have to want it. They have to do it themselves. Give it a break, okay?"

Marnie wrinkled her nose up, nodded and sighed deeply. Her eyes remained downcast on her covers, but she was listening, her snuffles easing.

"Marnie, are you tired of carrying the weight of the world on your shoulders? Are you tired of always trying to fix things? Are you tired of rescuing everyone – except yourself?"

Marnie lifted her head, looked tearfully into Carl's eyes and nodded.

"Good. I'm going to ask you to do something that I'm pretty certain that you don't want to do. That's your choice, but I do think it could be an excellent first step. Ready?"

Marnie shrugged in response.

"Okay, I want you to take the next few weeks off. Stay away from the office, and take care of yourself. Do things that you want to do, even if it's things that others consider work. If it makes you happy, go for it. Get ready for Christmas. Find a new house. Get some sage, and cleanse your house. Settle into Danny's cabin. Plan the parade. Take care of the toys for the kids. Sleep for a couple of days. Take Tater on long walks. The more outdoor, fresh-air time, the better. Do your shopping, wrapping and baking, and don't worry about anything but what you want to do. A change is as good as a holiday."

"What about my clients? Who is going to take care of them?" Marnie asked.

Carl grinned and glanced down at his watch. "Well, as of mail o'clock today, I have my license back. The letters that you and Giles wrote appear to have been the deciding factor."

Marnie threw her arms around Carl's shoulders again.

"Oh, Carl, that is wonderful news! That's the best news that I've heard in a long time!"

"Well, it has been a long process. I am so grateful to Giles. His own unfortunate experience with Claire van der Heyden, née Jones, is the biggest reason that I'm off the hook and back in business. Your Aunt Janet provided an affidavit supporting Giles's letter, and their lawyer chimed in as well about the restraining order that *they* had to get against old Claire. Did I tell you that her husband threw her out? She's gone from living in that magnificent manse to… Well, I 'm not sure where she is, but I do know that she is a thing of my past, *and* I've got my license back!"

"This is so exciting, Carl! We'll have to throw a party, get a fabulous frame for your license and put it up on the wall as soon as possible." Marnie squeezed Carl's hand warmly and nudged him lightly with her shoulder.

"Well, let's not go overboard. Don't go all crazy with 24 karat gold. Gold gilt would be fine." Carl flashed a cheeky grin.

Marnie laughed lightly and turned serious. She placed her hand on top of Carl's.

"Carl, I have to tell you about something – something that happened when I was locked in that trunk."

Carl leaned in closer. "What is it, Marnie?"

"Please don't think that I'm crazy." Marnie cast her eyes down on her blanket.

"I already know that you're crazy," Carl teased.

Marnie smiled, took in a breath and exhaled loudly. Her shoulders eased back, and she rested her head back on the pillows.

"I was trying desperately to get someone's attention. I kicked that damn trunk so hard. Did you know that I broke my toe? There's nothing that they can do for it, but I broke my toe because I was kicking so hard. Then I couldn't breathe. The air... the air was all gone. I thought that I was going to crawl out of my skin. I was suffocating!"

Carl nodded and waited for Marnie to continue.

"I died, Carl. I died. White light, tunnel, the whole shebang. I died."

Carl's face never changed expression. He nodded, waited, listened.

"Mom and Dad were there. They were standing right there. I thought that they were waving to me. I thought that they were welcoming me home. I just kept walking toward them. I just kept walking into the light."

"They weren't waving you forward, were they, Marnie?" Carl asked with a shake of his head.

"No! They were shooing me away. They were telling me to turn back, but I didn't know that, and I didn't want to! I was so happy to see them. Mom looked so beautiful, and Dad, well, I just wanted to run into his arms for a hug."

Marnie began to sniffle again. She grabbed a tissue out of the box on the nightstand and dabbed her eyes and then her nose.

"Carl, it was the most beautiful and terrifying thing that I've ever experienced. Mom and Dad and Gramma and Pa and Granny and Pops and William – they were all right there shooing me away. Oh, dogs do go to heaven, Carl. I saw them, and every person who I have ever lost in my life was right there. Except Ken, of course. Dad kept telling me to go back. 'Go back,

Marnie, it's not your time. Go back to Tater, Marnie.' He kept saying it over and over and over again. I could see Mom – she wanted to hug me. I know that she did, but she kept telling me to turn around – to live and be happy. You know, I think that I heard Danny talking to me. I know that I heard Tater bark. I'm sure of it, but I kept walking to Mom and Dad. When I crossed through the light, it was like a gossamer veil just floated around me, and I heard it whoosh gently behind me. Carl, it was beautiful, and Mom and Dad both shouted 'No, Marnie. Go back! Go back!' Then Dad held my shoulders tightly, he turned me around and he said 'Marnie, it's not time. You have to go back before it's too late. You have to go back before the veil closes completely.' It was like when I was little and he would wake me up from a bad dream. Then I started thinking about all of you, Tater and everyone who I loved and cared about on the other side of that veil. I kissed my parents and grandparents, and I ran, Carl. I ran as fast as I could. I could see the veil closing. I could see it closing, and I could hear Danny's voice and Tater's bark. I could see all of you gathered around me on the floor at the Station Hall. When I got to the veil, it was nearly closed, and I tore through the veil as fast as I could. I tore through the veil to come home to all of you. Then I was coughing, Tater was licking my face and..."

Marnie, exhausted and overwhelmed, burst into tears once again. Carl pulled her close. She wrapped her arms around him, put her head on his shoulder and cried herself to sleep.

-CHAPTER TWENTY-NINE-

Tuesday, December 8th

Allen awoke choking with a bad case of dry mouth in the early morning dimness; he had a terrible headache and immense pain in his left wrist. His right foot and leg throbbed and ached from toes to knee. He tried to sit up, but sunk back down into the pillow. He'd never felt this weak and drained in his entire life – not even when he had the flu last year.

Allen knew that he wasn't at home. He reached for his glasses to have a better look at his surroundings, but couldn't quite reach the nightstand next to his bed. He shifted to lean further toward his glasses. He still couldn't reach them because his left wrist was secured to the bedrail with a handcuff. Slumping back onto his pillow, the memories of the previous evening began to flood into his now sober and conscious mind.

As the sun began to rise, light slowly leaked through a crack in the curtain, revealing to Allen that his surroundings were, in fact, a hospital room.

Allen stared at the ceiling, fear and dread rising up from the pit of his stomach.

"So help me, God. What have I done? What did I do?"

~~~~~~~~~~~~~~~~~~~~

Just two floors away and in another wing, Alice struggled to reconcile the voices that intruded upon her. *Oh, no… I know where this is… nooo…* She was in intensive care and had regained consciousness in the early hours of the morning. She glanced around the room, but was unable to move easily.

As a lifelong asthmatic, she knew too well the mask on her face; she was hooked up to a nebulizer, but there were other wires and things attached to her chest and arms that made her nervous. Her breathing was not as labored as it had been when she arrived at the hospital.

I died last night! She knew that the EMTs had done an excellent job of resuscitating her on the way to the emergency room. Alice had seen the light of God and felt herself being pulled in a different direction. She had stretched her hand up to the light, and all went dark as she was pulled back to life. *Must not have been my turn – or what was the phrase? – my time… yeah, my time…*

Alice was fearful of death. She knew that she had not always done right by others. She knew that she was, as Marnie Reilly pointed out many times, a charlatan. She knew that she sold hope and duped people. She hadn't started out doing so. She really had wanted to be helpful a long time ago. The life that she led now was something that she fell into along the way.

Alice's thoughts drifted to the day that she'd met Grace Wilmot and her son. Alice met them at the library where she worked. Alice was a librarian. She loved her job and the people with whom she worked.

It was late fall and bitterly cold outside. Alice discovered Grace and Reuben hiding in the stacks on the third floor. They had come in to get warm.

Grace's husband and Reuben's father Stuart had died several months earlier. He'd left them with a pile of debt and no life insurance to cover the expenses. They had nothing. They lost their home, most of their belongings and just recently their car, in which they had been living for the past few months.

Alice's supervisor knew that the two had encamped themselves in the stacks and had twice caught them hiding just as the library was to close. Alice was sent to shoo them from a third attempt, but when Alice put on her serious face to tell them to leave, Grace broke down in tears and told Alice her woes. Alice couldn't imagine how horrible things had been for them. She had so much and was grateful for the life that she led. "Do unto others" was a mantra Alice lived by back then, so she opened her family home to Grace and her young son, a lad of just 10 years old.

Alice had no family and thought that it might be nice to have people visit for a while. In hindsight, it was the biggest mistake that Alice ever made. Grace and Reuben took control of her home. They frightened her – each incident worse than the last.

Alice came home from work one day to find that Grace and Reuben had moved all of her belongings out of her lovely turret bedroom where Alice had slept since she was 4 years old. Grace explained that the turret room suited her far more than Alice because she needed the natural light for her work. Alice scoffed and asked what work. Grace slapped her across the face so hard that Alice had a handprint on her cheek for days. After the slap, Grace calmly smoothed her hair and told Alice that she would be doing spiritual healings, tarot readings and white magic. The turret room was the perfect place for her to set up her consulting room. She told Alice that it was how she would pay her way – that she would start contributing to food and utilities.

Alice wasn't happy, but she was hopeful that this would be the end of Grace and Reuben sponging off her kindness, and maybe they *would* contribute to the expenses.

Alice tried to get them to leave a few times. She found work for Grace, but she used Reuben as an excuse for remaining at home. Alice didn't want to involve the authorities because she thought it would be mean to throw a widow and her child out on the street, so Alice adapted and allowed. Besides, she was frightened of Grace and her son – deeply, sincerely, horrifically frightened of them. Alice had been conned by the biggest charlatan in Creekwood.

Alice's memories danced back to the time of year when Grace and Reuben moved in because Creekwood had just put up the Christmas decorations in town. She also remembered that her Christmases were never the same after Grace and Reuben moved into her house. They alienated her friends, intruded on her time at the library and called her so often at work that she lost her job. They always had a problem that Alice needed to fix. Alice's boss felt horrible, but she just couldn't have "those people" hanging around the library. She tried to speak to Alice about it, but Alice had taken offense and shrugged off Grace's and Reuben's behavior, saying that they were victims of a series of unfortunate circumstances. Time and again, Alice defended her unwanted housemates.

The last straw came when Alice's boss informed Alice that she had also been told that Grace was a witch and was doing tarot readings and spells in Alice's home. Alice knew so little about what went on in her own turret room that she was embarrassed and angry at the notion that others in town had been talking behind and in front of her back. She didn't care about those mystical things, but many of the God-fearing people of Creekwood were frightened of Grace – for good reason.

As Alice lay in the hospital bed reflecting on the last few years of the Wilmot invasion, she felt tears forming in the corners of her eyes. They would shortly race down and into her ears.

Yes, Grace Wilmot will forever be the evilest, vilest, most contemptable human being I've ever had the misfortune to encounter.

Alice closed her eyes as tears started to flow down her face in streams.

Regrets were not something that she had experienced until Grace Wilmot had moved into her home. Regrets were all that she thought about now. Her heart ached for a simpler time. She needed help. She needed someone to understand. She needed to speak to Marnie Reilly and Carl Parkins. She desperately needed to speak to them. They would know what to do.

-CHAPTER THIRTY-

"Hi, Ellie. I am so sorry for calling you so early," Danny apologized, feeling a bit guilty. He parked his Jeep.

"Who is this?" Ellie responded, groggy with sleep.

"Oh, sorry. It's Danny Gregg – Marnie's friend," Danny replied.

"Oh. Hi, Danny. Is everything okay? Is Tater ill?" Ellie asked.

"No. No. Nothing like that. Marnie is in the hospital with a bump on her head. She's fine. She's going to be just fine. I'll be picking her up at 2:00, but I can't take Tater to work with me this morning. I'm wondering if he can come to your day care today?"

"Yes, of course. Tater is welcome anytime. I keep telling Marnie to drop him off. It would be good for him to socialize. You'll tell me about Marnie when you drop Tater off?"

"I will. What time can I drop off Tater?" Danny asked.

"The benefits of having the clinic in my home – you can drop him off anytime. We're awake. The phone woke us," Ellie said, with a hint of a grin in her voice.

"Yeah. Sorry about that, Ellie. I have to get to work early. We've got three cases in the air," Danny replied sheepishly.

"I was teasing. Bring Tater over now if you like. By the time you drive over, we should be dressed," Ellie said.

"Uh, Ellie?" Danny said.

"You're out front, aren't you?" Ellie asked.

"Yeah."

Danny watched as Ellie opened the front door, phone still to her ear. In her pajamas with her bathrobe cinched about her waist, Ellie stepped out onto the front porch and waved Danny and Tater into the house.

"Your mom has some very understanding friends, Tater." Danny reached back and scratched Tater's ears.

Tater barked and jumped from his usual seat in the rear into the front passenger seat. He smiled out the window at Ellie.

Danny stepped out of the Jeep and went around to the passenger side to get Tater. When Danny opened the door, Tater scooted out the door and ran straight to Ellie, dragging his lead behind him.

"Tater!" Danny shouted.

"Hello, Tater!" Ellie said, bending down to give Tater a warm hug and pat. "It's okay, Danny. He always comes right to the door. Marnie just opens the door and lets him run to me. He would never run into the road," Ellie said, easing Danny's fear.

Danny nodded and shrugged. "Yeah. It's just that, if anything happened to Tater, Marnie would be devastated. If it was my fault, *I* would be."

"Danny, I'm going to give you a 10-minute course on Tater when you have 10 minutes. You just need some of the basic commands, and you'll have control of this cheeky brat." Ellie ruffled Tater's fur.

"Ellie, that would be great. Not only would it be good for me to know the commands, it may just impress his mistress." Danny winked and grinned.

"How does Marnie resist those dimples, Detective?" Ellie asked.

"Beats me, but she does seem to be immune to them." Danny twisted his mouth and shrugged one shoulder.

"C'mon in, and we'll get Tater settled before you go. Time for a quick coffee?" Ellie led the way into her home.

"Yes, thank you. I can fill you in on Marnie's concussion while Tater settles in." Danny followed Ellie into the entryway.

As they walked through the door of Ellie's colonial home, four dogs ran into the entryway from four different directions.

"Settle! Sit!" Ellie commanded.

All five dogs sat, including Tater.

"Danny, please meet Barley, Chicken, Eli and Dewey."

"Wow! Tater's got some playmates. This is going to be great for him." Danny knelt to greet the canines.

"Barley is a Border Collie, too. Chicken, well, we aren't certain what he is, but we think he is part Australian Shepherd and part Corgi. We don't know. Eli is part Border Collie and part Rottweiler, and Dewey is part Border Collie and part Saluki. We've got a few rescues waiting for homes, too, but they're out in the day care area. I can't possibly have all of the pups in the house at once. It would be a madhouse!" Ellie laughed.

"Rescues? What kind?"

"One is a Border Collie, and he's just 8 weeks old. One Australian Shepherd. One Belgian Shepherd. We've got two Labs and three Terrier mixes. They're all under 12 months. We'll find homes for all of them soon, I'm sure." Ellie nodded with certainty.

Over coffee and a slice of toast, Danny filled in Ellie on the events of the past evening. He kept some of the details out, but since Ellie was such a good friend to Marnie, Danny shared what he knew about Marnie's condition.

"Poor Marn. Ha. Boy, she'd be furious to hear me say that." Ellie winced.

"She would. Carl was with her when I left the hospital last night. Giles seems to think that Carl may be able to get her to take some time off." Danny took a sip of coffee.

Ellie tipped her head in thought. "Hmm. You know, Giles may be onto something there. Marnie and Carl have a strange relationship. No matter how many tiffs they have, those two always find their way back to each other."

Danny frowned and raised one eyebrow. "What do you mean?"

Realizing that her comment could have alluded to a romantic relationship, Ellie quickly set the record straight.

"By relationship I meant friendship. There's camaraderie between those two – a professional understanding. I can't explain it accurately. They are close, but not "sleep together" close, if you know what I mean. They've never been involved in that way. You have nothing to worry about," Ellie said awkwardly, waving her hands uncomfortably.

"They do seem to have a mutual admiration club going on there," Danny responded uneasily.

An uncomfortable silence dragged a bit longer than Danny could bear. He pulled his gloves out of his pockets and was getting ready to leave, then he hesitated.

"Ellie? Have I read Marnie wrong? Is she interested in me?" he asked.

"Well, I could pass her a note during study hall, *or* you could just ask her yourself." Ellie's dry response made Danny's face redden just a bit.

He grinned awkwardly. "Yeah. That was a bit childish, huh?"

Ellie nodded. "A little bit, but I will give you a pass." She put a hand on Danny's arm and sent him a comforting smile. "Look, Marnie Reilly is… Marnie is… an enigma. She's frustrating, stubborn, precocious, loving, arrogant and humble all at the same time. She's infantile, trusting, distrusting, intuitive, empathetic, damaged, loyal, passionate and odd, *and* she is one of my dearest friends. Yes, Detective, I do believe that she is interested in you."

Danny dropped his gaze to the floor and nodded. "Okay. Okay. Um… Any tips?" Danny lifted his gaze to Ellie.

Ellie laughed. "Nope. You're going to have to figure her out all on your own. Just one thing – it's the little things with Marnie. Grand gestures don't work."

"Making her a cup of tea is good, but buying her expensive jewelry is bad," Danny suggested.

Ellie laughed. When she did, her eyes crinkled up, and her whole face lit up.

"Now, don't go overboard, Detective. All women like expensive jewelry if the intent behind said jewelry is honorable. Tea is good, but only in a proper teacup. Flowers are nice, but plants are better. Old cookware and crockery from an antique or secondhand shop – good. She would love a surprise outing to a flea market over brunch any day. Dinner and a movie at home in front of a fire over dinner at a fancy restaurant. Chat with her while she cooks. Buy her a book from one of her favorite authors. Breakfast is good, but not breakfast in bed. Marnie hates that. It's a crumb thing." Ellie shook her head lightly.

"Thanks, Ellie! That certainly helps. We were going on an outing tonight to go Christmas tree shopping. We have a tree trimming party planned for Friday night, but now I'm not sure if Marnie will be up for that."

"Friday? Yes, Marnie mentioned that to me yesterday afternoon when I called to check on Tater." Ellie puckered her brow.

"Ellie, is everything okay?" Danny asked.

"Detective, you do know that Friday is Marnie's birthday, don't you? Didn't Carl or Tom remind you?" Ellie raised an eyebrow in anticipation.

"Friday? Marnie's birthday? No. I had no idea!" Danny puffed out his cheeks and sighed.

"Well, we better make some plans then, shall we?"

~~~~~~~~~~~~~~~~~~~~~~~~

Sunlight streamed through Marnie's hospital room window. Carl woke from an uncomfortable night's sleep in one of the chairs in Marnie's room to find Marnie sitting up, knees up to her chin and covers wrapped tightly around her, staring off into space.

"Marnie, how are you feeling?" Carl asked through a yawn, as he stretched his legs and back.

Carl's question broke the stillness in the room and jolted Marnie from her trance.

"Carl Parkins, you scared the dickens out of me!"

Carl laughed and apologized.

"Sorry. I didn't mean to startle you. You appeared to be off with the fairies. Wasn't sure if you had seen a ghost or if you were just thinking." Carl winked and laughed lightly.

"I was just thinking about my friend William. Danny and Tom are working his case. I think that I told you that he was found by the old train tunnel. They should have the autopsy and forensic reports today." Marnie rested her chin on her knees.

"No, you didn't tell me." Carl stood and stretched his arms up toward the ceiling.

Dr. Markson pushed open the door and stuck his head into Marnie's room. "Anyone in here want a cup of tea?"

Dr. Markson entered with a picnic basket. He set the basket on the foot of Marnie's bed, pulled the table over and placed the contents of the basket on the table. In the basket were warm date scones; a freshly steeped pot of tea; a bone china cup and saucer; two coffee cups; a thermos of coffee; a pint of half and half; sugar packets; and pats of butter.

"Oh! Uncle Giles! You are the best!" Marnie clapped her hands.

"Don't thank me, Marnie. Thank your Aunt Janet. She rose with the birds to make these scones for you. She packed everything into the basket and gave me strict instructions on how to make your tea when I arrived at the office. I stopped at the diner next door for the butter and sugar packets."

"Oh, my gosh! I am so blessed! A proper cup of tea and date scones! It's the little things." Marnie happily munched on a warm date scone.

Dr. Markson held up a coffee cup in one hand and the thermos in the other.

"Carl, would you like a cup of coffee? I brewed it downstairs. It's not hospital coffee."

Carl laughed. "Yes, thanks! I would kill for a good cup of coffee!"

"Uncle Giles, have you finished William's autopsy?" Marnie asked.

"Perhaps we could have our tea, coffee and scones before we discuss the macabre aspects of my profession," Dr. Markson scolded.

Marnie took a sip of her tea. "Yes, sir. Sorry."

Dr. Markson sighed and set his cup down.

"Marnie, I haven't completed the autopsy yet. I will be writing my final report this morning. I'm sorry that I snapped; it's just important that you understand that I can't actually share that information with you. If the police choose to share, that's up to them."

"I know, Uncle Giles. I'm sorry," Marnie replied sheepishly.

"Now, what about your birthday, Marnie? Do you have plans? Would you like to do something special? Your Aunt Janet was asking me this morning." Dr. Markson took a bite out of a scone.

"Can we please just skip it this year? I'm really not in the mood to celebrate it." Marnie screwed her face up into a grimace.

Clearly uncomfortable, Marnie dropped her gaze to her tea and scone. Behind her and out of her line of sight, Carl started to say something, but Dr. Markson put his hand up.

"If you think that's for the best, Marnie, we don't have to do anything if you aren't up to it." Dr. Markson patted Marnie's arm softly.

"Thank you," Marnie responded quietly, lifting her eyes to meet her godfather's.

He nodded acknowledgement and sipped his coffee, only looking toward Carl when Marnie turned her attention back to her scone.

The unspoken words in the shared eye contact between Carl and Dr. Markson were simply, "We'll talk later."

"Now, Marnie, when do you plan to go back to work? Are you planning to give yourself a few days to mend that noggin of yours? As a doctor and as your godfather, I recommend that you take a bit of time off, if you feel that you can." Dr. Markson put on the best fatherly tone that he could muster.

Marnie glanced between Carl and Dr. Markson. She raised one eyebrow and assessed the two men.

"Why do I get the feeling that the two of you are in cahoots? Colluding? Conspiring? Who else have you two pulled into your devious plot?" Marnie narrowed her eyes, and the corners of her mouth lifted into a small grin.

Carl cleared his throat and bowed ceremoniously. "We are guilty as charged, your highness."

Dr. Markson simply nodded his head deeply in agreement.

"Aha! I knew it! The jig is up, boys!" Marnie pointed her finger at each of them.

Carl and Dr. Markson grinned at one another, and both turned to Marnie with questioning expressions.

Marnie threw up her hands in surrender.

"Yes! Yes, I will be taking some time off. Carl won me over last night with his droning chatter about taking time to enjoy the holidays. I'm taking the time off to do the things that I want to get done – baking; shopping; wrapping; organizing the children and float for the Christmas parade; and getting all of the toys organized and wrapped for Toys for Tots. All of the things that I really want to do. Besides, Carl has his license back. My clients will be in excellent hands until I'm better and actually able to help them. To be honest, right now, I don't think that I would be doing right by them."

"Well, I'm glad that my *droning chatter* was useful for something." Carl grinned.

"Yes, as am I! Marnie, I couldn't be more pleased that you are taking time for yourself. Your Aunt Janet will be, too. Perhaps you can spend some quality baking and shopping time with her. She would love to see you," Dr. Markson suggested with an expectant smile.

"That would be lovely! I would love to bake with Aunt Janet. I miss holiday baking with Mom. You know, I think about the amazing memories with my parents and realize how lucky I am. Too many people don't have wonderful memories like that." Marnie sipped her tea with a distant twinkle in her eye.

"Remembering the good times is important, Marnie, but making *new* good times is important, too." Dr. Markson's fatherly tone returned.

Marnie held up her teacup. "Cheers to a happy holiday season! God bless us all, everyone!"

In unison, Carl and Dr. Markson held up their cups and called, "Here! Here!"

-CHAPTER THIRTY-ONE-

The squad room was bustling with activity when Danny arrived at the station to review Dr. Markson's and Rick's preliminary reports on William Billy Williams. Danny had asked Officer Sam Jalnack to run a background on William. That report awaited him as well. Danny poured himself a cup of coffee, sipped it, grimaced, stuck his tongue out in disgust and went to work.

Tom bounced into the station about 20 minutes after Danny.

"Morning, children! How are we all today? It's a beautiful morning, isn't it?" Tom said, unusually chipper for this hour of the morning.

Tom deposited a box of donuts and a tray of coffee onto the corner of Danny's desk and then deposited his backside on the opposite corner. Danny glanced up with annoyance.

"Do you think that you could grab a chair?" Danny glowered at Tom.

Tom stood and held his arms out. "Sure thing, Danny. Why the grumpy face? Did you miss your roomie last night?"

"You're annoying me." Danny tipped his head and frowned.

"You're grumpy. Here, have a jelly donut, and turn that frown upside down, my friend." Tom pulled a bear claw out of the box and passed the box to Danny.

"I don't want a donut, thanks, but I'll take one of those coffees." Danny reached for a coffee.

"Suit yourself." Tom handed a coffee to Danny.

Danny took the lid off, sipped the coffee and smiled. "Good coffee. Thanks!"

"I walked to work and stopped by the bakery along the way. I figured that, if we're going tree shopping, you can drop me at home later. Besides, my car was covered with snow, and I really didn't have the energy to clear it."

"Yeah, well, I'm not sure about tree shopping. Let's see how Marnie is feeling, huh?" Danny replied.

Tom shook his head and licked sugar off his fingers. "She'll want to go. I'm sure of it. She's tough. She won't let what happened last night stop her."

"Well, let's leave it up to her. When were you going to tell me that her birthday is Friday?" Danny asked, eyebrows raised.

"Uh. Is it this Friday?" Tom, eyes wide, pulled out his phone to check the calendar.

"Yeah! Ellie told me this morning."

Tom drew a hand down over his face and puffed his cheeks out. "Shit. I'm sorry. I completely forgot. You know, Kate always reminded me a week or two before her birthday so that I wouldn't forget. Please don't tell Marnie that I forgot."

Danny nodded with empathy. "Well, I won't drop you in shit if you don't drop me in it. I had no idea it was her birthday. To be honest, I've never even asked her when it is."

Tom puffed out his cheeks again and shook his head. "We can talk to Giles. He and Janet will have some ideas. Any idea what you're getting Marnie for her birthday?"

Danny shot Tom a broad, mischievous grin. "I do. I know exactly what to get Marnie for her birthday, and she is going to love it!"

"Are you gonna share?" Tom asked.

"Nope. Now, let's get cracking on this case." Danny picked up a report and started reading.

~~~~~~~~~~~~~~~~~~~~~~~~~~

"What the hell was DEA doing in Creekwood? Is there some drug problem that we don't know about? We're cops. Wouldn't we know if there was a drug problem in our own backyard?" Tom scratched his head and twisted his mouth to the side.

Danny ran his fingers through his hair and shrugged.

"Well, look at Allen Schofield. He was zoned on something last night. I'm still waiting on that tox screen. I've got to get over to the hospital at 2:00 to pick up Marnie, but I may have to swing by earlier to see what they've got. I sent Jalnack over to interview him, but I haven't heard back from him yet. He was going to check in on Alice Wells, too."

"Yeah. Allen is one of those guys, you know. You just wouldn't expect it." Tom swirled his coffee around the bottom of his cup and creased his forehead.

Danny lifted his shoulders in a half shrug. "Nope. William Billy Williams was a DEA agent. He's been dead for two weeks. The tattoos were recent. Perfect health, so no need for pain meds, and he had injected enough morphine to kill a horse."

Tom rubbed his chin as he studied the report over Danny's shoulder. "Or someone injected William with the morphine. He had a nasty contusion on his temple. That knock on the head would have laid him out cold, and *then* someone could have injected him. Anything in there about the body being moved? If he's been dead for two weeks, there's no way that a body lies on the tracks for that long without something chewing a finger off."

Danny nodded. "This is only the preliminary report. The morphine isn't even in here. Rick called me when he got in to fill in that blank. He and Dr. Markson will have the full report over to us soon."

"Wouldn't there be more than one DEA agent in town? Would they only send one?" Tom cocked his head.

"I would think so. They typically travel in pairs. Do you want to talk to someone in Vice to see if they have any information? I need to check in with Jalnack to see what he's found out." Danny gulped the last of his coffee, crumpled the cup and shot it into the waste basket.

"On it!" Tom gave a brisk nod and went back to his desk to make a call to Vice.

-CHAPTER THIRTY-TWO-

Danny knocked on Marnie's hospital room door and poked his head inside. Carl was gone, and Marnie was nowhere to be seen. He glanced around her room and frowned. As he was backing out the door, the bathroom door opened, and Marnie came through it.

"Hey, Marnie! Are you ready to go home?"

Marnie pulled the back of the hospital gown tight and glared at him, her face flushed with embarrassment.

"Danny Gregg! Don't you knock?"

"I did knock," Danny replied sheepishly.

Tater poked his nose through the door at the sound of Marnie's voice and let out an excited bark. Danny let go of his lead, and Tater raced to Marnie's side. Marnie backed up to the bed, sat, pulled the covers around her backside and patted the bed, inviting Tater to jump up. Tater jumped up and covered Marnie's face with licks. Marnie giggled and hugged Tater tight.

"Tater, I missed you, boy!"

"Are you ready to go home?" Danny asked again.

Marnie glowered at Danny, and the rant began. "Well, if I knew where my clothes were, I would have been dressed hours ago. No one seems to know where my clothes are or my phone or my handbag. Do you have any idea how crazy it makes me to not have my phone and my handbag? Do you have any idea how it feels to be stuck wearing this backless thing?"

Danny held up an overnight bag and shrugged.

"I took your phone and handbag home with me last night. I didn't want anything disappearing from your room. Your clothes were collected as evidence because you were obviously assaulted. I'm sorry, Marnie. I brought you clothes from home, your phone and your handbag." An awkward grin spread across Danny's face.

Marnie reached out for the bag. "Oh. Well, thanks." She glanced at the bag in Danny's hand and frowned. "Wait a minute! You went through my clothes? You went through my underwear drawer? Oh, my God! You had my handbag, and you went through my underwear drawer! Two of the most personal things in a woman's life, and you violated both!"

Tater jumped off the bed and went under it. He poked his nose out and looked up woefully at Danny.

148

"Okay, Marnie. That's enough! You're not being rational. I didn't do it to upset…"

"Not being rational? Really?" Marnie huffed.

Danny rolled his eyes and set a piercing blue gaze on Marnie.

"Marnie, I didn't go through your handbag, and I certainly did not rifle through your underwear drawer! You had a laundry basket sitting on the foot of your bed with folded, clean laundry in it. I took things out of the laundry basket, and I grabbed the boots that you had sitting in the boot tray near the front door. I did not go through your things!"

Exasperated, Danny dropped the bag onto the foot of Marnie's hospital bed and stalked out of the room.

Tater poked his head out, and he raced out from under the bed and back up onto the bed. He turned in three circles and nestled in at the foot near Marnie's bag.

"Shit, Tater. Your mom is an idiot. A bloody idiot!" Marnie let out a long exhale.

She lay her head next to Tater's and rubbed his nose with her thumb. He scooched closer to her and licked her nose.

"I love you, Tater. You keep me sane."

Marnie picked up the bag and disappeared into the bathroom to change her clothes *and* her attitude.

~~~~~~~~~~~~~~~~~~~~~~

Marnie sat in the chair that Carl had occupied last night. She had missed a few calls, messages and E-mails. Three of the calls were from private numbers, and when she checked her voice mail, she knew exactly why the numbers had been blocked.

Voice mail #1 had a taunting singsong tone. *"Marnie, my beloved baby sister, why aren't you answering your phone? Don't you want to speak to your big brother? Cat got your tongue? We haven't spoken in days. Maybe you should come for a visit and check out my new digs. Three squares a day, an uncomfortable cot and a roommate who smells like a teenage boy's gym bag, but hey, I'm far away from general population. You know, they don't drop cops into general population unless they want them dead. Apparently, someone is shining some love on me from above. You suppose Mom and Dad are my guardian angels? Now, that would be somethin', huh? Come see me, Marn, and hey, pick up a book of Robert Frost's poetry. You know the one. I've misplaced my copy."*

Voice mail #2 was the same voice but a very different tone – menacing. *"Marnie, when I get out of here – and you know that I will – you're fucking dead! You, your friends, your mutt! All dead! I'm going to string you up and bash you like a piñata. No. Actually, I'm going to torture you first. I'm going to tie your hands behind your back, bind your feet together at the ankles, lock you in a box and drop you in the lake. Just when you're running out of air and you think that you're going to die, I'll pull you up and do it again and again and again until you lose your fucking mind. Then I'll string you up and use you as a piñata. Call me! I want my book back!"*

Voice mail #3 wasn't her brother Sam at all. It was Kate Parish. *"Marnie, I know that I shouldn't be calling you, but I really need to speak to you. Do you know who I saw here in Creekwood? You'll never guess! I saw Grace Wilmot! I don't know what she's up to, but you know that it can't be good. Listen, Marn, I'm worried about you. Grace isn't the forgiving type, and she was always into that crazy hoodoo voodoo nonsense. Isn't she a black witch or something? Anyway, Marn, watch your back. I saw her over by the tracks. You may want to have someone check it out, and don't you go there alone. I'd hate to think what she would do to you. You know the old saying, 'Hell hath no fury like a woman scorned,' and you certainly must be on the top of her you-know-what list. Anyway, if you could call me, that would be great. Bye, Marnie."*

Marnie looked down at her phone and tossed it onto the bed as if it was venomous. She did an involuntary heebie-jeebies dance next to the bed. She pulled her shoulders up to her ears and shivered. When she did this as a child, her father would laugh and ask if she had walked through a spider web. Marnie hadn't, but it certainly felt like she had. Every one of her senses was awake and on high alert.

Marnie turned to the window. Clouds had rolled into Creekwood. The sky had taken on an ominous shade of pale green. Marnie shivered again. When she turned away from the window, a knock came at the door, and it opened slightly. Danny poked his head in just enough to let her know that he was there. He could see her standing near the window fully dressed and he entered the room. Marnie turned back to the window as the first of the sleet tapped on the glass. She turned back to Danny with a vaguely familiar look in her eyes. Their gazes locked, and without any words – just Marnie's expression - Danny knew what was headed their way.

"Marnie, are you okay?" Danny asked, fearing the answer.

"Here comes the storm," Marnie replied in a faraway voice.

An icy trickle of dread ran down Danny's spine.

-CHAPTER THIRTY-THREE-

Tom sat at his desk reviewing notes and updating William Billy Williams's case file, known as a "murder book." He glanced from the notes to the board and back again. He had reached out to a friend in Vice Division, Detective Rodriguez, and got nowhere. Either Rodriguez wasn't talking, or she couldn't talk. A DEA agent in Creekwood must mean something. Even when Tom told her that they were investigating a dead DEA agent, she was quiet.

A call came up from the sergeant's desk.

"Hey, Tommy, you gotta lady down here flashin' a badge who wants to speak to someone in homicide. Says her name is Special Agent Hannah Patterson. Ring any bells?" Sergeant Beaumont inquired.

"No, Beau, it doesn't. I'll be right down," Tom said, grabbing his jacket off the back of his chair as he hung up.

Tom took the stairs two at a time on the way down and stopped dead in his tracks at the bottom. The woman who stood next to the sergeant's desk was familiar. There was something about her that he couldn't quite place.

Tom stuck his hand out and said, "Hi, Agent Patterson? Detective Tom Keller, it's..."

She cut him off.

"Special Agent Patterson will do nicely, thanks," she tossed her head and responded brusquely.

Tom threw her a sideways glance. "Okay, Special Agent Patterson, you got ID?

Special Agent Hannah Patterson pulled her credentials from her pocket and opened her coat to reveal a gold shield hanging around her neck from a lanyard. She handed the credentials to Tom.

"I understand that you have one of my colleagues in your morgue. I'm here to pick him up. I'll take any reports you have on the case as well. Not copies. I want the originals and any copies that may exist." Special Agent Hannah Patterson reached out for her credentials.

Tom handed the credentials back and sized up the agent in front of him. Special Agent Hannah Patterson was around 5'5". She wore charcoal gray slacks, a matching jacket, a burgundy scarf and a wrinkly white button-down shirt – all covered by a well-worn black wool overcoat with matte silver buttons. She wore low-heeled black boots that were in need of a polish. She had messy shoulder length mahogany hair and icy gray eyes shielded by rimless glasses with thin black stems that needed to be tightened; she was thinner than a law enforcement officer should be. Tom thought to himself that a strong breeze would knock her down.

"Officer Keller, I don't have time…"

Tom returned her rudeness and cut her off. "It's Detective Keller, and I need to speak to my partner *and* my captain before you get your hands on anything."

"I really don't have time for semantics. Officer, detective, what difference does it make? I need to head back to DC in the morning. Please make the arrangements, and call me at the Creekwood Lodge when you're through speaking with your partner and captain."

Ruffled, Tom shot back, "Well, Agent Patterson, you obviously do have time for semantics since you corrected me at the beginning of this exchange. I will speak to the people I need to speak to, and I will call you."

Tom spun on his heel and took the stairs three at a time on his way back up to the squad room.

Special Agent Patterson put a hand on her hip and shifted her stiffened posture to a frustrated slouch. "What an ass," she muttered softly. She was startled by Sergeant Beaumont loudly clearing his throat, obviously a reminder that she was in their house.

"Ms. Patterson, you may want to get a move on. That's sleet comin' down out there, and you don't want to be driving in that." Sergeant Beaumont smiled and nodded toward the door.

"It's Special Agent Patterson, and I know what sleet is. I grew up around here!"

She turned without a further word and pushed through the station door. She stepped onto the sidewalk, slipped, regained her balance, slipped again and fell on her backside onto the icy the sidewalk. She rolled onto her hip, and from this vantage point, she saw that her misstep had not escaped the notice of those whom she had just left.

Sergeant Beaumont stifled a laugh and called Officer Jalnack out of the coffee room to assist Special Agent Hannah Patterson.

Danny checked in with Tom as he and Marnie were driving to the cabin.

"Tommy, how goes it? Any new developments?" Danny asked.

"New developments? Hmm. Let me think. Yeah! A special agent from the

DEA is here to pick up William's body from the morgue and all of the paperwork and reports. She wants the originals and all of the copies," Tom huffed.

"Yeah. I kinda thought that would happen. Have you spoken to Captain Sterling?"

"No. He's out for the rest of the day. He didn't look well when he left. I think that it's the flu," Tom answered.

"Well, she can't take him until we get his sign-off. That's how it works at Creekwood PD." Danny reached to turn the windshield wipers down. The clunking of the blades was making it hard to hear Tom.

"Yeah. Well, tell Special Agent Hannah Patterson that! She's a piece of..." Danny cut him off.

"Who? Did you say Special Agent Hannah Patterson?" Danny asked.

"Yeah. You know her?"

"She's my sister," Danny replied, rolling his eyes and turning the Jeep around to head back to the station.

~~~~~~~~~~~~~~~~~~~~~~~

Special Agent Patterson sat in reception – her dignity shattered and her tailbone bruised.

Officer Jalnack brought her a glass of water. "Can I get you anything else, Agent Patterson? Can I give you a lift somewhere?"

"No. I have my own car, and it's *Special* Agent Patterson! Now, please, just let me be!" Special Agent Patterson sniped. She winced, shifting her weight from one hip to the other.

Jalnack took a step back with his hands out in front of him. "No problem. You're on your own." Jalnack turned to go upstairs.

Sergeant Beaumont shrugged as Jalnack walked by his desk.

"Can you please tell me who is in charge around here?" Special Agent Patterson queried.

"Uh, that would be Captain Sterling. He's out for the rest of the day." Beaumont picked up a roster and pretended to study it.

"Who is the CO when Captain Sterling isn't here?" Special Agent Patterson queried in a snotty tone.

"That would be Detective Gregg," Sergeant Beaumont replied.

Special Agent Patterson swung a stunned gaze of disbelief in Beaumont's direction.

"Detective Gregg? Detective Daniel Gregg?" Special Agent Patterson asked.

"Yes, ma'am. You know him?"

"Oh, brother, do I ever." Special Agent Patterson slumped and rolled her eyes.

"Well, that's him pulling up out front. I thought that he was gone for the day, too. Looks like your lucky day, Agent Patterson."

"Don't bet on it, and it's *Special* Agent Patterson, please!" she growled.

~~~~~~~~~~~~~~~~~~~~~~~~

Danny got out of the Jeep and carefully navigated the icy path from the curb to the door of the station. Marnie and Tater stayed in the Jeep with the heater running. As Danny pushed through the station door, Special Agent Hannah Patterson stood and visibly cringed.

Danny stomped his feet on the doormat, assessed his sister's mood and braced himself.

"Hannah, what are you doing here?" Danny stepped forward with open arms to embrace his sister.

Hannah took a step back to avoid Danny's incoming hug, which of course made Danny step closer. He bent at the knees, wrapped his arms around Hannah, picked her up off her feet and hugged her tight. Hannah patted his back with one hand and rolled her eyes.

"Why do you have to do that, Daniel? You know that I hate hugging," Hannah whined.

Danny hugged her a bit tighter and set her gently back onto her feet.

"That's why I do it – just to irritate my big sister," Danny teased, his dimpled smile broad and his blue eyes sparkling.

Hannah straightened her scarf, smoothed her jacket down around her hips and glowered at Danny.

"Don't let your happiness to see me overwhelm you, Hannah. Geez, it's been what, three years? Every time that I visit Dad, you disappear. Lucky for me, I don't have low self-esteem or I'd be a mess right now."

"I'm busy, Daniel. I have a demanding career. Besides, low self-esteem has never been your problem. Just the opposite. You've always erred more on the side of megalomania." Hannah narrowed her eyes, daring Danny to counter her verbal attack.

Danny smiled and shook his head. "Yeah, well, I'm okay with whatever it is you happen to think about me. If it makes you happy, Hannah, I'm okay."

Danny chuckled and reached his arms out to hug her again. Hannah pushed him away and gritted her teeth. "Stop it! Daniel, you are infuriating."

Danny grinned and winked at Beaumont, who was watching the interaction between the dueling siblings with great amusement.

"Look, I've got a friend waiting for me in the car. You want to come out to the cabin? We can discuss why you're here."

"I'm here to pick up my colleague. I want you to take care of that now!" Hannah ordered.

A few feet away, Sergeant Beaumont cleared his throat and ruffled papers in an attempt to appear busy with his own problems.

Danny's face hardened, he stepped closer to Hannah and he lowered his head and his voice. Danny slipped his arm through one of hers and growled, "Yeah. I think we both know that, uh, your tone, yeah... That's not gonna work with me. Your tantrums work with Dad, but not me. I've got the afternoon off, Hannah. Had you called, which is proper protocol, I may have been able to work with you. Now, you're gonna have to wait until tomorrow. I have plans." Danny stepped away and appraised her with a steely gaze.

Hannah scowled up at Danny and shook loose of his arm's reach. Danny smiled sweetly at Hannah and turned toward the door.

"Are you coming to the cabin where we can talk?" He raised an eyebrow and motioned his head toward the door.

"What's to talk about? I'm a special agent with the DEA, and you're only local PD." Hannah tossed her head and smirked.

"Until I see some paperwork telling me that you've got jurisdiction over this case, you've got squat!" Danny fired back.

Hannah chewed the inside of her cheeks and glared at her brother.

"Fine! I'll come to the cabin and talk, but I'll drive myself! My car is out front. I'll follow you."

"Suit yourself." Danny shrugged and lifted his chin to the desk sergeant. "Beau, I'll see you tomorrow!"

"Drive safely, detective, and please watch your step." Sergeant Beaumont grinned.

Special Agent Hannah Patterson glowered at Sergeant Beaumont's mirth and reached for her satchel. She straightened and stepped with as much dignity as her sore backside would allow. Once outside, she grabbed for railings to avoid another spill. She refused to give Beaumont any additional entertainment.

-CHAPTER THIRTY-FOUR-

Alice had been removed from the nebulizer, and the wires and beeping machines had been removed from her room. Her pallor was a bit gray, but better than last night. Alice asked the nurse if she could have her phone to call a friend. The nurse offered to make the call for her, but Alice shook her head.

"I need to make this call. Please, it's vitally important," Alice begged.

"Well, you really aren't supposed to have your phone, but I will make an exception. You haven't had any visitors. It must be lonely. Now, don't stay on the phone long, and you tell anyone who asks that you got it out of the cupboard yourself. Okay?"

Alice nodded and took her phone from the nurse. She waited until the nurse was gone and made her call.

"Hello?"

"Carl, it's Alice. I need your help."

"I'm sorry. You need my help? Alice, what could I possibly help you with that someone from The Collective wouldn't be better suited to handle?"

"Carl, it's about Grace Wilmot," Alice whispered.

"What? Did you say Grace Wilmot? Are you still at the hospital?"

"Yes," Alice whimpered tearfully.

"I'll be right there!"

~~~~~~~~~~~~~~~~~~~~~~~~~~~

Carl arrived at the hospital half an hour after Alice called him. He'd been at the office and needed to find an excuse to leave. He certainly couldn't tell Andrea that he was going to see Alice. Andrea would blow an absolute gasket if she thought that Carl was visiting Alice. Andrea didn't like the way that The Collective had treated Marnie, and she didn't trust any of them – especially Alice. He decided that he would use a visit to the drugstore as a reason for running out. The weather was terrible, and if the streets were closed off due to ice, he may not be able to get there before going home. He did have to pick up his blood pressure medication, so it really wasn't a lie.

Alice was resting her eyes when he arrived. He thought that she was asleep and didn't want to wake her, so he tiptoed into the room and sat in a chair next to her bed. When he sat, the vinyl squeaked, and Alice opened one eye. He sat quietly, checking messages on his phone.

"Carl?"

Carl raised his head at the sound of his name. He noted that Alice's pallor was paler than normal.

"Alice, hi," Carl said softly and scooted forward on his chair.

Alice extended one gnarled hand. Carl hesitated in offering his hand, then he did. Alice's hand was cold – icy.

"My goodness! Do you need another blanket?" Carl asked.

Alice shook her head. Tears welled up in her eyes, and her head darted from side to side, looking for a tissue. Carl grabbed the box off the side table and offered it to her. Alice plucked out two tissues and dabbed her eyes.

"Alice, do you want to tell me what this is about? You said something about Grace Wilmot. What has she done?" Carl's deep brown eyes softened.

"She's been back in Creekwood for some time now. She told me that she had come into quite a bit of money and that she came back to reclaim her glory. That's how she put it. Reclaim her glory. I don't know what she means by that, but that's her plan – to reclaim her glory. She's hell-bent on getting even with Marnie Reilly." Alice pulled her covers up and cast her teary blue eyes down to the blankets on her bed.

"Well, Alice, I think that *you* are hell-bent on getting even with Marnie Reilly, too – *and* me! What was that performance at the cemetery all about, Alice? Was that you or Grace? I'm asking because Grace Wilmot's name never came up in the list of attendees."

Alice squeezed her eyes shut. "You spoke with Patrick? He told you about that?"

"Yes, Alice, I have spoken with Patrick. Want to fill me in with your own words?"

Her head sagged to one side, and she sighed heavily. "I wish that Allen was here. He would be able to support me. He knows everything that happened. No one else in The Collective knows what Grace is up to. Most of them weren't even with us when she was still in Creekwood. They've all seen her skulking around, but they haven't got a clue. I didn't tell you because I assumed that you would tell Marnie. If Marnie knew that Grace was back, well, she probably would have blamed me!"

"Alice, Allen is in police custody. After his stunt on stage last night *and* after nearly running Detectives Gregg and Keller over at the cemetery, he's here in the hospital handcuffed to his bed. I think that it's time that you tell me everything that you know."

Alice's face dropped, and her eyes flooded with tears. Through bouts of hiccoughs and sniveling sobs, Alice filled Carl in on Grace Wilmot's activity in Creekwood.

~~~~~~~~~~~~~~~~~~~~~~~

Alice pushed herself up off her pillows and sat forward. Sharing her information with Carl brought a bit of her spark back.

"I know that she is trying to build up her customer base again. She's trying to take over The Collective, and she's making progress. Some of the younger folks are entranced by her. I know that she has been doing psychic and tarot readings for cash only over at Enlighten Crystals in Town Square the last few months. She's raking it in from what I hear and see. The people who own Enlighten Crystals weren't here when the whole fiasco happened with Grace. They don't know, and I am quite certain that people are afraid to tell them. I've seen the shoppers at Enlighten Crystals. They are mostly young locals or from Hudson or further away – not people I recognize – you know, like people from the library and the more God-fearing folks from around town. I guess that those people wouldn't go in there anyway. Everyone from The Collective shops there, but I haven't seen many townies of my age in that store. Grace's bad reputation seems to be nonexistent to the people who shop at Enlighten Crystals." Alice chewed on her bottom lip and sighed.

"What else can you tell me?" Carl pushed.

Alice took a deep, shaky breath. Tears welled up again, and she sniffled into her rumpled tissues.

"The ritual at the cemetery was supposed to satisfy Grace's need to destroy Marnie. She has pushed and pushed and pushed us for months, and I had to come up with something! It didn't work, though. Someone told her that I put salt into the ground with the rest of the ritual, so I don't know now what she's going to do to me *or* Marnie *or* you!"

"You put salt in the ground, so you didn't really do anything at all. You were just going through the motions?" Carl glanced up in thought.

Alice nodded and dabbed the tissue under her nose. "The rat in the grave was already dead. I didn't kill it. Justin found it in the cellar. I just jabbed the feathers into its chest. I stabbed a sprig of water hemlock, a sprig of holly and a sprig of mistletoe into the dirt on top of the ritual site."

"How many feathers, Alice?" Carl asked.

Alice sniffled. "Eight feathers in total – six crow feathers and two vulture feathers. I didn't hurt the birds! I found the feathers. I knew where to look."

A grin spread across Carl's face.

"Let me get this right. Eight feathers... Eight is the number of resurrection and new beginnings. Feathers are the symbol of freedom and divine connection. The salt cleanses. The sprigs of holly, mistletoe and water hemlock... well, that's three – the Holy Trinity. Alice, you crazy witch, you blessed us. You didn't curse us. You blessed us!"

Alice pulled the covers up to her chin and beamed. She held a finger to her lips.

"Shush. Don't tell anyone. My reputation will be ruined," Alice replied with a mischievous grin and an impish giggle. Carl squeezed her hand. Alice giggled again and relaxed into her pillows.

-CHAPTER THIRTY-FIVE-

The roads were becoming slicker by the moment. Danny sighed. Dusk was a miserable time of the day to be driving in an ice storm. His fingers tensed on the wheel. Marnie sat in the passenger seat with her head against the window. Danny worked hard to keep the Jeep on the road, his knuckles white from gripping the steering wheel. Tater sat on the back seat, tongue out, smiling.

Marnie turned to Danny, opened her mouth to speak, changed her mind and then turned back to the window. Danny caught the motion and frowned.

"Marnie, do you want to talk?"

Marnie shook her head.

"Well, I can see the wheels turning in that head of yours. What's on your mind?" Danny pushed.

Marnie turned to him. "Ken. Ken Wilder is on my mind."

Danny glanced at Marnie and quickly turned his eyes back to the road. He was a bit shocked at the mention of Ken Wilder's name.

"Why would you be thinking about him?" Danny glanced at Marnie again.

"Well, it's not that I have been *thinking* about him. He's been talking to me," Marnie responded.

"Why?" Danny pulled a face.

"Redemption." Marnie sighed.

"Okay. He wants to be forgiven?"

"Hmm… sort of. It's more that he wants to help." Marnie drew a question mark with her finger in the steam on the window.

"With what?"

"With what's coming our way." Marnie rested her window.

Danny shot her a sideways glance and turned his attention back to the road. "Have you heard from anyone else?"

"Mm-hmm. Danny, can we talk later? My head is pounding, and I just want to rest my eyes."

"Sure. We can talk later. Rest your eyes. We'll talk later." Danny reached across the console, put his hand on hers and squeezed gently. Marnie squeezed back and didn't let go.

They rode in silence the rest of the journey up Lake Road. Danny slowed the Jeep well before the turnoff to his driveway.

160

"Marnie, I need my hand back. I have to turn into the driveway. It hasn't been plowed, and it's icy."

Marnie sat up and let go of Danny's hand. Ice was built up at the entry to the long driveway from cars going past and pushing slush to the side of the road. Danny had his turn signal on and was waiting for oncoming traffic to clear.

"Will we get over the ice?" Marnie crooked her head around Danny and peered out his window.

"Yeah. We should be fine. Not sure about my sister, though. The car that she's driving looks pretty light."

Danny glimpsed into the rearview mirror. Hannah was right behind him with her turn signal on. As soon as the lane was clear, Danny turned carefully across the slush at an angle and made it into the driveway. Hannah followed at an angle and also made it into the driveway.

When they reached the security gate, Danny pressed the remote. The gate didn't move. He pressed the button again. The gate still didn't open. He put the Jeep in park and got out, leaving the car running and the door ajar. It was dark and cold, and it was spitting snow. Marnie glanced up at the security lights and wondered why they hadn't come on when they drove up to the gate.

She took off her seatbelt and leaned across the console and the driver's seat. "Danny, the security lights are out."

Danny looked up and frowned. He waved his hands in the air, but the lights didn't activate. He moved on to the gate. There wasn't any ice buildup underneath, and the gates were high enough to swing clear had they been operational. Danny opened the gate manually and got back in the Jeep. He drove through and waited as he waved Hannah through as well. He thought about closing it as long as he was right there. *Nah,* he grumbled to himself. *She won't be staying long.*

As they got closer to the cabin, Danny noticed that there was a wire down. He knew that the wire was for the garage, gate and security lights on this side of the house. He'd have to get someone in tomorrow to fix it, but he wanted to turn off the power at the breaker before anyone got out of their vehicles and were electrocuted.

Danny turned to Marnie. "Stay here. I want to turn off the power to the garage before you get out."

She nodded and turned around in her seat to see Tater smiling at her. She smiled back and scratched his head.

Danny skirted around the wire and went back to Hannah's car to tell her what he was doing. She simply gave him a bored nod and went back to looking at her phone. *She looks tired,* he thought. *That was a tough drive, and all that she seems to care about is that damn phone.* Danny disappeared inside the garage and returned a few minutes later.

Marnie grabbed her bags off the back seat and stepped out of the Jeep. Tater leapt easily out the door after her and ran to the front porch in the darkness. He had no trouble finding his way and wagged his tail with anticipation. Hannah parked her car, and pulling her coat around her shoulders, she plodded behind them, only glancing up from her phone for a second to find the bottom step. She limped a little from her earlier fall, but was more intent on her phone than looking for icy patches.

Danny opened the door, and Tater slipped inside. Marnie ducked under Danny's arm into the cabin. Vertically smaller than Marnie, Hannah easily walked beneath her brother's outstretched limb, not even noticing that he was holding the door – her eyes glued to her phone. Danny followed and pushed the door shut tightly. He caught Marnie frowning at his sister's bowed head and shrugged in response. Marnie pursed her lips and shrugged back.

Marnie kicked off her boots, left them in the tray by the front door and began to wriggle out of her coat. Danny took it from her and reached to help Hannah from hers, but his sister turned a shoulder from him. *Suit yourself,* he thought to himself and turned again to hang his and Marnie's coats on the coatrack. Tater happily ran into the living room and curled up under the pool table.

Marnie laughed at Tater's comfort at making himself at home and turned to Danny's sister to break the silence. Hannah was still standing by the front door staring down at her phone.

"Hi, Hannah. I'm Danny's friend, Marnie Reilly. It's nice to meet you."

Marnie offered her hand to Hannah. Hannah looked up from her phone briefly and just nodded. Marnie wrinkled her nose. She laughed again.

"Wow, Danny! I can see you didn't get all of the charm in your family. Your sister is such a delight!" Hannah looked up from her phone and shot Marnie a dismissive squint.

Marnie rolled her eyes and went into the kitchen to get Tater's dinner ready. Danny followed.

"Sorry about that. She's always been awkward." Danny's face colored pink with embarrassment.

Marnie raised her eyebrows in response. "Awkward? I'd call that rude, but whatever."

"Her social skills have never been strong. My father let her get away with it. I'm the only one who ever calls her out. Sarah never let her get away with it, either. Probably why they didn't get along." Danny opened the fridge and took out a beer.

"I think I would have liked your wife, Danny. She sounds like an exceptional judge of character."

A clatter from the living room was loud – the shriek louder. Danny nearly stepped on Hannah's phone lying on the floor as he and Marnie raced into the room to find Tater standing next to Hannah with his chin resting on the couch cushion next to her – Hannah grimacing with her hands waving over her head.

"Get it away from me! Get it away from me now!" Hannah screamed.

Tater sat back on his haunches, cocked his head to one side and stared at Hannah. Hannah kicked her foot at him. Tater leaped out of the way just in time, tucked his tail between his legs and ran to Danny and Marnie.

"Keep that dog away from me! Put it outside. I hate dogs!"

"Whoa! Whoa! Hannah, that's enough. Tater is Marnie's dog, and he's welcome in my home. He was just curious, and since when do you hate dogs? You don't hate dogs. You're just a pain in the ass!" Danny stood in front of his sister, his expression hard.

"C'mon, Tater. Let's get your dinner ready." Marnie called Tater to the kitchen and threw a scowl at Hannah over her shoulder.

Hannah looked at her brother with contempt and disgust. "God, Daniel! Do you take in every stray! Who is that… that… person? Why are she and her dog in your home?" Hannah waved a hand dismissively toward the kitchen, Marnie and Tater.

Danny's eyes grew wide, and his face darkened. "Wow! Hannah, you have crossed a line! Go one more step over it, and you will be out the front door on your ass in a snowbank. I promised Dad that I would never hit a girl, but I never promised that I wouldn't throw one out the door. Don't ever behave that way toward people I love… or dogs for that matter! What the hell is going on with you?"

Of course, Marnie was eavesdropping. She let out a little titter and skipped across the kitchen to feed Tater. She bent down and scratched his ears.

"Did you hear that, Tater? He loves us," she whispered and tittered again.

Tater put a paw on her leg and smiled.

Hannah looked slack-jawed at her brother. Danny held her stare then stalked across to the fireplace. He grabbed the log tote and disappeared out the front door to get firewood. When he returned, he laid a fire, lit it, turned and slammed his hand down on the arm of the couch so hard that Hannah flinched and dropped her phone again.

"Put the damn phone away, Hannah. Why are you here? *Don't* lie to me!"

Hannah placed her phone on the coffee table and glared up at her brother defiantly. Her ice-gray gaze locked on his steely blue eyes. Neither spoke. They just stared at one another with their jaws clenched, their shoulders tight. 1 minute, 2 minutes passed. Neither spoke.

Danny's own phone rang. He tried to ignore it, but knew it would be important. It was Tom. As a joke, Marnie had set Tom's ringtone on Danny's phone to The Three Stooges theme song of "Three Blind Mice." Hannah's face broke with a snort of disdain, and Danny wheeled away, pulling his phone out of his back pocket and distancing himself to the other side of the room.

"Yeah?"

"Danny?"

"Yeah, Tommy. What's happening?" Danny asked.

"Are you at the cabin? I assume tree shopping is off for the evening, you know, because of the sleet?"

"Yes and yes," Danny replied.

"We need to talk. Carl just stopped by the station and filled me in on some details. I think it's important."

"Okay. Um… My sister is here, but yeah. You and Carl should come over."

"You want me to bring Carl?" Tom asked, a hint of skepticism in his tone.

"Yeah! Words from the horse's mouth are better than secondhand."

"Um… well, you're gonna want to speak to Alice Wells and Allen Schofield. Carl spoke with both of them at the hospital today. There's something rotten in that proverbial state of Denmark, and all roads lead to Grace Wilmot," Tom replied.

Danny ran his hand over the top of his head and glanced up at the ceiling. He needed to think. He needed to deal with his sister. He needed to get Marnie settled in. He needed to eat; his stomach was growling.

"Tommy, I think this has to wait until morning. The roads are bad. Go home, and we'll go see Alice and Allen in the morning."

"If you're sure."

"Yeah. I'm dealing with something here. Thanks, Tommy," Danny said and hung up.

~~~~~~~~~~~~~~~~~~

Marnie stuck her head into the living room. Danny was on the phone, and Hannah was on the couch staring into the fire. As soon as Danny hung up from his call, she asked about dinner.

"Danny, do want me to fix us something for dinner? I haven't eaten since breakfast, and that was disgusting hospital food. What about you two?"

Danny nodded, touching his stomach instinctually. He felt the low rumble of hunger. "That would be great, Marnie, if you feel up to it. What did you have in mind?"

"Well, I can whip up some pasta if that sounds good to you. We're kind of short on supplies, but we do have pasta."

Hannah picked up her head abruptly and scowled in Marnie's direction. Her attention shifted quickly to Danny.

"*We*? When did this become a *we* situation?" Hannah pointed a finger between Danny and Marnie. "I've not heard anything about this. Has Father? Does he know that you have this woman living with you?" Hannah interrogated Danny in a condescending tone, all the while pointing a judgmental finger at Marnie. "Daniel, why *is* this woman here in *your* home with her dog? Are the two of you living together? Are you a couple? Is she homeless?"

Marnie's jaw dropped open. As she took a step into the living room and opened her mouth to defend herself, Danny crossed the living room in three long strides. He picked up his sister off the couch and carried her over his shoulder to the front door. Hannah shrieked and struggled, her mouth twisted fiercely in anger. Danny opened the door, stomped to the edge of the porch and dropped Hannah unceremoniously into a small snowbank.

Danny stomped back into the cabin, slammed the door and made his way to the kitchen. "Let's make dinner. I'm starving."

Tater peeked out from under the pool table – ears flat to his head, tail between his legs. Marnie hadn't moved, and her mouth was still open. Danny gently put his hand under her chin and closed her mouth. He took Marnie's hand and led her into the kitchen, Marnie double-stepping behind him. Tater slunk behind them – ears down and tail tucked.

Marnie approached the sink, but Danny turned and saw Tater's posture. He squatted down to Tater's level, held out his hands. "Come here, Tater."

Tater's ears perked up and he belly-crawled slowly to Danny. Marnie watched the pair from across the kitchen. Tater approached Danny cautiously – one step at a time – slowly, slowly. Danny held out one hand to Tater, who sniffed and licked it and then nudged his head under Danny's hand for an ear scratch. Danny sat back on the floor and patted Tater, hugging him only when Tater leaned his back against Danny's chest. Tater turned his head, licked Danny's face and then lay down between his legs.

"We all good now, Tater? Sorry if I scared you. I kinda scared myself a little bit, too," Danny said soothingly to the dog, but intending it for Marnie as well. "My sister and I have a complicated relationship. She hates me, and I don't hate her. That's about all that I know about that," Danny said. He gave Tater one last pat and got up to help Marnie with dinner.

Marnie cocked her head to one side. "Um, what about the 'snow princess?'"

Danny laughed easily. "She's a big girl. We'll let her cool off for a while. I didn't lock her out. Let her figure this out. C'mon. I'm really hungry now!"

Danny and Marnie chatted comfortably about the day, the craziness of the past few days, Tater and Christmas plans while they prepared dinner. Tater sat by the glass doors that overlooked the lake and watched the darkness. He'd been doing this a lot lately – watching the darkness.

"Do you want to sit at the table or by the fire?" Danny pulled two plates out of the cupboard.

"Hmm. Let's sit by the fire tonight," Marnie replied thoughtfully.

"Glass of wine?" Danny held up a wine glass.

Marnie turned the question over in her mind before responding. "No, thanks, my head is still a bit swimmy. I think wine may not be the best anecdote."

Danny nodded his agreement. He grabbed another bottle of beer from the fridge for himself and filled a glass with water for Marnie.

They settled in around the fire. Drawn by the smells and their comfort, Tater curled up on the hearth rug, nose tucked under his tail. Soon, Marnie heard the sounds of gentle snores emanate from the furry mound. They ate in companionable silence. Marnie glanced at Danny several times, wondering if he wanted to talk about what just happened with his sister. She knew that he usually needed a bit of time to cool down, and it had been a while since he had dumped Hannah in a snowbank. He was so quiet – too quiet – so she began softly.

"Do you want to talk?" Marnie asked.

"Nope."

"Okay, then," Marnie replied and returned her attention to her plate. *Let it be, silly.*

A loud knock on the front door made them both jump. Danny put his plate down a bit harder than he had planned, and linguini slipped over the side of his plate and onto the floor. Never one to let food go to waste, Tater dove onto the pasta like a shark to chum.

"Tater!" Marnie scolded.

"Fair game, huh, big guy?" Danny countered with a mild laugh.

The knock came again, harder this time. No longer amused by the theft of some of his dinner, Danny stomped to the door and, growling like a hungry bear, flung open the door.

"What?!"

Tom stood there with Hannah at his elbow.

"Hey, easy now, grumpy bear. I found this one sitting on the step turning blue. Can I come in?"

Danny stepped back from the door and motioned Tom inside. Hannah tried to skirt in around him, but Danny put up his arm to stop her. Hannah stared up at him. He saw tears on her eyelashes and cheeks, and she was trembling. He dropped his arm and let her inside.

Tom abandoned his rescued visitor to the wrath of Danny, shed his coat and boots and drifted to the fireplace, sniffing the air as he went. "Mmm. What smells good?" Tom asked Marnie. "Hey, Tater Tot! Hey, is that red sauce on your chin?"

Marnie laughed. "Yep. It's linguini with a sad Napolitano sauce," she answered, holding up her plate. "Want some?"

"I do. I do, indeed." Tom rubbed his hands together and made a beeline for the kitchen. He was accustomed to helping himself.

Marnie set her plate down and followed Tom. Halfway to the kitchen, she turned around.

"Hannah, would you like some pasta?"

Hannah faltered. She hadn't moved fully into the room. She was standing with her back against the door, ready to make an escape. Tater sat a few feet from her, wagging his tail. He didn't try to approach Hannah, but watched her closely. He also eyed Danny's plate, considering his options.

"If it's not too much trouble, thank you." She remained stiffly where she was. Danny eased past her and rescued his plate before Tater could gobble up any more pasta.

"Sure. No trouble at all. I think that you will have a hard time eating if you don't relax and sit down. Have a seat next to the fire, and I'll bring it in," Marnie replied cheerfully.

Danny smiled into his plate. Why did he think Marnie was up to something? Her mind worked in mysterious ways, and he hadn't figured her out just yet. He sat silently, Tater at his feet. Out of the corner of his eye, he watched Hannah. She stood stiffly at the edge of the room.

Danny could hear Tom and Marnie chatting as they busily pulled more plates from the cupboard in the kitchen and mounded the plates with warm pasta and sauce. He heard Marnie ask Tom to grab a tray, and he knew that, in just a minute, Tom and Marnie would return. *It's now or never...* he thought. Danny sat very still, assessing his sister's sudden change of attitude.

"Do you want to talk to me now? Tell me what's going on?" Danny set his plate safely out of Tater's range.

Hannah nodded tightly.

She took off her coat, hung it on a hook, kicked off her wet boots and then slipped into an overstuffed chair near the fire. There was a wool blanket at its back, and she eased forward to release it, fluffing it in front of her and over her legs. She kept her eyes low, unwilling to meet Danny's gaze. She was silent. She could feel her brother's eyes bearing down on her. Danny gave in.

"Not that it's any of your business, Hannah, but Marnie is a close friend. She and Tater are staying with me because I invited them," Danny said. "Now, how about you come clean with me? What's going on, Hannah? As I said before, don't lie to me."

-CHAPTER THIRTY-SIX-

A book of Robert Frost's poems lay open on a coffee table in the tidy living room of a small, comfortable apartment. The book of poetry had once belonged to Sam Reilly, Marnie Reilly's brother. He'd left it behind in a mad rush to get somewhere. The apartment was above a cozy bookstore at the end of Cobblestone Lane in Creekwood. Mrs. Backus, the owner of the bookstore, had been so kind about renting this two-bedroom apartment. Sam had stayed here for a short time and had highly recommended the location. It was perfect. It was close to almost everything. It was a stone's throw from the center of town, *and* it was just two blocks up from Marnie Reilly's office.

Flickering flames burned in a small fireplace, and lit candles of fragrant balsam dotted the end tables, the mantle, coffee table and sofa table. The heavy curtains were drawn against a draft, and a glass filled with whiskey and ice sat neatly on a coaster on the pine coffee table in front of the couch. Long legs, dressed in loose black pants, stretched from the couch to coffee table. The owner of the legs sat comfortably sipping whiskey while reciting poetry to a cat. The Siamese cat stretched languorously across a chintz-covered chaise lounge, basking in the warmth of the dancing fire.

The reader set the book open to the page just recounted to the cat. The reader eased back and repeated the poem softly. "Yes, Simon… "Fire and Ice." Listen…"

> *Some say the world will end in fire,*
> *Some say in ice.*
> *From what I've tasted of desire*
> *I hold with those who favor fire.*
> *But if it had to perish twice,*
> *I think I know enough of hate*
> *To say that for destruction ice*
> *Is also great*
> *And would suffice.*

-CHAPTER THIRTY-SEVEN-

Hannah's and Danny's conversation had no sooner begun when it was put on hold until after dinner. Marnie and Tom came back to the living room with plates of food and drinks, interrupting the discussion. Enough had been said that Hannah had visibly warmed and softened and even remembered some manners.

"Marnie, this pasta is lovely, thank you," Hannah said over her glass of water.

"You are welcome, Hannah. It's not much, but it's what we had in the fridge and pantry. Things have been busy, and groceries have been put off a bit too long." Marnie's apologetic smile received a warm nod of understanding from Hannah.

"This is really good," Tom said with a mouth full of pasta.

"Don't talk with your mouth full, Tom. It's disgusting." Marnie snapped her napkin at him. "Thank you. I'll run out and get some groceries tomorrow. Carl and Uncle Giles have convinced me to take some time off. From now until after Christmas, I am a lady of leisure." Marnie stretched out her long legs and hugged herself.

"That's excellent news!" Danny held up his beer in a cheering fashion.

"Yay! Home cooked meals for us!" Tom waved his fork in the air.

Marnie shook her head and shot Tom a grin. "No, Tom. During that time, I will be shopping, wrapping, decorating, baking and doing the things I want to do – not the things you want me to do for you."

"Will you help me pick out a Christmas present for my mother?" Tom smiled hopefully.

"Of course. Don't I always?"

"Yup. She would get a bottle of wiper fluid if not for you." Tom laughed.

"Will you help me pick out something for Gram?" Danny tipped his head and nudged Marnie's leg with his toe.

"Of course! I can't imagine Gram needing very much, but I'm sure that we'll find something perfect for her. I was thinking of getting her a nightgown, robe and slippers. Do you think that she would like that?" Marnie nudged Danny's foot with her own.

"Isn't that what Sarah always got for Grandmother?" Hannah asked, eyebrows raised.

Danny nodded. "Yes, it is, actually. I'm sure that Gram would be thrilled to receive them again."

"Oh, Danny, I'm sorry." Marnie's face reddened. "I didn't mean to be insensitive."

"You weren't. Sarah always bought Gram pajamas and slippers… and brandied eggnog. Gram loves brandied eggnog."

"Who doesn't? I mean, really!" Marnie grinned.

"I don't like brandied eggnog," Hannah replied bluntly.

Marnie glanced at Tom, who was making a face. She scolded him with her eyes.

"What do you like to drink, Hannah?" Marnie asked.

"Whiskey. Rye whiskey… with ginger ale."

"Would you like a drink?" Danny asked.

"I would, thank you." Hannah gave a curt nod

"Ice?"

"Yes, please."

Danny mixed a drink for Hannah and grabbed two beers out of the fridge for him and Tom.

"Marnie, do you want anything?" Danny asked.

"Hmm. Do we still have that bottle of port from Thanksgiving?"

"We do. I'll get you a glass."

"Thank you!" Marnie stretched, leaned forward and patted Tater's sleeping head.

Tom examined the label on his beer bottle. Marnie could see the gears turning in his head. He was sizing up Hannah and just how far he could push her with questions.

"So, Hannah, what was William working on here in Creekwood? Might be good to fill in the locals so that we can be on our game if there's a drug issue in town."

"Well, you're about as subtle as a brick through a window," Marnie shoved Tom's knee with her toe.

Hannah tried to cover the look of fear that washed over her, but she didn't manage it well.

"Hannah? Are you okay?" Marnie jumped to her feet.

Hannah put up a hand. "I'm fine. Everything is fine."

Marnie took a step forward. Hannah's eyes filled with tears, and she held up her hand again.

"Please, I can't get into it right now." Hannah turned to face the fireplace. Tears glistened in her eyes.

"Okay. That's okay. In your own time," Marnie replied in her best therapist tone.

Hannah just nodded her head and took a drink of her whiskey.

Danny returned with the port for Marnie. He turned to Hannah because both Marnie and Tom were focused on her.

"Everything okay?" Danny set the glass on the coffee table.

Hannah burst into tears. Danny glanced between Marnie and Tom, both shrugging in response to his inquisitive eyes.

"Hannah, you come in the kitchen with me and tell me what's going on," Danny pushed.

Hannah shook her head and turned her gaze to Marnie.

"Do you want to have a chat with me?" Marnie asked, pointing to herself with wonderment.

Hannah nodded, tears streaming down her face.

"Okay. Guys, you two go out to the kitchen, and let Hannah and me sit by the fire and chat." Marnie motioned Tom and Danny out of the room with her head. Danny started to protest. It was his sister, after all, but he relented, especially since Tom didn't give him a choice.

Tom and Danny disappeared into the kitchen. Tater got up from his spot next to the fire and belly-crawled over to Hannah. He stood, placed his head on her lap and looked up into her face. Hannah patted him on the head. Tater sat and put a paw on her knee. Hannah managed a small smile and leaned over to give Tater a hug.

Marnie watched the interaction between Tater and Hannah. She couldn't be all that bad if Tater was comforting her. After all, Tater was an excellent judge of character. He didn't do this sort of thing with everyone.

Hannah lifted her head and accepted the box of tissues that Marnie offered. She wiped her eyes and nose and hung her head for just a moment. She took a deep breath and began.

"William and I were involved. We were planning to get married, but I hadn't… we hadn't told anyone yet. He told me that he would be working undercover for a few months, but that, when he returned, we would tell my family and our friends. He would call me every couple of days, and all of a sudden, about three weeks ago, he stopped calling. He didn't check in with his boss, and he stopped sending information to the field office in Hudson. He just vanished. Then we received news that someone was searching his fingerprints in databases outside of the norm. Alarm bells started going off, and we knew that his cover had been compromised. Have you got any idea who would have been looking in databases outside of the normal PD databases?"

172

"I think so." Marnie nodded and scooched forward on the couch. "Rick Price is a forensics specialist. He has access to information that many of the cops don't. He's done work with the FBI, CIA, DEA, ATF – all of them over the years. He may have done the search if the local guys couldn't find anything."

Hannah nodded. "I'm not supposed to be here. I took vacation days and told my boss that I would be gone for a while. I have a ton of vacation time. I think that he knows what I'm up to; he just didn't stop me." Hannah raised her whiskey glass to her lips and took a long drink.

"I would have done exactly the same thing, Hannah. Something happens to someone you love, well, you have to find out. Nothing else matters." Marnie nodded in empathy.

"I should have just asked Daniel for help, but I couldn't. We have a complicated relationship, and I didn't want to ask for help. He would never let me forget it."

"That doesn't sound like the Danny I know." Marnie creased her forehead. "But he isn't my brother."

"It's a bratty little brother, overbearing big sister kind of thing." Hannah shrugged.

"Well, I'm quite sure that the bratty little brother has grown up and would be happy to help his overbearing big sister." Marnie leaned forward and gave Hannah's knee a reassuring squeeze.

Hannah smiled, her face softened and she nodded.

"Shall we get the knuckleheads back into the room and see if they can help?" Marnie asked.

Hannah nodded and grabbed for another tissue as her eyes welled up again.

Marnie stood and touched Hannah's shoulder gently. "I'll go get them and give you a sec to compose yourself."

"Thanks, Marnie. I'm sorry that I was so rude to you when I first got here," Hannah said sheepishly.

"That's okay. I'm a therapist. I deal with much worse on a daily basis, but thank you for apologizing. At least now, I know that you're not an asshole." Marnie shrugged and headed to the kitchen.

Hannah laughed, which was exactly what Marnie was hoping that she would do.

-CHAPTER THIRTY-EIGHT-

Allen sat in the local jail awaiting a hearing. His tiny cell had just a single cot, a sink, a toilet and ghastly LED lighting shining down from above. The cot was terribly uncomfortable, and he had no privacy. He now realized that he had taken so much for granted – until now. He had hit rock bottom. Grace Wilmot had brought him to this point. He'd been a content and successful pest exterminator when he'd met Grace Wilmot and her late husband Stuart. He had been to their home years earlier, taking care of a rat problem early one autumn.

He hung his head and sobbed quietly. If only he was alone, but he wasn't alone. Several other cells were housing some of Creekwood's finest criminals and characters. Old Joe Carter was in the cell next door – drunk again. Terry Lewis had a tussle with Dave Blanchard over a referee's call during a college basketball game that they'd been watching at the tavern; they were in cells at opposite ends of the jail, still yelling at each other. Becky Clark was the town kleptomaniac; she was in a cell once again, waiting for her husband to come pick her up. Jack Kelly, Terrance Carver and Pete Hernandez had been picked up behind the community center with beer and pot; all three teens were stoned, intoxicated and waiting for their parents to pick them up.

Allen glanced through the open bars at the row of cells caging his fellow incarcerated. Allen still wasn't sure what had happened last night. People – these miscreants, the cell chief, the weary matron who brought in morning coffee and stale muffins – some of these people told him – he just didn't remember much. When sparks of memories did rush into his head, he agonized over how much trouble he was in and where he would be for Christmas – at Alice's house for a lovely dinner or in jail. Alice – the very thought of her brought a fresh wave of tears to his eyes.

~~~~~~~~~~~~~~~~~~~~

Alice dozed fitfully in her hospital bed. She would be released tomorrow. Her mind was bombarded with images of Grace Wilmot. Her body twitched as she dreamed horrible nightmares. *Oh, the things… the things that Grace Wilmot would do…* Alice could not rouse herself to the surface. She fretted about what might happen to her if she went back to her house tomorrow. Carl told her that Allen was in jail; that meant that he couldn't stay with her and be

174

the buffer between her and the rest of the world. She couldn't bear being alone with members of The Collective. She didn't know whom she could trust.

~~~~~~~~~~~~~~~~~~~~~~~~~

Grace Wilmot sat in a comfy chair at the silo chanting over a totem of Alice Wells. Her cruel hands thumbed the forehead of the doll and twisted the neck from side to side.

A loud bang reverberated through the silo. Grace dropped the doll and rose to find the culprit of the din. She crept quietly through the candlelit silo, stopping and turning her head with each step – listening for sounds of an intruder. Another bang reverberated. Grace tipped her head to the side and realized that the noise was coming from the hatch. A moment later, Reuben came through the hatch soaking wet, face red and lips trembling.

"Reuben! What were you thinking making all of that noise? You know that my tinnitus is aggravated by noises like that!" Grace Wilmot shrieked at her son.

"No, Mother! Your tinnitus is aggravated by high-pitched noises – not loud bangs on metal. That noise was a clunk – not a ting. Your tinnitus has never been aggravated by clunks! There was a ton of ice on the handle out there. I had to hit it with a rock to open the door. It's sleeting!" Reuben fired back.

Grace turned her back on him and skulked to her chair.

"Make me a cup of tea, Reuben, and don't put too much milk in it this time," Grace ordered with a wave of her hand.

"Make your own tea, Mother!"

Grace turned around swiftly to meet the defiant glare in Reuben's eyes. Grace narrowed her eyes and took a threatening step forward toward Reuben. Reuben didn't move; he held his position.

"Excuse me! Did I hear you right? Did you tell me *no*?" Grace asked in a menacing tone.

Reuben laughed, shook his head and sneered. As Reuben spoke, he took a threatening step toward his mother with each statement that he spoke and every question that he asked.

"Mother, I have put up with your shit for way too long! You have ordered me around since my father died. You have lied to me. You have humiliated me. You have beaten me. You have used me. You have abandoned me time and again. What kind of mother leaves her child with strangers for days on end only coming back because you need proof of life so that you get money from social services to survive? What kind of mother buys only enough food for one person and eats it all herself? What kind of mother allows her child to go hungry while she stuffs her face like a gluttonous pig with her child looking on? What kind of mother threatens her child when he won't break the law for her? What kind of mother does those things?" Reuben retorted rebelliously.

Reuben now stood toe to toe with Grace. He looked down on her – his jaw set, his amber eyes piercing her forehead. She looked up into his face – shocked at first. Then, for the first time in his life, she was proud of the man whom she saw. He'd stood up for himself. He was actually frightening her a little – just a little. She knew that Reuben didn't have the courage to continue this tiny burst of bravery. He would disappoint her yet again.

Grace put her hands on Reuben's chest and nudged him to step back. Reuben grabbed her wrists and shoved her back. Her face exploded with anger, and she rushed toward him, arms upraised. Reuben stepped back and put his arms up in defense, bracing for impact. Grace stopped, cackled and retreated one step back.

"Don't touch me! You are nothing more than a vile, evil woman," Reuben sneered.

Grace smirked. "Reuben, be very careful. You and I both know that you won't last long without me out there to protect you. How will you take care of yourself, Reuben? How?"

"I've been taking care of myself since I was 10 years old. I have my own apartment. I do odd jobs. I have money saved. I get by, Mother. I don't need you. As a matter of fact, you need me more than I need you." Reuben sniggered. "How are *you* going to take care of yourself, Mother? Who is going to be there when you need something? I can tell you that it is not going to be me! I'm done with you! I. Am. Done." He wheeled about, arms crossed.

Grace shrugged and turned her back on Reuben. *Big show… he'll be back. Fool.* He was loyal like that.

"Do as you like, Reuben, but first give me the laptop." Grace spit at the broad back of her son, holding out her hand for the computer.

"I *will* do as I like, and I don't have the laptop. Justin has it, and you know that because you sent him to get it from my apartment last night… because you didn't trust me to bring it to you." Reuben glowered.

"What?!" Grace shouted. "I didn't send Justin to your apartment. You told me that you would bring it back. When you didn't return last night, I assumed that you were mad at me and wanted to make me wait. How could you have given the laptop to Justin? How could you?!"

"Well, guess what, Mother? If you were a little more honest with everyone and didn't play games with everyone, I may have realized that Justin was lying.

Since you have lied, cheated and stolen your way through life, I had no idea that Justin *was* lying to me." Reuben twisted his mouth and shrugged.

"Reuben, you have to find that laptop! You have to find it now!" Grace shrieked.

"No, I really don't. Have a nice night, Mother. I'm going home to relax." Reuben walked toward the hatch.

"Reuben Wilmot! If you don't have the computer, then why did you come here?" Grace shouted.

Reuben turned around and smirked.

"Why did I come here? I came here, *Mother*, to tell you to fuck off!"

Reuben lifted the handle and opened the hatch. He paused in the doorway and walked out of the silo. He heard the cackling echo of his mother behind the hatch. He made his way up the tracks to downtown Creekwood. He looked forward to returning home to his tiny apartment and a nice quiet dinner with Erin Matthews.

-CHAPTER THIRTY-NINE-

"Hannah, I don't understand why you just didn't come to me to begin with?" Danny studied his sister's face. "Did you really think that I *wouldn't* help you? Geez, Hannah! If you'd just been honest with me…" Danny left the last few words hanging. He was standing next to the fireplace, hands in his pockets, head back, rocking on his heels.

Marnie curled up on the couch near the fireplace. Tom sat on the other end of the couch sipping a beer quietly. Tater lay on his back on the hearth, his head lolled to the side and his tongue hung out – relaxed.

"Daniel, you and I have never had a conventional brother-sister relationship. We have always been at odds, and you know damn well that you would have asked me a thousand questions that I, quite frankly, didn't feel like answering! I just wanted to come here, see William – just to make sure that it's actually him – and then go back home and find closure. I don't know if I will ever find that, though, without digging in and finding out what happened to William!"

Danny pulled his hands out of his pockets and held up a hand in surrender. "Okay. Okay, Hannah. What can we do to help?"

Hannah threw up her hands. "I don't know. I don't know what you can do. I have a copy of William's file from the Hudson field office. I haven't reviewed it yet. I'm not even supposed to have it. I doubt that my boss would be mad or surprised, but I shouldn't have the file."

Tom stretched and stood. He walked over to the door and peeked out. "Hey, Danny, if you don't mind, I think that I will crash here tonight. It's lookin' pretty bad out there. The cars are covered with a couple of inches of ice, and it's spitting snow. I really don't want to navigate Lake Road in that crap." Tom turned, looking hopefully at Danny.

Hannah jumped up, ran to the window and looked out.

Danny nodded. "Yeah. I don't want either of you driving in that. We'll make up the beds. It's fine."

Hannah rolled her eyes and slouched. "I forgot how quickly weather can move in up here. We get snow in DC, but I don't think it gets as treacherous as that mess out there." Hannah stood by the window for a long moment. "Well, I better get my overnight bag out of the car." Hannah began pulling on her boots.

"Hannah, I'll get it for you." Tom pulled on his boots and jacket. "Is it in the car or the trunk?"

"Thank you, Tom. It's on the back seat. My briefcase is back there, too. Would you mind grabbing it?" Hannah smiled, relieved she didn't have to go back out into the cold.

"Sure thing!"

Tom opened the door, ventured out onto the porch and examined the steps and path to the cars. The ice gleamed under the glare of the porch light. Danny kept a barrel of sand on the porch. Tom scooped up some sand with a large cup, and he sprinkled the porch, steps and the path to the cars with sand. As he was stepping off the porch, he noticed a brown package tucked next to the railing. He picked it up and read the label. It was for Marnie. There was no return label. Tom raised his eyebrows. He turned over the package and checked the bottom. It didn't look suspicious, but not everything suspicious reveals itself immediately. Tom shrugged, set the box down and went to gather up Hannah's things from her car. He had to struggle to get the door open due to the ice, but finally managed to loosen the ice and pull up the latch. He grabbed Hannah's overnight bag and her briefcase, slammed the car door and then went to his truck to get his emergency overnight bag. On his way into the cabin, he stuck Marnie's package under his arm.

"Hey, Marn! There's a package here for you," Tom called out and set the bags down near the door.

Marnie appeared at the top of the stairs. "Huh? Couldn't hear you... Did you need something? We came up to make up the beds."

"No, I was just saying that there's a package here for you." Tom waved the package at her.

Marnie frowned. "A package for me? I didn't order anything."

Tom shrugged and replied, "I'll just leave it on the table."

"Thanks, Tom!" Marnie disappeared down the upstairs hall.

Tom went into the kitchen and started cleaning up the dinner dishes. While he was putting dishes in the dishwasher, he noticed that Tater had wandered into the kitchen and was sitting by the wall of windows and the glass door in the kitchen. He was staring out into the darkness.

"Tater Tot, what are you doing, boy?"

Tater turned around, acknowledged Tom with a twitch of his ears and then turned back to the window and the darkness outside. Tom shivered. He remembered the last time that there was activity in these woods. It was Marnie's brother stringing piano wire from tree to tree and scaling the cabin to get to the sunroof above the attic. The memory of this made Tom shudder again. It was just a few weeks ago that this happened. All of the events, beginning with the murder of Ken Wilder and the murders of Officers Webb and Weaver at Marnie's house, were seared into Tom's memory. Tom had been lucky. He had been knocked unconscious on the bridle trail beside Marnie's house. If not for Danny and Marnie, Tom may be dead now, too.

A whimper from Tater drew Tom out of his memories and back to the present. Tater whimpered again and touched his paw to the window. Tater stood and watched the woods beyond the glass. Tom heard a low growl building in Tater's throat. Tater stepped from front left paw to front right paw. He crouched low. He looked like he was ready to spring forward through the glass. Tom shook his head and grinned to himself. The security lights hadn't kicked on, so it must be a raccoon, a possum or some other woodland creature.

"Tater, come here. Come and see your Uncle Tom."

Tater's ears twitched, but he ignored Tom. Tom moved across the kitchen and stood at the window. He was a bit scared to look out into the woods. He knew that he was being silly. Thinking about the murders had just given him the willies, that's all.

Marnie walked into the kitchen with her port in her hand just as something smashed into the window.

Tom jumped back. "Fuck!"

"Jesus!" Marnie shrieked and threw her glass in the air.

Tater crouched and released a deep, threatening growl.

Danny and Hannah raced into the kitchen.

"What the hell was that?" Danny rushed to the window.

Hannah made her way to the window and peered out.

Tater sat back and returned to watching the darkness.

"Danny, why aren't the security lights on? Did that downed power line operate those, too?" Marnie asked.

Danny nodded. "Yeah, all of the security lights are on the same breaker." Concern lined his face as he crossed to the back door. He reached for the doorknob, but then thought better of it.

"Tommy, you got your gun?" Danny asked.

"Yeah. Of course. It's on the mantle. I put it there when I came in." Tom nodded.

"I've got mine, too," Hannah added.

Danny walked across the kitchen, reached above the hutch and pulled down a lockbox. He retrieved his gun and checked the safety. Hannah and Tom went back to the living room and returned with their weapons.

The sight of the three of them with their guns drawn prompted a nervous laugh from Hannah. "Might we be overreacting, Daniel?" Hannah smirked.

"Sis, you haven't been around here the last few weeks. Trust me when I say that I am not overreacting," Danny replied somberly.

Danny turned to Tom. Tom leveled his gun at the door. Danny turned the knob and opened the door slowly. Marnie grabbed the flashlight out of the junk drawer next to the sink.

She whispered, "Danny, take the flashlight." Marnie held it out to him.

Danny put his hand behind his back, and Marnie placed the flashlight in his hand. He turned it on and shined it out the door. He stepped out onto the ice-covered deck and shined the flashlight directly in front of him. There on the deck lay a bird. Danny couldn't be sure if it was dead. He took another step forward, knelt down and touched the bird with the flashlight. The bird didn't respond. Danny set the flashlight on the deck, reached out his hand and touched the bird's back.

Marnie stuck her head out the door and asked, "Danny, what is it?"

"It's a raven or a crow. I can't tell if it's dead or just stunned." Danny poked the bird gently with the flashlight again and shrugged.

"Well, bring it inside," Marnie responded.

"Don't bring it in here!" Hannah shrieked. "What if it's just stunned and it starts flying around?"

Marnie grabbed an old towel out of the pantry and handed it to Danny.

"What do you want me to do with that?" Danny screwed up his face.

"Wrap it around him, and bring him inside." Marnie mimed her directions.

Snow was piling up on Danny's head and back. He stared at Marnie – a bit in disbelief and a bit with understanding. He knew that she was an empath, and that meant that she was empathetic to all things great and small. He did as Marnie asked. He wrapped the crow in the towel, dutifully brought him inside and handed it to her. Marnie gently accepted the toweled bundle and went directly into the living room next to the fire to examine the still, feathered mound.

"Hmm. His neck is definitely not broken." Marnie studied the bird closely. "His beak looks fine, and he's somewhat warm."

Marnie gently unfurled the towel and carefully stretched one glossy black wing and then the other. "His wings seem fine. I think that he's just stunned." The bird's beady eye peered at her.

Marnie kept the bird's wings still in the towel, but allowed one finger to stroke the crow's head, neck and back under the towel. She felt his breast, hoping to feel a heartbeat. She smiled slightly and held the bird up to her ear.

A wing fluttered against her face. Marnie wrapped the towel around the crow and motioned to the others to keep their places. She went to the back door and then to the deck. She set down both the towel and the bird, unwrapped the bird from the towel and stepped away.

A few moments later, the crow hopped across the deck. It turned once toward Marnie and took flight into the darkness. Marnie gasped and wheeled into the warmth of the kitchen. She washed her hands cleaned up the broken glass and spilled port; poured herself a fresh drink; and returned to the living room with the others.

Tom, Hannah and Danny looked at her in silence as Marnie paced in front of the fireplace, thinking and moving back and forth while swirling her glass of port.

"Marn, everything okay?" Tom asked.

"Crows don't fly at night. They are not nocturnal. They gather at night. They don't fly," Marnie replied.

"Okay, so what are you saying? The crow didn't fly into the window?" Tom frowned.

"No. I think someone caught him and threw him at the window." Marnie pondered, hand on her chin and eyebrows raised.

"Aha, so you think someone is using birds as projectiles to... what? What would it mean?" Tom screwed his face up at Marnie.

"Tom, do you remember my dad's pet crow?" Marnie asked.

"Hey! I'd forgotten about that. He talked, didn't he?"

"Yes, he did. He did talk." Marnie smiled at the memory.

"Okay, Marn. I still don't see the point." Tom shrugged, and his eyes widened.

Marnie pointed at Tom. "There! You get it! You get it! I think that Sam is behind this. I think that he's put someone up to terrorizing me. It's what he does. He's always reveled in scaring me. Anything that could scare me, he would do. Like locking me in a trunk."

Marnie paced back and forth as she explained the possibilities of Sam's involvement in recent events. "He knows that I'm claustrophobic. He could have someone following me. You, Tom! He hates you as much as he hates me! Maybe more!" Marnie stopped pacing, put a hand on her hip and stared at Tom, her eyes wide, challenging him to counter her deduction.

Tom frowned. He thought about Marnie's hypothesis for a moment, agreed with her for the briefest of seconds and then changed his mind. He shook his head and countered. "Marn, I think that you're tired. I think that you're stressed. I think that you're just about around the bend. Sam's locked up. He hasn't had any visitors. I've checked. There is no way that Sam Reilly is trying to drive you crazy, my friend. You're already there!"

Hannah and Danny appeared to be spectators watching a tennis match, turning between Tom and Marnie and watching the duo's animated reactions to each other's words.

"Tom, you have no idea what you're talking about. Sam may not be receiving visitors, but he sure as hell is making phone calls!"

Marnie stomped across the living room, picked up her bag and pulled out her phone. Tom and Danny both followed her rapidly across the living room. Danny held out his hand for Marnie's phone. She gladly handed it over. Tom yelled at her, incredulous.

"Sam has called you? Sam has called you, and you didn't think it important to tell me? To tell Danny? For fuck's sake, Marnie! You should have told us!" Tom scolded.

"Can I listen to the message?" Danny handed Marnie her phone.

Marnie took her phone back from Danny, pressed both play and speaker so that everyone could hear the calls.

"Marnie, my beloved baby sister, why aren't you answering your phone? Don't you want to speak to your big brother? Cat got your tongue? We haven't spoken in days. Maybe you should come for a visit and check out my new digs. Three squares a day, an uncomfortable cot and a roommate who smells like a teenage boy's gym bag, but hey, I'm far away from general population. You know, they don't drop cops into general population unless they want them dead. Apparently, someone is shining some love on me from above. You suppose Mom and Dad are my guardian angels? Now, that would be somethin', huh? Come see me, Marn, and hey, pick up a book of Robert Frost's poetry. You know the one. I've misplaced my copy."

Danny and Tom exchanged glances.

"There's another one," Marnie said. She hit both play and speaker again as Tom and Danny raised their eyebrows at the fact that there was a second call.

"Marnie, when I get out of here – and you know that I will – you're fucking dead! You, your friends, your mutt! All dead! I'm going to string you up and bash you like a piñata. No. Actually, I'm going to torture you first. I'm going to tie your hands behind your back, bind your feet together at the ankles, lock you in a box and drop you in the lake. Just when you're running out of air and you think that you're going to die, I'll pull you up and do it again and again and again until you lose your fucking mind. Then I'll string you up and use you as a piñata. Call me! I want my book back!"

When the message finished playing, Marnie stuck up her index finger and said, "Hang on. There's another call that you should hear. This one's from Kate."

Danny and Tom both rolled their eyes and listened intently.

"Marnie, I know that I shouldn't be calling you, but I really need to speak to you. Do you know who I saw here in Creekwood? You'll never guess! I saw Grace Wilmot! I don't know what she's up to, but you know that it can't be good. Listen, Marn, I'm worried about you. Grace isn't the forgiving type, and she was always into that crazy hoodoo voodoo nonsense. Isn't she a black witch or something? Anyway, Marn, watch your back. I saw her over by the tracks. You may want to have someone check it out, and don't you go there alone. I'd hate to think what she would do to you. You know the old saying, 'Hell hath no fury like a woman scorned,' and you certainly must be on the top of her you-know-what list. Anyway, if you could call me, that would be great. Bye, Marnie."

Hannah glanced with mild confusion at Danny, Tom and Marnie. She finally turned to Danny.

Danny gave Hannah the short version of the Sam Reilly saga. Hannah shook her head in disbelief.

Hannah turned to Danny. "I thought that *our* relationship was fucked up."

Danny shook his head, puffed out his cheeks. "Sister dear, we ain't got nothin' on the Reilly clan."

Marnie nodded in agreement.

"Yeah," Tom replied with a roll of his eyes.

"What's next?" Hannah asked.

"We sleep on it," Danny replied. "We all get some sleep and discuss it in the morning. Tom and I have a day off, and Marnie is taking some time off. Let's get some sleep and circle back in the morning."

Everyone nodded in agreement.

"Go ahead up. I'll lock up and turn off the lights. See you all in the morning." Danny turned to check the lock on the front door.

No one argued – except Tater. He stayed downstairs while Danny made sure that the cabin was locked up and the lights turned off. When they reached the top of the stairs, Tater nosed his way into Marnie's room and jumped up on the foot of the bed.

Danny went to his room, brushed his teeth, washed up in the master bath and got ready for bed. Just as he was climbing under the covers, he thought about Marnie and how she would be coping with Sam Reilly's recent calls. He put on his slippers and bathrobe and ventured down the hall to Marnie's room. The door was ajar, and the light was still on. He stuck his head in the door.

Tater was stretched out along Marnie's legs, and Marnie was reading.

"Are you okay?" Danny asked softly.

Marnie nodded hesitantly. "I'm reading. Seasonal stuff, not anything macabre." Marnie held up her book – *The Complete Christmas Books and Stories of Charles Dickens.*

"Okay. I'll see you in the morning." Danny hesitated in the doorway.

Marnie looked down at Tater, and her eyes welled up with tears.

Danny stepped across the room softly, sat on the edge of Marnie's bed and pulled her close for a hug.

"It's going to be okay. I'll call the prison tomorrow and make sure that Sam doesn't get access to a phone again. Okay?"

Marnie nodded into Danny's shoulder. He pulled a tissue out of the box on her nightstand and handed it to her. Marnie wiped her eyes and her nose.

"Okay," Danny said. "If you need anything, I'm right next door. Okay?"

"Thanks. I'm being an idiot." Marnie stared down at her book.

"No, you're not. We've all been through a lot." Danny squeezed her arm.

As Danny reached the door, Marnie cleared her throat. "Danny, do you think that you could stay in here with me and Tater tonight?"

Danny half-turned toward her.

"You want me to stay with you and Tater?" Danny glanced around Marnie's room.

She nodded.

"Safety in numbers?" Danny raised an eyebrow.

Marnie nodded again with a slight grimace.

"Sure. Of course." Danny kicked off his slippers and threw his robe onto the foot of the bed. "Move over, Tater. Make some room."

Tater yawned, stretched, stood and curled up at Marnie's feet.

"Well, I guess that Tater is going to chaperone." Danny laughed.

"Yeah. You may as well get used to it." Marnie giggled.

"Really? Are you suggesting what I think you're suggesting?" Danny teased.

Marnie put her book on the nightstand, turned off the light and curled up close to Danny with her hand on his chest.

"Go to sleep, Detective Gregg. We'll talk more tomorrow." She sighed and grew silent, then she was gently snoring almost immediately.

Danny put his head back on his pillow and held Marnie's hand. Thoughts whirled through his head. How was it possible that Sam Reilly was still tormenting them? He knew that crows didn't fly at night. Someone had purposely thrown it against the window. This was probably why Tater had been staring out the windows every night. The downed power line had been bothering him since they returned home. Tater knew that someone was out there in the darkness, and so did Danny.

Danny turned his head, kissed Marnie's forehead and then closed his eyes. One minute later, he was wide awake, staring at the ceiling. Something was nagging at him. Kate's call was nagging at him.

"Grace Wilmot," he whispered. "Grace Wilmot was down by the tracks. Hmm... we found William on the tracks. I wonder if there's a connection, and what's the connection to Marnie being locked in that box?"

Marnie stirred and asked, "Danny, who are you talking to?"

"Hmm... no one. Everything's okay. Go to sleep," he said softly.

Marnie grumbled something and snuggled closer. Danny stared at the ceiling until dawn.

-CHAPTER FORTY-

Wednesday, December 9th

Marnie woke up to the smell of coffee and bacon. She stretched and snuggled back into her pillow. Last night was the first night since Ken Wilder's murder that she had slept through the night. She glanced at the clock and then out the window. It was 5:30 and still dark.

She could hear voices downstairs. Actually, she could hear Danny talking and Tater answering. She loved this about Border Collies – they're a chatty breed. She rolled on her side, stared out the window into the darkness and listened to Danny and Tater. She rolled onto her other side and buried her face into the pillow on which Danny had slept last night. Feeling silly or perhaps a little worried that she might be caught, she rolled onto her back and stared up at the ceiling. This was the first time in a very long time that she didn't need to rush to get out the door. She could just lie here and listen. After a few minutes, she realized that she really *did* like having something to get up for and that she really wasn't the type to lounge in her pajamas all day. She rolled out of bed, put on her slippers and went into the bathroom to get ready for the day.

As Marnie came out of the bathroom, there was a light rap on the bedroom door. Tater pushed the door open with his nose and waggled his whole body when he saw her. Marnie gave his neck a scratch and looked up to see Danny standing there holding a cup of tea in her favorite cup.

"We thought that you might like a cup of tea." Danny smiled and held out the cup and saucer.

"I would love a cup of tea. Thank you so much." Marnie graciously took the tea.

"How'd you sleep?" Danny asked.

Marnie took a sip of her tea and smiled. "That's the best that I've slept in weeks. Thanks for staying with us last night."

"Anytime, and I do mean that. Anytime that you need me to stay in here with you, I'm here."

Marnie grinned. "Point taken. I hope that our little chaperone didn't cramp your style too much."

Danny laughed.

"Tater and I had a long chat downstairs. We have a new understanding."

Marnie narrowed her eyes at Tater and lifted the corners of her mouth. "Oh, really? Are you two conspiring? Whose side are you on, Tater?"

Tater replied with a bark and a nudge of her hand with his nose.

"Is anyone else awake?" Marnie asked.

"Yeah. Tom came downstairs when I did. He kinda caught me sneaking out of here around 5:00."

Marnie shrugged. "Well, you didn't need to sneak. We're both adults, and if we want to sleep together, we can."

"That's pretty much what I told him, but he got all brotherly and gave me a twenty-minute lecture when we got downstairs. He was pretty mad."

"Please tell me that you didn't explain yourself to him," Marnie scowled. Danny could see the anger rising on her face.

"I did not explain myself or the situation to him."

"Good!" Marnie replied.

"Good!" Danny mimicked.

Marnie set her cup and saucer on the nightstand. Danny moved toward the door, hesitated and turned back to Marnie. She shot him a confused look. Danny took a step forward, pulled her to him and kissed her. Marnie rested her head on his chest for just a moment and looked up at him.

"Good morning," she said with a grin.

"Good morning," he replied. "I'll see you downstairs? I've started breakfast."

He stepped away, picked up the cup and saucer, handed it to her and retreated to the door.

"I'll be there in a sec." Marnie took a sip of her tea and gazed out the window dreamily.

Marnie appeared in the kitchen about 20 minutes later. She was dressed in a pair of faded, boot-cut jeans; a navy-blue, V-neck sweater over a white Henley shirt; and a pair of black boots. She wore just a touch of mascara, and her blonde hair hung straight and loose around her shoulders.

Tom was perched on a barstool at the counter, phone in hand, flipping through his messages and E-mails when she walked into the kitchen. He did a double take when he noticed her hair.

"Hey! Where's your ponytail? Why isn't your hair up?" Tom asked, motioning with his hand around the back of his own head.

"I don't have any place to be, and that means that I don't have to fix my hair. It's not going to be falling in my face while I'm in sessions, nor will it bother me while I'm writing reports." Marnie shrugged one shoulder. She squeezed Tom's arm gently as she walked to the windows.

Confused by the gesture, Tom looked at his arm where she'd squeezed and then across the room at Marnie. It was strange to Tom because Marnie normally poked him or punched him. He glanced down at his arm again and then back to Marnie. He studied her – thoughtfully.

"You know? I like it down. Your hair. It looks nice down. It just looks different, that's all."

"I'm so glad that you approve, Detective Keller. I was worrying about what you'd think the entire time that I was getting ready this morning." Marnie's dry response was followed by a friendly poke in the ribs.

"Ha! I think that you were more worried about concealing the fact that a certain detective was seen sneaking out of your room this morning," Tom teased.

"I don't believe that Danny was *sneaking* out of my room. He was just being quiet. He didn't want to wake me," Marnie replied, adding a head toss to enunciate her indifference to Tom's opinion.

Marnie scanned the room. "Speaking of… Where is Danny? Is Tater with him?"

"Uh… he and Tater went out to check on that power line that came down in the storm. They went out about 20 minutes ago. He should be back in a minute," Tom replied.

"You didn't go with him?"

"I asked if he wanted help. He said that he didn't. I stayed here. Drank my coffee. Read the news. Problem?" He raised his eyebrows.

"Well, yeah! It's a power line. He could get electrocuted."

"The breaker is off, Marn. He told me that he turned it off last night. He's not going to get electrocuted."

Marnie scowled. "Well, I'm going to see if I can help."

A raucous boom echoed through the cabin. Dishes clanked on the shelves, pictures shook on the walls, the water in Tater's bowl splashed over the sides and Tom dropped his coffee cup onto the counter. They could hear Tater frantically barking outside.

"What the hell?!" Tom shouted as he jumped up from the barstool.

Tom and Marnie raced for the front door.

A stunned and confused Hannah, dressed in her nightshirt, appeared at the top of the stairs.

"What the hell was that?"

Tom and Marnie didn't stop to respond. They raced out the door, following Tater's barks, yelps and "a-roohs" to the garage. As soon as they entered the garage, Tater raced across the garage to Danny's side and placed a paw on his chest. He nudged his nose under Danny's chin. Danny was sprawled out cold – wedged awkwardly against the back wall between a refrigerator and a large tool cabinet. Marnie ran to Danny, but Tom stood at the door frowning and sniffing the air.

"Do you smell that? I smell something hot – electrical hot." Tom glanced around the room looking for the source of the odor.

Marnie knelt next to Danny. "Danny? Danny?" She touched his face gently.

Marnie placed an ear to his chest and her fingers on his wrist. She heard his heart beating and felt a pulse. She lifted one eyelid. Danny's iris reacted to the light. She lifted the other eyelid. Everything appeared fine. She felt the back of his head. A bump was taking shape, but there was no blood. She checked his hands. There were visible burns on the knuckles of Danny's right hand. Marnie scanned his other hand quickly; it appeared to be fine. Assuming that he had been electrocuted, she moved to check the bottom of his feet when she heard him mumble.

Tom turned his direction to the breaker box. He was certain that he had heard a fizzling sound, then he saw the source of the sound. Sparks appeared. Tom raced to the breaker box, flipped off the main for the garage and then sprinted to the corner of the garage to retrieve the fire extinguisher.

Hannah ran into the garage wearing her nightshirt, Marnie's Wellingtons from the boot tray and Tom's jacket.

"What happened?" Hannah asked anxiously.

Marnie glanced up at Hannah. "Danny's been electrocuted, I think. He must have been thrown back into the wall. He has a burn on his hand and a bump on his head."

Hannah knelt down opposite Marnie. She felt Danny's neck for a pulse.

Danny mumbled again and turned his head.

Tater nudged Danny's chin with his nose. Danny lifted his left arm, reached across and patted Tater.

"Good boy, Tater. Good boy," Danny said hoarsely.

Marnie noticed a graze on Danny's cheek.

"Danny, what happened? Were you electrocuted?" Marnie's voice rose with fear.

Danny shook his head lightly – opened one eye and then the other. He shifted and pulled himself upright and leaned back against the wall.

Marnie held one of Danny's hands while Hannah held the other.

"Do you want some water?" Hannah asked.

Danny nodded. Marnie grabbed a bottle of water out of the refrigerator, took the cap off and helped Danny drink from the bottle.

"Okay," Danny said hoarsely. "I'm okay. I gotta get up off this floor. It's freezing, and there's somethin' jabbing me in the back."

Both Marnie and Hannah tried to help him, but he was too heavy. "Let me try to get up myself. You two won't be much help if I pull you over!"

Tom crossed the room, bent, put out his hand and braced his foot against the bottom of one of Danny's boots. Danny took his hand, and Tom pulled him to his feet. Danny stumbled, then Tom caught him and held him up until he gained his balance.

Tom peered into Danny's face.

"You okay?" Tom asked.

Danny gave a quick nod and continued to lean on his partner's shoulder. He reached his arm around to his back and winced.

"What the hell is jabbing me?" Danny winced with pain.

Marnie and Hannah stepped behind him. Hannah reached out and grabbed Marnie's hand. Both silenced a gasp and exchanged worried glances.

"Maybe we should go inside and have a look at it, Danny. We don't have much light in here. It's pretty hard to see." Marnie put a hand on Danny's shoulder.

"Tom, can you help Danny get to the cabin?" Hannah eyed Tom and nodded her head toward the door.

Tom frowned at both Hannah and Marnie, but shifted his hold on his partner to move behind Danny. He raised his eyebrows when he realized why they wanted to get out of the garage into better lighting and back into the heat of the cabin. There was an icicle spear protruding from Danny's back. Blood was beginning to ooze from the wound, which meant that the icicle was melting and not acting as a plug any longer.

"C'mon, big guy, lean on my shoulder, and we'll get you into the house to thaw out." Tom wrapped an arm firmly around Danny's back – above the icicle.

Marnie shot Tom her "that was inappropriate" face, and she and Hannah ran ahead to the cabin with Tater trotting behind them.

As they entered the cabin, Marnie ran to the downstairs bathroom and got the first aid kit, a bottle of extra-strength Tylenol and a couple of towels. Hannah poured a mug of coffee for Danny and set it on the counter. She considered the coffee, raced to the bar, grabbed a bottle of Irish whiskey and set it down next to the mug. Tater raced to the windows, sat and stared out into the forest. Tom helped Danny sit on a barstool at the counter, pulled out his phone, disappeared into the living room and called Giles Markson.

Marnie ripped Danny's shirt and moved it away from the icicle. She was examining his wound when Tom returned to the kitchen. Tom took a closer look, grimaced and went around the other side of the counter.

"I just spoke with Uncle Giles. He said to take Danny to urgent care as soon as possible. I think that we should get moving," Tom urged.

"Pfft! It can't be that bad." Danny tried to reach around, and Marnie pushed his hand away.

Marnie cleaned around the wound with a towel and placed the bloody towel on the counter next to Danny.

"Danny, it really can. I agree with Uncle Giles and Tom. It isn't all that deep, but we need to get to urgent care. Isn't there one just up Lake Road going toward Hudson? Let's get moving." Marnie put a hand on Danny's arm, urging him to get up.

Danny stared at the bloody towel sitting on the counter. His face paled, and he wobbled on the stool. Marnie put her shoulder under his arm and held him up. Tom came around the counter and helped Danny to his feet.

"C'mon, Danny. It's off to urgent care with you, young man." Tom tried to keep concern out of his voice for Danny's comfort.

"Yeah. Yeah. I think that's a good idea," Danny replied weakly.

"I'll stay here with Tater. You all go ahead," Hannah volunteered.

"Are you sure, Hannah?" Marnie asked.

Hannah nodded. "Yes, I want to review those files that we discussed last night. Please call me when you have information."

Hannah jotted her number down on a Post-it note and shoved it into Marnie's waiting hand.

"We'll call you soon! Thanks, Hannah!"

As soon as the door closed, Hannah fell back onto the couch. Tater jumped up and sat next to her. She called Tater closer and wrapped her arms around him. Tater stretched and snuggled into her neck.

"He's going to be okay, right, Tater?"

Tater licked her nose in response and curled up on the couch next to her.

Hannah opened her briefcase and pulled out her laptop, a notepad and the files that she had photocopied before leaving the office the previous morning. She turned on her laptop and opened the digital files that she had downloaded to her desktop from the Hudson field office.

"Well, Tater, it's time to find out what William was doing that got him into so much trouble. Do you want to help?"

Tater edged closer to Hannah, stared at her laptop screen and barked.

Hannah inhaled deeply. She was good at her job, and she knew it. Her job was the only thing that she had ever been good at, and that was okay. It was enough for now.

"Let's get this done. Let's catch the asshole who killed William!" Hannah hissed.

-CHAPTER FORTY-ONE-

They took Danny's Jeep to the urgent care center because it was the only vehicle that had been partially under cover overnight. The windshield would defrost quickly. Also, Danny had bought himself a new toy last year – a plow attachment, thinking that it might come in handy should the driveway and entrance be a mess. Tom drove. Danny sat in the front with him, and Marnie was in the back seat. She wadded a towel to keep the icicle from pushing further into his back, and she encouraged Danny to sit forward grabbing his knees. She told him that he would get blood on the tan leather seats if he leaned back. She knew that he was particular about his vehicle and hoped that he was as much of a neat freak as she believed. Tom kept the temperature low, and when Danny reached out to turn on the seat warmer, Tom swatted his hand away. Danny glowered at him, and he reached for the switch again. Tom swatted his hand away again.

"Hey! I'm freezing!" Danny yelled, reaching forward again.

Tom covered the switch with his hand and glared a "do something" face at Marnie in the rearview mirror.

Marnie put a hand on his shoulder and calmly said, "Danny, please don't turn the seat warmer on. We didn't want to alarm you back at the house, but you have an icicle protruding from your back. That's what you felt jabbing you. It's not too bad. It's not terribly deep."

Danny turned to face her. "I what? An icicle? Are you freaking kidding me? An icicle? You mean like the ones hanging off the roof?"

Marnie nodded. "I'm afraid so. Danny, what happened this morning?" She felt herself lurch forward and realized that Tom had braked.

Tom stopped and dropped the plow at the top of the driveway. Ice and snow were built up at the exit to Lake Road. The plows had been down Lake Road and had pushed snow and slush into the driveway. Tom wasn't sure if he would break through, but two swipes later, he cleared the path sufficiently to proceed onto Lake Road. Danny tried to relax, but he was growing more and more uncomfortable. Marnie prompted him to tell them what happened, hoping to distract him as Tom drove as quickly as he felt safe.

"I went out to check that downed power line. I figured that, if it wasn't too difficult, I could fix it myself," he replied. "When I got into the garage, the door was unlocked. I know that I locked it last night. Anyway, I remembered that I wouldn't be able to turn the lights on, so I went rummaging in the dark for my hunting lantern. I heard Tater growl. I heard Tater's growl get louder, and I saw someone move toward the door. I grabbed him by the jacket, spun him around and punched him, then I got punched. I saw Tater leap toward me. I heard clothes tearing, but then I saw someone standing just outside the door. As I went to the door, someone else pushed me back. I heard Tater snap and cry out. I turned to find Tater, and I remember feeling a pain in my back. I turned around again. I was shoved back into the garage, then I was shoved again. That's it. That's all that I remember."

"There were two people?" Marnie concluded.

Danny turned to her, and he nodded slowly. "There must have been. Tater snapped and yelped behind me, and I got stabbed at the same time. There must have been two people. I'm tellin' you right now, if Tater hadn't been with me, I'm not sure what would have happened."

Tom had the Jeep on Lake Road heading to the urgent care center. He glanced at Marnie in the rearview mirror. She read his thoughts. He should have gone out with Danny to fix the power line. Neither had to say it. He could read it on her face, too.

"Not to sound morbid, Danny, but if they wanted to kill you, they would have." Tom glanced at him out of the corner of his eye and turned back to the road.

Danny turned to Tom. "Yeah, well, they stabbed me in the back with an icicle, and I'm not feeling too great. If you could step on it, I'd really appreciate it."

Tom glanced at Danny and stepped on the gas. Marnie took her seatbelt off, scooted to the center of the back seat and put her hand on Danny's arm. He took her hand and held it tight for the rest of the drive.

Tom used the Bluetooth to call the urgent care center on the way. He told them that he was coming in with a police officer who had been stabbed. When they arrived, they were met outside by several aides, and Danny was rushed into a consult room immediately. Marnie and Tom filled out his paperwork as fast as they could. Danny had been here once before, so they had much of his information available. Tom and Marnie took seats and waited impatiently for news.

Tom sat, elbows resting on his knees and his head in his hands. He stared at the floor. Marnie sat next to him with her arms around his waist and her head on his shoulder. The waiting room was a busy place at 7:00 in the morning. People bustled here and there. A small artificial Christmas tree sat tightly in a corner. Christmas decorations were strewn haphazardly around the room, and a festive sign listed Christmas greetings in several languages. A coffee machine stood in another corner.

Marnie nudged Tom with her shoulder. "Tom, do you want some coffee?"

Tom shook his head without looking up.

"Hot chocolate?" she suggested.

He shook his head again.

"Bourbon?"

Tom turned his head and scowled at her.

Marnie rubbed his back gently, stood and went to the desk. The nurse glanced up.

"Yes?"

"Just wondering if there is any news on Detective Gregg?" Marnie smiled hopefully at the nurse.

"When there's news, we'll give you news," she replied brusquely with a frown. Marnie turned and stuck her tongue out at Tom and gestured with her thumb over her shoulder.

Marnie stepped away from the counter, went to the window and peeked out through the blinds. The sun was coming up. The sky was pink, and Marnie knew that couldn't be good. She recited the poem in her head. *"Red sky at night, sailors delight. Red sky in morning, sailors take warning."* She pulled her phone out of her pocket to check her weather app. Snow flurries were in the forecast for later in the day. She rocked on her heels and turned to Tom. He hadn't moved. He was still staring at the floor.

Marnie paced. She paced from one side of the waiting room to the other. She checked her watch. She paced. She checked on Tom. She paced. Her chest was starting to get tight, so she counted the balls on the Christmas tree. When she ran out of those, she counted the magazines on the table, and she paced. When she ran out of magazines, she counted her steps. When she reached 988, a doctor emerged from the consult room hallway. He spoke to the grumpy nurse briefly. Grumpy nurse pointed to Marnie and then Tom.

Marnie quickly crossed over to Tom and touched his shoulder. He looked up at her, and she pointed to the doctor. Tom stood and ran his fingers through his hair.

"Doc, what's the good word?" Tom asked.

The doctor nodded to Marnie and addressed Tom.

"Detective Gregg is doing just fine. The icicle didn't damage any organs. The puncture wasn't deep – but deep enough. I'm glad you brought him in. He does have a bump on his head and a few other minor contusions, but he is going to be just fine. He's going to be sore tomorrow, no doubt, but other than that, he'll be fine. We're stitching him up, and he can go home with you in about 30 minutes. He will need to have a prescription filled – just antibiotics and mild pain pills in case he needs them. His wound will need to be cleaned and dressed every day. Can one of you help him with that?" the doctor asked, turning to Marnie.

Marnie nodded. "Yes, I can help with that."

Tom stuck his hand out to shake the doctor's hand. "Thanks, Doc. We're grateful to you for taking care of him and relieved that it isn't serious."

"A quarter of an inch in any direction, and we would be having a very different conversation. Detective Gregg is very lucky," the doctor replied somberly. He turned to head back down the hallway and turned back to Marnie and Tom. "He told me that there's a dog at home who very likely saved his life. A Border Collie, he said. I have two at home. Amazing breed."

"Yes, sir. His name is Tater. He's a brave boy." Marnie beamed with pride.

The doctor stared at Marnie for a moment, then his face broke into a wide grin.

"You're Marnie Reilly. You're the gal organizing the toys for the underprivileged children, is that right?"

"That's right." Marnie nodded.

The doctor smiled. "I've always donated to that fund, then Ken Wilder was murdered. I didn't know where to send the check or if I should continue to support the charity. Such terrible business. Mr. Wilder wasn't of the best character, but he did do quite a lot for the kiddos. Penance, I suppose, for evil deeds. Complicated man. I shouldn't judge. Apologies for my crassness," the doctor said. "Anyway, I would love to help. Do you have a card? I can call you early next week?"

Tom quickly pulled his wallet out of his pocket and handed the doctor one of his cards.

"You can call me, Doc. I'm helping Ms. Reilly. She left her handbag at home."

The doctor took Tom's card between two fingers and smiled.

"Thank you, uh..." The doctor looked down at the card to search for a name.

"Tom Keller. Detective Tom Keller. Detective Gregg's partner."

"Ah, well, thank you, Tom, and thank you, Marnie. I'm Dr. Fleming – Dr. Addison Fleming. Helping children is an honorable endeavor. There are so many here in Creekwood who need support. I'll reach out next week, Tom. It was lovely to meet you, Ms. Reilly. I'm sure that we'll see one another again."

Dr. Fleming disappeared down the hallway, and Marnie poked Tom in the side with her elbow once he was gone.

"What's up with you? Why did you do that? My bag is right over there. I could have given him one of my cards," Marnie hissed and scowled.

Tom stared down the now-empty hallway. "Yeah, sorry about that. Somethin' about that guy… Maybe I'm just jumpy, but something about him made me uncomfortable. I didn't like the way that he looked at you. I didn't like him bringing up Ken Wilder. It's like a light bulb went on when he realized who you are." Tom raised one eyebrow and shivered.

"Of course a light bulb went on! He realized who I am! Duh!" Marnie retorted, rolling her eyes. "It's like a nightmare that never ends. Will I ever be rid of Ken Wilder?" She stomped to a seat and dropped down on it with a thud.

It was Tom's turn to pace from one end of the waiting room to the other. He had crossed a line, and he knew it. He stopped in front of Marnie on the fifth circuit.

"You better be careful when Danny comes out and we're able to leave." Tom's serious tone brought Marnie's gaze up to his.

"Why's that?" Marnie glowered up at Tom.

"You'll trip over your lip on the way out." Tom smirked. She recognized his playful attempt to make amends and relented by kicking his shin gently.

The sound of heavy boots on tile made Tom turn around. Marnie popped up from her seat. Danny appeared at the entrance to the hallway. He looked pale and exhausted. A nurse followed behind him, his hand under Danny's elbow.

Tom and Marnie moved quickly to Danny's side.

"We'll take him from here," Tom offered. "Thanks for your help!"

Marnie put her hand under Danny's elbow where the nurse's had been. "Thank you!" she said to the nurse.

"Here is Detective Gregg's prescription and instructions for cleaning and dressing his wound. I've jotted down the dressing and other things that you may need to pick up at the drugstore." The nurse handed the list to Marnie.

Marnie took the list. "Thanks so much. We'll get him home to rest, and one of us will run out to fill the prescriptions."

Tom and Danny went to the counter to speak to the grumpy nurse to see if they were good to go. She dismissed them unceremoniously with a grumpy nod.

"Make sure that he doesn't overdo it. He needs time to heal," the nurse warned.

Marnie nodded. "We'll take good care of him. Thanks again."

"Let's get out of here. I've had enough of this place," Danny complained.

Tom and Marnie walked in pace with Danny out the door of the urgent care center. Once alongside the truck, Danny opted for the back seat. He huddled into the corner behind Tom's seat, he stretched his legs behind Marnie's seat and wrapped his arms around himself. He had on the same long-sleeve T-shirt he'd worn in the garage that morning, and in their haste to get to urgent care, they had rushed out without grabbing his jacket. Tom took his jacket off and dropped it over the seat into Danny's lap. Danny accepted it gratefully, pulling it around himself like a blanket. Marnie settled into the front seat after moving the bloodied towel from the seat to the floor.

Tom started the Jeep and waited for it to warm up. Marnie turned on the radio to the local station to hear the 9:00 AM news. Tom nudged the heat up for Danny's sake. It was a cool 25 degrees outside on this wintry autumn morning.

They drove in silence back to the cabin. Danny snoozed and mumbled incoherently most of the way. Marnie sat sideways in her seat with one arm extended to the back seat. Her hand rested on Danny's knee. His hand rested atop hers.

Marnie lay her head against the back of the seat – her head was full of voices at the moment. She couldn't clear the voices away. Her clairvoyance was a gift to be sure. There were times that she wished that she had better control over it, and *this* was one of those times. She could hear Mom and Dad and Ken. She could hear Ken's voice above all others. He had been speaking to her – warning her. He'd warned her about the trunk. He'd told her that Danny would have an accident. He said Kate's name many times, but with no clarity of reason.

Marnie closed her eyes to concentrate. When Ken spoke to her, it didn't sound the same as when her parents spoke to her. It was muffled. It was different. She knew that he wasn't with her parents. She was certain that he was in the in-between – that place between heaven and earth – not earthbound – more like purgatory – a waiting room for people who had done bad things in life. Ken was being judged. He was using this time to show that he could be good.

Marnie didn't believe in Hell, and she didn't believe in the devil. She did believe in good and bad, and she did believe that bad people's souls stayed in the in-between when they died. They were exiled. They could never go home until they redeemed themselves. Perhaps helping Marnie was Ken's chance – his penance.

Everything was jumbled and then again not. Marnie could not get the Robert Frost poem "Fire and Ice" out of her head. She had been reciting it to herself for days. *Of all of his wonderful work, why THAT poem?* She didn't even like the poem all that much. She thought that it was somewhat morbid. It did bring back a memory, though. She remembered a time when she was little. She, Tom and Kate would go sledding or ice skating behind her house. Her father would build them a bonfire, and her mother would bring them hot chocolate with mini marshmallows. Her brother Sam would stand by the bonfire and threaten them with icicles that he had pulled down from the eaves of the shed. He would pretend that he was going to stab them if they came too close to the fire. They thought that it was a game and would run away screaming and giggling. She was pretty certain now that he would have stabbed them given the chance. Hindsight.

Ken had shown her pictures of fire and ice over and over again, but until now, she could not make the connection. Had someone tried to set the garage on fire and stabbed Danny with the icicle to mimic the poem? Was the icicle meant for her and *not* Danny? Ken wasn't making much sense, but he hadn't in life, either. He had loved her and loathed her in equal measure.

Marnie stirred from her concentration and shifted in her seat. She closed her eyes again and focused on William. Perhaps he could clear things up. She didn't want to disturb him on the other side of the veil. She just felt that he could connect the dots. Maybe her parents could help. Maybe they could get William to help. Surely, they had been there to welcome him home.

-CHAPTER FORTY-TWO-

Grace Wilmot awoke with a shiver. Her electric blanket was working, but the air outside was cold, and the silo had no insulation. Grace rolled out of her bed and checked her heaters. Two had gone out through the night, the gauges reading empty. She stomped her foot and cursed Reuben.

"Damn you, Reuben! You were supposed to fill these heaters yesterday. Damn you to Hell!"

Grace lit a candle and searched the silo for the kerosene cans.

"Silly! What am I doing? Have I lost my mind? Searching for kerosene with a lit candle?"

Grace blew out the candle and turned on a flashlight. A tap sounded on the hatch. She stood still and listened. Another tap. She listened and scurried to her bed to get her bathrobe. She wrapped it around herself and moved toward the hatch.

"Grace, it's Justin. Let me in! The latch is frozen out here. Turn it from the inside!"

Grace turned the handle. It wouldn't move. She put the flashlight on the ground and tried again with both hands. This time, it did turn just a bit. She wiggled the handle and tried again. Finally, the latch turned. Justin pulled the hatch, and as he stepped through into the silo, a bluster of wind and ice crystals followed him.

"Shut the hatch! Shut the hatch! You're letting the cold in!" Grace shouted, dancing back and forth while waving her arms.

Justin entered the silo with a large knapsack and a briefcase. He set them on the ground, pulled off his gloves off and then took off his jacket.

"Jesus, Grace! It's cold in here!"

"That damn Reuben didn't fill the heaters yesterday. I was looking for the kerosene when you knocked," Grace complained.

"I'll fill the heaters for you. Do you know where he put the cans?"

"I don't know what he was thinking – leaving an old, defenseless woman without heat. It's his responsibility to take care of me. I took care of him all of his life. It's his turn to take care of me. He should have been here by now to heat the water for my bath. He is never where he should be!" Grace whined.

Justin smirked. "You have a bathtub in here?"

Grace snapped, "Of course I do. I'm not about to live in filth now, am I? Of course I have a bath. Reuben fills and empties it for me."

"Where does the water come from?" Justin turned and surveyed the silo for water pipes.

"We rigged up a hose that runs from the town water line. It runs under the silo to the filtration plant. Reuben dug the trench for it last summer. He and Allen got it all hooked up, *and* the hose is below the frost line. That was my idea. There isn't a whole brain between the two of them. Did you hear that Allen is in jail?"

Justin shook his head and gave Grace a long side-eye stare. He was starting to understand Reuben's issues with his mother. He was getting a much clearer picture of Reuben's childhood.

"The cans are here! I've found the cans. Justin, be a dear and fill up the heaters for me," Grace ordered sweetly.

Justin loped to the cans and picked up one. He shook it. It was empty. He picked up another – also empty. He picked up a third – maybe half full. The fourth can was full. He filled the heaters with the remainder of the fuel and put the empty cans next to the hatch.

"You'll need to get kerosene the next time that you go out. You have maybe enough for today – that's it."

"Justin, be a dear. Run out, and fill the cans for me. I don't have a car, and I couldn't possibly fill those cans and carry them back here on my own."

Justin shook his head. "I have to pick up a friend, Grace. I can't run errands for you. I stopped to bring you the things that you wanted from Alice's house and, of course, a copy of the files from the laptop. I don't have time to run around looking for kerosene."

Grace scowled. "What do you mean you can't get the kerosene? Of course you can, and you will! You will leave me the laptop! What am I going to do with a *copy* of the files? I don't even know what that means. I need the laptop!"

"I'm afraid that I won't get the kerosene for you. Call Reuben, and you can't have the laptop. It's mine. It doesn't belong to The Collective." Justin held firm.

Justin removed several items from the knapsack and set them on a table. Grace had given him the key to the turret room and asked him to bring her several of her belongings that she left behind years ago. Sitting on the table were her crystal ball, a black tablecloth adorned with gold pentagrams, assorted crystals, boxes of incense, two decks of tarot cards, a Ouija board, a black-hooded velveteen cloak, a smoky quartz wand, two pendulums, bundles of sage and a plethora of other "spiritual" paraphernalia.

Grace glared at Justin while he unpacked the knapsack.

"Last but not least, here's the thumb drive. This holds all of the information relevant to The Collective," Justin said, handing the thumb drive to a scowling Grace. "You really need to get caught up on technology, Grace. Get yourself a laptop, and I'll show you how to use it."

Grace raised a fist and launched an attack on Justin. Justin caught her arm mid-swing and held tight. Grace shrieked in pain.

"I'll destroy you, you smarmy little bastard!" Grace shrieked.

Justin smirked. "Au contraire! When will you learn that you only have power over people who believe your bullshit." Justin pushed Grace gently away from him. "I'm not afraid of you, Grace. I've seen power, and you don't have it."

Justin lifted the latch and stepped out, leaving Grace all alone with her empty kerosene cans.

-CHAPTER FORTY-THREE-

Hannah was at the coffee table in front of the fire, files and paperwork spread out on the table and the couch. Tater lay on his back, legs in the air, on the hearth. Hannah couldn't help but laugh. She had never in her life seen a dog sleep in this position. She opened the camera on her phone and snapped a picture. Normally, she would have sent a silly picture like this to William. She set her phone on the coffee table and leaned back into the cushions. Tears welled up in her eyes. She reached for a tissue, wiped her eyes and watched Tater sleep. She scooted down the couch closer to Tater.

She spoke softly, not sure how this sleeping dog reacted to being woken. "Tater. Tater," she murmured softly.

Tater stretched his long legs, turned his head toward her and rolled onto his side.

"Come here, boy."

Tater stood, stretched, yawned – his spine in a downward dog – and then walked to Hannah. She scratched his neck and ears. He put his paw on her knee, licked her chin, sat back and smiled at her.

"You're a beautiful boy, Tater."

Tater's ears shot up, his tail wagged, he whined and then he raced to the front door. Hannah heard the car pulling into the driveway and got up to see if it was Danny, Marnie and Tom. She stood at the window, breathed a sigh of relief and watched them get out of the Jeep.

Danny looked terrible. Marnie had an arm around him gingerly and led him up the steps. Tom followed, clutching his jacket in one hand with his other hand under Danny's elbow. Hannah saw Danny shrug his arm away from Tom.

Outside, Danny grumbled loudly. "I'm not an invalid," Danny griped, glancing over his shoulder at Tom.

"I was just helping. Marnie's helping you." Tom stepped back, a hurt look on his face.

"Yeah, well, Marnie smells better than you. She can hold me up all that she wants," Danny shot back.

Tom moved ahead of them and opened the front door. Tater waggled and whined when they came through the door.

"Settle down, Tater. No jumping. Get in your house." Marnie pointed to the pool table.

Tater ran across the room and lay down under the pool table. From his "house," he smiled and watched as Danny settled onto the couch.

Hannah stared expectantly at the trio. "Is everything okay? Good prognosis?"

Danny nodded. "Yeah. I'll be fine. I'll need to be waited on for the next few weeks, but I'll be fine." He managed a weak cheeky grin.

"Good. I'm glad that everything is okay. You should call Gram. She called here earlier. I didn't tell her anything, but she was confused by my presence." Hannah creased her forehead and glanced down at the floor.

"I'll call her after I've cleaned up a bit. I need to wash my face, change my shirt and wake up." Danny puffed out his cheeks and sighed.

"Do you need help?" Marnie asked.

"If you're offering to give me a sponge bath, I am all in!" Danny tipped his head and winked.

Marnie laughed. "You are feeling better. C'mon. Let's get rid of that bloody shirt and find you something loose that won't stick to your stitches and bandage."

Tom called out as they went upstairs. "Do you want me to run in and get your prescription filled? Maybe stop by the station and tell Cap what's happened?"

Marnie turned back. "Oh, Tom, wait for me. I want to go into town to get my car. I need to drop by my house to pick up Christmas ornaments and a few other things, too."

"Yeah. Sure. I'll wait." Tom nodded.

Danny leaned over the railing at the top. "Hey! We need to go see Alice and Allen today. By the way, Cap isn't in. He's still out with the flu."

Tom frowned. "That's two days in a row. Cap is never sick. It must be serious."

Danny put his hands up. "I don't know. Beau texted me when I was outside earlier."

"We should get the crew out here to dust for prints, Danny. We should give that garage a good once over," Tom suggested.

Danny agreed. "Yeah. I was thinking that, too. We should have them check that power line too while they're at it. It's probably a good idea to get that organized sooner rather than later. We're supposed to get more snow later."

Tom pulled his phone out of his pocket. "I'll take care of that. You'll have to call Creekwood Power. They'll only speak to the account holder."

Danny nodded. "Yeah. I'll do that. Thanks, Tom, and hey, I'm sorry that I snapped at you out there."

"No problem, Iceman!" Tom chuckled.

Danny turned and glared at him.

Tom shot him a sheepish grin. "Too soon?"

"Too soon," Danny growled.

~~~~~~~~~~~~~~~~~~~~~~~~~~

"Let me help you up the steps, Alice." Justin held Alice's arm and guided her around the patches of ice. "I'll come back out once you're safely inside. Someone should have shoveled and put some sand down."

"That's kind of you, Justin. I can manage it later. I want to have a cup of coffee and a shower, then I can take care of the snow and ice." Alice patted his hand.

Justin shook his head. "I don't think that's a good idea. You had a severe asthma attack, you've been in the hospital and you shouldn't be out in the cold exerting yourself. Besides, Detective Keller called. He and Detective Gregg will be coming by around 11:00 to speak to you."

Alice's face dropped.

"It's gonna be okay, Alice. Just tell them everything that you've told me. Everything is going to be okay." Justin unlocked the door and led her inside.

Alice stepped in and gazed around her home. The members of The Collective had been disrespectful. There was clutter everywhere. The hardwood floors were dirty and in bad repair. Not one of them offered to clean or tidy up, nor did they respect her furniture – water rings on tables, dirty feet on the coffee tables and couch cushions. Her once grand Victorian home was in need of a good clean, polish and several repairs. Her couches and chairs needed a steam clean, and the walls needed paint. Sadness and shame overwhelmed. She hung her head, but she didn't cry. She was out of tears. Justin helped her out of her jacket.

"C'mon, Alice. Let's make that coffee." Justin led the way to the kitchen.

Alice followed, her mind spinning. She wanted out of this life. She wanted everyone out of her house. She wanted out of The Collective. She wanted her job back at the library, and she wanted to get on with her life on her terms. This was never the life that she wanted. This was her house. Grace Wilmot be damned!

Alice stopped at the kitchen doorway. "Justin, I need your help. I wouldn't ask if I didn't have to, but I need your help – maybe Detective Keller's and Detective Gregg's help, too."

Justin glanced up as he made the coffee. "What do you want?"

"I want to be a better person, Justin. I want all of these people out of my house. You, Allen, Carl and Marnie are the only people who have never taken my home for granted. None of you just moved in and took over. Actually, Patrick didn't, either. I want Grace's crap out of *my* turret room, and I want out of The Collective unless we commit to doing honest to God good things for people!"

Justin listened. Alice sank into a chair at the breakfast table. He didn't respond until after he had poured out two cups of coffee and set them on the table.

"Alice, I can help you with all of those things, but I need something from you first."

"You need something from me? What can I help you with?" Alice asked, a bit surprised by the request.

"Yes. I need you to help me get Grace off my ass. She's been harassing me for months. Alice, she's been blackmailing me. That evil bitch has found things out about my past. I have no idea how she's done it, but she has."

Alice raised her eyebrows and took a sip of her coffee.

"Justin, what did you do? What is Grace holding over your head?"

Justin dropped his head and stared into his coffee. He couldn't look at Alice. The guilt that he felt was unbearable. Rather than face Alice, he continued to stare at his coffee cup while he confessed.

"I accidentally helped someone do something bad. I gave someone information that got another person killed."

"Oh, dear." Alice brought a hand to her mouth. "Then maybe we can help each other?"

-CHAPTER FORTY-FOUR-

Tom and Hannah sat at the coffee table in the cabin reviewing the files and Hannah's timeline.

Tom scratched the top of this head. "You know, we need a case board here. We need to be able to stick all of this stuff up on a board so that we can view everything at once and also add to it."

Hannah nodded. "I was thinking that earlier, but I didn't want to go snooping around Daniel's house."

"We could set all of this up in Danny's study," Tom suggested.

"There's a study?" Hannah asked.

Tom nodded. "Yeah. It's off the kitchen. He had an office in one of the bedrooms, but I helped him move it downstairs to the study a few weeks ago after we finished the walls. C'mon, let's go check out what he's done with it, and we can figure out how to set up everything. I do know that he has a couple of whiteboards."

"He won't mind?" Hannah raised her eyebrows in doubt. She remembered how territorial he was about his room when they were kids.

Tom shook his head and stuck his bottom lip out as he thought about it. He went to the bottom of the stairs and shouted up. "Hey, Danny! You mind if we go into your study to set up a murder board?"

"No! Go ahead. Whiteboards and bulletin boards haven't been hung yet, but you can hang them for me."

"Wall preference?" Tom yelled.

"There's only one wall that they'll all fit on!"

"Okay, thanks!" Tom answered.

Tom grabbed a toolbox from a cupboard in the kitchen, and he and Hannah went into the study to set up the murder board.

~~~~~~~~~~~~~~~~~~~~~~~~~

Danny and Marnie were making a pot of coffee when Tom stuck his head out the study.

"Hey, Marnie! I just remembered that package that I brought in last night. Have you opened it?"

"No! I forgot all about it. With the commotion last night with the bird and Danny this morning, I forgot."

Marnie went into the living room, got the package and returned to the kitchen. Tater trotted behind her and took up guard at the windows. She took a knife out of the drawer and sliced the tape.

"I haven't a clue what this could be. I haven't given out your address." Marnie studied the package – turning it over looking for a return address label.

"You haven't ordered anything?" Danny asked.

Marnie shook her head. She opened the package and took out a smaller white box with a red ribbon. She set it on the counter and just stared at it.

"What's wrong?" Danny asked.

Tom poked his head out of the study again. "She's worried that there's a bloody finger or ear in there," Tom quipped.

Marnie nodded and poked the package with an index finger. "That's exactly what I'm worried about. With everything that's been going on, I'm just a bit nervous about opening the box."

Marnie removed the ribbon, pulled the top off the box and removed tissue paper from the top of the box. She reached in and pulled out a small ceramic bird and held it up.

"It's a crow," she said nervously.

"Is there a note?" Tom walked out of the study and stood opposite her.

Marnie pulled more tissue out the box. "No. No note," she replied, knitting her brows.

"Hmm… Anything else in the package?" Danny picked up the box and looked inside.

Marnie sat on a barstool and pushed the crow away.

"Marnie? What are you thinking about?" Danny asked.

"Well, maybe I'm making too much of this, but it takes three crows to make a flock. Um… a flock of crows is called a murder. Two crows… um… there aren't enough crows for the gathering to be called a murder. It takes three crows. Two crows are what? Attempted murder. What happened to Danny this morning? Well, it just kind of lines up, doesn't it?"

"What do you mean two crows? There's only one in the box." Tom laughed.

Danny smirked. "Marnie, I think that you might be reaching."

Marnie turned to Danny and Tom. The look on her face – they both knew it. Danny shivered a little, and Tom put his hands up and backed away a bit.

"Marn, don't make that face. That face gives me the willies. Do. Not. Make. That. Face. Just don't." Tom shook his head slowly.

Marnie shrugged. "Well, technically, it's two crows – one here in the box and the one that was thrown at the window last night."

Both Danny and Tom turned to the window and then back to Marnie. They knew that she was right.

"That's just silly!" Hannah said loudly from the doorway. "Marnie, you can't honestly believe that anyone other than you would know that a flock of crows is called a murder? Who knows that sort of trivia?"

Marnie stared off into the corner of the kitchen near Tater's bowls and responded, "My brother."

~~~~~~~~~~~~~~~~~~~~~~~~~~

Kate Parish knocked on the silo hatch. She was about 10 minutes early, but she had to park a few blocks up and walk the rest of the way. There was not a chance that she was going to park her car in this neighborhood. Kate shivered as a north wind blew between the silo and an outbuilding. She felt like she was standing in a wind tunnel. She shivered again and clapped her hands together before wrapping her scarf around her neck and ears. She knocked again. This time, the latch turned, and Grace stuck her head out.

"Get in here! Quickly!" Grace ordered.

Kate stepped through and sauntered toward the couch like she was on a catwalk. Grace rolled her eyes and sauntered behind her mockingly.

"Why did you want to see me?" Kate asked. "I have a full schedule today. I'm opening my law firm. It's something that I've always dreamed of doing."

"Well, isn't that nice," Grace replied sarcastically. "You're here because I need help. Your law firm can wait. Let's be honest, Ms. Parish, you're opening your own law firm because no one will employ you after the stunt that you pulled."

"I didn't do anything! I was coerced! Sam Reilly is a very bad man!" Kate tossed her head and stuck out her bottom lip.

"Hmm… well, that's not the full story, and we both know it. People in this town talk, and you, Ms. Parish, are not liked by many people. Marnie Reilly, on the other hand… Well, people like her. When I say people, I mean other people. I hate her. There isn't another person on this earth that I hate more than Marnie Reilly. You come a close second." Grace pointed a gnarled finger in Kate's direction.

Kate feigned shock. "But Ms. Wilmot, I thought that we were becoming fast friends. I can't believe that you would say such a thing!" Kate's eyes grew wide with faux drama. Her face changed in an instant to one of sheer disdain. "Okay, I don't care much for you, either, but we need each other."

"Don't flatter yourself, Kate Parish. The only reason that you're still alive is because I want Marnie Reilly dealt with as much as you do. With my brains and your knowledge of Marnie's life, we could be a formidable team."

"Yes, well, you must remember that Sam Reilly is her brother and I am her best friend. If we couldn't beat her, what makes you think that you and I can?" Kate responded with a toss of her hair.

Grace let out an ungodly cackle and twisted her mouth into an evil grin.

"You and I, Ms. Parish, are going to do the one thing that Marnie Reilly fears most. We're going to torment the people whom she loves most." A sinister smile spread across Grace's face.

"What's that supposed to mean? Marnie is a severe claustrophobic, and other than losing the people whom she loves, which she already has, there's nothing else that Marnie Reilly fears. Unless you're referring to Tom Keller and Detective Gregg... or *Tater*. You want to kill her dog?" A confused expression clouded Kate's face.

Grace threw her hands up in the air and shouted, "No! You stupid woman! The veil! That damn veil that she's always going on about."

Grace skulked to the dining table that she had set up in the middle of the silo and motioned for Kate to draw nearer. Kate moved slowly toward the table and examined the items sitting atop it. She raised an eyebrow. It was an impressive assortment.

Kate casually waved her hands above the items. "What are you planning to do with all of this?"

"We, Kate Parish. We. Together, we're going to have a séance. We're going to call in the people whom Marnie loves. We're going to call in your Ken Wilder. We're going to call in anyone Marnie Reilly knows on the other side of that precious veil. We're going to torment their souls so that they cry out in pain and Marnie hears them cry. She will hear them cry; she's a clairvoyant. They will call out to her and beg her to stop us, and it will destroy her. She won't be able to find us. She'll never find us here. All of the souls will be stuck between here and there." Grace pointed up and waved her hand across the table. "Except for Ken Wilder. We both know where his is, don't we, Kate?"

"Grace, I don't understand. What will that do? What will it accomplish?" Kate scrunched up her face.

"That veil that Marnie Reilly pretends to protect will be torn to shreds!" Grace sniggered and cackled for a few moments, then she glanced over at Kate, who was smirking. Grace fell silent, then she peered closely at Kate. *Kate wasn't smirking at the plan. She's laughing at me!*

"Okay, Grace. I'm not buying everything that you're saying, but we can play this your way," Kate soothed. She tried her best to hide her disdain, but didn't manage it well.

"Are you mocking me?" Grace squinted her eyes. "How dare you mock me!" Grace's voice rose and echoed in the silo.

Kate composed her most serious courtroom face. "I'm not mocking you, Ms. Wilmot. I'll help in any way that I can."

"Good! I need you to get me something personal that belongs to Marnie, and I need a ride to a place where I can buy kerosene and a large kettle."

"Okay. I have a sweater of Marnie's and a pair of earrings that I borrowed and never returned. Will those do?" Kate replied.

Grace sneered and nodded, her fingers steepled in front of her.

"Kerosene. Hmm… I think that we can get that at the feed and grain store at the edge of town. You said a large kettle? Like a cauldron?" Kate asked, furrowing her brow.

"A cauldron? What would I do with a cauldron? I want a kettle to boil water for my bath!" Grace snapped.

"Ah. A kettle. Of course, a kettle will be easy to find, but wouldn't it be easier to purchase one of those dojiggies that you plug in and place in the water? Like the ones for tropical aquariums?" Kate suggested.

Grace smiled. "Why, yes, I know what you mean. We'll have to go to a pet store to get one of those, then, won't we?"

"Let's go! We'll have to walk to my car. I parked a few blocks away. I didn't want anyone to see me in this part of town."

"Good thinking. A princess like you wouldn't be caught dead on the other side of the tracks. Just don't make me angry, or that is exactly how and where they will find you," Grace threatened.

It was a threat that Kate Parish took seriously.

-CHAPTER FORTY-FIVE-

Marnie and Danny stood at the kitchen counter sipping tea and coffee respectively; they were planning the remains of the day. Original plans for the day had been scattered by the unfortunate events of the last few days.

Danny moved slowly around the counter and sat on one of the barstools, placing his elbows on the countertop with his coffee mug between his hands. Marnie thought that he looked exhausted. She reached across the counter and gently stroked his cheek with the back of her hand. "You need a shave," she grinned. "Those whiskers could cause some serious damage."

Danny rubbed his face and sighed. "Yeah. I didn't get a chance to shave this morning. I'll shave tomorrow."

Marnie rested her elbows on the counter and looked up into his face. "We're a sad pair —me with my bruised temple and you with your grazed cheek and your poor back." She giggled.

Danny took one of her hands in his and kissed her palm. "Okay, we need to get organized. Tommy and I will drop you off at your office so that you can pick up your car. I'll call Gram on the way in and invite her to dinner tonight. You're going to pick up my prescription and get groceries. Tommy and I will interview Alice and Allen. I've got to set up a meeting with Rick, Dr. Markson and Jalnack. We'll meet you at Gleeson's at 3:00 to pick up the Christmas tree for the party. What am I forgetting?" Danny double-checked his list.

Marnie leaned closer, glanced over Danny's list and replied, "I have to drop by my house to get Christmas decorations. We need to make sure that we have invited everyone we wanted to invite to the tree trimming party, and I have to go over food with Gram. Danny, are you sure that you still want to do the party? You may not feel up to it by the time Friday rolls around."

"What do you mean me? You're the one with the concussion," Danny reminded her. He reached across the counter and pushed her hair away from the bruises on her temple. "It could have been much worse, Marnie. We're just going to have to look out for each other, huh?"

Tom and Hannah strolled into the room just as Danny reached out to kiss Marnie.

"Well, well, well! What have we here? Two star-crossed lovers comparing stories of war?" Tom teased. "Hey, not to interrupt your good time, but we gotta hit the road. Hannah and I have the board set. She's going to hang here with Tater and keep going on the board."

Marnie shook her head. "Tater is coming with me. I have to go to my house, and I don't want to go there alone. Call me silly, but having Tater with me gives me a bit more confidence," Marnie reasoned.

Hannah filled her coffee cup and listened quietly to the conversation. She observed the comradery that Danny, Tom and Marnie shared. She smiled to herself. It was nice being in this group of friends who so obviously cared dearly for one another. She knew that she was an outsider looking in, but she was certain that, with a bit of work, these people would trust her someday.

"Marnie, how about if I come with you and Tater?" Hannah blurted out.

Surprised by the offer, Marnie nodded. "Sure. That would be great, Hannah."

"Marnie, I hate to ask, but would you possibly have clothes that I could borrow? A sweatshirt and sweatpants maybe? I'm fairly certain that your jeans won't fit, but a pair of sweatpants might. I only have this suit and one other. Probably not appropriate for a day out in the cold."

Marnie nodded again. "Of course! My jeans will be a bit too long, but I'm sure that we can find something for you."

As Marnie went upstairs to get her grocery list and find options for Hannah, Danny turned to Hannah and quietly suggested, "Hey, Hannah, you might want to bring your firearm. You know… just in case."

Hannah raised her eyebrows at her brother. "Seriously? Did you think that I would leave the house without it? I never leave home without my gun."

"With a backup," they both added in unison.

~~~~~~~~~~~~~~~~~~~~~~~~~~

Danny dropped off Marnie and Hannah a block from Marnie's office. He was dropping Tater at Ellie's for a day of socializing, and Marnie would pick him up before driving back to the cabin. The town crew was busy adding an array of decorations to Town Square for the upcoming Christmas parade and was blocking the entrance to the square. Marnie wrapped her scarf a bit tighter around her neck and closed her jacket. Hannah pulled her borrowed jacket down over her hips, glanced down at the boots and jeans that Marnie had lent her and sighed.

Marnie heard the sigh and turned. "Everything okay?"

Hannah nodded. "Yes. I think if I stay much longer, I will need to get some clothes."

"Borrow anything you like," Marnie replied.

"Um... Maybe we could just run to a department store. I'd be more comfortable in clothes that fit, and no offense meant, but your feet are a lot bigger than mine and my ass is a lot bigger than yours." Hannah laughed.

Marnie giggled. "Well, I can understand that. We have a couple of department stores near the grocery store. I can drop you at one and go get groceries."

"Perfect! I'll call you when I finish or vice versa. Can I have your number?" Hannah asked.

Marnie dug in her bag and produced a business card. "Here you go. This has my cell and office numbers."

As they walked through town, Hannah found herself delighted with the little town of Creekwood's holiday spirit.

"They do a lot of decorating for a small town." Hannah beamed.

"Yes. Creekwood spares no expense during the holidays. We'll have stalls lining the streets in a few days. It's my favorite holiday shopping experience. All of the local retailers have a stall here – some from outside of the area, too. It's quite a spectacle, and the food vendors are fabulous. Roasted chestnuts, caramel apples, cotton candy, funnel cakes, you name it. Right here in Town Square!"

"That sounds wonderful," Hannah agreed. "Um, Marnie? I don't want to be morose, but do you think it may be possible for me to see William?"

"Uh, gosh, Hannah. I'm so sorry! I wasn't thinking," Marnie replied. "Yes, I'm certain that we can arrange that. My godfather is the ME – Giles Markson. I'm certain that he would make arrangements for you."

"Thank you, Marnie. It doesn't have to be today. If tomorrow is possible, I would greatly appreciate it."

"No worries. I'll call Uncle Giles and take care of it." Marnie nodded.

They arrived at Marnie's office and walked through the front door to the jingle of bells above. Marnie glanced up and smiled. Andrea looked up and smiled, too.

"Hey, boss! How's your head? Oh, my, look at those bruises! Are you okay?" Andrea crossed the office and stared into Marnie's face.

"I'm fine, thanks. Is Carl here? By the way, this is Danny's sister Hannah. Hannah, this is Andrea."

Andrea offered her hand to Hannah. "It's good to meet you, Hannah."

Hannah shook Andrea's hand with a smile. "You, too."

"Carl's in his office. Go ahead in. He's alone. By the way, Marn, I'm really glad that you're going to take a bit of time off. I think that it's a good thing," Andrea said. "Hannah, would you like a coffee or tea?"

Marnie waved her hand above her head, acknowledging Andrea's concern. She knocked on Carl's door and entered. He was at his desk reading through files.

"Who have you got there?" Marnie sat on the credenza.

"Hmm... It's Connor Daugherty's file. Just reviewing your notes. He'll be here in about an hour."

"Hmm... What do you think?"

Carl pursed his lips in thought. "I think that your notes are meticulous, and I agree with your plan. I hate seeing files like this for someone so young. His home life sounds typical of a father who drinks and a mother who's an addict. Are you planning to recommend family counseling? It sounds like the parents aren't taking responsibility at all." Carl looked at Marnie over the top of the file.

"Oh, I've tried. They don't think that *their* behavior has anything to do with Connor's. His mother actually called him a sociopath. When I asked her if she knew what the word meant, she gave me a lecture on questioning her prognosis and informed me that the only reason that Connor was seeing me was because the judge suggested it. Let me tell you. The judge didn't suggest it; he mandated it. Maybe you'll have better luck with her. Charm her, Carl. You've always been good at that." Marnie winked.

Carl closed the file and dropped it on top of the desk.

"How are you feeling, Marn?"

"Better. I'm feeling better. Hey, are you still coming over Friday night for the tree trimming?"

"Is it still on? If it's still on, then yes. Let me know what I can bring."

"I'll text you tonight. We're putting the final list together over dinner tonight. Gram is coming, and Danny's sister is visiting. We had a bit of an issue at the cabin this morning. Danny was stabbed with an icicle out in the garage. The police are there now gathering whatever it is that they are gathering."

Carl grimaced. "He was stabbed? With an icicle?"

"I'll tell you more later. I've got to run. Hannah's waiting for me out in reception. I'll call you in the morning, or you could come out and have coffee with me tomorrow."

"I'm free first thing. How about I stop at the bakery and be there at 8:00?"

"Perfect!" Marnie turned the doorknob to leave.

"Hey, Marn! Did you tell Danny?"

Marnie turned back. "About what?"

"The veil," Carl responded.

"Not yet," Marnie replied, and she left.

~~~~~~~~~~~~~~~~

Marnie and Hannah raced around the corner to her ice-covered car. Marnie pulled on the door and was pleasantly surprised that it opened so easily. She started the car and got out again to clean it off. Hannah used a mittened hand to wipe down the side windows as best as she could.

"Get in the car, Hannah. No point in us both freezing our asses off," Marnie said with a laugh.

Hannah laughed as well. "I'm not going to argue." She ducked into the passenger seat and turned on the seat warmer.

Marnie climbed in a few minutes later, adjusted the heater and defroster and turned on her seat warmer. "Okay. We should go to the pharmacy first. It's not too far, but I think that we'll drive. Then we'll go to my house for the decorations, then to the grocery store and the department store. Do you want to stop at Gram's diner for lunch?" Marnie looked expectantly at Hannah.

Hannah shook her head. "No. I'd rather not. She and I don't have the same relationship that she and Danny have."

"Okay. If we get hungry, we can stop somewhere for a quick bite." Marnie checked her rearview mirror and backed out of her spot. She noticed Kate Parish's car on a side street, and Grace Wilmot was getting out of Kate's car. Marnie raised her eyebrows. "Interesting."

"What? What's interesting?" Hannah sat forward and peered out the windshield.

"Oh, nothing. It's nothing important." Marnie stepped on the clutch, shifted into first and drove off.

~~~~~~~~~~~~~~~~~~~~~~~~

Hannah waited in the car while Marnie ran into Drake's Drugs. She checked her messages and her E-mails.

Marnie took Danny's prescription to the pharmacy counter. She passed the usual group of women at the coffee counter. Corinne Hooper, Irene Hazelton, Carol Chadwick and Susanne Connor were all chattering away with over-exaggerated gestures and long, knowing glances.

"Oh, look! There's Marnie Reilly! Hi, Marnie!" Irene Hazelton called out.

Marnie waved and smiled. "Hi, Mrs. Hazelton. Hello, ladies. How are we all today?"

"Come have coffee with us, Marnie. We haven't spoken with you in weeks." Corinne Cooper's syrupy sweet voice always made Marnie cringe inwardly.

"I really can't today. I have a loaded schedule. Thanks for the lovely offer, though." Marnie pasted on her best smile.

"Marnie Reilly, what can I do for you?" Mr. Drake asked. "How have you been? That nasty business a few weeks ago. Are you coping?"

"Yes, sir. I just popped in to get a prescription filled for Detective Gregg. I believe that he called and told you that I would be picking it up." Marnie smiled and handed the prescription to Mr. Drake.

"He did. Indeed, he did. Let me get that for you." Mr. Drake studied the prescription that Marnie had just handed to him. "Do you need anything else today?"

"No, sir," Marnie replied. "Oh, actually, I do. I need melatonin. I'm going to run out soon, and I need all of the help that I can get with counting sheep these days."

"I'm sure. Nasty business with your brother and those poor police officers... *and* Ken Wilder. Just nasty business. I'm sure that you're having nightmares as well."

"Hey, Marnie!" Marnie turned to see Erin Matthews sashaying down an aisle.

"Hey, Erin!"

Erin gave Marnie a warm hug and whispered, "I hear ya got a bump on your head the other night. I'm whisperin' because I don't want the chatterin' monkeys over there to hear."

Marnie pulled a face and nodded. "I did. Who did you hear that from?" Marnie narrowed her eyes, wondering who had been gossiping about her – again.

Erin shrugged one shoulder, grinned and waved her hand. "Oh, I overhead it. Giles and Janet Markson were in for lunch yesterday. I heard Giles tellin' Janet. Don't worry. Mum's the word. I won't tell a soul." Erin pretended to lock her lips and throw away the key. "A little advice. Ya might want to pop a bit of concealer on those bruises if ya don't want people askin' questions."

Marnie put her hand up to her temple and nodded. "Yeah, that's a good idea. I didn't even think about that this morning. Thanks."

"That's what friends are for," Erin replied with a smile. "Are we still on for Friday, or have y'all cancelled? You know, because of your little accident."

"We're still on. We're going to get the tree later today," Marnie replied. "Have I sent you the address?"

Erin frowned. "I think so. Didn't ya text it to me?"

"I can't remember. If you need the address, send me a text, and I'll send it. I'd forget my head at the moment if it wasn't attached." Marnie rolled her eyes and laughed.

"Well, I hope you have a wonderful day. I'll see you Friday night. Let me know if ya need me to bring anything other than wine, beer and chips," Erin drawled.

"I will. Thanks, Erin. I'll see you Friday around 6:00." Marnie waved.

Erin waved. "Buh-bye!"

Mr. Drake cleared his throat. "Marnie, Detective Gregg's prescription is ready."

"Thanks, Mr. Drake." Marnie walked back to the counter to pick up the bag.

"Now, I've put a bottle of melatonin in there for you. It's the same one that my wife uses. She swears by it. Only thing that helps her fall asleep these days. Ever since that nasty business at your house, she just hasn't been able to sleep. She worries about everything, you know. Your poor parents. Lordy, if they were still with us, they would be heartbroken," Mr. Drake lamented, shaking his head.

Marnie grabbed the bag off the counter. "Well, please do send my best to Mrs. Drake, and please assure her that my brother is locked up. He won't be going anywhere soon." Marnie forced smile.

"Take care of yourself, Marnie." Mr. Drake waved and nodded goodbye.

"You, too. Have a lovely day." Marnie turned to get away fast.

Erin Matthews was at the checkout when Marnie got to the front of the store.

"I'm really lookin' forward to Friday, and I can't thank you enough for the invitation. It means a lot to me." Erin's eyes sparkled as she rang up Marnie's purchases.

"It'll be a good night. I'm looking forward to kicking off the Christmas season. I can't wait to get the tree up. Christmas trees always make a home smell so good!" Marnie's eyes danced as she thought about the tree and decorating for the holidays. "Thanks, Erin. See you Friday night!"

Out on the street, Marnie took in a deep breath and exhaled. Busybodies drove her nuts. Mr. Drake had been a friend with her folks, but he was a bit gossipy for her liking. Everyone in Creekwood would now know that she had picked up Danny's prescription and that she was having trouble sleeping. She didn't really have much choice. Drake's Drugs was close by. The next closest pharmacy was 30 miles away. Thank goodness that Erin had some discretion. She had never told Erin something that had gotten back around.

Hannah was listening to Christmas music when Marnie got into the car. A beautiful rendition of 'Have Yourself a Merry Little Christmas" was drifting happily through the car.

"I love that song!" Marnie said cheerily.

Hannah nodded in agreement. "It's one of my favorites. To be honest, I think that all Christmas music is wonderful. I play it on my radio at night. It helps me sleep."

A memory flooded in, and Marnie smiled. "My mom used to put me to bed this time of year with the stereo playing Christmas music. She would be downstairs baking, wrapping or decorating. Christmas music would play on the stereo or radio, and Dad would hum along. I could hear Dad and Mom chatting about the day. I loved falling asleep to their voices and Christmas music. It was magical."

Hannah joined Marnie in reminiscing. "Mother would do the same at our house. We would sneak out of bed, sit at the top of the stairs and listen to Mother and Father. Oh! Mother made the most amazing gingerbread men. Daniel and I would sneak down the back stairs, and if we were lucky and Father wasn't in the kitchen, Mother would give each of us one and send us back up to bed."

"How much of an age difference between you and Danny?" Marnie asked.

"Oh, just a few minutes. I was born at 11:59 PM, and he was born at 12:04 AM. It's good. We actually do have different birthdays, which is quite nice," Hannah said casually.

"Wait a minute! You and Danny are twins?!" Marnie asked.

"Yeah. Fraternal, obviously. I thought that you knew," Hannah said with a shrug.

"Uh. No. I'm learning more about your brother from you than him." Marnie tipped her head and glanced at Hannah. "It will be interesting to find out what else Danny hasn't told me."

~~~~~~~~~~~~~~~~~~~~

Marnie and Hannah didn't speak on the way to Marnie's house. They listened to Christmas music and sang or hummed along. Marnie was pleasantly surprised to see her driveway and porch steps clear of snow. She thought that it was incredibly kind of her neighbor to do that for her. She opened her mailbox at the top of the driveway, gathered her mail, set it on the back seat and then parked her car near the front steps.

Hannah glanced around when they got out of the car. "This is charming, Marnie. Why aren't you staying here?"

Marnie pointed to the police tape that still hung in spots. "That story will require at least two bottles of wine." Marnie grimaced.

"Okay. Perhaps we can do that some night. I'll tell you tales of how horrible Daniel was as a child and teenager, and you can share your horror stories," Hannah snickered.

Marnie simply nodded and unlocked the front door. She glanced around, closed her eyes and inhaled. She did love the smell of her house. It smelled of timber and lemon Pledge. It smelled exactly like her childhood home.

"Okay. Let's head down into the dungeon to get the Christmas stuff." Marnie led the way to the cellar.

One by one, they brought all of the boxes labeled Christmas to the front entryway. At the end of it, there were 10 large boxes. Marnie assessed the boxes and shrugged. "Well, this is a job for Thomas Keller and his truck. These boxes are not going to fit in my car. No way." Marnie shook her head and pulled her phone out of her handbag. "I'll text Tom. I'll see if he can come by and pick them up after work. He's coming up for dinner anyway. Hopefully, it isn't a problem."

Marnie texted Tom while Hannah wandered through the house. She stopped in front of Marnie and pointed upstairs. "Do you mind? I just love exploring old houses."

Marnie nodded. "Knock yourself out. Excuse the dust. I haven't been here much the last few weeks."

While she waited for Tom to answer her text, Marnie went into the kitchen to check if anything in the fridge needed to be thrown out. She opened the door and frowned. She couldn't remember buying bologna, three dozen eggs or chocolate milk. She turned and scanned the room. A mug, glass, knife and plate sat on the draining board. She opened the freezer and frowned again. Beef pot pies, frozen Salisbury steak dinners and peanut butter ice cream? She did eat pot pies, but not beef – she liked turkey. She never ate frozen dinners, and she hated peanut butter ice cream. She moved to the living room and glanced around the room. Nothing *seemed* out of place. As Marnie headed toward the stairs to check upstairs, she heard Hannah yell and feet hitting the floor.

"Who the hell are you?!" Hannah screeched.

Marnie ran up the stairs three at a time and saw Hannah just outside the back bedroom with her gun drawn. A familiar voice strained out of the room.

"I-I-I'm sorry. I'm P-P-Patrick. I won't hurt you. Lower your gun."

"You bet your ass you won't hurt me. Sit down on that chair, put your hands on your knees where I can see them and don't move!" Hannah shouted.

Marnie moved quietly behind Hannah. "Hannah, I know him. He's harmless."

"Did you know that he was in your house?" Hannah asked quietly.

"No, but I think that I know why he's here. He was trying to protect me and my friend Carl and probably didn't have any place to go," Marnie replied.

"What do you want me to do?" Hannah asked.

Marnie put a hand on Hannah's arms and gently lowered them. "Lower you gun. Let me talk to him, but stay here."

Hannah lowered her weapon and scowled. "Patrick, I am lowering my firearm. I will shoot you if you do anything that I find threatening. Are we clear?"

Patrick assessed Hannah carefully.

"Crystal," replied Patrick, his right eyebrow lifting slightly.

His reply surprised Marnie. It was mildly defiant.

-CHAPTER FORTY-SIX-

Danny and Tom were back at the station after their interviews with Alice and Allen. Both were skeptical of what they had learned. Tom went up to his desk to write reports and dig a bit deeper into Alice's and Allen's stories. Danny made a quick trip to evidence.

The evidence room was in the bowels of the station. It was dark, dreary and smelly, and it had horrible lighting that made everyone look like a ghoul. The officer on duty had the appearance of an undernourished gothic cartoon character. Standing behind the cage and looking absolutely bored to death, Officer Garcia smiled and jumped up from her tall stool when she saw that she had company.

"Hey, Garcia, can you help me out?" Danny asked.

"Detective Gregg, what's your wish today?" Garcia smiled warmly.

"Hey, I hear that you're taking your detective exam. Is that true or just a rumor?" Danny asked.

Garcia nodded and crossed her fingers in front of her. "I've been studying. The test is in January. I gotta get out of this box. I'm thankful for the experience, but I go stir-crazy down here. I gotta get back on the streets. Captain Sterling thinks that I'm not detective material, and he's been discouraging me from taking the exam." Garcia's face dropped into a frown.

"Well, if you need any support, just let me know," Danny said. "Captain Sterling probably doesn't want to lose you. You run evidence better than anyone ever has."

"Thanks, detective. Now, what can I get for you?" Garcia leaned forward and made a few keystrokes on her keyboard.

"We brought some evidence in on Monday night – Allen Schofield and Alice Wells," Danny said, sliding Garcia a slip of paper with the case numbers through the evidence cage window. "Can you get me everything that has been logged into evidence for both, please?"

Garcia tapped her keyboard and hummed "Last Christmas" while she searched. "Sorry, detective, this system is slower than death. Give me a sec." Garcia went back to humming and tapping. "Here we go. I'll be back in a sec."

Danny nodded his thanks and waited. He texted Ellie to see if Tater was getting along with the other dogs. The reply that he received made him laugh.

"He's been teaching my four how to open doors! Good grief! He's now

busy herding the puppies into their kennels. He's gorgeous!"

"Detective? If you can sign these out, that would be great," Garcia requested, sliding a clipboard through the cage window.

Danny put his phone back in his pocket. "Yeah. Sure. Thanks, Garcia, and good luck with your studying."

Danny signed out the evidence and headed upstairs with the cartons. He ran into Sergeant Beaumont along the way.

"Hey, Beau, any word on Cap?"

Sergeant Beaumont shook his head. "No. We haven't heard anything from him since his text early this morning. I'm getting a bit worried. He usually calls in to check on things, and it's not normal for him to send a text. He doesn't like texting." Sergeant Beaumont twisted his mouth and raised an eyebrow. "Isn't this your RDO? What are you and Keller doin' here on your rostered day off? Hey, one more thing. Why did forensics go out to your place today?"

"We've got a lot happening. You know that we're short-staffed." Danny shifted the cartons that he was holding and grimaced. "Forensics was at my place because someone broke into my garage and assaulted me."

"What? Who? Assaulted you? Detective, you'd better stop hanging around Marnie Reilly. She's bringin' crazy people out in clusters," Sergeant Beaumont teased.

Danny laughed and waved off the comment. "Has Rick been by? I've got a few things to discuss with him."

Beaumont pushed out his bottom lip and shook his head. "Have not seen hide nor hair of the man."

"Okay. Hey, if you're worried about Cap, maybe you should send somebody out to do a welfare check."

Sergeant Beaumont gave a curt nod and picked up his desk phone.

Tom was settled into his reports when Danny arrived upstairs. He dropped the cartons on his desk and winced.

Tom jumped up from his chair when he heard the cartons hit Danny's desk. "Hey, you shouldn't be carrying heavy shit around. I could have gotten those for you."

"Nah. I'm fine. I just... I... it's only when I move a certain way. It hurts like a son of a bitch." Danny puffed out his cheeks and managed a pained smile.

"Why don't you head home? I can work through these reports, and we can finish the rest in the morning." Tom took one of the cartons and removed the lid.

"I need to catch up with Rick. He and Giles have finished with William

Billy Williams's reports, and I need Rick to walk me through." Danny took the lid off the second carton and peeked inside.

"Okay, but don't come cryin' to me if your stitches pop. Seriously, don't pick up heavy stuff. Speaking of heavy stuff, Marnie asked me to pick up some boxes at her house before heading up to the cabin. What time are you meeting her to get a tree?"

Danny rolled his eyes and stared up at the ceiling. "Dammit! I forgot about that." Danny ran his fingers through his hair and glanced down at his watch. "Okay. It's 1:45. I've got time."

Rick Price strolled into the office waving several folders in the air. "Hey, Danny! Tom! I've got some goodies for you."

"What have you got for us, Rick? Anything in there that's gonna make our jobs easier?" Danny asked, rubbing his hands together.

"Okay, I've got a lot of things to go over with you, but I am tight on time. Here's the short version in layman's terms. One, William Billy Williams died of an overdose – morphine, to be exact. It was administered directly into the left popliteal vein – that's the big one behind the knee. Two, his tattoos were new – one week old from our estimation based on healing. Yes, all of the tattoos were done in one visit. Again, based on healing, they would have been done within hours of one another. Three, he did not have the tattoos by choice. Someone restrained him and did the art. Four, yes, he did have ligature marks on his wrists and ankles. We also think that he may have been slipped something to knock him out. Nothing showed up in the tox report, but it wouldn't show up that long after the fact. The artwork is too good. If he had been thrashing about, there would have been slips of the needle. We didn't see slips or mistakes like that, and both Giles and I looked over the tattoos carefully."

Rick stopped for breath, peering over his glasses and anticipating questions from Danny and Tom.

Tom glanced up from his notepad. "Is that it?"

Rick shook his head. "Nope. Just letting you catch up. On to number five. Five, we found no DNA or other trace evidence on the victim. Whoever did this cleaned up carefully – nothing under his nails. He was not killed where we found him. He'd been moved based on coagulation on the right side – almost like he'd been in the trunk of a car on his side before being placed at the dump site. Something curious to note… there were small traces of Epsom salts and clay in his hair. The clay is cosmetic grade – the type of clay used in facials. That's the short version. Your vic, William Billy Williams, was definitely murdered."

Danny puffed out his cheeks and dropped his chin to his chest. "Okay. What about at my house? What'd you find?"

Rick closed his folder and shrugged one shoulder. "Not a lot yet. I had a call from the sheriff's office that I had to tend to, so I haven't tackled the evidence from your garage yet. Ah, but the power line was definitely manipulated. We did gather some blood at the scene. We're running tests to see if it's yours or somebody else's."

Danny sat in his chair and pushed the evidence carton to the side. "Yeah, I think that Tater may have bitten someone. I'm not sure."

"Well, we'll know real soon if Tater needs to worry about rabies. The blood samples are in the lab. We'll have those back by morning. Thanks for leaving your clothes for me. The lab has those too." Rick tapped his folder on the corner of Danny's desk and glanced between Tom and Danny. "Anything else, gents?"

Danny pulled an evidence bag from the carton on his desk. "Can you do something else for me?"

"Not today, but I can tomorrow," Rick replied.

"I've got some evidence here from Station Hall from Monday night. These are the nicotine patches that Allen Schofield was using on the night he was arrested and overdosed. Can you have a look to see if these have been tampered with?" Danny held out the evidence bag containing the foil packets.

Rick took the evidence bag and puckered his brow. "Yeah, sure. I'll get these in tonight. Tampered with? What are you thinking?"

Danny threw up both of his hands. "I don't know. Things aren't adding up." Danny turned to Tom. "Hey, Alice's puffer isn't in evidence. You know, the one Marnie got out of Alice's jacket pocket. Any idea where it is?"

Tom pursed his lips, thought about the questions for a moment, then shrugged. "Nope. You think that maybe Marnie put it in her pocket? There was a lot going on that night. She may have just put it in her pocket."

"Well, we need to find it. Something's going down in Creekwood, and I've got a bad feeling." Danny turned to the window and growled. "Dammit! It's snowing again!"

~~~~~~~~~~~~~~~~~~~~~~~~~

Marnie finished her grocery shopping and packed everything into the car. She glanced up at the sky, and snowflakes landed gently on her forehead. She called Hannah and met her outside the department store. Hannah got into the car with three large bags.

"I went a bit overboard. There were so many amazing deals, and I can't get clothes or shoes this cheaply in DC." Hannah turned and put the bags into the back seat. "I wanted to have something nice to wear when I see William. I know it's stupid, but I just…"

Marnie put her hand on Hannah's arm and smiled warmly. "It's not stupid. You want to look nice for him. I understand. Uncle Giles said that you can go in tomorrow. I'll give you the address tonight."

"Thanks, Marnie. I have enough clothes to last me a few days. I hope that's okay if I stay a bit longer. Do you think Danny would mind?"

Marnie turned to Hannah and smiled. She thought back to just a day ago when Hannah didn't want to spend time with her brother. "I don't think that he'll mind at all. You can ask him yourself. We're going to pick out a tree. Danny is meeting us there."

A text pinged on Marnie's cell. It was from Ellie.

"Heading out for about 30 minutes. Tater is fine. See you at 4:00. x Els"

Marnie thumbed back a quick reply.

"Thanks. Hope he hasn't been too bossy. x Marn"

Marnie smacked her hand on her forehead. "Oh, no! I forgot to tell Tom that Patrick is at my house! I better text him before he goes to get the boxes."

Marnie thumbed out a text to Tom telling him about Patrick staying at her house. She asked him not to tell Danny because she wanted to explain it to him. She received two thumbs up in response.

"Okay. Let's go get a tree, then we'll pick up Tater and go home!" Marnie turned up the Christmas music, shifted and pulled out of the parking lot.

~~~~~~~~~~~~~~~~~~~~~~~

Gleeson's Tree Lot was surrounded by white fairy lights strung from candy cane-striped poles. This was the quintessential Christmas village. Every year, the Gleeson family opened the lot just a few days after Thanksgiving. Gleeson's shipped in and grew every type of Christmas tree imaginable. There was a quaint chalet right in the middle that housed their sales office; a small counter for coffee and hot chocolate; a little stall with poinsettias, pine cone balls and red-ribboned balsam and cedar wreaths; a food stall with gingerbread, sugar cookies, shortbread and chestnuts; and a large section that sold ornaments, lights and other holiday decorations. There was even a barn at the back of the lot with a petting zoo full of reindeer. Marnie's father always said that, if Santa ever needed a new home, he could move into Gleeson's chalet.

Marnie and Hannah stood chatting at the entrance while waiting for Danny. The sun was dipping as quickly as the temperature. The air smelled like Christmas, and while some people laughed at her, Marnie believed that snow did indeed have a smell of its own. She described it as clean sheets with the tiniest hint of nutmeg. Marnie tilted her head back, hugged herself and breathed in the scents of the season.

"I love this time of year. It really is quite magical." Marnie smiled up at the snowflakes dancing in the street lights.

"Christmas is okay. It's not really my favorite," Hannah confessed, her mouth screwed up to the side. "It was fun when Mother was with us, but that all changed. I don't know how much Daniel has told you about Father. He's an old curmudgeon. Ever since Mother died, well, he's not easy to get along with."

"Danny doesn't really talk about family, but we haven't known one another all that long." Marnie shifted uncomfortably. This was Danny's information to share with her. Then again, his sister did have a right to speak her mind. "What does your dad do?"

"He's a cop. He's the chief of police in a small city in the Adirondacks where we grew up."

Marnie turned to comment, but was hit in the arm with a snowball before she could. She turned and saw Danny walking up the sidewalk with a broad dimpled smile on his face that became a grimace.

"You shouldn't throw snowballs, Daniel Gregg! You'll pop your stitches." Marnie frowned and giggled.

Danny walked to Marnie's side and draped an arm over her shoulders. "Carry me. I'm injured," he whined.

"Carry yourself, Detective Gregg. You threw a snowball at me. You're lucky that you're hurt, or I'd have to show you a thing or two about snowball fights." Marnie poked him gently in the side.

"Okay! What kind of tree do we want?" Danny rubbed his hands together as he looked around the lot.

Marnie glanced around at the trees. "I love balsams and Fraser firs."

"Balsam it is. They're my favorite," Danny replied. "Now, let's remember, I have very high ceilings, so let's get the biggest one that we can find. I'm sure that they deliver."

"They do. Where are we going to put it?" Marnie asked.

Danny rubbed his jaw and thought about it for a minute. "I was thinking that we could put it to the left of the fireplace, closer to the window. What do you think? The ceiling is 12 feet there."

"That's pretty much where I was thinking." Marnie nodded in agreement.

"Have you got enough ornaments to go on a tree that big?" Danny glanced around looking for a salesperson.

Marnie grinned. "Shouldn't be a problem. You've got some, too, right?"

"Yeah. Most of them are Sarah's and mine." He paused. "You know, I haven't had a tree since she died." He gazed off for a moment, remembering Christmases with his late wife. Sadness used to overwhelm him, but not this year. This year, it wasn't as lonely.

Hannah shifted uncomfortably at the mention of Sarah's name. The two had never gotten along.

Marnie gave his arm a gentle squeeze. "You know, I bet that she would be thrilled to know that you're decorating this year."

Danny glanced down at her and smiled. "Been talking to her again, have you?"

Marnie grinned. "Just a bit of girl talk." She shot him a sideways, knowing glance and a wink.

Danny faked a shiver. "Ah… just what I need. My late wife giving my girlfriend advice. That's a new one."

Marnie pulled a face and glanced up at Danny. "Girlfriend?" Marnie asked quietly. "Did you just call me your girlfriend?"

He took Marnie's hand, nodded and smiled.

It took 15 minutes to find the perfect tree, a tree stand and a bottle of tree preservative. It was a gorgeous fragrant balsam that would stand gloriously between the front window and the fireplace. Mr. Gleeson said that he could deliver it on his first run in the morning and that he would be at the cabin around 9:00 AM.

"Thanks, Mr. Gleeson!" Marnie waved goodbye as they left the lot.

"See you in the morning!" Mr. Gleeson waved back.

Marnie giggled to herself. Mr. Gleeson looked much like a lumberjack version of Santa. He wore a Santa hat on his head, old dungarees, a green-and-blue plaid flannel shirt, work boots, leather gloves and a vintage Carhartt jacket. He was Paul Bunyan with white hair and a beard.

"Hannah, do you want to come with me to get Tater or go with Danny?" Marnie pulled her keys out her bag.

Hannah glanced between Danny and Marnie, trying to decide.

"How about you come with me, Banana. We haven't had much time to talk," Danny suggested.

"Fine, but don't call me Banana. You know how much I hate it." Hannah narrowed her eyes and gritted teeth.

Danny waved to Marnie. "We'll see you at home, okay, Marnie?"

"You will. I'm just going to run in and get Tater and be right behind you. Drive carefully!"

~~~~~~~~~~~~~~~~~~~~~~~~~

"What's the story with you and Marnie?" Hannah asked.

Danny rubbed his chin with his thumb and glanced at his twin. "The story? Well, I like her. She likes me. That's about it."

"Uh huh. I think that there's more to it." Hannah raised her eyebrows.

Danny shrugged. "It's new. I don't know what else to say."

"Okay." Hannah pressed her head against the window and watched the falling snow. She thought that it was quite pretty, then she thought about how much she dreaded returning to her tiny, overpriced apartment in DC.

"Do you want me to turn to Christmas music?" Danny asked, hand hovering over the radio.

Hannah nodded.

Neither spoke the rest of the way home.

~~~~~~~~~~~~~~~~~~~~~~~~~

Marnie turned onto Lake Road. Tater was in the passenger seat, biting at the guide rails as they passed. Big, white, wet snowflakes fell onto the windshield. Marnie turned her wipers on high. Christmas music played on the radio, and she sang along with Perry Como. She glanced in her rearview mirror and saw a truck's lights coming up on her fast. Marnie touched her brakes lightly to see how icy the roads were tonight. The sanders must have been up through recently because she didn't feel any slip when she braked. She checked her mirror again. The truck had slowed down a bit, but it was close enough for Marnie to see the red Rudolph nose and antlers in the front grill. She smiled and felt safe. Her best friend had her back. It was Tom following her.

Her phone rang, and she hit answer on her steering wheel without looking to see who it was. "Hello!"

"Hello, sister dear. Where's my book?"

"Sam, I don't have your damn book, nor am I going to buy you one. Stop calling me. Stop trying to torment me, and fuck off!" Marnie hung up.

Her phone rang again. She disconnected the call. The phone rang again. She disconnected. It rang again. It was Tom.

"What?!"

"Hey, lady, are you drunk? You're swerving all over the road!"

"No, I'm not drunk! My brother keeps calling me, and I keep hanging up on him!"

"Okay, Marn, calm down. Stay on the phone with me, and he can't call you back," Tom said calmly.

"He *will* call back, and he'll leave me another psycho message! How is he getting a phone? Who's giving him a goddamn phone?"

"Danny called today and asked that he not be given phone access. I don't know how he's doing it, but he is. I'll make a call tomorrow. Don't worry, Marn. I'll take care of it," Tom reassured her.

"Thanks, Tom. Did you have time to stop at the house?"

"I did. How many Christmas ornaments can one person have? Geez, Marnie!"

"I love the holidays. Besides, some of that stuff belonged to my parents and grandparents on both sides. We probably won't use all of it."

Marnie turned on her signal light when she spotted the reflector marking Danny's driveway. Tom's clicked on a few seconds later. They both slowed down and turned into the drive. Partway to the cabin, Marnie saw a flash of light that seemed to hover in the mist, and she slammed on her brakes. Tom braked as well. Leaving the car running, Marnie shifted into neutral, pulled on the parking brake and opened her door. Behind her, she heard Tom's door open, too. Tater's ears perked up, and he stared off into the woods. Marnie and Tom peered into the mist.

She heard Tom shout, "What the hell is that?" The white, translucent specter floated along the edge of the marsh and drifted into the woods behind the cabin.

"Holy shit! Did you see that?" Tom shouted. Marnie could hear Tom through the Bluetooth of the phone connection as well as behind her.

"I did see that. It must have been a will-o'-the-wisp."

"It was what, you say?" Tom screwed up his face and threw up his hands.

"Swamp gas, Tom. A will-o'-the-wisp is just a more romantic way of saying swamp gas," Marnie replied.

She sat back in her car, pushed down on the clutch, released the parking brake, shifted the gear into first, took her foot off the brake and accelerated.

She reached over and gave Tater a pat. "Good boy, Tater. Good boy for not barking."

Tom followed. "That wasn't swamp gas, Marnie. That was a person. Living or dead, that was a person."

"No, it wasn't," Marnie replied tightly.

"What do you mean? I saw it with my eyes. That was not swamp gas!" Tom argued.

"Swamp gas!" Marnie shouted into the phone.

"Ghost!" Tom shouted back.

"Thomas Keller, don't you think that I know a ghost when I see one? That was not a ghost. Swamp gas!" Marnie chided.

"Yeah, okay, whatever you say, Good Witch of the North," Tom said sarcastically.

"What did you call me?"

"You heard me. That was a freakin' ghost, Marnie Reilly, and you won't convince me that it wasn't. The hair on my arms and the back of my neck stood straight up. That was a fucking ghost!" Tom argued.

"Swamp gas!" Marnie again hit her brakes hard. "What the hell! Tom, did you see that?"

Tom braked, skidded and stopped short of Marnie's bumper. Marnie glanced into her rearview mirror to see Tom's face.

"I saw it. I don't believe it, but I did see it!" Tom replied, his mouth hanging open and his eyes transfixed on a large globular black mass moving beyond a stand of pines at the edge of woods.

They both sat speechless in their vehicles. Neither spoke for several seconds. Tater's nose fogged up the window, and he whined.

"Tom?"

"Yeah."

"I think that we better get to the cabin," Marnie said.

"Marn, you sound spooked. Are you spooked, Marn?" Tom asked.

"Yup."

Marnie pushed in the clutch, shifted into first and rolled forward. Tom stayed tight on her tail the rest of the way up the long dark driveway. When they reached the cabin, the security lights came on, and the gate stood open. Danny was just pulling his Jeep into the garage. Marnie followed him in and parked in the spot next to the Jeep. Tom parked at the edge of the driveway and sat in his truck for a long moment, processing what they had just seen.

Marnie clasped Tater's lead onto his collar. Something was telling her that he wouldn't run to the front porch tonight. The hair on the back of her neck was standing on end. The will-o'-the-wisp probably hadn't been swamp gas. She was now quite certain, considering the shadow figure lurking near the stand of pines. She had never seen a spirit roaming the woods around Danny's cabin. *"What are Grace Wilmot and Kate up to?"* she asked herself.

Danny opened her door. "Are you okay? You look like you've seen a ghost – literally!"

"Uh. I think that we may have." Marnie's mouth was a grim line across her face.

"I was just kidding." Danny grinned.

"Well, I'm not." Marnie's tone was also grim.

"Really? You're not joking?" Danny's eyes grew wide.

"I'll fill you in later. I don't want to freak out Tom any more than he already is." Marnie grabbed her bag and Hannah's bags from the back seat and slammed the car door.

Danny nodded and took the bags that Marnie handed to him.

~~~~~~~~~~~~~~~~~~~~~~~~~~~

They put Tater inside and fed him his dinner early to keep him occupied. Danny helped with the groceries. Hannah, Marnie and Tom brought the Christmas decorations into the cabin and put them on the far wall near the pool table.

Danny was unpacking groceries when Marnie went into the kitchen.

"I'm just going to put a stew together in the pressure cooker. It won't take long." Marnie took the pressure cooker out of a cupboard and set it on the counter.

"That sounds good to me," Danny replied. "You gonna tell me what happened?"

"Let's wait until later. I don't want Tom walking in while I'm telling you. He's a bit fragile when it comes to the otherworldly." Marnie winked.

"Okay," Danny replied with a shrug.

"Can you hand me that chuck roast, please?" Marnie reached across the counter and Danny handed her the roast. "I'm starving! We never stopped for lunch. I had a little bag of cinnamon bears in the car, but that was not enough." Marnie giggled.

Tater sat near the windows, staring off into the darkness, a low growl escaping every few minutes. Then he settled into a furry mound, but his ears, nose and watchful eyes stayed vigilant.

Hannah and Tom joined them in the kitchen a few minutes later.

Hannah plopped her elbows on the counter. "What can I do to help?"

Marnie handed her a bag of baby potatoes and a bag of baby carrots. "Could you rinse these for me? The colander is hanging in the pantry."

"Sure. Is that all that I can do?" Hannah asked.

Marnie handed her a package of mushrooms and grinned. "Thanks, Hannah."

Tater's ears twitched, and he spun around. He let out a bark and raced through the kitchen to the living room.

"Gram is here!" Danny announced cheerfully.

Marnie saw Hannah visibly shrink. She couldn't imagine Gram not having a good relationship with Hannah. It just seemed impossible.

Gram bustled into the kitchen with Tater at her heels. She patted him on the head and bent to give him a hug.

"Hello, Tater, my little lad. Sit and be a good boy while I unpack my basket." Gram set her basket on the table.

Marnie stepped from behind the counter and gave Gram a hug, and Tom dropped a kiss on top on Gram's head. Gram reached her arms out to Danny for a hug.

"Danny boy! How are you feelin', love?"

"I'm okay, Gram. Just being careful not to pop my stitches." Danny bent his knees, wrapped his arms around his grandmother and gave her a weak bear hug.

"Hannah, darlin'! Oh, lass, it's so good to see your beautiful face. Come here, lass. It's been too long between hugs." Gram held out her arms to her granddaughter.

"Hello, Grandmother." Hannah gave Gram a quick hug.

Gram teased, "Is that all you've got? Give me a big squeeze, child."

Hannah burst into tears, smiled awkwardly and wrapped her arms around Gram, giving her a proper bear hug. Hannah sniffled and hastily reached for a tissue from the box on the counter.

Gram patted Hannah's back. "I love you, lass. It's so lovely to see you. Bygones be bygones, lass. Bygones be bygones."

~~~~~~~~~~~~~~~~~~~~~~~~~~~~~

They ate heartily and finalized the plans for Friday night between bites. The stew was scrumptious, and Gram's apple upside down cake with homemade whipped cream finished the meal brilliantly. Gram and Marnie chatted about the children's float for the Christmas parade. Danny and Gram whispered between themselves several times and called "Christmas secrets" when anyone asked what they were talking about. They regaled in family stories of Christmases past. They laughed and giggled the evening away, and poor Danny winced in pain often from laughing.

Gram and Tom left together after the kitchen was tidied up. Tom probably wouldn't admit it, but he was quite happy that Gram would be heading up the driveway with him. Safety in numbers. Danny poured a brandy for himself and Marnie and a whiskey for Hannah, and they sat down in front of the fire. Tater curled up on his matt on the hearth and snoozed peacefully.

"I love evenings like that," Hannah confessed. "It's been so long since I've had a good laugh. Thank you!"

"Well, Hannah, if you can, we'd love for you to stay through Christmas," Danny remarked offhandedly.

Hannah sat up, surprised, tears welling up in her eyes. "Really? I would love to stay. I think that we should get Father to come for Christmas. Do you think that he would?"

Danny clenched his jaw. "Hmm. Maybe. Let's not go overboard. He hates Christmas. He really won't be good company."

"Oh, come on, Daniel! Father can't be on his own, and I if don't go to him like I normally do, he will be alone." Hannah scooched forward on her chair and waggled a finger at Danny. "Bygones be bygones, as Grandmother said."

"Okay. We can invite him, but only if I can call you Banana for the rest of your time here," Danny teased.

Hannah rolled her eyes. "Pfft. Do I have a choice?"

Danny grinned. "Nope."

"Fine. Fine. Call me Banana. I'll just call you Buck! You hate that as much as I hate Banana, so we'll be even. Okay, Buck!" Hannah teased.

"Okay! Truce! Hannah it is!" Danny laughed.

"Sorry to spoil this soiree, folks. I am exhausted. I'm off to bed." Marnie stood, arched her back and stretched.

"Me, too," agreed Hannah.

"Me, three," chimed Danny. "C'mon, Tater. Let's go out one more time."

"I'll go with you," Marnie volunteered quickly. "I don't want Tater to pull you if he sniffs a deer on the trail or something."

"Okay," Danny replied. "Let's go."

~~~~~~~~~~~~~~~~~~~~~~~~~

Huge, wet snowflakes fell from the sky. Danny and Marnie walked Tater toward the lake. Marnie tugged up her hood and put on her mittens. Tater shook snow off his back and watched the darkness. He was aware of every snap of a twig, hoot from an owl and moan of the trees as the gentle wind moved through the branches.

"Okay, give." Danny nudged Marnie gently with his elbow. It was the first opportunity that they had had to chat.

Marnie puffed out her cheeks and let out a long exhale.

"Well, I think that Grace Wilmot and Kate are up to some of Grace's old shenanigans. You know, black magic. I've had an uneasy feeling most of the evening. When Tom and I were coming up the driveway, we saw a ghost. I told Tom that it was a will-o'-the-wisp. He didn't believe me, of course. As we got closer to the cabin, we saw a black mass moving near a stand of pines. It was strange. I've only seen a black mass once before. It frightened me then, and it frightens me now. Before you ask, it definitely was not our resident black bear Percy. It appeared to float, and it was globular."

Danny furrowed his brow and stared off into the woods, considering what Marnie just said.

"What the hell is a will-o'-the-wisp?" Danny wrinkled his forehead.

Marnie rolled her eyes. "Gosh, you and Tom really need to read more. A will-o'-the-wisp is basically swamp gas."

"Okay. First, I've never seen swamp gas up here. I've seen fog, but never swamp gas. Second, I think that swamp gas is easier to say than will-o'-the-wisp. Who uses those words?" Danny quirked his mouth.

Marnie grabbed Danny's arm and turned quickly to the path back to the cabin. "Shh. Listen," Marnie whispered.

A soft, mellifluous tune drifted on the wind. The hair on Tater's back spiked up, and he stood stock-still, a low growl starting to build in his throat.

"What is that?" Danny whispered, crinkling his face.

"We better get inside," Marnie replied quietly. "C'mon, Tater. Let's go." Marnie pulled his lead gently. Tater resisted, then he trotted along beside them, his eyes holding steady on the path ahead.

"That sounds like a woman singing," Danny whispered. He stopped on the path to listen.

Marnie grabbed his hand. "C'mon. Let's get inside. I'll explain." Marnie pulled Danny to the porch steps.

As they reached the porch, a wailing scream pierced the darkness. Marnie pulled Tater's lead and Danny's hand toward the door. "Get inside!" Marnie implored, pushing the door open.

Danny turned back to the path and listened. Another mournful screech echoed through the night.

"Danny, get in here! If that's what I think it is... Just get inside, please, now!" Marnie begged.

"What is it?" Danny asked as he felt her pull him into the cabin with her.

"Get in here!" Marnie pleaded. "I think that it's a banshee. I think that Grace Wilmot conjured up a banshee!"

"Did you say banshee?" Danny shut the door and pressed his back to it.

"Yes. A banshee. It's Irish folklore. It's a harbinger of death." Marnie peered out the window and snapped the shutter closed.

"Stop it. Banshees are a bunch of malarkey, Marnie. Gram told us stories about banshees when Hannah and I were kids. They're not real." Danny frowned.

"You know, I normally wouldn't think so, but after what happened to William, what happened with Sam a few weeks ago and the fact that you got stabbed with an icicle, I'm not taking any chances. Grace and Kate are up to something. They're playing with fire, Danny. The images that I have been getting the last few hours... I'm telling you – she is stirring things up. Real or not, I'm just not taking chances."

"Stop. Look at me," Danny ordered. He placed his hands on Marnie's shoulders and stared into her face. "Do you believe in black magic, Marnie?"

Marnie shook her head. "No, of course not. My rational mind knows truth from fiction. I know that Grace Wilmot is a charlatan, but if you do things with intent, well, intent can go a long way to wreaking havoc. It doesn't matter what I believe. It matters how many of her hooligans she has involved in her little scheme and whether their intent for evil is strong. Dark energy begets negativity, and once it catches, it spreads like wildfire."

-CHAPTER FORTY-SEVEN-

Candles sputtered and sparked in the drafty silo. Fingers perched above the planchette, Grace Wilmot and Kate Parish focused all of their energies on the Ouija board. Six members of The Collective stood, circling the table where Grace and Kate sat. All six wore horned goat masks, symbolizing the devil. The masks were Grace's idea so that Kate Parish wouldn't recognize them should she see them in the future.

Kate leaned across the table and whispered, "Is it working?" Behind them, the masked folks murmured and moaned.

In a thunderous roar, Grace shouted, "Quiet!"

Smirking, Kate leaned back in her chair. She glanced at all of the masked people standing around the table. Soulless eyes peered back at her. Kate shivered and accidentally touched the planchette.

"Be still!" Grace shouted.

Kate smirked again and glanced past Grace into the gloom of the candlelit silo. She was certain that she saw movement in the living area behind the couch; it was difficult to see, but it was clearly a human figure. A candle blew out, then another and another until the living area was shrouded in blackness. Kate continued to watch the shadowy figure slink through the room. Dressed all in black, it was lithe and ominous. It crept closer, candles extinguishing in its path. Kate grew nervous. Her hands began to tremble. One by one, the masked six stepped away from the table and disappeared into the darkened living area. One by one, Kate saw the shadowy figure move stealthily between them, and one by one, she heard the masked ones cry out and thump to the floor.

Kate turned back to Grace, who was staring intently over Kate's head. Kate snapped her head to the side in a wave of panic to see what had Grace's attention when an ice-cold hand gripped her neck. Kate screamed, felt the prick of a pin and fell forward onto the table. She was still.

"Ah, if it isn't my ninja friend!" Grace mocked. "Tell me, to what do I owe the pleasure of this visit?" Grace croaked, eyes narrowed.

"I know how, I know when and I know where," answered the shadowy figure.

Grace sneered and rubbed her hands together. "Tell me! Tell me!"

"I am expecting further intel in the short term. I will visit you again on

238

Saturday at midnight. Keep your mouth shut, and we will both get what we want. Understood?"

Grace nodded excitedly. "Have they gotten any closer to solving that little murder?"

"Pfft! I wish them luck. There is no way to trace any of *my* activity. I am warning you, Grace Wilmot, do not fuck this up with your crazy antics!"

Grace scowled. "Crazy antics? You're the one dressed up like a ninja. You obviously don't know who you're dealing with."

"Shut up! Just shut your stupid mouth! You don't know who *you* are dealing with. Trust me when I say that I will kill you if you fuck this up. If any of my planning goes haywire because you have been sloppy, well, a sharp knife to your carotid will be my little Christmas gift to you. Are we clear?"

Grace swallowed hard and nodded.

"Are we clear?" the shadow asked again.

"We're clear," Grace hissed.

"Excellent! I'm going home to my cat, a cozy fire and a glass of whiskey on the rocks." The shadowy figure disappeared into the darkness. The hatch door opened and slammed shut, leaving Grace with a room full of drugged colleagues.

~~~~~~~~~~~~~~~~~~~~~~~~~~~~~

Marnie's sleep was restless. Visions of Grace Wilmot and Kate Parish in front of a Ouija board haunted her sleep. As the visions faded out, voices faded in – voices from the other side of the veil. Voices delivering encouragement. Voices delivering warnings. Her parents were desperately trying to tell her something. They faded in and out – reception between this life and the hereafter was weak tonight. Most disturbing to her was that Ken continued to send images her way – the same thing over and over again. Fire and ice. Ice and fire. She rolled onto her back and stared up at the ceiling. She checked her watch. 4:00 AM glowed back at her. She glanced down at the foot of the bed. Tater was awake, looking back at her.

"Hey, buddy. Can't sleep?" Marnie asked with a yawn.

Tater yawned and crawled on his belly to Marnie's outstretched hand. She scratched his ears and rubbed his tummy. He stretched his head up and nuzzled into the crook of her arm. Both sat up when they heard footsteps in the hall – then nothing. Tater gave a low woof and watched the door. Marnie swung her legs out from under the warm covers and onto the floor. She searched for her slippers first, then she reached for her sweatshirt and pulled it over her head.

"C'mon, Tater. Let's go downstairs. Maybe some warm brandy…"

Marnie opened her door and jumped back, stifling a scream. Danny was standing outside her room, hand raised.

"Sorry. I didn't mean to scare you. I was going to knock," Danny whispered.

"Geez, Danny. You scared the bejesus out of me. We thought that we heard footsteps. Are you okay?" Marnie asked, clutching her chest.

"I can't sleep, and thought that I heard you moving around."

"No. Tater and I were in bed. I can't sleep, either. We were just getting up to go downstairs," Marnie whispered.

"Want some hot chocolate?" Danny offered.

"Do you have peppermint schnapps?"

"I think so." Danny nodded.

"Let's go." Marnie grabbed Danny's hand and headed for the stairs.

They tiptoed down the hall and stairs so that they wouldn't wake Hannah. When they reached the bottom, the living room was softly lit by the still-glowing embers in the fireplace. Danny crossed to the fireplace, stirred the ash and embers and put a couple of dried pine cones into the fireplace. Once the pine cones caught, he placed two small logs into the fire. While Danny tended to the fire, Marnie and Tater went into the kitchen to make the hot chocolate. Tater went directly to the window and peered out into the woods.

Danny joined them in the kitchen a few minutes later carrying a bottle of peppermint schnapps. He set it down on the counter and sat on a barstool.

"It's been one of those days. My mind is racing. No matter how many times that I fluffed my pillow or how many times that I kicked my blankets off or pulled them back up, I just tossed and turned. I couldn't fall asleep." Danny leaned his elbow on the counter and put his chin in his hands.

"Well, my mind is racing, too. Voices, visions, feelings – none of it makes sense," Marnie commented. She stirred milk in a pan on the range top and glanced over her shoulder at Danny. "The voices, visions and feelings – I'm feeling, well, discombobulated to say the least. One minute, I think that things are starting to make sense; the next, everything is jumbled."

Danny nodded in Tater's direction. "What do you suppose Tater sees?"

Marnie shrugged. "I'm not sure. I feel like there are a series of events that are going to collide. That probably doesn't make sense. I don't know how else to explain it. My parents, Ken and Sarah, they're all trying to tell me something."

"What about my mother?" Danny asked expectantly.

Marnie shook her head. "No. I haven't heard from her lately, but I am getting other voices who I don't normally hear. It's confusing. Everybody wants to say something, but they keep interrupting one another. It's all jumbled – like 10 people all trying to talk to me at the same time through a tin can phone."

Marnie took two mugs out of the cupboard and set them on the counter. She chopped up chocolate and put it into the pan with the warming milk. She stirred until the chocolate had melted. Danny poured peppermint schnapps into each mug, and Marnie poured in the hot chocolate and stirred. They took their mugs into the living room to sit by the fire. Danny added another log to the fire and sat on the couch next to Marnie. Tater curled up on his mat and tucked his nose under his tail.

"How're things going with William's investigation?" Marnie asked.

Danny inhaled deeply – ready to respond - but winced with pain and breathed out loudly. "Damn, my back hurts – every time that I move. Hey, do you have my prescription?"

"Oh, I forgot about that. It's in my bag upstairs. Actually, Mr. Drake gave me some melatonin to help me sleep. Can't believe I forgot about that. Geez! Full brain. I'll get it for you." Marnie sighed and sat up.

Danny put a hand on her arm. "We'll get it when we go back upstairs. Sit. Relax." Danny took a sip of hot chocolate and grinned. "Good hot chocolate." He took another sip. "So, yeah, I met with Rick today, and he reviewed the final autopsy and forensics report. We have a lot to follow up, but we do know that he died of a morphine overdose. We also know that the tattoos were recent." Danny didn't go in to the fact that William was most likely tattooed against his will. He didn't want to upset Marnie.

"Hmm. There really aren't that many tattoo parlors in Creekwood. I would think that finding the artist should be easy. There's a goth tattoo parlor over near the old railroad tracks. I can't imagine William going there, but who knows. If the artist is good, maybe." Marnie sipped her hot chocolate and closed her eyes. "This is so good! The peppermint schnapps makes it exceptional."

"It sure does," Danny replied, taking another sip. "What's happening in your world tomorrow, Ms. Reilly?"

"Carl is driving out for coffee at 8:00. The tree is being delivered, so we should probably figure out the exact spot for it before you take off in the morning. Um… I'm going to go shopping for wrapping paper, ribbon, tape and all of the things that we'll need for the toys. I'm thinking brown craft paper, bright red and green ribbons and candy canes as a decoration for each package – tags, of course. Let's keep it simple."

"That sounds like a full day," Danny replied.

"Yes, and I need to put some food together for Friday. Gram, Hannah and I have it all sorted. Carl, Andrea, Ellie and Erin are all bringing food and drinks, too. Have you invited anyone from the station?" Marnie asked.

Danny nodded. "Jalnack, Rick, Garcia, Tony and Beau. I was going to invite Captain Sterling, but he hasn't been in the last few days. I may invite a few more of the guys tomorrow. We'll see. Anyone else you want here for the party?"

Marnie shook her head. "Nope. My group is small. I like it that way."

"Okay. Hey, want some more hot chocolate? I could use another."

"Yes, please!" Marnie finished what was left in her mug and wiped off the chocolate mustache with the back of her hand.

"Charming," Danny teased.

Marnie laughed and followed Danny to the kitchen. "How did your interviews go with Alice and Allen?"

"Ah. That was something that I wanted to ask you. Do you have Alice's inhaler? The one from Station Hall?"

Marnie thought about it and nodded. "Yeah, actually. I think that I stuffed everything into my coat pocket."

"Everything?" Danny raised an eyebrow.

"Uh huh. The inhaler was in a bag. I think that I took it out of the bag and stuffed the bag, box and receipt in my pocket," Marnie replied, walking to her coat, hanging next to the door in the living room. She rifled through her pockets and called out, "Yup. I've got it."

Marnie returned to the kitchen and handed the bunched papers, box and inhaler to Danny. "Here you go."

Danny examined the contents of Marnie's pocket while she made another batch of hot chocolate.

"I'm waiting for Rick to analyze the nicotine patches Allen had in his pocket, and I'm going to get him to analyze this, too. I think that someone tampered with Allen's patches and Alice's inhaler." Danny looked up at the ceiling and hypothesized.

Marnie's eyes widened in disbelief. "Are you serious?"

Danny held up the inhaler and smelled it. "I don't know. That's what Rick is going to tell us. It's just a hunch. Hey, if Casper or one of your other ghostly connections could give us a lead, I would be grateful." Danny winked.

"You're not joking, are you?" Marnie raised an eyebrow. They had this conversation when they first met, and Danny's skepticism had evolved into confidence and belief. There was just no denying that Marnie had a gift.

"Not really." Danny shrugged.

"I'll see what I can do. If William would reach out, that would be helpful." Marnie glanced up, willing contact.

"Is that hot chocolate done yet?" Danny leaned over to look in the pan.

"Yes. Pass me the mugs."

Danny poured peppermint schnapps into the mugs. Marnie poured out the hot chocolate, then held up one finger and grinned. She opened the fridge, pulled out Gram's whipped cream and put a dollop of cream into each mug. They each took a sip and laughed at the matching mustaches.

Marnie suddenly grew serious. "Hey, Danny, I wanted to talk to you about something, and I don't want you to get all overprotective."

Danny narrowed his eyes and sighed. "Okay. What's up?"

"Patrick is staying at my house. He needed to leave Alice's, and he had nowhere else to go, so he's staying at my house temporarily," Marnie said quickly, then braced for his protest.

Danny shrugged. "It's your house. If you trust him not to trash the place, I've got no beef with Patrick. I think that he's probably an okay guy. What does Carl think?"

"I haven't asked Carl. I will in the morning. I think that we should probably invite Patrick on Friday night. Introduce him to some people. What do you think?"

Danny scrunched up his face and tipped his head. "I don't know. I'd definitely ask Carl about that."

Danny thought for a moment about the Station Hall incident. Patrick's behavior at Marnie's office and at the cemetery had been entirely different from Patrick's behavior when Marnie was trapped. It changed – he changed. Danny recalled Patrick stepping up when he, Tom and Carl were all racing around. It was Patrick who found the screwdriver. It was Patrick who removed the lid of the trunk. It was Patrick who lifted Marnie out of the trunk and placed her gently on the floor. It was Patrick who checked her vitals and began CPR. He was cool and levelheaded, *and* it was Patrick who had ultimately saved Marnie's life.

"Danny?" Marnie interrupted his thoughts. "What's traveling through that gray matter in your noggin?"

"Uh. You know, maybe inviting Patrick would be a good idea," Danny said. "I was just remembering something that Carl said about him. He said something like Patrick always wants to do the right thing. Anyway, I remembered something else from that night at Station Hall. I think inviting him would be okay – just check with Carl to be sure."

Marnie nodded, picked up her mug and headed back to the comfy couch and fire.

Danny followed her into the living room and continued chatting about his day. "Hey, Marnie, what can you tell me about Alice's history with Grace?"

Marnie glanced over her shoulder and shot him an expression that said more than words ever could. Danny shuddered in response.

"That bad, huh?" Danny asked.

"Uh, yeah!" Marnie replied.

"Tell me," Danny coaxed.

Marnie turned a bit and sat with one leg under her. She faced Danny straight on, and he could see by her expression that she was mulling over what to share.

"Marnie, just tell me everything," Danny pushed.

"Well, I can tell you that Grace Wilmot is a bad person, and I am not simply saying that she is not nice. I'm saying that she is rotten – rotten to the core." Marnie took a sip of her hot chocolate and gathered her words in her mind. "She's a user, a blackmailer, a manipulator, a liar, a thief, a charlatan and a nasty, vile human being. Those are just her positive attributes. What she did to poor Alice, well, she should be locked up in the loony bin for the rest of her days. *Grace* should be locked up, and maybe Alice, too. She's quite damaged from years of Grace's abuse. Reuben and Grace terrorized her. Plain and simple, they terrorized her."

Danny shook his head, trying to grasp the severity of damage that Grace Wilmot had caused.

Marnie took another sip of hot chocolate and continued. "You know, she tried to blackmail me once. When she was forced to leave Creekwood, she sent me letters after she was gone – told me that, if I didn't send her money, she would put a curse on me. I still have the letters somewhere. You never know when that type of evidence may come in handy." Marnie shared a knowing look over her mug and took a sip of her hot chocolate.

"Are you offering to give me the letters, Ms. Reilly?"

"I am, Detective Gregg. Those letters just so happen to be in my office file cabinet in a folder labeled 'Threats and Persons of Concern.'"

Danny raised his eyebrows. "How many letters are in that file?"

Marnie stuck out her bottom lip, looked up and tallied up the letters from memory. "Oh, probably 50 or so. All from Grace or The Collective. Oh, there a few from Ken in there as well." Marnie shrugged. "Anyway, if Alice told you that Grace terrorized her or caused her emotional, physical or psychological harm, believe every word of it. Alice Wells was once a well-respected librarian here in the town of Creekwood."

Danny considered Marnie's estimation of Alice's relationship with Grace. "Now, hypothetically, if Allen told you that Grace had tormented both him and Alice to the point of them having to fake a ritual damning you and Carl at the cemetery to get her off their backs, would you believe it?"

"Absofuckinglutely," Marnie replied with a firm nod.

Danny laughed. "Okay. You answered that a bit too quickly – didn't even have to think about it. Would you also believe that Alice and Allen really didn't want to do you harm? Would you believe that Alice purposely messed up the ritual by adding salt and, um, she said something about the number three. I can't remember, and I didn't fully understand it at the time, but that's all in my notes."

Marnie crinkled her forehead, sipped her hot chocolate and considered what Danny was telling her. "You know, I'm trying to work through a timeline in my head of when Alice started sniping at me more than usual. I'll have to check my diaries to see if there is a correlation between Grace returning and Alice's snarkiness escalating. To answer your question, salt cleanses and could reverse negativity. You said three?"

Danny nodded. "Yeah, I think that she said three."

"Hmm. The only connection that I can make to that is the Trinity – you know, Father, Son and Holy Spirit."

"She was actually blessing you, not trying to hurt you?" Danny quirked his mouth to the side.

"Well, I wouldn't go that far with it, but yeah. She was probably trying to protect us while appearing to damn us. Make no mistake, Danny, I am not one of Alice's favorite people." Marnie took another sip of her hot chocolate and looked at Danny over the rim of her mug.

"Okay. I'm going to get her inhaler tested tomorrow, and I will hopefully have results from Allen's patches tomorrow afternoon." Danny shifted sideways to get comfortable. "Marnie, Alice wants to see you. She wants to apologize to you. I think that she is trying to make amends. I'm cynical, so I maybe don't buy it. It's up to you how you handle it."

Marnie shrugged. "Forgiveness is divine. I'll talk to her. Maybe we can forgive each other. I did trash and crash events where they were speaking quite regularly." She giggled, remembering their faces when she would turn up in the program. No wonder Alice was bitter.

Danny laughed. "You, Ms. Reilly, are a rabble-rouser!"

Marnie grinned. "Thank you. I will take that as a compliment."

"Okay. One more thing." Danny held up an index finger. "What the heck was really going on tonight when you and Tom drove in? Swamp gas? What else?"

"Ah, the specters trouncing about the woods," Marnie replied with a nod. "I think – I could be wrong – that Grace, Grace's assorted hooligans and Kate were playing around with a Ouija board. Now, that's the kind of stuff that nightmares are made of, and that is how the veil between this life and the hereafter gets torn. It's absolutely crazy that people mess around with Ouija boards. They are quite dangerous, especially if you don't close the session. I do think that what we saw and heard in the woods were, well, yeah, real. I'm not worried, though. I'm more afraid of the living than the dead."

"What if they conjure up a demon? Would that worry you?" Danny shifted closer to Marnie to get a better line on her expression.

Marnie shook her head and pushed out her bottom lip. "I don't believe in demons or the devil or Satan or Hell for that matter. I believe that there are good, bad and evil. People are good, bad or evil. I don't believe that people are sent to an eternity in Hell."

Danny frowned. "Do you believe in God? In Heaven?"

Marnie crossed her legs beneath her, took another sip of hot chocolate and considered her response carefully. "I do believe in God. In my mind, heaven is a place where most people go after they die. When I say most people, I mean that people who have done evil, terrible things like murder go to a different place – a purgatory of sorts until such time that they redeem themselves. If they do redeem themselves, then the veil between purgatory and Heaven opens for them. If they don't redeem themselves, they stay in purgatory until they do redeem themselves. They could be there forever. I call the space the in-between. It's kind of like a therapy clinic for the damned, but I like to think that everyone is welcome in Heaven at some point. Some people can be rehabilitated. Perhaps some can't, but I like to think that they can. Besides, isn't God supposed to be forgiving? Doesn't everyone deserve a chance to go home in the end?" Marnie shrugged and took another sip of hot chocolate.

Danny sat, silent. Sipping his cocoa, he mulled over Marnie's words.

Marnie recalled, "Alexander Pope wrote, 'To err is human; to forgive, divine.' I'm not saying that he had a direct line to God when he wrote that in 'An Essay on Criticism,' but I'd like to think that he had some divine guidance."

Danny considered Marnie's opinion for several moments. He stirred the fire and threw another log onto the grate. "I like the way that you think, Marnie Reilly." Danny smiled and swirled the hot chocolate left in his mug. "Hmm... I need something stronger than hot chocolate."

Marnie giggled. "It's 5:30 in the morning."
Danny grinned. "I was thinking coffee."

-CHAPTER FORTY-EIGHT-

Thursday, December 10th

Kate once again awoke on her couch in her apartment, her aching head foggy. She glanced around the room. It was still dark. She looked at her watch. It was 5:30 AM on Thursday morning. She stood to get a glass of water, but wobbled back down onto the couch. Her head swam, the events of last night twirling in her memory. She stood again. This time, she made it to the kitchen, got herself a glass of water and collapsed into a hard-backed chair at the kitchenette. She felt her neck where the needle had pricked her and found a healing scab. She put her head into her hands and broke into sobs. As she sobbed, her anger boiled. She hated her life. She hated what Sam had coerced her to do. She hated herself for doing it. She hated Grace Wilmot for tricking her again. She hated her boss for firing her, but most of all, she hated Marnie Reilly. She hated Marnie for being happy. She hated that Marnie always managed to land on her feet. She hated that Detective Gregg and Tom Keller watched over her. She hated that Sam's thoughts were consumed by her. She hated her life.

Her self-pity was interrupted by the soft sound of her phone ringing. Kate stood, grabbed the back of the chair to get her balance and walked sluggishly to the living room. Her phone was in her bag and had stopped ringing by the time that she retrieved it. She stared at the screen. The call had come from a private number. She set the phone on the coffee table and turned to go into her bedroom to lie down. The phone chimed again. She turned and stared down at the phone. It was from a private number again. She answered.

"Hello?"

"Kate, don't hang up on me! I want you to come see me today! Don't you dare say no. I swear, Kate, if you don't start doing as I tell you, well, your life may be cut short like Ken's."

"Sam, I'm not feeling good. I was going back to bed when you called the first time. I can't possibly come see you today," Kate replied weakly.

"I don't care if you're sick. You get here to see me today! I've had enough of the games, Kate. You've been telling lies about me!" Sam's menacing tone had amplified since their last call.

"Sam, I haven't told any lies about you. I've told the police everything exactly as it happened. You and I both know that you can be forgetful sometimes. You've had too many bumps on your head over the years, and that explosion, well, that knocked more than sense out of you."

Sam's voice rose, both in pitch and volume. "Don't try gaslighting me, Kate. You were the mastermind behind killing Ken and pinning it on Marnie. You knew every detail. You were the one who knew about that Johnny Cash song. You were the one. You were the one who knew about Ken, Marnie and the piano wire. You were the one with the key to her house and the code to her alarm. That was all you, baby!" Kate could hear Sam's spittle strike the mouthpiece with each word that he spewed.

"Sam, please stop this nonsense. I'm tired, and I need to rest. Please stop badgering me. I will come see you on Friday or maybe Saturday. I can't make it today. I really can't, Sam." Kate choked up and started to cry.

"Oh, poor, Katie. You know, don't worry about it. I've got a lawyer coming to see me today. He's one of those guys who can get anyone out of a jam. A connection of mine hooked me up. I'm going to reverse everything that you've done. Everything that I tell him will be the truth, and I've volunteered to take a lie detector test to back it up. What's that gonna do to your story, Katie?"

"Sam Reilly, you are absolutely hateful. I'm crying, and you're being horribly hateful!" Kate whined and sniffed.

"C'mon, baby! Throw a tantrum. You always get your way when you throw a tantrum. That pretty face of yours has gotten you out of trouble over the years, but not this time. You're as good as dead, Kate. You're as good as dead."

Sam hung up.

Kate stared at her phone and threw it across the room.

~~~~~~~~~~~~~~~~~~~~~~~~~~~~~

While Danny made a pot of coffee in the dim light, Marnie took Tater out for a quick walk down to the lake. A light wind blew, and snow drifted down from the tree branches above. A light dusting of snow had fallen overnight, and there was a wintry chill in the air. Marnie wrapped her coat around her and took in the peaceful hush of morning.

Marnie made a snowball and tossed it gently at Tater. He turned and sniffed the ground where the snow had fallen.

"Hey, Tater! Do you want to go spend some time with Ellie today? I've got Christmas shopping to do."

Tater trotted to Marnie's side, sat, put a paw on her leg and smiled up at her. "Okay, boy, let's get inside. We'll come back out once the sun comes up."

Marnie and Tater headed back to the cabin. The security lights to the side of the garage lit their path. They both turned to a rustling in the woods and watched as a buck and a doe burst from the brush and galloped gracefully through the snow, disappearing into the darkness behind the cabin. Ears up and eyes alert, Tater let out a high-pitched bark. Marnie patted his head.

"C'mon, Tater. I need coffee." Marnie climbed the steps and pushed open the door. The warmth of the cabin was welcoming. The smell of sausage and sizzling bacon was even more welcoming.

~~~~~~~~~~~~~~~~~~~~~~~~~

Justin stood in front of Reuben's apartment building, hoping to see some sign of life – a light, a curtain opening – anything. He walked around to the rear of the building and saw a light on in the back. He trudged back through the snow and around to the front of the building. He stood looking up, gathering his thoughts – the words that he would use to gain Reuben's trust and help. He walked up the steps and rang the bell. A sleepy voice came through the speaker.

"Yeah?"

"Reuben, it's Justin. I need to speak to you for a few minutes. It's about your mother," Justin replied.

After a long moment, the door clicked. Justin pushed the door and went into the small lobby. He climbed the stairs to Reuben's floor, knocked on the door and waited. A glower on his unshaven face, Reuben opened the door and stepped back to allow Justin into the apartment.

"Make it quick. I have company," Reuben snapped.

"Sorry, Reuben. I didn't want to disturb you, but I think that we need to discuss your mother and her... uh... activity," Justin stammered.

Reuben rolled his eyes and glanced up toward the ceiling. He puffed out his cheeks. "What has she done now?"

"Reuben, I'm sorry about the other night. Really, man, I'm sorry. I was out of line. Your mother has been threatening me – blackmailing me is more like it." Justin hung his head.

"That's Mother's specialty. The amount of money that she has stashed from blackmailing people throughout the years – well, let's just say that she has a lot of money tucked away somewhere. I've never been able to find it."

Reuben went into his tidy kitchen and started making coffee.

"Do you know that she let me go hungry when I was kid? She had more than enough money to buy food for both of us, but she would eat and I wouldn't. Did you know that? Alice used to sneak food to me in my room. She'd sneak in after Mother went to bed. Honestly, Alice was more of a mother to me than Grace. After we left Alice's, well, I... I... Anyway, that was a long time ago." Reuben stared down at his bare feet.

"Man, I didn't know. I'm sorry." Justin looked away and stared at the brewing coffee maker. "Look, I gave someone information about a guy who I saw rummaging in a dumpster in the alley behind the drugstore. I gave a description of the guy to Mr. Drake and said where the guy lived because I followed him. I was curious about what the guy was doing digging in a dumpster and thought that maybe Mr. Drake would pay me to give him information." Justin shrugged. "He didn't, but I think that someone else overheard the conversation because this guy turned up dead near the tracks just a few days ago. I told your mother, and now, she's blackmailing me – telling me that she's going to the cops and that, with my past, I'm as good as convicted. Jesus, Reuben, I don't need anyone digging into my past. There was a lot of questionable stuff – identity theft, securities fraud, hacking – in my college days. I did my time. I'm on parole, and I didn't kill this guy. I swear it!"

Reuben poured himself a coffee and held up a mug to Justin. "You want coffee?"

Justin nodded. "Yeah. Coffee would be good, thanks."

"Justin, the first thing that you need to remember is this: my mother isn't gonna go to the cops. She will never go to the cops because they won't believe her. The second thing that you need to remember is that she only has as much power as you give her. Stop giving her your power."

Justin nodded. "I did stop giving her my power yesterday. I told her that I couldn't help her and that I wasn't afraid of her. You know what? Today, I woke up the middle of the night with a dead rat on my chest!"

Reuben chuckled softly. "Like you, my mother is very good at picking locks. She always has been." Reuben grinned. "You have to install special locks to keep her out. Look, Justin, I don't know what you want me to do to help you, but how about you tell me so that I can get back to my company." Reuben nodded in the direction of his bedroom.

"Uh, yeah, sure." Justin nodded. "You see, I was speaking with Alice yesterday. I picked her up at the hospital and helped her settle in. She needed groceries and things like that, and she needed a bit of moral support because the detectives came around to question her. Anyway, she thinks that, if we speak to Marnie Reilly…"

Reuben choked on his coffee and rolled his eyes dramatically. "Are you nuts?"

Justin held up his hand. "Hang on! If we speak to Marnie, we may all be able to figure out a plan that would settle everything – once and for all. Alice thinks that Marnie Reilly may be able to help us put your mother away in a home where she can get help and where she can't hurt people."

Reuben scoffed. "Why would Marnie Reilly help us? Seriously, Justin, why would she? We haven't exactly ingratiated ourselves to her, have we? For fuck's sake, I knocked her out and locked her in a trunk. Besides, I think that Alice is a bit crazy herself. Maybe she and Mother could be locked up together. It sounds like a bad plan." Reuben side-eyed Justin and shook his head.

"Maybe. Maybe not. I asked Alice the same question. Alice said that Marnie won't be able to help herself. She said that Marnie lives for fixing things. Besides, you and I both know how mean your mother was to Alice. From what Alice tells me, she's scared of Grace. I think that Alice is a bit of a kook, but crazy? Hmm… I don't know. She knew enough to feed you, didn't she? Remember that Marnie doesn't know that you stuck her in that trunk. What if you confess and apologize? Maybe she'd like that."

Reuben scratched behind his ear and considered what Justin was suggesting. "Look, you get Marnie to agree to meet with us, and I'll be there. I think that we tell her about the database that we've got. That might make a better case for us. We feed her some info for her cop friends, she makes nice and helps us. That database should be worth something. I'll bet that my mother is blackmailing the people from the events."

Justin stuck out his bottom lip and shook his head in doubt. "Nah. She's got the thumb drive, but she doesn't have a computer. How would she access it?"

Reuben huffed. "She's very resourceful, Justin. Mother's got everyone in The Collective working for her, and she's got Kate Parish hangin' around for some reason. Any of them could and would help her. Yeah. She's got a plan, and she's making money off those people. You know it. She'd do anything for money. Anything!"

~~~~~~~~~~~~~~~~~~~~~~~

Marnie bounded down the stairs, wearing warm jogging pants and an oversize sweatshirt, her blonde hair running sleekly through the back of a baseball cap. Tater was on her heels and ran into her when she stopped abruptly at the bottom of the stairs. They clattered to a halt just as Tom arrived.

"Hey, Tom! You're here early." Marnie greeted him cheerfully.

Tom pulled his jacket off and threw it on the couch. "Yeah. I couldn't sleep. I went to the station around 5:30 and found out that Captain Sterling is in the hospital. He's in an induced coma. Fell down the stairs at home. It's bad. Where's Danny? Beau has tried to call him a few times."

Marnie turned toward the stairs and shrugged. "I think that he's in the shower. I was just heading out for a run with Tater, but I'll wait. Want coffee?" Marnie asked.

Tom nodded and followed Marnie into the kitchen. Tom dropped onto a barstool and leaned his elbows on the counter. Marnie poured him a cup of coffee and switched the kettle on to make herself a cup of tea.

"Where's Hannah?" Tom asked.

"She's in Danny's office." Marnie nodded toward the closed office door.

Tom took a sip of his coffee. "How's she doin'? Are you two gettin' along?"

Marnie poured water into a teapot and nodded. "Yeah. After the first night, she's been fine. I actually like her. She can be bristly, but can't we all."

Danny came into the kitchen dressed in jeans and a red Henley, and he carried a worn black leather jacket in his hand. "Hey, Tommy! What are you doing here so early?"

"Captain Sterling had an accident. Beau has been tryin' to reach you. Why haven't you answered your phone?" Tom responded, unusually snappy.

"Hey! I was in the shower, and before that, I was shoveling. Before that... Oh, wait! I don't have to explain myself to you," Danny sniped back. He poured himself a cup of coffee and glared at Tom.

Tom put a hand up. "Sorry. I'm sorry. I didn't sleep last night. I keep running through the cases in my mind. I think that there are connections with William, Alice and Allen. There's somethin' nagging at me, and I can't put my finger on it. Now this with the captain? Remember when I told you that there was something rotten in the state of Denmark? Yeah. That feeling is still there. Nagging and niggling at me every second of every day!"

Danny nodded in agreement. "Yeah. I've been trying to piece it all together, too." He took a long drink of his coffee and pulled his phone out of his pocket. He didn't have a missed called from the station. "Are you sure that Beau tried to call me? I don't have any missed calls from the station, only one from a private number." Danny hit both play and speaker on the message.

"Hello, sister dear! Where's my book? I've been waiting patiently. You hang up on me; you won't take my calls. I'm beginning to think that you don't love me. That makes me so sad. Boo hoo! Why don't you just swing by to visit me and bring me my book? I have something important to tell you about your friend Kate Parish."

Marnie frowned, pulled a phone out of her pocket and checked the screen. "Danny, I think that you've got my phone. Do you have the same security code as me? Mine is 1109." She handed the phone that she was holding to Danny.

Danny took the phone and scowled. "Your code is 1109? Same as mine." Danny shot her a strange and confused look. "Anyway... How the hell is he still calling you? I've called the prison and asked that his phone usage be monitored. I told them that he wasn't to call you again. Ever!"

"He called when we were driving up last night, too. I have a note to call the prison today to make the same request," Tom added. "Why do you two have the same code for your phones? What's 1109? The date you met or something? Pfft." Tom rolled his eyes.

Marnie stared into her cup of tea and smiled, not wanting to make eye contact with Tom.

Danny raised an eyebrow in Tom's direction. "Can we move on? Can you call the prison now while I call Beau?"

Tom shrugged, pulled his phone out of his pocket and disappeared into the living room. Danny called Sergeant Beaumont at the station.

"Sarge, it's Danny Gregg. What's happening?"

"When can you get to the station?"

"Uh, I can be there in about 20 minutes – tops. Any word on Cap?"

"No change. He's in an induced coma. The fall caused internal injuries, contusions, a compound fracture of the ulna, a fracture of the femur and head and neck trauma. I'm reading this off the report," Sergeant Beaumont said.

"He was alone when this happened? Our guy doing the welfare check was the discovery?" Danny asked.

"Yeah. Jalnack and Garcia went over at the end of their shifts. Jalnack broke down the door when he saw Cap on the floor through the window," Sergeant Beaumont replied.

"Has Rick gone over with a team?" Danny inquired.

"No. Why?" Sergeant Beaumont asked.

Danny ran his fingers through his hair and considered the possibilities. "Call it a hunch. I want everything bagged and tagged. Anything in the garbage, his medication. I want blood samples. Beau, I don't think that this was accident. Something has been eating at me and Tom for a couple of days. Cap has been distracted, and he's disappeared from the precinct a lot over the last few weeks. Maybe he was in meetings. Maybe not. I think that we need to check out everything. Who's at the hospital with him? Any one on his room?"

"Someone on his room? What? Like guarding his room?" Sergeant Beaumont asked.

"Beau, I think that Cap was on to something. You know, he hears a lot of the whispers that we don't hear because of the circles he moves in. He has calls with agencies that we don't know about. I want a 24-hour protection detail organized starting now."

"Agencies? Danny, what are you talking about?"

"We've got DEA officers roaming around Creekwood at the moment. We've got a dead agent in the morgue. My sister is DEA. She's here trying to figure what happened to her pal. Something's going on that we don't know about," Danny warned. "Look, Beau, Tommy and I are trying our best to piece this together. Can you please get Rick and his team over to Cap's house, and can you please organize protection for Cap? I think that it's bigger than we know."

"Yeah. Sure, Danny. I'll get onto it. Anything you need, let me know. By the way, you're the officer in charge of the precinct with Captain Sterling incapacitated. You might want to dust off the uniform, Lieutenant," Sergeant Beaumont said. Danny could imagine Beau's weak grin.

"Thanks, Beau, but I'm not putting on my uniform. Cap will be back in no time, and we've got a lot of work to do out on the street. Roll call and briefings as per usual. Tommy and I are heading out of here. We've got things to follow up. If you or anyone else needs me, call." Danny signed off.

Danny turned around to ask Marnie about the tree delivery, but she was gone. He went through to the living room. Tom was just finishing up his call.

"Where's Marnie?" Danny asked.

Tom pointed to the door. "She and Tater left a few minutes ago. They've gone out for a run. It's barely light. They won't be long."

Danny glanced at the clock on the mantle. It was 7:05 AM. The tree would arrive in about 2 hours. He hated leaving before Marnie returned, but he didn't have a choice.

Marnie and Tater burst through the door just a few minutes later. Marnie's cheeks were bright red, and Tater was smiling. "Oh, my God, it's cold out there! That wind cuts right through you. I should've dressed warmer." Marnie shivered and sat down to pull off her running boots and to catch her breath.

"Marn, we've got to head out. You're okay to deal with the tree delivery?" Danny asked.

Marnie nodded. "Yeah. Carl should be here soon. If I need help moving anything, I'm sure that he will help me. How's Captain Sterling?"

"Not good. I'll tell you about it later." Danny pulled on his jacket, grabbed his keys off the table and put his phone in the inside breast pocket of his jacket. He dropped a kiss on the top of Marnie's head on his way out the door.

"See ya later, Marn," Tom said as he zipped his jacket and pulled his gloves and keys out of his pocket. "We'll check in later." He jokingly tried to kiss Marnie on the top of her head, but she brushed him away.

"Ass!" Marnie giggled.

Tom tapped her on the arm with his gloves. "Be safe, kiddo. Call if you need anything."

"You, too!" Marnie called out.

~~~~~~~~~~~~~~~~~~~~~~~

Hannah was at the counter drinking coffee and doodling in a steno pad when Marnie returned downstairs after changing from her short run. Hannah glanced up and went back to doodling.

"Are you heading out to the morgue soon?" Marnie asked.

Hannah nodded. "Yes. Dr. Markson is expecting me at 10:00. I thought that I would stop at the diner to see Grandmother first." Hannah shrugged. "A bit of moral support couldn't hurt." She managed a weak smile.

256

Marnie squeezed Hannah's shoulder gently as she walked past. "Are you sure that you don't want me to go with you? I can change my plans with Carl. I'm sure that he would wait for the tree, or I can call Mr. Gleeson and ask him to leave it on the porch."

"No. I need to see William on my own. I would like a distraction later, though. Maybe I can help you with the party and shopping."

"Sure. That would be great," Marnie replied. "Call me when you're ready, and we can plan from there. I'm heading to town after the tree is delivered."

Hannah nodded.

~~~~~~~~~~~~~~~~~~~~~~~~

Carl knocked on the cabin door at precisely 8:00 AM. Marnie pulled open the door, and Tater ran to greet Carl.

"Good morning! I come bearing donuts!" Carl said cheerfully, handing a box of donuts to Marnie. "For Tater… let me see what's in my pocket. It's a chicken treat!" Carl knelt, patted Tater's head and handed him a treat. Tater took his treat and settled in under the pool table.

"You want coffee?" Marnie asked.

"Oh, yes, please!" Carl followed Marnie into the kitchen. "Was that Hannah who flew by me in the driveway?"

Marnie nodded and poured coffee. "Yes, she's off to town. Do you want to sit here or in the living room?"

Tater trotted into the kitchen with a tennis ball in his mouth. He dropped it at Marnie's feet and waited for her to toss it.

"Here is good. Now, catch me up on Danny's accident." Carl rested his elbows on the counter.

Marnie filled Carl in on the events of the previous day, tossing the ball to Tater throughout the conversation. They chatted about clients; Marnie tossed the ball. They discussed the upcoming tree trimming party the following night; Tater brought back the ball. They chitchatted their way through current events; Marnie tossed the ball, and Tater brought it back.

"Mr. Gleeson should be here soon with the tree. Want to help me move a few things around in the living room?" Marnie asked, glancing down at her watch. Tater dropped the ball at her feet. Marnie tossed the ball to Tater.

"Sure. Did you get a big tree? Danny's got the perfect home for it." Carl followed Marnie into the living room.

Tater dropped the ball at Marnie's feet. Marnie tossed it back.

"Wait until you see it. It's gorgeous!" Marnie beamed.

Tater dropped the ball at Marnie's feet. Marnie picked up the ball and put it on the edge of the mantle. Tater stared. "Tater, settle. We'll play ball later."

Tater ran upstairs and came down a few minutes later with Danny's slipper. He ran under the pool table and used Danny's slipper as a pillow.

Carl laughed. "He's settling in nicely, isn't he?"

Carl and Marnie moved a sofa table to the other side of the living room. They moved the couch a few inches closer to the coffee table, the coffee table a few inches closer to the club chairs and the club chairs just a few inches back toward the kitchen door.

"That still looks somewhat centered, doesn't it?" Marnie stood back and assessed the rearrangement.

"Yeah. I think that it looks good." Carl nodded.

Tater let out a small, soft woof. Marnie and Carl turned to the windows and heard the truck on the gravel driveway. They both stepped out onto the porch. Mr. Gleeson and his son wrangled the tree into the house, put it in the stand and gave Marnie instructions on feeding and watering the tree. When they left, Carl and Marnie stood back and admired the tree that overwhelmed the corner of the living room. Tater sniffed around the tree and curled up underneath the branches.

"That's some tree, Marnie." Carl looked up at the huge balsam and smiled.

"Do you think that it's too big?" Marnie asked, tipping her head to the side.

"C'mon, Marnie. I ask you… Can a Christmas tree ever be too big?" Carl glanced down at Marnie and then back up at the tree.

"Hmm… I suppose not." Marnie stepped back a bit further and smiled. "I think that it's perfect!"

"There you go!" Carl glanced down at his watch. "Hey, I gotta go. I've got appointments. I'll see you tomorrow night."

-CHAPTER FORTY-NINE-

The long driveway from Danny's cabin to Lake Road was a bit messy. Marnie concentrated on the road and was careful not to catch her tires on the shoulder. Tater sat in the passenger seat snapping at the trees they drove past on the side of the road. Marnie's phone rang, and she looked to see who was calling. The screen lit up "Erin."

"Hi, Erin!"

"Hi, Marnie. Hey, I just thought that I would offer my services tonight if you need help gettin' ready for the party. I've got the night off and nothin' to do," Erin offered.

Marnie thought about it for a second. "Ah. Well, help is always appreciated. We've got a few dips to make, and I wanted to bake a few batches of cookies. Danny's got a cleaner coming in tomorrow morning, so that's one thing that we don't have to worry about. I'm really trying to keep it simple. Finger foods, a big charcuterie board, dips, veggies, maybe some chicken wings. We can drink wine and make food. That's always a nice evening. Sorry, Erin. I'm rambling." Marnie laughed.

"Bless your heart! You've got so much happenin'. How are you doin' with the toys and the parade? Anythin' I could do to help?" Erin asked.

"I will keep you posted on that kind offer. I'm heading into town right now to finish shopping for the kids. The parade float is under construction. Danny and Tom have recruited some of their friends to build it. We've got wrapping to do – a lot of wrapping. Do you like to wrap presents?" Marnie asked hopefully.

"I'd be happy to give you a hand," Erin agreed.

Marnie did a little fist bump. She had a volunteer to help wrap. "Perfect! Okay, so how about we say 6:00 tonight at the cabin. We're having Chinese buffet here for dinner. Danny is picking it up on the way home so that we aren't cooking dinner, too. Does that sound good?"

"See you at 6:00! Buh-bye!"

Marnie switched the radio station to Christmas music. Bing Crosby was singing "The Little Drummer Boy," and Marnie sang along. Tater started to howl, so Marnie stopped singing. "My singing isn't that bad! Geez, Tater!" Marnie's phone rang again. She didn't recognize the number, but she knew that it was local. She turned down Bing.

"Hello!"

"Uh… hello! Marnie, it's Alice – Alice Wells. I'm sorry to bother you and would understand if you hung up on me…"

"Hi, Alice. I hope that you're feeling better. What can I help you with, Alice?" Marnie replied stiffly.

"Marnie, I… uh… I have some information about Grace Wilmot. I thought that maybe you could help me figure out what to do about it. I want to talk to you before calling Detective Gregg. To be honest, I feel a bit uncomfortable asking you for help, Marnie. It's just that… well, I think that working together may be our best chance to get rid of Grace." Marnie heard a loud sigh from Alice.

"Alice, if this is a game… if this is a trick, I want no part of it. I've had enough…"

"Marnie, I swear that this isn't a game. I promise that this isn't a trick. I really do need your help. I'm terrified that she is going to hurt someone else," Alice replied tearfully.

Marnie could hear the sincerity in Alice's voice and thought, *what harm could it do to just listen to the old loon?* "Fine. I can be there in about 40 minutes. I have to drop off Tater at his vet's office and pick up some dry cleaning."

"Is Tater sick? I hope that he isn't sick."

"No, Tater is fine. Just spending some time at doggy day care so that I can get my shopping done."

"Well, that's good. I'll see you in about 40 minutes then. Bye," Alice said and was gone. Alice turned to Reuben and Justin at the end of the call and gestured a thumb up.

Marnie stared at her phone for just a second, waiting for it to ring one more time. She knew that it was going to – she sensed it. It did.

"Hello!"

"It's P-P-Patrick returning your call."

"Hi, Patrick. We're having a tree trimming party tomorrow night at Detective Gregg's cabin. Just calling to see if you would like to join us. Carl offered to pick you up and take you home – that is, if you'd like to come."

"Tree t-t-trimming? Y-Y-You're inviting me?" Patrick asked.

"Yes, of course, Patrick. We would love to see you, and I owe you a huge thanks for all of your help at Station Hall. Will you please come tomorrow night?"

"Y-Y-Yes, thank you for inviting me," Patrick replied.

"Great! I'll have Carl pick you up on his way over. He'll call and let you know what time. See you tomorrow night." Marnie clicked off before Patrick could change his mind. She grinned ear to ear. She really wanted Patrick to meet some nice people – people who would properly welcome him to Creekwood.

"Tater, your friend Patrick is coming tomorrow night."

Tater smiled and wagged his tail in reply.

~~~~~~~~~~~~~~~~~~~~~~~

Marnie dropped off Tater at Ellie's, picked up her dry cleaning and then drove to Alice's house. She sat outside in the driveway and looked up at the foreboding mansion. She'd been here many times over the years, but she never felt comfortable. It had dark energy. She shivered as she went up the walk – not because she was cold, but because she dreaded the feeling that she always got as soon as she crossed the threshold.

Marnie rang the doorbell, and Alice greeted her warmly. "Marnie, I can't tell you how much that I appreciate you coming. You could have said no, and I am so grateful that you didn't. Come in," Alice said, stepping back to allow Marnie to cross the threshold.

Marnie stopped and stood just inside the door. She glanced around. "Hmm… something has changed. What have you done, Alice? I don't mean to be rude, but the energy is much lighter in here."

"I dumped all of Grace's things onto a trailer and asked Reuben and Justin to take them away. I took back my home. Everyone from The Collective is gone, and I've taken back my house." Alice smiled proudly.

Marnie sniffed the air. "You've smudged the house, too. Wow! It makes such a difference."

Alice beamed with joy. "Yes, I did, and that completes a long and toxic cycle."

"Okay, Alice, what can I help you with? I've got a full schedule, so if we could get to it, that would be great."

"Of course. Would you like a cup of tea or coffee?" Alice offered.

Marnie sighed deeply. "Uh. Okay. Tea would be lovely."

Alice nodded brightly and walked down the hall to her kitchen. Marnie followed. Marnie couldn't get over the change in the house. It was bright and airy, and everything felt… happy. Was happy the word? Hmm… happy was the word.

Reuben and Justin were both in the kitchen when Marnie walked through the door. She stopped and frowned.

"What are you two doing here?" Marnie demanded.

"We're here to help Alice. My mother has hurt a lot of people, including me. It's time. It's time that she was stopped," Reuben proclaimed. He stood at the table, hands on the back of a chair with a look of determination on his face.

Marnie turned to Justin. "And you?"

"Grace has been blackmailing me, and I want it to stop. She's lost her mind, Ms. Reilly. She's crazy!" Justin commented, eyes bulging in what looked like fear.

"Please, Marnie, sit and have tea with us. I promise – not that my word is worth much – that this isn't a trick or a trap. It is, quite honestly, three people who want to escape Grace Wilmot forever," Alice pleaded.

Marnie nodded, pulled a chair out and sat. Alice put a pot of tea; cups and saucers; cream; and sugar in the middle of the table. She poured cups of coffee for Reuben and Justin and poured tea for herself and Marnie.

"Oh! Wait. I made these for you this morning!" Alice said excitedly. She turned to the counter, picked up a plate and set it near the teapot.

Marnie looked at the plate and then up at Alice. "Is that lavender shortbread?"

Alice nodded. "I know that it's your favorite."

"Well, thank you for remembering." Marnie stared at the shortbread, wondering with what Alice may have laced it.

Alice picked up a shortbread and took a bite. "I promise that it isn't poisoned."

Marnie laughed, picked up a cookie, took a bite and set the rest on the edge of her saucer.

Over the next hour, Alice explained everything that Grace had done to her over many years. She told Marnie that Grace had stolen most of the money from all of the events that they had held. Grace's name was on The Collective's account. They had never been able to remove her name because Grace was one of the original account holders.

Reuben gave her the short version of his childhood, highlighted Alice's kindness and filled her in on what Grace was currently up to in a rambling of revelations.

"Ms. Reilly, she has money stockpiled somewhere. I do know that she's working part time at Enlighten Crystals, and I think that she's got some ring running. I don't know. I'm not sure what she's involved in, but I've seen her with Kate Parish a few times, and I know what she did to you and Ken Wilder.

My mother blackmails people, too. I know that she's had Allen helping her with things that he didn't want to do. I don't know the full story, but she knows something about him that he doesn't want other people to know. As for Mrs. Wheeler over at the pawn shop... My mother knows somehow that Mrs. Wheeler assisted with her husband's death. I remember my mother saying assisted suicide. I don't know how many other people she's doing that to, but she's been doing it for years. Maybe she gets information when she's reading for them. Maybe they confess, or maybe she really is psychic and sees it. I don't know."

Reuben took a deep breath. "Ms. Reilly, I want to apologize for something. I'm the person who hit you and shoved you into that trunk at Station Hall. I was scared. I... I... am so sorry. I honestly don't have any other excuse. If you want to tell Detective Gregg, I understand." Reuben's face was flushed, and sweat glistened on his upper lip and forehead. His fists were clenched so tightly that his knuckles were white. He hung his head and looked down at the table.

Marnie slunk back in her chair like the wind had been knocked out of her. She sat quietly for a moment, studying the contents of her teacup. She turned to Reuben, her aquamarine eyes blazing with anger. "You know, this could be much worse than it is, Reuben. Did you know that I died that night? Did you know that I suffocated that night? If not for Patrick and Danny – Detective Gregg - I wouldn't be sitting here right now. They would have caught you, Reuben. They would have figured out who put me in that trunk, and you would be facing murder charges." Marnie clenched her jaw tightly and held Reuben's gaze. "Look at me, you little toad!" Marnie hissed, furious that he would not meet her gaze.

Marnie heard a strange groan, and Reuben Wilmot couldn't take it anymore. He lay his head on the table and burst into tears. Alice patted his back gently.

"Reuben, you need to tell Detective Gregg what happened. I think that, if you do, it will help you start a new chapter. I think that you need to speak to him, dear," Alice cooed.

Reuben picked up his head. "I'll go to jail. I'll get locked up for attempted murder – probably assault, too. I'm so sorry, Ms. Reilly. I am so very sorry." Reuben stood and went into the bathroom. When he came out, he had a box of tissues under his arm, and he was blowing his nose.

Reuben took a thumb drive out of his pocket and handed it to Marnie. "Ms. Reilly, this has information for every person who has attended one of our events for the past several years and also our financial records. Justin has been collecting information for quite some time. We think that Grace may be blackmailing some of these people. We think that it's where she gets some of her money."

"Thank you. I'll give this to the detectives. We'll call it a sign of good faith." Marnie glanced down at the thumb drive, the she picked it up and shoved it into the pocket of her jeans.

"Oh, dear. Marnie, can I freshen up your tea?" Alice asked.

Marnie nodded and turned to Justin. "Did you know that Reuben had locked me in the trunk?"

Justin nodded meekly.

Marnie rolled her eyes. "Why would the two of you do that? What have I honestly, *honestly*, done to you? Over the years, I have tried to keep you honest. I have most certainly butted in because I didn't want innocent people to be harmed. If you want to be pissed at me for caring about people, then fuck off! I am so sick and tired of The Collective hurting people. People come to you for help, and what do you all do? You sell them hope. You sell them a whole lot of bullshit that will cause them further damage in the long run! Why would you do that?"

"You took away our livelihood – a livelihood that we needed to keep Grace happy. She was pulling the strings from Pennsylvania, Houston, Vermont and everywhere else where she relocated over the years. Any time that we made legit money, she stole it out of the account, and she came back here and started blackmailing everyone, including me!" Justin shouted.

"Why didn't you just open a new account?!" Marnie shouted.

"We did. She had Reuben hack into it and link the new account with the old account. We even tried a different bank. She just kept finding the money and stealing it. You don't get away from Grace Wilmot! You don't!" Justin replied. "She's blackmailing me, Ms. Reilly. I'll tell you what I told Reuben and Alice. I gave someone information about a guy who I saw rummaging in a dumpster in the alley behind the drugstore. I gave Mr. Drake a description of the guy and talked about where the guy lived because I followed him. Someone had to overhear the conversation because this guy turns up dead. I saw Detective Gregg with his buddy near the tracks just a few days ago. I told Grace, and now, she's blackmailing me – telling me that she's going to the cops because I ratted out the guy and he got killed. With my past, Ms. Reilly, I'm as good as convicted."

Marnie studied Justin closely. "Did you kill this man?"

Justin pushed back from the table hard. His eyes bugged out, and he shook his head tightly. "No! No, I didn't kill him. I would never kill anybody!"

"Then stop acting like you did," Marnie said sternly.

Justin hung his head and nodded meekly.

Marnie turned to Alice. "I'm guessing that you told Detectives Gregg and Keller much of this?"

Alice nodded. "Well, yes. I did tell them about Grace. They don't know what the boys just told you." Alice glanced between Reuben and Justin sympathetically.

Marnie stared at Reuben for a few moments and then Justin. "Okay. I'm going to speak to the detectives, and I am going to encourage them to speak to you. Come clean, guys. Tell them everything that you know. Don't hold back because they will know if you're lying."

Justin gulped. "Ms. Reilly, um… I did something really stupid. That night at Station Hall, I may have put on a police uniform and may have blended in so that I wouldn't get caught trying to leave the building. I spoke with the detectives, Carl and Patrick showed up and I had to get out of there. They would have recognized me, so I took off. I was scared."

"Well, that was stupid!" Marnie snapped. "This just gets deeper and deeper!"

~~~~~~~~~~~~~~~~~~~~~~~~

Danny and Tom walked the railroad tracks to the tunnel. They shone a light into the tunnel and took a step inside.

Tom scoped it out, took a few steps and stopped. He looked up at the ceiling and stepped back into the sunlight. "I don't think that this is safe, Danny. It looks like it could collapse at any minute."

Danny agreed. "Yeah. I don't think that it's going to collapse today, though. Let's keep going. I know that I saw someone in here the day that we found William. The message that Kate left for Marnie said that she saw Grace Wilmot down here."

Tom scoffed. "Do you really think that Kate Parish is going to tell the truth or do anything that would help Marnie? Kate told Marnie that tidbit to see if she could lure Marnie down here. She wasn't banking on Marnie sharing the information with us."

"You're probably right, but I think that this is worth a look. You saw someone down here, too. Maybe we should've checked it out that day." Danny stepped forward into the tunnel. He moved the flashlight beam carefully over the bricks, searching for any irregularities in the masonry. Tom did the same on the other side of the tracks.

"Danny, look at this! These bricks look like they've been moved. The mortar is loose." Tom leaned close to the bricks to examine them. He pulled one of the bricks, and it gave just bit. He pulled his keys out of his pocket and pried the brick, loosening it a bit more.

Danny stood over his shoulder and handed him a Leatherman. Tom rolled his eyes. "Thanks, Eagle Scout." Tom wedged in the knife, pushed down and pulled out. The top brick gave. Tom grasped it with his fingertips and pulled hard. The brick was free from the wall. He grasped the bottom brick, and it released easily.

Danny shone his light into the gap and whistled. "What have we here?" He put on a glove, reached into the hole and pulled out a black satchel. Inside were twelve vials and about a dozen syringes. Danny shone his light on the vials and glanced up at Tom. "Morphine, fentanyl and midazolam. Four of each."

Tom glanced up and down the tracks. "We've got somebody's stash. Do you suppose that Grace Wilmot stashed that here?"

Danny thought about what Alice and Marnie had told him about Grace. "I don't think so, but what the hell do I know. She could have returned to Creekwood for the express purpose of dealing drugs. What connections does she really have here in Creekwood anymore? We'll need to dig into that. Let's keep going. Let's check the rest of the tunnel."

Alice saw Reuben and Justin to the door and came back to the kitchen. Marnie was standing at the sink, looking out the window into Alice's backyard. It was overgrown with dead vines, the bird bath was tipped over and broken, the lawn furniture was dilapidated and the patio was crumbling. It hadn't been this way years ago. It had actually been a peaceful setting for meditating and parties. She gazed over at Alice.

Alice stood in the doorway. Sadness overwhelmed her once again. Her backyard had once been a point of pride for her. Her flower garden had won awards. The Collective had enveloped her and her home, and she had lost sight of what had once been important to her. Her house needed paint, her kitchen required updating and the plumbing was in need of repair. Every penny that The Collective made was either siphoned away by Grace or spent on frivolities. She hung her head.

"Marnie, I'm going to tidy up the garden in the spring, and I'm going to find a job – an honest job. I'd like to go back to the library, but I doubt that they would have me. Maybe I can find a nice boarder or two for extra money. The house is certainly big enough." Alice's eyes glistened with tears, and her bottom lip trembled.

Marnie turned around and saw what she always saw when she looked at people. She saw potential. She saw the person whom Alice could be. Maybe Alice just needed someone to believe in her. Maybe that's all that it would take. Marnie ran the thought through her mind several times.

"I'm probably going to regret this, but I have a job for you. I have a mountain of Christmas presents that need to be wrapped for Toys for Tots. I have deliveries that will need to be made and cookies that need to be baked for the Christmas fair. Do you think that you can help me with that, Alice?" Marnie asked.

Alice's face lit up. She clapped her hands together, skipped across the kitchen and wrapped her arms around Marnie. Marnie stared up at the ceiling and removed herself from Alice's grasp.

"Now, look. We aren't hugging friends quite yet, Alice. If you can help me, you don't let me down and you don't get into trouble, we can work on that. If you do anything to muck this up, we're through. You understand?"

"I understand. Oh, Marnie! You have no idea how happy that this makes me. I'll work hard, and I won't let you down. I promise. I will not let you down!"

Marnie tried to hide her doubt. "Okay. I'm going shopping now. I'll drop back here with wrapping paper, ribbons, tape, tags and candy canes before I go home. I'll ask that the presents be delivered to you in batches so that it doesn't overwhelm you. Do you still have that huge dining room table?"

"Yes, I do. The dining room will be a perfect wrapping station. I'll run in there and get it cleaned up right away. I'll have everything ready for when you come back."

Marnie glanced around the kitchen and frowned. "Alice, do you have food? Have you been shopping for groceries?"

Alice shrugged. "Grace took the last of the money from the account while I was in the hospital. I was able to transfer a small amount before the event started, but not much. I wanted to make sure that she didn't steal it all."

Marnie nodded. "Okay. I'm going to pick up some groceries for you while

I'm out. I'm only getting basics, but it will give you enough for a few days until you can get to the grocery store. You obviously have an account separate from The Collective's account."

Alice nodded.

"Good," Marnie replied. She took her wallet out of her bag, counted out several twenties and handed them to Alice.

Alice stared at Marnie's outstretched hand and shook her head. "I can't take that, Marnie."

"Yes, you can. It's an advance on your pay." Marnie pushed the bills at Alice. "Please, Alice, take it. You need to eat, and you need to take care of yourself."

Alice's face reddened, and she reluctantly took the money. "Thank you, Marnie. I... I..."

Marnie waved her hand. "Don't mention it. There was a time when you were kind to me. I never forget kindness."

~~~~~~~~~~~~~~~~~~~~~~~~

Marnie pulled away from Alice's house and took a detour. She wasn't going to go snooping in unsafe territory, but she was going to take a drive down to the tracks to see if she could spot Grace Wilmot or Kate Parish rambling around.

As she turned the corner onto Railway Street, she saw Danny's Jeep and Tom's truck parked at the curb. "Shit!" She slammed her hand on the steering wheel, did a quick U-turn and headed in the opposite direction. She glanced in her rearview mirror several times to ensure that they hadn't seen her. She really wasn't doing anything wrong, but she just didn't want them to know that she was scoping out the other side of the tracks. She didn't need a lecture from either of them.

~~~~~~~~~~~~~~~~~~~~~~~~

Marnie parked her car between the grocery store and the department store. She dropped her bag into the seat of the shopping cart, dug out her list and then put her bag over her shoulder. She surveyed the department store and spotted the Christmas section with ease. It was in the back-left corner where all of the people were milling about. She took a deep breath and pushed her cart forward.

Marnie heard Mrs. Drake before she saw her. She couldn't escape.

"Hello, Marnie. How lovely to see you!"

"Hi, Mrs. Drake. How are you?" Marnie asked politely.

"My husband mentioned that you were in a few days ago to pick up a prescription for your friend. Detective Gregg, isn't it?" Mrs. Drake fussed over and rearranged items in her cart, then she looked at and appraised Marnie over the top of her glasses.

"I think that everyone in town knows that I'm staying with Detective Gregg through the holidays, Mrs. Drake." Marnie rested her foot on the undercarriage of her cart, tipped her head and slouched slightly.

"Oh, dear, Marnie, I wasn't implying anything. Frank just mentioned that he'd seen you and that you had a bruise on your head. I was going to call to see how you are, but I don't have your number."

"Thanks for your concern. I'm fine. I hope that you and Mr. Drake have a merry Christmas, Mrs. Drake. I have a busy day ahead, and I don't have time to confirm gossip. Have a great day!" Marnie said, waving dramatically. She heard Mrs. Drake's sudden gasp, but she quickly pushed her cart in the opposite direction. She hated being rude, but she was quite tired of the Creekwood rumor mill using her life as fodder.

Marnie saw several people whom she knew while pushing her cart to the back of the store. She smiled graciously, wished a number of town folks "Happy holidays!" and then continued without stopping. She loaded her cart with brown paper, tissue paper, ribbon, tape, tags shaped like mittens, snowmen and stockings. Her next stop was the candy aisle where she picked out candy canes, chocolate bells and a box of ribbon candy for herself. She checked out of the department store, packed her car and did a quick trip into the grocery store for Alice.

Her phone rang as she stood in the checkout line. She pulled it out of her bag and checked the screen. It was Hannah.

"Hi, Hannah. I'm just going through checkout. Do you want to go back to the cabin and have some lunch?"

"How about the diner?" Hannah suggested.

"Yeah, sure. I've got to drop off a few things first, then I'll meet you there. I won't be long," Marnie said.

"See you soon," replied Hannah.

Marnie drove to Alice's house. She gathered one load of bags and rang the doorbell. Alice greeted her at the door. Her face was pink, and her smile was wide.

"Come on in! I've been organizing the dining room into a wrapping station."

Marnie followed Alice into the dining room and set the bags in the corner of the room. Marnie remembered this room. It was huge, and the table was perfect for wrapping a truckload of toys.

"I've got two more loads in the car. I'll be right back!" Marnie turned and headed back to the door.

"Let me help." Alice followed Marnie out of the room.

They hauled in the remaining bags, and Marnie separated out the groceries. "Alice, you may want to get some of this stuff into the fridge. I've got to head out. I'm meeting a friend for lunch. Will you be okay?"

"Yes, I'll be okay." Alice nodded.

Marnie noticed that Alice seemed sad – forlorn. "I'll pop over tomorrow morning around 10:00, if that's okay. I've got some of the toys at my office, and I can pick them up and bring them over. We can figure how best to tag them with the names of the kiddos on the list. I was thinking that we could put each family's presents all together in one bag – a garbage bag, maybe. I don't know, but we can figure that out in the morning."

Alice cheered up a bit and nodded. Marnie felt horrible leaving her here all alone, but didn't know what to do.

"You know, Alice, I can call Carl. Maybe he'll bring a batch of toys over on his way home from work tonight. That would certainly make the load lighter for me tomorrow. Does that sound okay?"

"I would appreciate that. You know, Marnie, I think that I have yards of old sackcloth up in my attic. It's left over from Halloween many years ago. I've got a small sewing room, and I could make Santa sacks for the presents to go in. That would be a good project for me tonight."

Marnie nodded with enthusiasm. "Well, that certainly sounds better than garbage bags. That's a great idea, Alice, if you think that you have time."

"Of course. I'm going to get onto that now. Bags are easy to make. It's good to have a project." Alice beamed.

"Okay, I'll see you in the morning." Marnie waved and left.

Marnie called Carl once she started the car. She told him that Alice was going to wrap the presents and asked if he could drop off some of the packages on his way home. He wholeheartedly agreed that it would be a good project for Alice and also agreed to drop off the packages.

Marnie turned up the radio and listened to Christmas music on her way to the diner. When she arrived, she saw Danny's Jeep and Tom's truck parked at the curb. Hannah's rental was tucked in behind them.

Danny, Tom and Hannah were sitting at their favorite booth at the back of the diner. They didn't see Marnie arrive, and when she scooted into the booth next to Danny, Hannah and Tom both jumped.

Danny grinned at her and nudged her gently with his shoulder. "Fancy meeting you here, Ms. Reilly."

"Oh, you know. I thought that I'd give you losers a treat and sit with you today." Marnie giggled.

Gram's faithful waitress Dorie took their order. Marnie asked Hannah if there was anything that she could do; Hannah shook her head in response. Danny and Tom were tight-lipped about their visit to the railroad tracks. They did share that they were awaiting information on Captain Sterling, that they had no leads on William – but were working several angles – and that the lab tests on Alice's inhaler and Allen's patches were taking longer than expected.

Danny put his arm across the back of the booth behind Marnie. "What have you been up to today, Marnie?"

Marnie glanced up, gathered her thoughts and filled them in on her eventful morning. When she was finished and she saw the consternation on their faces, she tried to calm the situation.

"Danny? Tom? You need to hear the guys out. They've basically admitted that what they did was wrong and that they are both terrified of the consequences. Just meet with them. Hear what they have to say. Grace is a… a… puppet master! She's been pulling everyone's strings for years. Please, just talk to them."

Marnie shot a stern glance at Danny and then Tom. They weren't affected – both continued to fume. When calming them down with words didn't work, she remembered the thumb drive. She pulled it out of her pocket and slid it across the table.

"Here, this has all of records for The Collective for the past several years. Reuben gave it to me and asked me to pass it along to you. He and Justin believe that Grace Wilmot is most likely blackmailing a number of the people on the list, either for money or… or… um… deeds."

It didn't work. She watched their anger build like a thunderstorm. Danny clenched his jaw tightly, and his gaze turned steely. Tom curled his hands into fists and chewed on the insides of his cheeks.

Dorie brought their food before either exploded… or imploded. She set down the plates with a smile and said that she'd be right back with Marnie's side of fries and Tom's side of onion rings.

Tom scowled. "Deeds? What the hell does that mean?"

Marnie rolled her eyes. "It means that they think that Grace is getting people to do favors for her because she has damaging information on them."

"Give me a for instance." Danny growled and studied his sandwich, lifting the top slice of bread to examine the pastrami, pickle, mustard and cheese.

Dorie set French fries and onion rings on the table. Marnie waited for her to leave and tried to remember one of Reuben's examples. Marnie thought for a minute and snapped her fingers.

"Mrs. Wheeler over at the pawn shop. Reuben told me that Mrs. Wheeler assisted with her husband's death. He said that Grace called it an assisted suicide. There's some exchange of money or favors for what Grace knows."

Tom interjected, "Yeah. Well, Mr. Wheeler had terminal cancer. He suffered for a long time. I'd be surprised if Mrs. Wheeler hadn't helped him out of his misery. I'm not saying that it's legal. I am saying that it happens more often than we know."

Danny picked up one of Marnie's fries and pointed it as he spoke. "How would Grace Wilmot know that bit of information?"

Marnie reached for a French fry. She mimicked Danny as she spoke. "Reuben's thinking is that maybe she gets the details when she's reading for them. They either give her the information during a reading, or she really is psychic, which she's not. Trust me. She. Is. Not!" Marnie popped the fry into her mouth. "She gets them to spill their guts and blackmails them. She's no more a psychic than... than... I don't know. I can't come up with a good analogy."

"Than anyone is." Hannah scoffed. "There's no such thing. It's all just trickery and control."

Marnie stared at Hannah for a moment. Danny and Tom picked up their sandwiches and started eating.

Marnie picked up her sandwich. Before taking a bite, she tipped her head and glanced between Danny and Tom. "We're just gonna leave that comment hanging out there for a while." She took a bit of her sandwich and chewed, watching Danny and Tom for a reaction.

A confounded expression spread across Hannah's face. She looked at Marnie, Danny and Tom. "Have I missed something?"

Danny nodded. "I'll tell you later." He took another bite of his sandwich.

-CHAPTER FIFTY-

Marnie ran a few more errands, picked up Tater and arrived back at the cabin at 5:00. Hannah's car sat in the driveway, and the overhead garage door was open with the light on. She paused for just a moment, shrugged and then thought, *"Did I forget to close that this morning?"* She pushed her garage remote, but it didn't work. She shook it and tried again. She was certain that she had shut it when she left to go shopping. She put on Tater's lead, she got the few bags of shopping and dry cleaning from the back seat and she and Tater headed for the front door.

"Hey, Hannah! We're back!" Marnie called. "Did you open the garage door?"

Hannah appeared at the top of the stairs, towel-drying her hair. "The garage door? No. It was closed when I got back." Hannah thought for a moment. "I'm pretty sure that it was closed."

Marnie twisted her mouth to the side and turned to the door. "Ah, well, Danny will be here soon with dinner. I'm going to start a few things for tomorrow night. Do you want a glass of wine?"

"Yes, thanks. I'll be right down. I need to dry my hair. 10 minutes!" Hannah disappeared down the hall.

Marnie fed Tater, opened a bottle of wine and heard the crunch of tires in the driveway. She went out to help Danny with the Chinese food and the bags of ice that he promised to pick up for tomorrow night.

"Let me help!" Marnie called from the porch. She raced off the porch and turned the corner into the garage.

"Why was this open?" Danny asked, pointing to the door.

"It was open when I got home. I asked Hannah. She said that it was closed when she got here. I am pretty sure that I closed it this morning, but when I tried to close it a few minutes ago, my remote wouldn't work. I knew that you'd be right here, so I didn't worry."

"Huh." Danny searched his memory. "Anyway, let's put the ice in the freezer out here. I don't think that we have room in the cabin."

"Let me get it. You'll pop your stitches." Marnie grabbed two bags of ice from the back of the Jeep.

"Really, Marnie, I'm fine." Danny laughed and handed her two more bags of ice. He slammed the back door and retrieved the Chinese food from the back seat.

They stepped out into the driveway, and Danny pressed the remote fob on his keychain. The door didn't move. He tapped the remote and tried again. The door moved slightly.

"Shit! I'll bet that electrical issue has fucked up the door. We'll have to close it manually. Marnie, I'm going to need your help. If I reach up to get the rope, I *will* pop my stitches."

"Yeah, of course." Marnie nodded.

Danny set the food on the porch, and he and Marnie went back into the garage. Danny hit the release button to manual, and Marnie reached up and pulled down on the rope. It was a heavy door, and she braced herself to give the rope a good pull. She struggled a bit, but with the second pull, the door came crashing down.

Marnie's bloodcurdling scream echoed through the garage.

~~~~~~~~~~~~~~~~~~~~~~~~~

"Oh my God! Oh my God!" Marnie screamed. Justin Chambers's body had rolled off the door, onto the top of the Jeep and to the floor with a sickening thud at Marnie's feet. Justin's lifeless face stared up at her.

"Marnie, come here, come here." Danny gently took Marnie's arm and pulled her close. He glanced down at the body on the floor. He recognized him as the Officer Johnson from Station Hall. "Marnie, is that Justin?"

Marnie couldn't catch her breath. She couldn't speak. She just nodded and buried her face in Danny's jacket.

"C'mon. Let's get you out of here." Danny guided Marnie toward the side door of the garage, unlocked it to allow them to pass, locked it behind them and led her to the cabin.

Hannah was on the bottom step when they walked through the door. She took one look at Marnie and froze. "What's wrong?"

Danny glanced up and motioned Hannah to them. "Can you get Marnie a drink of water, wine, tea or whatever she wants? I've got a situation in the garage." He pulled his phone out of his pocket.

Hannah pulled a face. "A situation?"

Danny nodded. "A body." Danny turned and stomped out of the cabin and off the porch, phone to his ear.

"Marnie? What happened?" Hannah crossed the living room, took Marnie's arm and led her to the kitchen.

Marnie sat on a barstool and turned to Hannah. "Justin Chambers is dead. He's been killed. Someone put him on top of the garage door, and when I closed it, he fell off the door onto the garage floor. Hannah, I saw him this morning. He... he... I don't know. I don't know what to say." A wave of nausea hit, and Marnie raced to the bathroom. She closed the door, splashed cold water on her face and stared at herself in the mirror. "What the hell is going on? Mom! Dad! Give me something! Talk to me!"

~~~~~~~~~~~~~~~~~~~~

At the same time that Justin rolled from the garage door onto the floor of Danny's garage, Carl Parkins was on the phone with Alice Wells making plans to drop off Christmas presents.

"Okay, Alice, I'll be there in about 15 minutes. I'm just packing the car now."

Carl heard a crash in the background. "Alice, what was that?"

"I don't know. It sounded like it came from the kitchen," Alice replied. "It sounds like someone broke the glass out of the back door. Oh!" There was a muffled scurrying in Carl's ear, then he heard Alice whisper, "Someone is in my house!"

"Alice! Alice!" Carl shouted.

"Shush... Someone is in the kitchen. I'm hiding under my dining room table. Please call the police, Carl. I need to hide."

Carl stared at his phone for a second and called the police. He tossed the remaining bags into his car and sped to Alice's house.

~~~~~~~~~~~~~~~~~~~~

Alice reached up and searched for a pair of pinking shears that she'd placed on the dining room table earlier. She grasped the handle, pulled her hand under the table and crawled to the back wall of the dining room near her china cabinet. She set her phone and the shears on the floor, and with her palms flat, she pushed a section of wainscoting. A hidden panel popped open. She clapped her hands quietly, put her phone in her dressing pocket, grabbed the pinking shears and crawled inside. She pulled the panel back into place and quietly climbed a narrow set of stairs to the third floor turret room. She could hear someone running up the stairs and doors being thrown open on the second floor. She heard feet shuffling down the hallway below her. Alice crawled under her bed and removed a revolver that she had stashed inside her box spring. Rolling over onto her stomach, she belly-crawled to the foot of the bed. Alice cocked the revolver and waited.

~~~~~~~~~~~~~~~~~~~

Carl burst through Alice's front door. "Alice! Alice! It's Carl! I'm here!" He raced through the house, turning every light on as he went.

A patrol car screeched to a halt out front, and two officers ran up onto the veranda and into the front foyer.

"Hello! Creekwood PD!"

Carl ran back to the front foyer. "I'm Carl Parkins. I called you. I can't find Alice anywhere! I haven't checked upstairs – just down here."

"Sir, please wait on the porch."

Carl stepped outside and paced the veranda from one end to the other. He jumped at the sound of a gunshot and raced back to the door. The sound of running feet echoed through the house. A moment later, a figure dressed in black raced down the front stairs, slammed into Carl, shoved him off his feet and ran out onto the veranda. One police officer sprinted down the stairs and off the front steps. The second officer trailed not far behind, but stayed in the house. Another patrol car pulled up out front, and two officers joined the first officer in pursuit of the suspect.

"Sir, we told you to wait on the porch." She held out a hand and assisted Carl to his feet. "No sign of Alice Wells, but we did hear a shot. We think that she may be hiding. We didn't fire. It had to be her or the suspect. I'm Officer Chavez. My partner is Officer Owens. I'm not sure who joined the chase out there, but I think that they were Officers Tartello and Connor."

Carl held out his hand. "As I said before, I'm Carl Parkins, a friend of Alice Wells."

Officer Owens returned a few moments later – winded and scraped. "I chased that fucking ninja into the next block. He climbed over a chain link fence like it had stairs. We've got Tartello and Connor out there now. We'll have to search the area. I swear to God that I've never seen anyone so fast or nimble – right over the goddamn fence."

~~~~~~~~~~~~~~~~~~~~~~~~~~~

Danny heard sirens screaming up Lake Road. A few minutes later, Tom drove into the yard, lights blazing. A patrol car and a sheriff's deputy were on his tail. Rick and his team pulled in a few minutes behind them, and Dr. Markson was the last to arrive.

Danny stood at the garage door. He explained what had happened and told them that the side door to the garage was locked when he and Marnie exited the garage earlier. The overhead door remained closed to keep the cold out so that the scene wouldn't be further contaminated.

An old, beaten up Ford Bronco pulled up alongside the forensics wagon. It idled in the driveway for a few minutes, and the driver turned off the truck. Erin Matthews stepped out of the vehicle – eyes wide.

Tom crossed the driveway, holding his hands up in front of him. "Ma'am, could you please state your business?"

Erin fanned a hand in front of her face. "I beg your pardon. I'm here to help Marnie with the party tomorrow. I was invited," she drawled.

Erin's pronounced drawl took Tom by surprise. "I'm sorry, ma'am. I didn't know. Marnie is inside. C'mon, I'll take you to her."

Erin's green eyes grew wider. "What in the blazes is happening?"

Tom didn't miss a beat. "Emergency equipment training. We do this about once a month."

Tom lead the way to the front door. He held the door for Erin and walked in behind her.

Tom called out, "Marnie!"

Hannah shouted back, "In the kitchen!"

Tom and Erin went into the kitchen. Marnie was back on the barstool drinking a glass of wine. Hannah was next to her doing the same.

Tom tapped Marnie's shoulder. "Hey, kid, you all right?"

Marnie nodded. "I'm good. Thanks, Tom. The cavalry has arrived?" She tipped her head back and looked up at Tom.

"Yeah. The usual suspects. We're all here," Tom replied. "Your friend, um… I'm sorry. I didn't catch your name."

"Erin. Erin Matthews."

Marnie turned around and saw Erin for the first time. "Oh, Erin! I'm sorry! Can we get you a glass of wine?"

"Uh… Am I interruptin' somethin'? I can leave…"

"No! No, it's fine. The guys are going to be tied up out there in the garage for quite a while. You know, boys and their toys. We can just stay in here and have something to eat, and we'll make… um… things," Marnie replied awkwardly. Her bottom lip started to tremble.

Tom gave her shoulder a tight squeeze. "You need anything, we're outside. Okay?"

Marnie nodded. "Yeah. Sorry. I'm being silly."

"No, you aren't," Hannah soothed. "Tom, I've got this. Go ahead."

Tom left, and Erin stood at the counter looking perplexed.

"It's just police business. Everything is fine," Hannah assured her. Hannah patted Marnie's arm, filled a glass with wine for Erin and topped off her own and Marnie's wine.

"Okay." Erin shrugged. "Tell me what I can do to help?"

Marnie handed Erin the wine that Hannah had just poured for her. "Have a drink with us. That's a good place to start."

~~~~~~~~~~~~~~~~~~~~~~

Danny sidled up to Rick. "Hey, you got anything on Cap?"

"Yeah. I got somethin'. We ran all of the screens like you asked. He had midazolam in his blood. I've been shaking my head on that one most of the day. I talked to his doctor, too. He checked out the Captain – went over him with a fine-tooth comb. He's got bruising on his ankles and wrists, and – wait 'til you hear this – somebody branded him on the back of the neck. Had to hurt like a son of a bitch!"

"What's the brand?" Danny asked.

Rick took his billfold out of his pocket, opened it and pulled out a one-dollar bill. He looked at it, flipped it over and pointed. "That's the brand."

Danny's eyes widened. "The Eye of Providence. Son of a bitch. They are connected."

~~~~~~~~~~~~~~~~~~~~~~

Carl called out for Alice once again. "Alice! It's safe! You can come out now!"

Carl and the two police officers heard a shuffling sound coming from the dining room. They all stepped into the room and watched as the wainscoting opened and Alice Wells emerged from the wall, revolver in hand.

Carl exhaled. "Alice, you *are* safe. Did you fire that revolver?"

Alice nodded and laid the gun on the table.

Officer Owens crossed the dining room and examined the wainscoting and the trapdoor. "I always knew that these old houses had trapdoors. Look at that, will ya!" He turned to Alice. "Ma'am, are you all right?"

"Yes, I'm fine. I crawled in there and went up to my bedroom to get my gun. It is registered, I assure you," Alice responded firmly.

Officers Tartello and Connor pushed through the front door and stepped into the foyer. "Creekwood PD! Owens, you in here?"

"Yeah! Yeah! I'll be right with you." Owens turned to Alice. "Officer Chavez is going to stay here with you and get a statement. She also needs to see where you discharged your weapon. I'm going to help my colleagues do another sweep and find that ninja."

Alice nodded. "Yes, of course. I'll make a statement. I'm fairly certain that I missed. I don't think that I shot anyone. I was under my bed and fired at the wall to scare him off."

Carl turned his head and grinned. The picture of Alice in her fuzzy purple housecoat and fuzzy pink slippers holding a revolver and coming out of the wall made him chuckle. He couldn't help it.

~~~~~~~~~~~~~~~~~~~~~

Danny received a call at 7:30 PM from Officer Chavez. She was reporting to him regarding the incident at Alice's home. After she provided the pertinent details, he asked if Carl Parkins was still on site. She confirmed.

Carl's phone rang a few moments later. He glanced down at the screen and answered it. "Detective Gregg, it's been a busy evening."

"Yeah. Listen, Carl. I need you to do me a huge favor," Danny said.

Carl frowned. "What's that?"

"Do you think that you could make sure that the glass is fixed or at least covered before you leave Alice's house? If possible, could you get a locksmith to change her locks? I'm happy to pay for the locksmith and the glazier. I know that Alice is short on cash. We've got a few cases at the moment, and they all seem to be connected. I just want to make sure that Alice is safe. I've instructed Chavez to stay with Alice until the shift change, and we'll have another officer on her all night."

"Danny, is everything okay? Is there anything that I can help with?" Carl asked.

Danny thought about it for a minute. He had to admit that Carl had been a good friend to all of them of late, and he needed to trust him. Besides, an expert's opinion could be helpful without dragging Marnie into it.

"Yeah. I think we could use some help. We've got a nut job on the loose, and we need to catch him before he hurts anybody else," Danny replied.

"Okay. Well, I do specialize in that field. Let me know what you need."

Carl listened carefully as Danny explained the cases that Creekwood PD was working. He asked Carl if he could come down to the station in the morning to review the files.

"Danny, I have a jammed schedule in the morning, but if you want to drop off the files, I will review them between appointments, if that works. Perhaps we can catch up at 1:00 to review after my last appointment."

Danny thought for just a moment. "Deal. I'll see you at 8:00?"

"8:00 is fine. I'll have the coffee on." Carl hung up.

Danny stepped back to the garage. "Have you guys got everything that you need?"

Rick nodded. "Yeah. We've dusted everything. There aren't any fingerprints different from the ones that we gathered after your accident. Whoever it is wore gloves. That's what I hate about this shit in the wintertime. Everybody wears their damn gloves. Makes it difficult. Have you got anyone at Justin's apartment, or should we head over there now?"

"Nah. I've got it secure. If you can hit it first thing in the morning, I would appreciate it," Danny replied. "It's been a long day, guys. Drop off everything at the station, and go home to your families." Danny ran his fingers through his hair and glanced up at the ceiling, looking for something. Anything.

Rick snapped a forensics case closed. "No problem. We've got the address. We'll head over first thing. Once I'm back at the station, I'll give you a shout. We can go see Doc Markson together."

"Yeah, thanks, Rick." Danny ended his reply with a long yawn. "Tommy, can you stick around a minute?" Danny asked.

"Yeah. I'm starving, and Marnie was baking cookies the last time that I ducked in to use the bathroom." Tom grinned.

Tom and Danny stood on the porch. They were tossing out hypotheses to see if they'd stick.

"Who do you like for this?" Tom asked.

"I don't know. What kind of sick person tattoos someone against his will, brands someone else on the back of the neck and shoots up both of them with drugs?"

Danny and Tom didn't have to think about it. In unison, they said, "Sam Reilly!"

-CHAPTER FIFTY-ONE-

Marnie was taking another pan of peanut butter cookies out of the oven when Tom and Danny came into the kitchen. Erin was bagging up carrots, celery, peppers and radishes that she had prepared for a vegetable tray. Hannah was loading the dishwasher while sipping a glass of wine.

"Wow! Something smells good in here!" Danny straddled a barstool and lifted a wine bottle to see how much wine was left. He frowned and went to the wine rack to get another bottle.

Tom grabbed a cookie off the tray before Marnie could slap his hand away. He put the whole cookie in his mouth and grinned.

"This is so good! I need a glass of milk and a dozen more."

Danny opened the wine and filled Marnie's glass. "Have you got much left to do?" He offered to freshen Erin's glass.

"No, thanks. I've got to drive," Erin declined.

"We've been busy. We have two types of chili simmering. The dips are made, the veggies are ready and this is the last batch of cookies." Marnie nodded, pleased with their productivity. "We'll pick up the fixings for the charcuterie boards tomorrow. Everything else is arriving with Gram and Carl."

"I'm picking up beer and soft drinks tomorrow," Tom added.

"We've got a wine delivery coming tomorrow around noon," Danny advised. "Marnie, will you be here then?"

Marnie shook her head. "I'm not sure. I've got some things to take care of in town."

"I'll be around tomorrow," Hannah replied. "I can take the delivery."

"Thanks, Banana." Danny put a hand on his stomach and glanced around. "Hey, is there any Chinese food left?"

"Yup." Marnie nodded, pulling the takeout containers out of the fridge. "I was just going to warm it up for you and Tom."

"Okay, I really need to be heading home. I have to work in the morning," Erin announced.

"Thanks, Erin. I look forward to you actually visiting tomorrow night." Danny stood and smiled.

"Yeah, sorry. We were tied up all night. We'll see you tomorrow," Tom said.

"'Night, Erin," Hannah replied.

"Thanks so much for all of the help, Erin. I'll walk you out." Marnie walked Erin to the door.

When Marnie returned to the kitchen, she heard the men's muffled voices mixed with Hannah's that stopped as soon as she walked in. She knew that she had walked in on something.

"What's going on in here?"

Danny turned to Hannah and gave her a warning glance.

"I'm sorry, Marnie. I was just telling Daniel and Tom that I don't particularly like your friend Erin. She's too... too sweet. I don't trust that." Hannah crinkled her nose.

Marnie raised her eyebrows. "Oh, really? Well, that's cool. We can't possibly like everyone. I thought that about her when I first met her, too." Marnie shrugged. "She's always been nice to me."

Danny broke in before Hannah could counter. "Anyway, I'm going to run up and have a shower while the food is warming up. I can't eat with the smell of death on my clothes tonight. It usually doesn't bother me. I must be getting sensitive in my old age. I'll be right back."

"Hey, Marn, is my bed still made up from the other night?" Tom asked.

"Yeah. The cleaner comes tomorrow. Danny asked her to strip the beds and make them up fresh."

"Great! Then I'm going to crash here tonight. Danny and I still have some things to discuss, and I want a glass of wine. I really don't want to think about driving home." Tom poured himself a glass of red.

~~~~~~~~~~~~~~~~~~~~~~~~~~~~

Danny and Tom sat on the couch eating warmed-up Chinese food, drinking wine and discussing the intricacies of the recent spate of homicides. They wondered how the cases correlated with Captain Sterling's "accident" and the break-in at Alice Wells's house.

Hannah had gone up to bed. Tater was asleep under the pool table with Danny's slipper, and Marnie eavesdropped from the corner near the Christmas tree while unraveling Christmas lights. Her sounds of exasperation and bouts of cussing to herself gave Tom and Danny reason to grin.

"I swear to God! It's impossible to put the lights on the tree without swearing at least once!" Marnie groaned.

"15 times, actually. I've been counting," Tom teased.

"Marnie, are you free for lunch tomorrow?" Danny asked, winking at Tom.

Marnie glanced up and frowned, thinking about her plans. "Um. Yeah, I think so."

"Well, I just thought that I could take the birthday girl to lunch, that's all." Danny winked again and grinned.

Eyes wide, Marnie pointed at Tom. "You told!" she accused.

Tom threw up his hands in defense. "'Twasn't me! Our friendly neighborhood vet let that cat out of the bag. Hey, that's kind of a pun isn't it? Vet. Cat. Yeah!" Tom snickered. "Besides, since when is your birthday a big secret?"

"Oh, I really just wanted the date to fly by unnoticed. Let's not make a big deal." Marnie frowned.

"Does that mean that you won't have lunch with me?" Danny turned, eyebrows raised.

"Of course I'll have lunch with you, but not because it's my birthday."

"Have it your way. Gram is making a cake." Danny grinned and shook his head.

Tom glanced at Danny and pulled a face. "Cake? Marnie doesn't like cake."

Danny's face dropped. "What? Who doesn't like cake?!"

Marnie raised her hand and grimaced. She walked to the couch with a wad of Christmas lights in her hand and sat. "Hey, is Alice okay?"

"You were listening?" Danny cocked his head and raised an eyebrow.

Marnie wrinkled her nosed at him. "Of course I was listening."

Danny smirked. "Of course, and yes, Alice is okay. We have an officer with her now."

Tom shifted forward, hands on his knees. "Hey, Marn, did you know that Alice's house has secret passages?"

Marnie nodded. "Yup. I wouldn't think that many people do know that, though. I found one purely by accident once, and Alice hushed me." Marnie continued detangling the lights. "She told me that it was the only way that she could get away from Reuben and Grace. She begged me not to tell, so I didn't."

"Reuben and Grace don't know?" Danny turned to face Marnie.

"Not that I know of. Why?" Marnie furrowed her brow.

"Marnie, do you know if Reuben has any martial arts training?" Tom asked.

Marnie stared up at the clock on the mantle and searched her memory. "You know, something tells me that he does. I remember a kid running around Alice's house roundhouse kicking everyone at some point. I think that it was

Reuben. I can check with Shaun to see if he remembers Reuben Wilmot. He's the shifu master who owns the local training kwoon."

Tom held up a hand. "That's okay. I know Shaun. I'll go see him tomorrow. Thanks, though."

Marnie shrugged. "Okay. Suit yourself."

"Marn, we're trying to keep you out of harm's way on this. We're grateful for your help, but we just don't want you to be targeted." Danny nudged her gently with his foot.

"I said 'okay,' and it really is okay. I've got enough to do without playing Scooby-Doo," Marnie replied. She gave Tom and Danny a sideways glance and continued detangling the lights.

Tom and Danny exchanged a glance. Danny shrugged a shoulder as a "go ahead, what have we got to lose" gesture.

"Marn, do you know if Kate has ever practiced any martial arts?" Tom asked.

Marnie burst out laughing. "Oh, my God! That is hilarious! Kate? Kate Parish? That is the most ridiculous thing that I've ever heard! Kate? Break a sweat? Kate wouldn't do anything that might break a nail. No! I tried to get her to come with me, and she never would. Why are you asking about martial arts? Have you got a ninja running amok in Creekwood?" Marnie giggled at the thought.

Danny and Tom replied in unison, "Yes."

~~~~~~~~~~~~~~~~~~~~~~~~~~~~~~

Grace sat in a comfy chair with an electric blanket wrapped around her shoulders. She shuffled a beaten-up deck of tarot cards. Candles burned throughout the silo, and the kerosene heaters were cranked. She knew that Kate would be by in the morning to fill them. She wasn't worried. Kate would do anything that she wanted. She had to, and Grace had seen to that. Kate Parish was terrified.

"Sleight of hand. A willing accomplice and the prick of a pin. Kate Parish is terrified and is all in!" Grace cackled.

Grace laid out tarot cards on the hassock in front of her. The Death card was the answer to her question. She examined the surrounding cards and frowned. The Ten of Swords, Judgment, the Six of Swords, The Tower and the Three of Swords all appeared in the spread. Grace scooped up the cards and put them back in the deck. She shuffled the deck again. She focused and asked the question with intent. She did a new layout with a similar result. This

284

time, the cards before her were Death, the Four of Swords, the Three of Swords, the Ten of Swords and The Tower.

"Well, that can't be! That can't be!" Grace frowned. She stared at the cards and went to her cabinet to take out her pendulum. She steadied the pendulum over the cards and asked the pendulum if the readings had been accurate. The pendulum responded with a resounding "yes." Grace's blood ran cold. "How can this be? We have planned everything so perfectly. How can this be?!"

Grace sat back down and scowled. She knew that anyone who reads the tarot knows that the Death card alone does not foretell a physical death. Such a death is only signified when combined with three other cards – any combination of the three: Judgment, The World, The Tower, the Ten of Swords, the Six of Swords, the Four of Swords, the Three of Swords or sometimes the blank card for those decks that include the blank card. Grace knew that only three of these were *needed* to signify an actual, physical death, but in each spread, she had four. She'd asked her pendulum to confirm that a physical death was imminent. It did. Now, Grace Wilmot was terrified, too.

～～～～～～～～～～～～～～～～

"Tommy, if you can get Jalnack onto the brand first thing in the morning, that would be great. If he can find a supplier, we are one step closer." Danny glanced down at his notepad and put a check next to another item.

Marnie was putting the lights on the tree in preparation for tomorrow night's party and listening to Danny's and Tom's conversation. "Um, brand? As in branding iron?"

Danny turned around and responded. "Yes."

"Well, you can special order those at a stationery store, or there are several online businesses that sell them. Before you ask, I bought one a few years ago to burn Halloween party invitations. Suppliers are everywhere. You can get electric branding irons or the traditional kind that need a fire."

"You can have them customized?" Danny asked.

Marnie stuck out her bottom lip and nodded. "Oh, yeah. You can have pretty much any design or text that you want. The custom ones take about a week to be delivered, but yeah, you can get anything you want."

"Well, the more specific the brand, the easier it will be to find our suspect," Tom commented.

Danny nodded.

"What's the design?" Marnie asked.

"The Eye of Providence," Danny replied.

Marnie tipped her head. "Maybe you should check in with the Masonic Lodge. The Eye of Providence is one of their symbols. Perhaps they have had something stolen. I don't think for a minute that it's anyone there – they are all peaceful men doing good work for the community. They donate thousands to kids' wellness programs. It's just a thought. Maybe it's just a redirect. People have all of these conspiracy theories about Masons being evil. It's not true. My dad was a Mason, and Tom's dad *is* a Mason."

"My dad, too. It comes with law enforcement sometimes." Danny jotted down a note. "We'll look into it."

"By the way, Marn, my folks will be home for Christmas this year. Mom wants a white Christmas, and as much as Dad would prefer a golf course, Mom won." Tom took a sip of wine and stretched out his legs onto the coffee table.

"That's great news! I would love to see them over the holidays," Marnie said with a wide smile.

Tom nodded. "We'll make that happen. You can make pot roast and raspberry pie. They would love it!"

"How did their visiting turn into work for me?" Marnie grinned.

"You cook better than me." Tom winked.

"Ah. Well, with that said, the lights are on the tree, and I am off to bed. C'mon, Tater. Let's go out one more time and then go to bed." Marnie grabbed Tater's lead from the back of the door.

"I'll come with you." Danny winced as he stood.

"You stay. I'll go with them." Tom got up from his comfy chair and pulled on his boots.

Danny nodded and dropped back onto the couch. "Thanks." He puffed out his cheeks and relaxed.

It was a chilly, clear night, and the moon was nearly full. Marnie looked up at the sky – thousands of stars shined back.

"When do your folks get into town?" Marnie asked as they walked.

"They arrive Saturday. It's going to be a long few weeks," Tom replied.

"You'll get through it. Your folks are great."

Tom sighed. "They are. They're staying at the house with me, and it will be two weeks of them asking me when I'm going to settle down and get married. You know the routine. It gets old after the first day."

"You'll settle down when you're ready. For the record, I don't think that you're a commitment-phobe. I think that you're just waiting for the right person." Marnie gave Tom's arm a squeeze.

"Yup."

"C'mon, Tater. Let's get back inside where it's warm," Marnie coaxed. Tater trotted back to the cabin with Tom and Marnie.

"Hey, Marn? Do you really think that Sam has anything to do with what's going on?"

Marnie turned to him and looked beyond him with a thoughtful gaze. "I've been asking my parents that all day. I think that the line between here and there is clogged. I'll try again tomorrow."

-CHAPTER FIFTY-TWO-

Friday, December 11th

Marnie rolled over and looked at the alarm clock. It was 12:01 AM, and she thought, *"Happy birthday to me."* She rolled onto her other side. Tater groaned and repositioned himself at the foot of the bed. She rolled onto her back and stared at the ceiling. Tater got up, hopped off the big bed and stretched; he sighed and curled up in his bed on the floor next to the windows. "Sorry, buddy. I can't sleep." Tater yawned in response and tucked his nose under his tail.

Marnie willed her parents to speak to her. She closed her eyes and waited for some sign that they could hear her. She started wondering and worrying if she had broken something when she crossed back through the veil. *"I wonder if that tear is stopping them from speaking to me?"* She sat up, swung her legs onto the floor and paced – because pacing sometimes helped.

Tater popped his head up and went to the door. He sniffed under the door, tipped his head and stood on his hind legs. With both paws on the door lever, he pushed down and slowly hopped back. He poked his nose around the door jam and peeked out. His ears went up, he woofed quietly and his tail wagged. Marnie turned to the door. Danny poked his head inside and laughed.

"Ellie told me that he could do that. I've just never seen it." Danny laughed quietly.

"I'll have to install locks on all the doors from now on. It looks like he's perfecting his art," Marnie replied with a giggle.

Danny pushed the door open, scratched Tater's ears and glanced up at Marnie. "Can't sleep again?"

"No. I've been trying to get my parents to talk to me. Tom asked me if I think that Sam has anything to do with all of this. I don't know, Danny. I thought that my parents could help, but they aren't. I can't get them to respond." Marnie sat on the edge of the bed and sighed in exasperation.

"Why do you think that is? Them not talking to you?"

Marnie sighed again. Her fists were clenched in her lap, and she was finding it hard to breathe. Finally, she exhaled, and her words raced out. "Danny, can we talk about something that happened? Are you okay to have a bit of a long chat? I've wanted to talk to you about this, but the time hasn't really seemed right... until now."

Danny took a step and puffed out his cheeks. "I'm not gonna like this, am I? Look, if it upset you when I called you 'girlfriend,' I'm sorry. I don't mean to rush you. It's just, well, we've been doing this dance for nearly a month now, and I don't know…"

Marnie grabbed his hand and pulled him to the side of the bed. Danny sat, and Marnie leaned in and kissed him. The kiss lingered. Marnie put her hands on Danny's chest, pulled away and explained, "I'm not upset about you calling me your girlfriend. I think that we're a bit too old for that term, but what other word is there? It's a perfectly good word. I do think that maybe we should go on a few more dates first. Have we ever really been on a date? Just the two of us? Anyway, that's not what I wanted to talk to you about."

Danny brushed Marnie's hair from her face. "That was a nice kiss." He smiled.

"It really was." Marnie grinned and lay her head on Danny's shoulder. "Danny, I really need to tell you something."

"Okay. I'm listening. I'm not at all distracted by that kiss."

"Danny, please!" Marnie sat up and looked him in the eyes. "Please," she said softly.

Danny shifted down the edge of the bed and put on his serious face, even though he didn't want to at that moment.

Marnie took a deep breath and exhaled. "Okay. That night at Station Hall. When I was locked in the trunk. Remember?"

Danny nodded. "Yeah, I remember. You could have died."

Another deep breath. Another big exhale, and in a rush of words, she told him.

"Danny, I did die. I saw the light of God. It was so calming and warm. I followed it down a long hallway, and the veil – oh, Danny, the veil. I've never seen anything so beautiful – ever –
gossamer and every color of the rainbow and silver and gold glimmered within it. It was… it felt like the wind had been knocked out of me, but I wasn't scared. It didn't matter because I didn't need to breathe – it doesn't make sense, I know. Then I saw my parents, William, my grandparents and all of the people I have known who have passed. My dogs – my dogs from my childhood – they were there, too. I know that I saw your mom and Sarah. Sarah."

Marnie stopped for a breath. Danny put his hand gently on her cheek and brushed her tears with his thumb. He gave her a light nod, and she continued.

"Mom and Dad kept telling me that it wasn't time and that I needed to go back. Hugging them was all that I could think of, you know? Wanting a hug from my parents – it's something that I think about all of the time. I miss them, and I just wanted them to hold me – even if just for a minute. They kept telling me that the veil was closing, and if I didn't go back, I wouldn't be able to return to all of you. They just kept shouting at me. I was confused, and I didn't know where to go, then someone grabbed my hand and pulled me down the hallway and back to the veil. Danny, it was Sarah. She took my hand, she dragged me back down that long hallway and she pushed me back through the veil. It was nearly closed. She pushed me, I jumped and I heard the veil tear. I keep thinking that the reason my folks aren't talking to me is that the veil is torn and it's my fault. I should have turned back when they told me to, but I was being selfish and childish. I wanted a hug. I was selfish. Telling you all of this seems cruel and selfish because it's bringing up Sarah again, and if this is upsetting you, I am so sorry. I am so sorry."

As tears streamed down Marnie's face, Danny turned away from her.

"I don't know how to process this. I… I'm not sure what to say."

Marnie reached for a tissue off her nightstand. She dried her eyes and wiped her nose.

"If you want me to leave, I understand. Telling you that… I didn't want to upset you, but something inside – in my heart – thought that you should know. I know that you know Sarah was… is… an amazing person. For me – at this moment – it's more. I don't mean that she means more to me than you. That's not what I meant. Oh, gosh!" Marnie paused and caught her breath. "She saved me, Danny. I heard you calling to me. I felt Tater lick my face, and I heard him bark. I know that you were holding my hand, and I know that Patrick helped. I know because I saw everything. It was… um… surreal and scary and amazing, and I am so sorry."

Tears streamed down her face, and she buried her face in her arm. Danny turned to her, wrapped his arms around her and hugged her as tight as he could.

"Marnie, I don't want you to leave. I have never wanted you to leave. From the minute I met you, I've thought that you were the most annoying, beautiful and peculiar control freak who I have ever met. I don't want you to leave, Marnie. I'm falling in love with you. Didn't you know that?"

Marnie sniffled and pushed away from Danny's arms. "What? You're not mad at me?" Marnie gazed up at Danny, her eyes wide and stunned.

"No, I'm not mad at you." Danny shrugged. "I am mad that you took off upstairs at Station Hall and went poking around, but that's because… we nearly lost you."

Marnie sniffled and wiped her nose with her wadded up tissue. "I told Carl some of this, but I didn't tell him everything. I didn't tell him about Sarah. That was information for you. It seemed like it would be… um… a… I don't know. A betrayal. That's not the word, but you know what I mean. It doesn't concern anyone else, I guess."

"It's an intimate detail that you didn't want to share with Carl," Danny offered.

"Yes, intimate." Marnie nodded, then she grinned. "Hey, did you just tell me you're falling in love with me?"

"I was wondering when that was going to register." Danny tipped his head back and laughed.

"It registered. I feel the same. I think that I started falling for you when you stopped calling me Ms. Reilly."

"Gee, that long ago?"

"Hmm… It may have been when you kissed me on the forehead in the cellar at my house."

"Mmm… Good memory. Hey, as soon as we've got the cases under some control, you and I, we'll go on a real date. I know this… us… it's been somewhat complicated, but we'll go on a real date without phones or Tom."

"Something to look forward to," Marnie responded with a broad smile.

"Hey, Marnie! It's 12:45. Happy birthday!"

Marnie threw her head back and made a face. "Yuck! I hate my birthday! It's not the same without my parents."

Danny hugged her. "What do you want for your birthday, Ms. Reilly?"

Marnie considered his question for just a moment, tilted her head back, stared into his eyes and whispered, "You."

Danny kissed her and kicked the bedroom door closed.

~~~~~~~~~~~~~~~~~~~~~~~~

Tater barking was the first thing that Marnie heard when she awoke. She glanced at the clock. It was 6:30 AM. She snuggled down into the covers and smiled. She heard Tater bark again. It wasn't a bad bark. It was his "I've just come in from the cold, and I want to play" bark. Marnie reached down to the floor and grabbed her sweatshirt. She pulled it on and went into the bathroom to wash up. When she came out of the bathroom, Danny and Tater were sitting on the bed with a tray.

"Happy birthday!"

"Oh! Breakfast in bed! Thank you!"

Danny frowned. "You don't like breakfast in bed, do you? Ellie did tell me that. I forgot, and I can tell by the look on your face."

"It's lovely, but not so much." Marnie giggled, wrinkled her nose and shook her head. She sat next to Danny. "It's all that trying to balance everything, not spilling anything and the crumbs."

"Happy birthday, control freak. C'mon. Let's go have breakfast in the kitchen." Danny picked up the tray.

Marnie stood and stared up at him. "Aren't you forgetting something?"

Danny gave her a sideways glance, the corners of his mouth lifting just a bit. "I don't think so."

Marnie took the tray, set it on the bed and draped her arms around his shoulders. "What does a girl have to do to get a birthday kiss around here?"

"Ah. I did forget that, didn't I." Danny dipped her and gave a long, lingering kiss.

"That's better." Marnie buried her face in his neck.

"Hey, Marnie?"

"Yes?" she murmured.

Danny grimaced and took a step back. "Aw... Ow... I think I just popped my stitches." Danny groaned.

"No! Let me check." Marnie went around behind him and lifted his shirt.

"I'm fine. I was just teasing, and even if I did, it was worth it."

"Ass! Let's go. I'm starving!" Marnie picked up the tray.

Danny held the door. "After you, birthday girl. Hey, I'll be down in just a sec."

Danny had lit a fire in the living room and one in the kitchen. A homey warmth radiated in every room. Marnie glanced over at the undecorated Christmas tree sitting in the corner. It was a grand tree. The smell of balsam drifted into the kitchen. Marnie closed her eyes and took in the smell of the tree. It brought back so many wonderful Christmas memories with her family. She hadn't known a home to be filled with that much love until now.

Marnie set the tray on the counter and carried her mug of coffee to the windows. Tater had taken up guard in his favorite spot, his eyes fixed on two deer who bounded across the snowy path to the deer trail.

"Happy birthday, Marn!"

Marnie spun around. Tom walked into the kitchen with a rather large package. It was beautifully wrapped, and it even had a bow.

"Aw. Thank you, Tom."

"Hang on! You can't open it yet. We have to wait for Danny and Hannah."

Hannah rushed into the kitchen a few minutes later and skidded to a halt. "Sorry! I don't want to miss anything," she puffed and shot Tom a knowing grin. "Happy birthday, Marnie!"

"What are you people up to?" Marnie accused with a smirk.

"Hey, Marnie! Look who I found running around in Tom's room!" Danny called from the living room.

Danny strolled into the kitchen with a puppy running behind him.

"Oh, my God! It's the Border Collie pup from Ellie's!" Marnie sat on the kitchen floor and called over the pup. He ran into her arms, squiggled and squirmed and licked her face. Tater appeared next to them. He sniffed the puppy's ears and then his backside. He sat back for a moment and put a paw on top of the puppy's head.

"Oh, my goodness, Tater, isn't he beautiful? Do you love him?" Tater licked Marnie's face and went back to his window to watch the deer.

"Uh oh. I guess that the jury is out. Tater's nose may be out of joint." Tom pulled a face.

Danny shook his head. "No, he's been playing with this pup when he's been at Ellie's this week. Tater will be fine. What do you think, Marnie? Good present?"

"You couldn't have picked a better present. Thank you so much! He's beautiful!" Marnie grinned and cuddled the pup in her arms.

Tom set down his package and squatted down to give the puppy an ear scratch. "He slept on my bed all night last night. He snores. Ellie dropped him off last night while you were all in the kitchen. We kept him in the garage and snuck him into the house. Here, Marnie, open this one. It's from me and Hannah. We conspired. Oh, Hannah wrapped it. You know me. I'm useless with things like that."

"You are not useless. You just don't wrap presents often. Volunteer to help with the toy wrapping, and you'll pick up your game." Marnie smiled warmly at Tom.

"Open it!" Hannah blurted out. She bounced on her toes and looked unusually animated.

Marnie unwrapped the box. Inside the box were a dog bed, two ceramic dog bowls, a tube of tennis balls, a stuffed lamb and a bag of puppy food.

"Wow! You guys! This is perfect! Thank you so much!" Marnie said tearfully.

"What are you going to name him?" Hannah asked.

"I don't know. It's good to wait a few days to see what pops in their personality. I love his little face. Split-face Borders are beautiful. A bit of Yin and Yang – he's perfect." Marnie held the pup up and stared into his face. "Let's see what you do over the next few days, little mister. Then we'll give you a name that fits."

The pup licked her nose, squirmed out of her hands and went straight to Tom.

"Tom, maybe you should get a puppy," Marnie suggested. "You've always loved dogs."

Tom held the pup in his arms and shrugged. "Oh, Marn, I'm so busy with work that it would be cruel."

"Yeah. I hadn't thought about that." Marnie shrugged. "A pup could go to day care. I'm planning to take Tater there more often in the future."

Tom stuck out his lower lip in thought and nodded noncommittally.

"Anyway!" Danny clapped his hands. "We need to have breakfast, then we need to get to work."

Marnie stood and thanked everyone for the gifts with a hug. "Thank you all so much for this. It's been a perfect birthday already."

-CHAPTER FIFTY-THREE-

Marnie left the cabin at 8:30 and drove into town with Tater and the new puppy. Tater sat in the passenger seat, and the pup was on the back seat chewing on a Kong dog toy that Ellie had given to Danny for him. Marnie had stuffed the Kong full of peanut butter to keep him busy.

Marnie's phone rang. It was a private number. She took a deep breath and answered in a snarky tone.

"Hello."

"Marnie? Marnie, it's Erin."

"Oh, hi. Are you okay? You sound like you've been crying."

Erin sighed. "Marnie, Mr. Drake just fired me, and I just need someone to talk to while I walk home."

"Oh, my gosh! Erin, I'm so sorry!"

"I don't understand. I was out back stockin' shelves in the pharmacy, you know, before we opened. Anyway, he was fillin' a prescription for a customer, and he was fillin' it with the wrong medication. I notice details, and I know what *that* customer always gets, 'cause I ring up the orders at the register. You know, I told him that he was givin' her the wrong medicine, and he just about took my head off. He told me that I was a busybody, I was too chatty with customers, some customers complain about me and *I* gossip. How dare he! Me? Gossip? He and that brood of hens that sit at the coffee counter do the gossipin'. I just don't know, Marnie. I was about as angry as a raccoon treed by a hound. I told him that he was bein' unfair and that I was just tryin' to help. He fired me right there on the spot." Erin stopped for a breath.

"Erin, I am so sorry that this happened. Maybe Mr. Drake is just having a bad morning, and maybe he took it out on you. I don't think that's appropriate, but it does happen. I'm on my way to a meeting. Can I call you back in a little while? I won't be long. I'll be heading home right after the meeting to finish getting things ready for tonight. Can I call you on my way home?"

"I would appreciate that. I'm headin' home to update my résumé and look for a job. There must be somethin' this time of year. Retail should be busy enough," Erin speculated.

"Great idea! Hey, I'll call as soon as I'm through. Again, Erin, I'm really sorry, but I am sure that, if we put our heads together, we'll find you something better," Marnie comforted.

"Thanks, Marn. Buh-bye." Erin stared down at her phone and glanced up the street. There were several little retail shops bursting with customers this time of year. It shouldn't be so hard.

~~~~~~~~~~~~~~~~~~~~~~

Marnie's first stop was the diner. She had to drop off a box of disposable platters for Gram, and Danny would pick up full platters before going home. Gram was making sandwich trays for the party tonight.

Marnie ran into the diner with the box, set it on the counter and raced back out to her car to get Tater and the pup. When she returned with Tater and the pup, Gram was behind the counter serving customers.

"Good mornin', lass! A happy birthday to you, dear Marnie!" Gram bustled from behind the counter, reaching out to hug Marnie. "Oh, and who do we have here? Who is this wee one?" Gram patted the pup's head. "Good mornin' to you, Tater. How's my boy?" Gram ruffled the fur of Tater's white shawl and patted his rump.

Marnie grinned. "We don't have a name for him yet, but we're working on it. Danny gave him to me this morning. Isn't he beautiful?"

"Ah, indeed he is. Such a sweet face. Look at that shepherd's lantern. Such a beautiful little tail. Tater's is quite grand, too, of course. The lads could lead a flock to safety with their tails in pitch blackness."

Marnie giggled. "They certainly could, but I think that we need to give this little one a bit more time before we send him into a field."

"Tea, Marnie? Would you have a cup of tea with me?" Gram asked hopefully.

"Yeah, sure. I've got time if you do." Marnie nodded.

"I'll make the time. Let's go upstairs. It's cozier by the fire." Gram led the way with Marnie, Tater and the pup following.

~~~~~~~~~~~~~~~~~~~~~~

"You know where she lives?" Danny asked.

"Yeah. You want me to go pick her up?" Tom replied.

"Take somebody with you. Take Garcia. She's bored as bat shit down in Evidence. Ask Sarge who can fill in for her while she's out. He knows the routine," Danny suggested.

"Okay. I'll talk to Sarge and roll. What path are you taking?" Tom picked up his keys and jacket.

Danny glanced up from his paperwork. "The path to Forensics. I've got some questions, and Rick's the guy with the answers. Catch ya!" Danny replied with a nod. He pushed back his chair, swung on his jacket and pushed through the doors.

Tom pulled on his jacket and went downstairs to speak to Sergeant Beaumont. "Hey, Sarge, can you free up Garcia? Danny wants her to come on a pickup with me?"

Sergeant Beaumont checked the roster. "Ah, yeah. We've got Danvers training with her this week. Might be good to give him a few hours on his own. Where are you off to?"

"I've got a date with the one and only Kate Parish. It's time for her to answer a few questions about the whereabouts of Grace Wilmot," Tom replied.

"That one? She's a freakin' piece of work," Sergeant Beaumont grumbled. "I see her walkin' my way, I move to the other side of the street."

Tom furrowed his brow. "Grace Wilmot?"

"Pfft. That Kate Parish. Never trusted that one. All looks, but nothin' nice about that one – manipulative and moody." Sergeant Beaumont rolled his eyes. "Yeah. She dated my son for a brief time. Used him, if you ask me. All right, Garcia is clear. I just E-mailed her. She'll be ready to roll in a few minutes."

"Thanks, Beau. Appreciate it."

~~~~~~~~~~~~~~~~~~~~~~~~

Marnie and Gram sat in front of the fire with cups of tea. Tater and the pup wrestled behind them. Marnie loved to sit with Gram. She was one of the most interesting people whom Marnie had ever met. She sat watching her – Gram's eyes always gleamed with a bit of mischief.

"Are you excited for the party tonight, Marnie?" Gram asked.

"Yes, I think it's going to be a lovely night. We've got a great group of people coming. My friend Erin just called, though, and I'm afraid that she's going to cancel. Mr. Drake fired her this morning." Marnie twisted her mouth and frowned.

"Oh, dear. That's not a decent thing to do this time of year. Well, I think Mr. Drake has some problems of his own. Perhaps your friend should be glad to be rid of it – that job," Gram replied.

Marnie was surprised by the comment. "Mr. Drake? Problems?" Marnie frowned.

"Never you mind, love. It will all come out in the wash," Gram predicted. "Now, tell me about this lovely new pup. Have you given him a name?"

"Not yet. I'm waiting to see what his personality tells us to call him." Marnie turned to see if Tater and the puppy were getting into anything that they shouldn't.

Tater and the pup raced through the apartment, and the pup came to a sliding halt in front of Gram's chair. The pup had one of Gram's slippers, and Tater had the other.

"Tater! What are you teaching him?" Marnie giggled. Tater dropped the slipper into Marnie's lap and smiled. "Come here, puppy! Come on. Give me the slipper."

The pup raced up the hallway toward Gram's bedroom with Tater following.

"Oh! This is going to be an interesting time. Tater and a puppy running my life." Marnie set down her tea and raced up the hallway after the dogs.

Gram hurried along behind her. "Marnie, don't worry. There's nothing that they can hurt."

"I just don't want the pup chewing on anything. Tater doesn't do that, but this one might." Marnie's reply was muffled. She was halfway under the bed trying to coax out the pup. "C'mon. I think that it's time for us to go. We have errands to run. C'mon, puppy!"

Gram went to the other side of the bed and snatched up the puppy. He squirmed and squiggled and let out a little bark. Gram set him on the bed, and he grabbed up one of her throw pillows and rolled across the bed with it. A smile lit up Gram's face, she picked up the puppy again and looked into his face. "Oh, you are a little dickens, aren't you?"

Marnie's face lit up. "Dickens! That's a perfect name for him, Gram."

"I think that it may be. What do you think, puppy? Is Dickens your name?" Gram held him up and looked into his face again. He squiggled and growled, and Gram set him on the floor. He raced back to the living room, sliding on the hardwood floors as he went. Tater raced after him and ran into him halfway to the living room. They tumbled across the floor wrestling.

Gram and Marnie stood watching them play. Gram wrapped her arms around herself and smiled. "I love puppies. They certainly make a house a home, don't they?"

Marnie agreed. "They sure do."

"Now, Marnie, before you leave, I want to give you your gift."

"Oh, Gram. You didn't need to get me a gift. Spending time with you has been the best gift."

"Hush, child. Now, where did I put it?" Gram glanced around the living room. "Oh, there it is."

Gram went to the dining room table, returned with a large box and set it on the coffee table. It was wrapped beautifully, just like the gift that Hannah had wrapped. "Now, it's not new. I've had this for years, but I think it's time that it had a new owner."

"Oh, Gram. Thank you!" Marnie sat and unwrapped the gift.

"That was made for me by my grandmother – my grandmother on my father's side. I've fixed it in a few places over time, but it's still as beautiful as the day that she gave it to me," Gram said proudly.

"This is amazing, Gram. Wow! I don't know how to thank you," Marnie eyes glistened with happy tears. Marnie tipped her head and examined the gift a bit closer. "Gram, is this a wedding ring quilt?"

Gram snickered and beamed. "You're not the only one around here who can foretell the future."

Marnie smiled and placed the quilt back into the box. "Gram, don't you think you're jumping the gun a bit?"

"No, I do not! That's the last that we'll speak of that," Gram declared.

"You don't think that Hannah might be upset that you're giving this to me?" Marnie asked.

"Hannah has one of her own. I gave her one when she got married. I don't see why she would be upset."

"Hannah was married? Ah… Wait. Her last name is Patterson," Marnie commented.

"Yes, she was married. Her husband, Mark, was killed in a terrible accident. It's my only regret – letting them drive away that night. I asked them to stay, but they wouldn't. I had a feeling, and Hannah told me that I was being silly. Hannah blamed me for a long time. She said that, if I had used logic rather than hooey, they would have stayed. She thought that I should have tried harder to convince them. I did try – several times. She thinks, or perhaps thought, that anything having to do with psychics, clairvoyance and the paranormal is all 'hooey,' as she put it."

Marnie nodded. "She said as much the other night. I didn't argue with her. Arguing with people who don't believe is pointless. Sooner or later, well, there's always that one moment when they realize that not believing is actually hooey."

"Well said." Gram nodded. "Marnie, I do want to talk to you before you go. I don't want to frighten you, dear, but there is something blowing in the wind. I've felt it for days. I think that Danny senses it, too. Be mindful of your surroundings and wolves in sheep's clothing. You'll know what I mean, lass."

Marnie sighed. "Yes. I've had a feeling for a few weeks. To quote the bard, 'Something wicked this way comes.'" Marnie shivered. "I don't have all of the pieces together, but I know that fire and ice have something to do with it. Visions… I've been having visions." Marnie stared off into the fire for a moment.

"Do you think that the ice you've been seein' was Danny's accident?" Gram asked.

Marnie tightened her mouth and shook her head. "No. I think it's something evil. Pure evil."

"The wolf, perhaps?" Gram asked.

"Mmm." Marnie nodded.

~~~~~~~~~~~~~~~~~~~~~~~~~

"You know, Danny, there's been a serious uptick in overdoses here and in Hudson for about four months. Obviously, we have a growing drug problem. Has Cap talked to you about investigations or activity?" Rick Price peered at Danny over the top of his readers.

"Nah. Cap keeps a lot of stuff to himself. I asked a few of the Vice guys. They say nothing. Absolutely nothing." Danny looked over the reports for Alice's inhaler and Allen's nicotine patches. He whistled. "This says that Alice's inhaler was filled with distilled water. Was that a manufacturer's mistake?"

"No. The canister did have traces of corticosteroid and a LABA. Uh… LABA is a long-acting beta-agonist. Anyway, we think that someone emptied it and filled it with distilled water." Rick stuck out his bottom lip and shrugged. "Did you look at Allen Schofield's nicotine patch report? Those patches were laced with enough fentanyl to take down a horse."

Danny raised his eyebrows. He rocked back in his chair as the pieces starting falling into place. He narrowed his eyes. "*And?*"

"*And* the patches and the inhaler both came from Drake's. You might want to look into that," Rick suggested. "I'm going back to work. Let's see if I can find you some answers. See you tonight, Danny."

"Yeah, see ya." Danny picked up his phone and called Marnie.

"Hi, Danny. I'm just leaving Gram now, and I'm on my way to see Alice," Marnie said, not giving him time to speak.

"Marnie, would you be terribly upset if I had to cancel lunch? We've got some interesting developments, and I want to follow them up before I meet with Carl this afternoon."

"No, I understand. I need to get back home to take care of things for the party anyway. No worries," Marnie replied. "Uh... Danny, you're meeting with Carl? Did he do something wrong?"

Danny laughed. "No, Carl didn't do anything wrong. As a matter of fact, he's going to use his powers for good today. I need a profiler. I don't have one, and Carl may be able to help. What do you think?"

"I think that's wonderful! He'll do everything that he can to help. He really is a good man, Danny," Marnie replied.

"Good. Hey, you have a great afternoon. I'll see you later, and I won't forget to pick up the sandwiches." Danny glanced around the squad room and lowered his voice. "I've been thinking about you all morning."

"Yes, that's been my morning, too."

"Gram is right there, isn't she?" Danny teased.

"Yes, I'll see you in a little while," Marnie replied with a giggle.

~~~~~~~~~~~~~~~~~~~~~~~~~

Danny called Tom next.

"Hey, Danny. She wasn't home or wasn't answering the door. I'm goin' over to Reuben's to see if I can scare that little turd into telling me where his mother is," Tom reported.

"Okay. Well, don't go to Grace's without me. I don't trust her, and I don't want you and Garcia going in there, wherever it may be, without backup."

"Yeah. No problem," Tom replied. "How'd it go with Rick?"

Danny filled him in on the details from his meeting with Rick. "I'm heading over to Drake's now. Keep me posted, huh?"

"You, too." Tom hung up.

Danny stood behind his desk for a moment. He turned and stared at Captain Sterling's office door. He called Sergeant Beaumont. "Hey, Beau! It's Danny. Can you tell me how I get into Cap's office?"

"You're the CO. If you want into Cap's office, I can let you into Cap's office. Is that an order, Lieutenant?" Sergeant Beaumont responded.

"Yeah. That's an order. Thanks, Beau."

"Come get the key."

Danny took the stairs down two at a time and back up three at a time. He grimaced with pain as he opened Captain Sterling's door. "Damn stitches!"

Danny turned on the lights and stood in the doorway. He glanced around and went straight to Captain Sterling's desk. He examined everything on top of the desk and in the drawers – nothing relevant to drugs in Creekwood. He eyed the filing cabinet and credenza. He tried them both, and they were locked. Captain Sterling's admin, Stacey, was as on vacation and wouldn't be back until Monday. A temp hadn't been assigned because Captain Sterling didn't trust anyone other than Stacey. Danny tapped his fingers on the captain's desk. He pulled out the middle drawer and felt the underside of the drawer. Two keys were taped to the underside, exactly as he had hoped.

~~~~~~~~~~~~~~~~~~~~~~~

Marnie's meeting with Alice was quick and fruitful. Alice knew exactly what to do and was already going gangbusters on the wrapping by the time that Marnie was ready to leave. Alice hadn't needed any direction at all. She had figured out a system for tracking which package went with which child before Marnie had even arrived. On top of it, Alice had already sewn a stack of Christmas sacks as discussed the previous night.

"These are wonderful, Alice! I can't believe that you made so many in one night," Marnie complimented.

Alice beamed. "Yes, I thought that maybe we could get some of that chunky yarn in red and green and tie the bags closed once they're filled."

"Perfect! That's a great idea, Alice." Marnie nodded enthusiastically. "Maybe we can go to the yarn store in Town Square and see if they have the right colors. We could do that on Sunday after the parade or Monday, maybe."

"You want me to go, too?" Alice seemed confused by the suggestion.

"Yeah. It *is* your idea. Wouldn't you like to help me choose the colors?" Marnie asked.

"I would. Yes, I would – very much," Alice replied.

"Great! I'll call you Sunday morning, and we can pick a time." Marnie nodded.

"Marnie, before you go, I have something for you. Hang on!" Alice disappeared down the hall and into the kitchen. Alice came back a few minutes later with a round plastic-lidded container.

"Happy birthday, Marnie! This is that lemon tart that you liked so much. I know that you don't like cake. I thought that you would enjoy this with your detective friends."

Marnie's eyes welled up with tears. "Alice, I can't believe that you remembered my birthday. Thank you so much! This is so thoughtful."

Alice smiled. "I remember kindness, too, Marnie. I hope that you have a wonderful birthday."

Marnie and Alice said their goodbyes, and as Marnie was stepping off Alice's veranda, a thought occurred to her. She turned to see Alice smiling in the doorway.

Marnie raised an eyebrow. *"Hmm... wolf or sheep?"*

-CHAPTER FIFTY-FOUR-

Danny unlocked the credenza first. He flipped quickly through the file folders in the left-hand drawer. Nothing pertinent or obvious jumped out at him. He moved on to the right-hand drawer, which delivered the same result as the first. The middle cupboard section delivered the same.

The large filing cabinet was next. The top two drawers contained personnel files and forms. The third drawer contained press clippings related to commendations, good and bad press that the department had received, a bottle of scotch, a bottle of rye and whiskey glasses. The fourth drawer produced press clippings of a different kind. Captain Sterling had been putting together a dossier.

Danny stood and set the file on top of the file cabinet. He skimmed through the file folder. "Whoa, Cap! What the hell were you doing digging into this?" Danny closed the folder and glanced around the office, talking to himself. "He must have found the East Coast supplier, and the East Coast supplier found out, drugged him and dropped him down the stairs. I gotta get into his house." Danny leaned his elbow on the file cabinet and considered the situation. How was he going to get Vice to cooperate with Homicide? "I'm in charge until Captain Sterling returns. I guess that I could pull rank." He raised one eyebrow and considered that fact for a moment.

Danny picked up the phone and called Detective Rodriguez. She pushed back and told him that she couldn't help him. "You know, Danny, I've already had this call with Tom. I've got the same answer for you that I had for him. I've got nothing to share."

Danny clenched his jaw. "Uh huh. Well, you see, Captain Sterling is in the hospital, and while he's in the hospital, I'm the CO. I'm the ranking lieutenant in this precinct, and that means that, if I ask a question, you answer it."

"C'mon, Danny! You know that it doesn't work that way!" Rodriguez argued.

"Sergeant Beaumont says it does, and he knows everything about protocol. I'm in Captain Sterling's office. C'mon up, and let's chat."

Tom and Garcia arrived outside of Reuben Wilmot's apartment building. Garcia asked Tom if she wanted her to be the good cop.

"Oh, Garcia! You've been in Evidence too long!" Tom laughed.

"What? I thought that was a fair question," Garcia huffed.

"Okay. How about you be the badass cop? I'll be the fun-loving larrikin that I so easily portray. That's how Danny and I do it," Tom replied.

"Hmm. I'm not sure that I can badass as well as Detective Gregg. He's pretty scary. Have you ever seen him slam his hand down on a table in the middle of an interview?" Garcia shuddered at the thought. "His eyes turn that steely blue. I wouldn't want to be interrogated by him."

"Indeed, I have seen it. That move is a finely tuned art form. C'mon! Let's go scare the shit out of Reuben Wilmot." Tom opened the door to the unmarked car.

Garcia and Tom walked up the sidewalk and the steps to Reuben's building. Tom pushed the button on the call box and waited for a response.

"Yeah!"

"Reuben Wilmot, this is Detective Keller and Officer Garcia from Creekwood PD. We'd appreciate a minute of your time."

Reuben didn't respond, but the door clicked open. Tom gave Garcia a surprised glance, pushed the door and ascended the stairs to Reuben's apartment. Reuben was standing in his doorway when they reached the top. Dressed in sweatpants and nothing else, he appeared disheveled, confused and scared.

"C'mon in." Reuben ran his fingers through his hair and stepped back from the door.

"New art, Reuben?" Tom gawked at the tattoo on Reuben's back.

"Uh, yeah. Got it last night." Reuben waved a hand nonchalantly.

"Who's the artist?" Garcia asked.

"Uh, there's a place over in Hudson. Uh, Dragon Ink," Reuben replied.

"You sure that's where you got it?" Tom questioned. "Hey, Reuben, what are you on? Your eyes have that, um, dull drugged look to them. Pinpoint irises, and those dark circles are tellin' a story, too."

"I don't do drugs. I used to, but I don't anymore. I haven't in years." Reuben puffed out his chest defiantly.

"Uh huh." Tom stared at Reuben, waiting for him to break.

Garcia stood next to Tom, looking up at his set jaw, cold violet eyes and rigid stance. She was impressed. Tom Keller, the fun-loving larrikin, *was* a badass detective.

When Reuben didn't break, but instead swayed, wobbled and stared down at the floor, Tom changed tack.

"Hey, Reuben, why don't we go sit down. I've got some questions for you," Tom moved toward the living room area. "You look like you're about to lose your breakfast, fall over or both."

Reuben led the way to a small seating area in the living room. He slumped down into a shabby recliner. Tom sat on a hassock in front of him, and Garcia stood at Tom's shoulder.

Reuben ran his hand over his face and yawned.

"Reuben, where's your mother?" Tom asked.

"What? My mother?" Reuben breathed out and worked hard to focus on Tom's face.

"Yeah, your mother. We've got some questions for her."

"I don't know. I haven't seen her in a few days." Reuben doubled over and breathed deeply. He took a sip from a half-full bottle of cranberry juice that he had on the end table next to his chair.

"Reuben, you don't look well, man. What are you on?" Tom asked again.

"I'm not on anything. I've been feeling like shit the last few days. It comes and goes," Reuben replied weakly and doubled over again.

"Maybe tell me about how you got that tattoo, Reuben. I'm thinkin' that there's a story behind how you got it. I'm also thinkin' that you're afraid to tell me how you got it." Tom pushed and scooted the hassock closer to Reuben.

Reuben sat back and tried to focus. "Look, I can't help you. The tat was a spur of the moment thing. I don't know where my mother is, and I'm not on anything. I've got the flu or somethin'." He took another sip of the juice.

Tom glanced back at Garcia. "Hey, Garcia, call an ambulance. We're getting Mr. Wilmot to the hospital. Tell them suspected poisoning."

Garcia stepped back and made the call into her radio.

"Poisoning? You're crazy. I don't need to go the hospital. I'll be fine," Reuben argued. He reached for the bottle of juice, and Tom took it away from him.

"Ambulance is on the way. It won't be long," Garcia confirmed.

"I gotta go to the bathroom," Reuben complained.

"Okay. Go. As soon as the ambulance is here, you are going to the hospital. I'll break down the door if you're in there too long." Tom stood and stared down at Reuben.

Reuben stood and wobbled. He regained his balance, and he staggered out of the room and into the bathroom.

"Garcia, go downstairs and around the back where the bathroom window is. Make sure that he doesn't make a run for it. I don't know how big the bathroom window is, but if it's big enough, he might try," Tom ordered.

Garcia replied with a nod. She raced from the room, and Tom could hear both her police-issue boots thumping down the stairs and the faint wail of a siren heading their way.

~~~~~~~~~~~~~~~~~~~~~~~~~

Marnie dropped by the deli to pick up her order for the charcuterie boards and headed over to her house to pick up Tater's old kennel. Based on the chewed ice scraper and car blanket in the back seat, Dickens was already living up to his name. The kennel would save everyone a lot of worry and frustration. It would also save the legs on Danny's furniture.

Marnie pulled into the driving circle at her house and saw an old red Chevy pickup parked off to the side. She frowned. Patrick was at the side of the house stacking firewood into a tote. He waved, and she waved back and got out of her car.

"Hi, Patrick! Is that your truck?" Marnie asked.

Patrick nodded. "Y-Y-Yes. I picked it up today. Mr. Gleeson over at the tree lot was selling it. He said that, if I help him make deliveries, he'll give me a good deal."

"Nice! You've got a truck and a job. That's really great, Patrick." Marnie walked over to the truck to take a look. "It's in great shape. What year is it?"

"N-N-Ninety-nine, b-b-but it's got low mileage." Patrick smiled proudly.

Marnie nodded. "Hey, I just dropped by to pick up Tater's old kennel. We've got a new puppy, and he's going to need a place to take time-outs."

Patrick set the log tote into a rack on the front porch and walked over to Marnie's car. He peeked in the window. Tater smiled out the window at him, and Dickens growled.

"He's g-g-got character," Patrick said with a grin.

"Yes, he's going to be a handful," Marnie replied. "The kennel is in the cellar. I'll just be a sec. Do you mind staying here with them? I have a bag from the deli on the passenger seat floor. I don't want Tater filling up on cheese and salami." Marnie laughed.

"Sure," Patrick agreed.

Patrick got into the back seat of Marnie's car, pulled Dickens into his lap and then reached over the seat to scratch Tater's ears. Dickens chewed on Patrick's thumb until he fell asleep.

"How are things, Tater?" Patrick asked. "Are you keeping your mom safe?"

Tater stood on the console and stepped onto the back seat with his front paws. Patrick put up his hand, and Tater high-fived him.

"You're a smart boy, Tater. I'll bet that you could be trained to do just about anything," Patrick commented. Tater nudged Patrick with his nose. "Good boy, Tater. I'll see you tonight."

Patrick set Dickens down onto the seat and got out of the car just as Marnie came out of the house with the kennel. Patrick raced to the steps and took the kennel from her. She popped the back door, and Patrick put the kennel into the cargo area.

"Thanks, Patrick. We'll see you tonight?" Marnie asked.

"Y-Y-Yes. I'll be there," he nodded.

Marnie climbed into her car and headed back to the cabin.

Marnie's phone rang. It was from a private number. She stared at the screen for a second and thought that it might be Erin. She answered.

"Hello!"

"Happy birthday, baby sister! When are you coming to see me? Don't you miss your big brother?" Sam Reilly taunted.

Marnie disconnected the call and called Erin as she had promised. Erin answered on the first ring.

"Hi, Marnie, thanks for calling me back."

"No worries. How are you feeling?"

"Uh, I'm okay. I popped into the bookstore, and Mrs. Backus gave me a part-time job through the holidays, so that's good," Erin responded. "She's a gem, isn't she?"

"That's good news. When do you start?"

"Monday mornin'. She doesn't want to start trainin' me on a weekend. She's afraid that it will be too overwhelmin'. I'm okay with that. At least I have a job, and I won't be panickin'."

"Are you still planning to come tonight?" Marnie asked.

"Yes. I'll be on my own. I was goin' to bring my boyfriend, but I caught him with someone else last night. What is it with some men? I thought that things were goin' great, I drop by to surprise him and this raggedy floozy is just hangin' everything out – she was in his kitchen in nothin' but her underwear."

"Oh, Erin! That's horrible! I'm so sorry," Marnie replied.

"Ah. That's all right. There's a heap of fish in the ocean. I'll catch a keeper one of these days," Erin replied. "Do you need any help today? I'm just sittin' around feelin' sorry for myself."

The call waiting beep came through, and Marnie rolled her eyes. It was a private number, and she knew that it was Sam again.

"Do you have to take that, Marnie," Erin asked. "I can hear the beep of another call comin' through."

"Absolutely not. It's just my brother, and I don't want to talk to him," Marnie replied sternly. "I don't actually need any help. Everything is under control, but if you want to come on out a little early, that's cool. Maybe around 6:00? I'd say earlier, but I'm going to go home to take a long hot bath and relax for a while. It's been a busy few days."

"I understand entirely. I'll see you around 6:00. See ya later, Marnie." Erin hung up.

Marnie felt terrible. She wanted to be there for Erin, but she also knew that her own plans were important, too. She and Carl had discussed this at length. She didn't have to fix everybody. Taking time for herself was important. Her thoughts were interrupted by another call. She glanced down at the phone, smiled and answered.

"Hello, Detective Gregg!"

"Hello, Ms. Reilly! How's your day?" Danny asked cheerfully.

"I'm just on my way back to the cabin. I picked up Tater's old kennel. I think that we're going to need it for Dickens," Marnie replied.

"Dickens? Is that what you've named him?"

"Actually, Gram named him. Sort of. He most certainly is a little dickens. He's chewed my ice scraper, my car blanket and his Kong. You name it, he's chewed it."

Danny laughed. "He's a puppy. That's to be expected. Just calling to let you know that I'm heading over to meet with Carl at 1:00, then I'll pick up the sandwich trays from Gram. I'll be home around 3:00. Unfortunately, I will have to work tomorrow for a while. Fortunately, we have gotten a few breaks today."

"It sounds like you're in the car?"

"Yeah. I've got a few questions that need to be answered," Danny replied.

"Okay. That was vague. I won't ask," Marnie said with a giggle.

"You don't want to know." Danny hoped that she wouldn't push.

Marnie sensed that further questions may poke the bear, so she didn't push. "Okay. I'm going to take Tater and Dickens for a walk, pour myself a glass of wine and have a bubble bath. I haven't done that in ages."

"You know that my bathroom has a big, old, claw-foot tub? It's a damn sight bigger than the one in your bathroom. Feel free to go for a swim." Danny laughed."

"You don't have to tell me twice. See you soon!"

~~~~~~~~~~~~~~~~~~~~~~~~~~

Garcia rode in the ambulance with Reuben. Reuben had passed out in the bathroom. Tom had heard a thump and was relieved to find that Reuben had not locked the door. He was out cold on the floor and had been carried out of his apartment on a stretcher. Tom drove to the hospital in the unmarked police car and called Danny along the way to update him.

"Are you sure?"

"Yeah. He has similar marks on his wrists to William. I couldn't see his ankles, but I'll bet that we've got the same marks there. The tattoo is the Eye of Providence – exactly like the one on William's chest, except it's on Reuben's back. I didn't see a brand, but that doesn't mean that there isn't one. Danny, he looked drugged. Pinpoint irises, vague – you know the look. It wasn't until he drank juice that I wondered if he had been poisoned." Tom checked traffic on the cross streets and pulled through the intersection, following the ambulance as closely as possible. "I'm getting him checked out – blood tests and the rest. I'm going to get a search warrant for his apartment."

"Yeah. Find an easy judge. Maybe try Judge Lawrence. She's a bit sweet on you," Danny suggested.

"What can I say? Older women like me." Tom laughed.

"Okay. I'm on my way to ask Mr. Drake a few questions. Call me when you know something."

"Yeah. You, too."

~~~~~~~~~~~~~~~~~~~~~~~~~~

Grace Wilmot sat in her chair with her electric blanket wrapped around her. A candle burned on a small table near her chair. The heaters had no fuel, and she was freezing. Kate should have arrived hours ago. Kate wasn't answering her phone, Reuben wasn't answering his and neither would return her calls. Grace threw her blanket off in a huff and turned on the kettle to warm enough water for a basin bath. She needed to get to Enlighten Crystals. She had clients to see today.

"If someone doesn't come to help me, I'll just have to go back to Alice's. She wouldn't dare throw me out," Grace mumbled to herself. "I'll pack a small bag and go directly to Alice's when I've finished with my clients."

Grace fussed about getting ready to go into town. When she was finished dressing in black tights, a black wool skirt and a red cable-knit sweater, she pulled her gray wool cape around her shoulders. She picked up her overnight bag, her handbag and her gloves; blew out the candle; and used a small flashlight to light her path to the door. She unlatched the hatch. She looked left and right, stepped out of the silo and padlocked the hatch. She pulled on the padlock twice to ensure that it was locked. Grace walked up the tracks, through the tunnel and onto the street, checking carefully for watching eyes. Once she was out on the street, she went into a shady diner, ordered a coffee to go and called a cab.

-CHAPTER FIFTY-FIVE-

Danny parked outside of Drake's Drugs. It was a busy store, and he knew that the lunch counter would be brimming with gossipmongers. He got out of his Jeep and went to the side entry by the pharmacy. Mr. Drake was behind the counter serving a customer, but there didn't appear to be anyone waiting for prescriptions. Danny had purposely come at 11:00 AM to beat the afternoon rush of people filling prescriptions on their lunch break. When Mr. Drake finished, Danny went to the window.

"Detective, what can I do for you today? Your prescriptions shouldn't have run out yet." Mr. Drake furrowed his brow.

"No. I'm here on a different matter," Danny replied.

"Has Marnie run out of melatonin already? That shouldn't be." Mr. Drake frowned.

"No. No, this has nothing to do with Ms. Reilly. I'm here to ask you a few questions about Allen Schofield and Alice Wells."

Mr. Drake shook his head. "Well, I think that we both know that I can't discuss either of them with you, Detective. There is a degree of confidentiality where prescriptions are concerned."

Danny casually leaned on the counter and lowered his voice. "You can talk to me about their prescriptions, Mr. Drake, here or at the station. It's your choice. I want to know why Allen Schofield's nicotine patches were laced with enough fentanyl to kill a horse and why Alice Wells's inhaler was full of distilled water instead of corticosteroid and a LABA?" He raised his eyebrows. "You got a good answer for either of those questions?"

Mr. Drake's jaw dropped. "Maybe you should come back here, Detective."

Danny smiled. "I thought as much." Danny waited for Mr. Drake to open the door, then he pushed through into the pharmacy.

"Look, Detective, I had to let Erin Matthews go this morning. She's been... uh... interfering, shall we say. I don't remember filling a prescription for Alice Wells's medication, nor do I recall Allen Schofield coming in for nicotine patches."

Danny pulled a puzzled face. "Erin Matthews? I wasn't aware that she's a pharmacist. What was she doing filling Miss Wells's prescription? How would she get her hands on fentanyl?"

"Well, she isn't a pharmacist, and she shouldn't have been back here at all, but she would sneak in while Susan, Carrie or Peter were away from the counter. Me, too. We've all caught her back here." Mr. Drake shifted uncomfortably.

Danny raised one eyebrow. "Is that so? Isn't that door supposed to be locked at all times? You know, so people from out *there* who shouldn't be back *here* can't come back here?"

"Well, yes, but we do get lax sometimes when it's busy," Mr. Drake admitted.

Danny rubbed his jaw. "Hmm. Well, I'll have to ask Susan, Carrie and Peter to corroborate that story. Maybe you could have them all come in tomorrow, say around 11:00?"

"Do you think that's necessary?" Mr. Drake whined.

"Yeah. I think it's necessary." Danny pursed his lips and nodded. "Get them in here, Mr. Drake, and don't try to coerce them into backing you up. I'll know if you do. Reading people is a big part of my job. I know BS when I hear it." Danny pushed through the door without giving Mr. Drake an opportunity to answer.

Danny had some time to kill before going to see Carl. He stopped at the deli and ordered a sandwich and a cup of coffee. He sat at a corner table by the window, ate his sandwich, drank his coffee and read his E-mails. He glanced out the window and saw Mr. Drake on the street outside the pharmacy door. He was speaking with an older woman wearing a gray cape. He watched as they had what appeared to be a disagreement. The woman put her hand up in front of Mr. Drake's face, closed her eyes and said *something*. Danny couldn't make out what she was saying. Mr. Drake rushed away in the opposite direction of his store. The woman laughed and walked up through the Town Square.

"That's Grace Wilmot," Danny said to himself, and he raced out of the deli. When he got outside, he searched left and right, but she was gone. He turned in a circle and dropped his shoulders. "Dammit! Where did she go?"

Danny walked through the square and went into a number of stores trying to spot her, but he finally gave up. He had to meet with Carl, and he didn't want to be late.

"Danny, do you want to sit in my office or the conference room?" Carl asked.

"That's up to you. Where will we be most comfortable?"

"Conference room chairs are more comfortable. Let's go in there." Carl led the way.

Andrea ducked her head into the conference room. "Danny, do you want coffee?"

"Thanks, but no. I'm wired on caffeine. I don't think that more is going to help." Danny smiled.

Andrea ducked back out.

Carl shook his head. "No, thanks, Andrea, I don't want coffee. Thanks for asking, though."

"She's not getting any better?" Danny pulled out a chair and sat.

"No. I don't think that she ever will. She's loyal to Marnie, and I'm the big, bad wolf." Carl scowled as he took a seat. "Anyway, let's discuss the cases."

"That would be great. I really appreciate this, Carl." Danny opened the files and pulled out a notepad. "Okay. We have William Billy Williams's death, Captain Sterling's alleged accident, Alice's inhaler, Allen's laced patches and Justin Chambers's death. Give me your thoughts in layman's terms, please. Did you have time to review the information that I sent over this morning?"

Carl nodded. "Yes. Justin Chambers was a bit of shock. I didn't know him well, but he was young. I don't think that the use of the brand *and* the tattoo of the Eye of Providence has any significance to the actual meaning of the symbol. I think that it's a threat that someone is watching and knows everything. The fact that all have been drugged tells me that their attacker has a need to control or dominate. The cases of William Billy Williams and Captain Sterling show that restraints were used. That again would be control or dominance. I think that there are esteem issues – as in low. I think that the attacker has been in and out of abusive situations right back to childhood. The disfigurement of William, as seen with the tattoos, makes me feel that it was personal, as if there was a preexisting relationship prior to the murder – a relationship of trust and compassion. When the trust was betrayed, the disfigurement was payback. I would guess that William was not a believer in tattoos. The symbols are all related to protection. Maybe William was supposed to be the protector in the relationship and betrayed the other person. Captain Sterling's case, well, that speaks to me as someone who was in the way or getting too close. There was nothing personal about it. It was just…

drug him, brand him, knock him down and incapacitate him to slow him down. Justin's death is a bit different. He was drugged, branded and placed up on the garage door – alive. The fall from the garage door onto the car and then the cement floor killed him. Acute subdural hematoma. His tongue had been slit down the middle, but not removed? That's mutilation, and it suggests that he snitched, but didn't tell the whole truth. The forked tongue could be symbolic. I didn't know Justin well. We need to ask ourselves, as well as others, 'Was Justin a duplicitous person?' Only then will we have a better understanding."

Danny shrugged a shoulder. "I don't know. I didn't know Justin. Marnie believed that he was being genuine when she spoke with him at Alice's house. Problem is…"

Carl cut off Danny and finished his sentence. "Marnie sees the potential in everyone. Whether they meet that potential is another thing." Carl looked at Danny over the top of his notes.

Danny nodded. "Yeah, she does see the potential in everyone."

"Now, let's discuss what happened to you." Carl skimmed the report and gathered his thoughts. "The stabbing with the icicle was purely defense. I think that you startled someone who was certainly planning to do damage to your property. Whether arson or something else, I don't know. The power line was purposefully cut – that's stated in the report." Carl considered his words carefully. "Danny, have you thought that Sam Reilly has someone working for him? Have you considered it? Justin falling off the door and nearly hitting Marnie. Marnie being locked in a trunk. Sabotaging the garage power and the security lights. Marnie and Sam both knew William. Maybe you are getting too close to something. What else has happened? Has Tom been targeted? Could Kate Parish be working with Sam? What about Grace Wilmot? She's back in town, and she would have twisted reasons for going after Marnie."

"If you had to give me a profile of the person doing these things, what would you say? Who would we be looking for?"

"I would say that you're dealing with a highly damaged persona. Someone who likes control. Someone who enjoys inflicting pain. Someone who has a wide network. Someone who watches and waits. Someone who blends into the woodwork. Someone who either has the capacity to take on a different persona or who is so terrifyingly charming that you would never know what's hidden beneath. I don't like Grace for this. She's up to something, but not this. Kate Parish is a possibility. Grace's son Reuben – possibly." Carl stuck out his bottom lip and sucked his teeth.

Danny twirled a pen around his fingers – thinking, considering everything that Carl was saying. "Let me throw a name out, and tell me if it sticks."

"Okay," Carl replied.

"Patrick," Danny said, pushing his chair away from the table.

Carl raised his eyebrows. "I wasn't expecting that name."

Danny tapped the folders on the table. ""He had access to Allen's patches. He had access to Alice's inhaler. He knew Justin. He's obviously dealing with PTSD. He had a rough childhood. He's got physical and psychological scarring. I don't have a connection to Captain Sterling or William yet, but who knows what digging will uncover. What's Patrick's last name?"

"Kowalski," Carl replied.

Danny tapped the folders one more time. "Carl, thanks. I may want to go over some theories a bit later. This has been helpful. Are you coming tonight?"

"Yes. I'll be there." Carl drummed his fingers on the conference table. "Danny, could I hang on to those folders a bit longer? I'm free for the rest of the afternoon. Another review or perhaps a deeper dive may be helpful."

Danny set the folders on the table and pushed them to Carl. "Knock yourself out. Can you bring them with you tonight? Maybe come a bit early so it's not a thing – you know, you handing me the folders."

"Of course. I'll put them in an envelope. Discretion is good." Carl nodded.

~~~~~~~~~~~~~~~~~~~~~~~~~~~~

Garcia and Tom sat in the waiting room at the hospital for news about Reuben Wilmot. The nurse at the desk was avoiding eye contact with them. Tom's patience was wearing thin just as Danny walked down the hall. Danny saw Tom and Garcia, but went directly to the nurse's station. Garcia and Tom sat up straight and listened

"I'm Lieutenant Gregg with Creekwood PD. Officer Garcia and Detective Keller have been waiting for information regarding a patient, Reuben Wilmot. We are working two murder investigations, and we require your cooperation. Could you please let me know to whom we may speak? Now."

The nurse glanced up at him and made a phone call. A doctor appeared a few minutes later.

"Lieutenant Gregg? I'm Dr. Klein. I understand that you're inquiring about Reuben Wilmot."

"Yes, doctor. As I explained to the nurse, we're working two murder investigations, and we believe that Mr. Wilmot was about to become the third murder victim. My detective and officer were with him when they noticed that he may have been given poison. Garcia came to the hospital with him, and Detective Keller escorted the ambulance. What can you tell me?"

Tom and Garcia leaned forward so that they could hear the conversation. Dr. Klein hesitated. "You know that I can't tell you much."

"Actually, Doc, if he was poisoned, you can tell me as much as you want. Someone tried to kill Reuben Wilmot, and we're trying to find out who did it."

Dr. Klein worried his jaw for a moment and then conceded. "All right. Reuben Wilmot has ingested thallium, which is essentially rat poison. We've administered Prussian blue, which is the antidote, and he should be fine. We want to hold him overnight to keep an eye on him. He could be dealing with damage to his nervous system, lungs, heart, liver or kidneys, especially if large amounts were eaten or drunk over a short period of time. We don't know the duration of the poisoning."

"Thank you. We're searching his apartment, and we will advise if other items in his cupboards or refrigerator have been tampered with. We'll put an officer on his room overnight."

"Thank you, Lieutenant." Dr. Klein nodded. "I'll let the nurses know."

Danny turned to Tom and Garcia. "Let's get out of here. I'll call the station and get someone on Reuben's room overnight. We'll check back tomorrow morning."

~~~~~~~~~~~~~~~~~~~~

After having settled Dickens into the kennel, Marnie steeped in a hot tub of bubbles in Danny's claw-foot tub. She had a glass of champagne sitting on the seat of an old ladder-back chair. The champagne bottle was next to the glass; the bottle rested conveniently in a bucket of ice. Tater sprawled in front the of the closed bathroom door. A burning church candle in an old mason jar lit the bathroom. Marnie closed her eyes and allowed her mind to drift into the meditation music playing on her phone.

~~~~~~~~~~~~~~~~~~~~

Danny arrived home at 3:30. Hannah was in the kitchen, and she glanced up when Danny came in with a stack of sandwich trays.

"What are you doin'?" Danny asked, putting the trays into the refrigerator.

"I was thinking about Saturday dinners when we were kids. Remember when Father would make stew? He always made it on Friday evening and warmed it up on Saturday. That extra day made all of the difference." Hannah turned to the stove and stirred the contents of a cast-iron Dutch oven.

"Rabbit or beef?" Danny asked.

"Rabbit," Hannah replied.

"Did you get it at the butcher shop or from the freezer?" Danny asked.

Hannah turned to look at him, and her jaw dropped. "You have rabbit in the freezer?"

"Yeah!" Danny replied, pulling a face at his sister. "Have you seen where I live? There are rabbits everywhere, including my freezer."

Hannah giggled. "True. I'd forgotten that you like to hunt woodland creatures. Hadn't even thought to check the freezer. Anyway, this will be done in about 45 minutes if you want to try it."

"That would be great! I only ate half of my lunch today. A lot going on." Danny leaned against the door jam. "Hey, what have you got happening tomorrow? I would like your input on the cases we're working. I thought that maybe you, me, Tom, Carl and Marnie could all sit around, eat leftovers *and* stew and share theories."

Hannah's jaw dropped again. "You want *my* input?"

"Don't look so stunned, Banana. I used to ask you for advice when we were younger," Danny replied over his shoulder as he left the kitchen. He returned a second later. "Hey, is Marnie home?"

Hannah nodded. "She's upstairs. She took a bottle of champagne and a glass up with her. She said something about taking a swim – whatever that means."

Danny went to the cupboard and took out a champagne glass. "I know *exactly* what that means."

Danny ran upstairs into his bedroom and tapped on the bathroom door. Tater let out a low woof, and Dickens whined. Danny cracked open the door. Earphones in, Marnie appeared to be asleep. He went to the edge of the tub, sat on the floor and knocked on the side of the tub. Marnie opened one eye, smiled and took out her earphones.

"Good afternoon, Detective. Are you going to sit there perving at me, or are you going to get into this tub and wash my back?"

Danny tipped his head back and rolled his eyes. "I just remembered. I'm not allowed to have a bath with my stitches. I'm going to have sit here, have a glass of champagne and admire the view." Danny frowned and poured himself a glass of champagne.

"I was just about to get out anyway. I'm getting pruney." Marnie sat up and pulled the plug from the bottom of the tub. Danny handed her a towel. She stood in the tub and toweled off. Danny wrapped his arms around her and swung her out of the tub.

"Didn't want you to fall in that slippery tub." Danny hugged her close.

318

"Mmm. Of course not." Marnie wrapped her arms around him as he dried her back. "You know, that bath was exactly what I needed. My folks are talking to me again."

Danny took the clip out of her hair and brushed her hair gently away from her face. "Maybe not so much with the chatter about your parents right now."

"Why? Did you have other plans, Detective?" Marnie stared up at him innocently.

~~~~~~~~~~~~~~~~~~~~~~~~~~~

Tom arrived at five o'clock to help Danny set up a table and to bring chairs in from the garage. He found Hannah in the kitchen sampling her stew.

"Whatcha got there?" Tom asked.

Hannah turned around and smiled. "Irish stew. Want some?"

Tom shook his head. "Later, thanks. I had a burger on the way here. Where's Danny?"

"I think that he's upstairs."

They both turned when they heard Danny's voice in the living room.

"C'mon, Tater! C'mon, Dickens! Let's go out!" Danny pulled on his jacket and picked up Dickens to carry him outside.

"Hey, you want help bringing in those chairs?" Tom asked.

Danny spun around. "Yeah. Let me get these two taken care of, then we can do that."

Marnie came down the stairs slowly, carrying the kennel. "Danny, I'm going to put this over by the pool table. Is that okay?"

Tom met her halfway on the stairs and took the kennel from her. He carried it to the pool table and set it down next to Tater's favorite spot.

Danny laughed. "Yeah. We may need to lock up the little dickens before the night is over. I'll be back in a sec."

"Thanks for your help with the kennel, Tom." Marnie walked into the kitchen. She picked up a spoon and stirred one pot of chili. "Tom, how was your day?" She picked up another spoon and stirred the other pot of chili.

"Did Danny tell you about Reuben Wilmot?" Tom asked.

"No. What's happened? Is he okay?" Marnie's eye widened.

"We, uh, Garcia and I, went over to question him. He looked like shit, and he passed out. Thallium poisoning. He's under watch at the hospital." Tom picked up a spoon and tasted the chili. "Mmm. That's good. Oh, Hannah, I'll try your stew while we wait for Danny."

"Sure." Hannah scooped a ladle full of stew into a bowl and set it in front of him, then she grabbed a spoon out of a drawer.

"Wow! Hannah, this is amazing! Marnie, you have to taste this." Tom held a spoonful up for Marnie to taste.

Marnie leaned in and took a bite of the stew from the spoon. Her eyes opened wide, and she smiled while she chewed. "Hannah, this is so good! Is that mustard that I taste?"

"It is!" Hannah beamed. "Nobody ever guesses that."

Tom sniffed and glanced up at Marnie. "You smell good. What are you wearing?"

"It's milk-and-honey lotion." Marnie giggled. "I relaxed in a milk-and-honey bubble bath for about 40 minutes today." Marnie disappeared into the pantry and came out with serving trays.

Tater raced into the kitchen and put his paw on Tom's leg. Dickens scurried in behind him, slid on the floor and ran into Tom's boot. Danny walked in behind them, bent and scooped Dickens up into his arms.

Tom leaned over and sniffed Danny. "You smell like Marnie's lotion."

"What?" Danny scowled. "C'mon. Help me get the chairs and the table out of the garage."

"You're avoiding me, Daniel!" Tom called out, chasing Danny through the living room to the front door.

Hannah smirked.

Marnie frowned. "What?"

"He does smell like your lotion. Wonder how that could be?" Hannah teased.

~~~~~~~~~~~~~~~~~~~~~~~~~~~

Erin arrived early and helped set out the food. Gram arrived shortly after Erin and took charge in the kitchen so that the "young folk" could visit. They listened to music, decorated the tree, told stories, compared notes, drank merrily, ate heartily and wished Marnie a happy birthday. Marnie blew out candles on a birthday cake that Gram made, and she ate a piece of raspberry pie that Ellie made. At the end of the evening, the tree was half-decorated, the sandwiches were all gone, one pot of chili was finished, the other pot was half full and many bottles of beer and wine had been consumed.

As guests were preparing to leave, Danny checked to see if everyone was okay to drive. "Is everyone okay to drive?" Danny asked. "Does anyone need to crash here?"

Marnie held the door and said goodbye to their guests. Tom was the only one who raised his hand to stay. Gram, Hannah and Marnie cleaned up the kitchen, while Tom and Danny took care of the living room.

"Thanks, Gram, for cleaning up throughout the night. It has saved us a ton of work." Marnie gave Gram a hug.

"Paper plates and disposable bowls certainly helped," Hannah added. "We've got most of the glasses and silverware in the dishwasher. The rest will only take a few minutes."

Tom and Danny carried a few glasses into the kitchen. Tom went back to do a quick check to see if they had missed anything.

Danny put a few glasses into the sink. "We're good in there. We'll have to finish the tree tomorrow. Everybody was so busy chatting and eating, it's only half done."

Marnie peeked into the living room at the tree and smiled. "That's okay. It's a nice, quiet Saturday morning distraction."

"Hey, Marn! There were a few birthday gifts on the bench near the pool table." Tom carried a few bags and three boxes into the kitchen.

Danny checked his watch. "You've still got one hour before your birthday is over. Open your gifts, Marnie."

Tom handed her a box. "I saw Uncle Giles and Aunt Janet bring in this one."

Marnie clapped. "Yay! They always get me a gag gift." Marnie unwrapped the box. She burst out laughing. "The note card says, 'For the girl who has everything, here's a little something for emergencies.'"

"What is it?" Danny asked.

"A hand auger and a snorkel," Marnie laughed.

Everyone frowned except Tom. He burst out laughing. "It's better than the time that they bought your father the fire extinguisher after he caught the kitchen curtains on fire with the blowtorch."

"Oh, my gosh, I forgot about that!" Marnie giggled. "Poor Dad! The pipes froze, and he was using a blowtorch to thaw the pipes. Mom said something to him, he turned and the curtains went up. Mom sprayed Dad and the curtains with the hose from the kitchen sink."

"I still remember your dad's face – standing there, dripping wet with the torched curtains behind him. Your mom laughed so hard!" Tom doubled over with laughter.

Danny, Gram and Hannah started to laugh because Tom and Marnie were laughing so hard.

"Oh! What about the time that they gave your mom the box of adult diapers because she wet herself laughing when your dad fell off the dock at the Fourth of July party?"

Marnie spit a mouthful of champagne and doubled over giggling. Her face was red, and she finally squeaked out, "That went up my nose."

"Fits of giggles are the best on a birthday." Gram had tears streaming down her face with laughter. Watching Marnie and Tom reminisce about her parents was a wonderful treat. She'd never seen either of them laugh this hard.

"C'mon, Marn!" Tom handed her another package. "Just a few more gifts to go."

Marnie finished unwrapping all but one. "These are all so thoughtful. I can't believe that people remembered that it was my birthday." Marnie smiled, picked up the last box and unwrapped it. Her face dropped, and she put the box on the table.

"What is it, Marn? Fake vomit? Rubber dog poo?" Tom teased.

"It's a sick joke," Marnie scowled. She shoved the box across the table to Tom.

Tom peeked inside and glowered. "It's sick all right. A sick fucking joke!"

Tom grabbed a napkin off the table, stuck his hand into the box and produced the offending item.

Hannah gasped. "It's a murder!"

Tom held up a small stuffed crow, an arrow piercing its back.

Danny's hand went to his back where he had been stabbed with the icicle.

Tom put the bird back into the box. "We'll see about prints tomorrow. Sorry, Marn. This is one present that you can't keep."

"Good riddance! I was going to see if I could exchange it anyway. I already have two." Marnie managed a forced laugh.

~~~~~~~~~~~~~~~~~~~~~~~~~~~~~

Gram shooed them out of the kitchen. "Go, sit by the fire. Enjoy what's left of Marnie's birthday. No more of this murder nonsense. We'll finish Marnie's blessed day with happiness and joy."

They all traipsed into the living room and plonked down on couches and chairs. Gram came back with a bottle of Irish whiskey and five glasses. Gram poured out five healthy servings.

"Lift your glasses to Marnie! May the most you wish for be the least you get! Lá Breithe Shona dhuit! Happy birthday, Marnie!" Gram toasted.

"Happy birthday!" Tom, Hannah and Danny toasted in unison.

322

"Drink up!" Gram ordered.

"Gram, you should stay the night with us," Hannah suggested. "You can drive home in the morning."

"It's a good idea, Gram," Danny agreed. "I noticed that it was snowing when I looked out the window a few minutes ago."

"You can have my room, Gram," Tom offered.

"I won't be puttin' anyone out of their room tonight," Gram said. "I'll sleep down here on the couch. No arguments."

Marnie gave Danny a knowing glance. He nodded. Marnie cleared her throat. "Gram, you can take my room. Tater, Dickens and I will crash with Danny."

Tom's eyebrows shot up, and he raised his glass. "Well, then, Marnie *will* be ending her birthday with happiness and joy."

Danny and Marnie responded in unison. "Shut up, Tom."

-CHAPTER FIFTY-SIX-

Saturday, December 12ᵗʰ

Alice sat at her kitchen table drinking a cup of cocoa. She glanced up at the clock every few minutes, and it seemed to never change. It was 12:05 AM. Grace Wilmot had invaded her home once again. When the knock came a little past 6:00 PM, she thought that it might be Justin or Reuben or maybe even Marnie or Carl. She'd opened the door without checking, and there stood Grace Wilmot, demanding entry into her home. Alice tried to shut the door, but Grace had overpowered her and shoved her way into the foyer.

Tears welled up in Alice's big eyes. How could this be happening again? Grace had ridiculed her from the moment that she arrived. Grace questioned her motives for helping Marnie and reminded Alice that she was assured eternal damnation for past actions. Grace told her that helping Marnie Reilly wrap a few Christmas presents for the kiddies wasn't going to get her a sainthood. Worst of all, Grace had once again – ever so unceremoniously – thrown Alice out of her prized turret room.

The more that Alice thought about Grace shoving through her door, the angrier she became. She slammed her hands down on the kitchen table, stood and stalked into the dining room to get her pistol. "That's enough, Grace Wilmot! You are going to leave my house, and you will never come back!"

Alice stopped in the front entryway, turned on the outside light and unlocked the front door. She clomped up the stairs and stomped down the hall to the turret room where Grace was asleep. Alice reached for the doorknob and found it to be locked. She pulled the key out of her bathrobe pocket, unlocked the door and threw the door open. She planted her feet, leveled her pistol and fired one shot above the headboard.

"Get out of my house! Get out now, you horrible, evil woman!" Alice shouted.

Grace shot up and clutched her chest. "Alice, what are you doing? Get out of here! How dare you!"

Alice fired another round into the wall next to the nightstand. "Get out! Get out of my house! Get out! Get out! Get out!" Alice stomped her feet with every word and aimed the pistol at Grace's head.

Allowing the pistol to hang loosely on her index finger by the trigger ring, Alice pulled her phone out of the pocket of her bathrobe. She pressed 911 on her phone and did her level best to sound terrified and pathetic. "Yes, someone has broken into my home. Could you please send help? Please, please send help. The woman is threatening me. She's broken in before. She overpowered me at my front door and threatened me. Please… My address? 88 Pine Valley Drive, Creekwood. Yes? Alice Wells. Thank you." Alice muted the phone and dropped it in her pocket, never breaking the connection.

"Get out of my house, Grace Wilmot. Get your ass out of my bed, pack up your nasty things and get out! Get out! Get out! Get out!" Alice shouted again, gripping the pistol with both hands.

Grace swung her legs over the edge of the bed and stalked toward Alice. "You didn't call the police, Alice. You sniveling coward. Put that gun down! Put it down now, Alice, and we can forget this ever happened."

"I'm not afraid of you, Grace. Don't come near me! I will shoot! Don't you dare take another step!" Alice warned, her eyes wild.

"I'm going to kill you!" Grace screamed. Grace lunged for the gun. Alice stepped to the side and Grace ran into the door frame and hit the floor.

Alice looked down at Grace laying on the floor holding her head in her hands. "No, Grace. You are not going to kill me. I've been waiting for this day for a very long time. You are done! You will never, ever, *ever*, threaten me again!"

Grace reached out a hand, grabbed Alice's ankle and dug her nails into the skin. Alice in turn cracked Grace on the head with her pistol. Grace slumped back onto the floor. Alice stepped out into the hall, took the phone out of her pocket and calmly waited for the police, never taking her eyes off of Grace.

Alice heard the police on the veranda and then heard them call out from the entryway. She called down for the police to come upstairs. As the police came down the hall, she held her hands out in front of her with her pistol hanging from one finger. "Officers, she's right here. Grace Wilmot. That's her name. She tried to attack me, and I hit her on the head with my pistol."

An ambulance was called. Grace was removed from Alice's house. The police said that they would be back in the morning for a full statement. Alice changed the sheets, crawled into her bed in the turret room and slept like a baby.

Marnie awoke at 6:00 AM. Danny was still asleep. Tater had made his way up onto the bed in the middle of the night and was snuggled between her and Danny – his nose on Danny's pillow. Dickens was stirring in the kennel. Marnie peeked down, and he was peeking back. He put his paws up on the side of the kennel and whined.

"Okay. I'll get up and take you out." Marnie pulled on a pair of sweatpants, a sweatshirt and socks and lifted Dickens out of his kennel. "Tater, want to go out?" Tater groaned and rolled onto his back.

Danny rolled onto his side and opened one eye. "Where are you going?" He stretched and smiled.

"Dickens needs to go out. He just woke up. Go back to sleep. Tater isn't ready to get up yet. He's happy to stay and snuggle." Marnie giggled.

"I don't want to snuggle with him, and how did he get up here? Wasn't he in his bed?" Danny asked, reaching over to rub Tater's tummy.

"Oh, Danny! You will soon learn that Tater finds a way up onto the bed *every* night." Marnie went around the foot of the bed and slipped her feet into her slippers. "We'll put the coffee on and bring you a cup."

"Hmm. No, I'm getting up. I'm starving. Maybe Gram will be up already making a good old Irish breakfast for her favorite grandson." Danny sat up and looked out the window. "We got snow overnight. Look at the trees."

Marnie kissed him on the forehead and ruffled his hair. "Okay. You make the coffee. I'll take out Dickens and Tater." She tossed him a pair of sweatpants off a chair and disappeared downstairs.

Danny turned to Tater, who was still sprawled on his back. "She's pretty bossy, isn't she?"

Tater rolled over, barked once and nudged Danny with his nose. Danny laughed. "You're pretty bossy, too."

~~~~~~~~~~~~~~~~~~~~~~~~~~~~

Gram was in the kitchen when Danny and Tater went downstairs. Pans were sizzling, coffee was bubbling in the percolator and the kettle was whistling.

"Gram, something smells amazing!" Danny gave his grandmother a hug. "I kind of like it when you stay the night. An Irish breakfast is my favorite."

"Everyone should start their day with a proper fry-up," Gram replied. "What time do you suppose that your sister and Tom will be stirrin'?"

"Hmm. I wouldn't count on either one of them for at least another hour or two. Hannah still likes to sleep in, and Tom is pretty bushed. We've had a lot

happening. Captain Sterling has been out. We've both been picking up slack."
Danny sat at the counter and reached for the coffee that Gram poured for him.

"What about you? You must be tired, love?" Gram asked, brushing his hair away from his forehead with her hand.

"I'm okay, Gram. I've got you, Marnie and Hannah looking after me. Geez! Marnie does my laundry for me, she cooks and I clean up. Yesterday, we hired a cleaner to come through and sparkle everything up for the party. It makes a big difference when you have people taking off some of the load."

Gram nodded. "It does. I believe that you and Marnie look after Tom, though, too."

"We do," Danny replied. "His folks are coming into town today. He always gets edgy when they visit. As soon as he picks his folks up at the airport, that's it. He's nonstop until they go back after Christmas. I feel kind of sorry for him."

"Oh, his mother does like to shop. Poor, Tom. She'll drag him to every shoppin' center, outlet center and boutique within a 20-mile radius." Gram laughed and patted Danny's hand.

Marnie came into the kitchen with Dickens. "Oh, my goodness! It's chilly out there!"

"What are the two of you doin' today?" Gram asked.

Danny scratched the back of his head and yawned. "Busy day ahead, Gram. I have to go into town for a chat with a few of Mr. Drake's employees. Then we've got a powwow set up here with Tom, Carl, Hannah, Marnie, Rick and me. We're going through the current cases, and we're going to figure out what the hell is happening in Creekwood."

"You know, Danny, your old grandmother is privy to town chatter at the diner. I may be an asset to your powwow. I hear things that I shouldn't, and I hear things that I wish that I hadn't. That's the life of a publican." Gram took a sip of her coffee and winked at her grandson.

"Hmm. I've never thought of you as a mole, Gram. I bet that you know more about the dirty underbelly of Creekwood than anyone else in town."

Gram's eyes twinkled. "To be sure, Danny. To be sure."

Marnie sat on the couch pulling on a pair of warm socks when Tom came downstairs.

"Morning, Tom! Gram has a plate ready for you. It's in the oven. She made an amazing fry-up."

"Mmm. I just want a cup of coffee. I have to go the office and get groceries. My parents arrive later today, and my refrigerator is empty. What time are we all gathering here?"

"Um, Danny said that Carl and Rick would be here at 1:00. Do you want me to get your groceries? I have to run into town for a quick meeting with the float-and-parade committee. That won't take long."

"Nah. I don't have a list or anything." Tom twisted his mouth to the side.

"That's okay. I can wing it. Bread, milk, cereal, eggs, chicken, beef, pork, vegetables, fruit, toilet paper, laundry soap, dish soap, hand soap. Even if I just get a bit of everything that I normally buy, you'll at least have food and essentials in the house when they arrive."

"If you don't mind, that would be great. You have a key, right?" Tom asked.

Marnie nodded. "You should take your folks to the parade tomorrow. It starts at 2:00. Everyone in town will be there. Think about it. Anyway, I'm taking the knuckleheads out, then I'll head into town."

"Is Danny still here, or did he leave?" Tom asked.

"He's shoveling. Wouldn't let me do it, but I don't think that he should be doing it. He's going to pop his stitches." Marnie shrugged.

"I'll go make him let me do it." Tom pulled on his boots and jacket.

"Thanks, Tom."

Marnie slipped on her jacket and boots, gathered Dickens into her arms and headed out onto the porch with Tater following. Wind whipped across the lake and made her eyes water as soon as she stepped off the porch. Tater ran toward the lake, turned and waited for Marnie to catch up. Marnie set Dickens down in the snow.

"I'll watch the little guy," Danny offered. "You go with Tater. He's waiting."

"Thanks. We won't be long."

Tom called out, "Hey, Danny. Have you been around the side of the garage? There are footprints going behind the garage and down behind the cabin. Have you been back here?"

Danny went around the corner of the garage. "No. I haven't been over this way."

Tom glanced up. "Well, someone has. Someone with about a size eleven boot," Tom said, placing his size twelve boot over top of one of the prints.

Danny ran his hand over his face. "What the hell? You know, I thought when Sam Reilly went to prison that all of this shit would stop. Did anyone here at the party last night set off your cop sensors?"

Tom pursed his lips and shook his head. "Nah. I was watching, and I know that you mean Patrick from our chat yesterday. I don't get a bad vibe from him. He fits the profile. I just don't see it."

Danny sighed. "I don't know, but someone brought that damn package! Someone had to bring it in with them."

Tom shrugged. "I don't know, but these tracks go all the way back behind the cabin and down the deer run. Somebody's been skulking around. I wonder what time it stopped snowing? These tracks look fresh. The deer have run through some of them, but these were made after the snow stopped."

"I don't know." Danny shook his head then glanced down at his watch. "I have to go into town and speak to Mr. Drake's people. I'll be back for 1:00. Are you okay to come back? I know that you're expecting your folks."

"Yeah. I'll be back. Marnie is going to do my grocery shopping for me and drop them at my place. That gives me some extra time."

"I hope that we can figure all of this out, Tom. There are too many moving parts, and I'm afraid that we're going to miss something important." Danny rubbed the back of his neck.

"You look stressed, Danny. Maybe you should get your girlfriend to give you a backrub," Tom teased.

"I would, but she's busy. She has to go grocery shopping for her loser best friend," Danny replied dryly.

"She volunteered!" Tom shot back.

Marnie and Tater came around the corner of the garage. Tater was covered in snow. He ran straight at Dickens and rolled the pup over with his nose. Dickens hopped up and barked at Tater.

"Oh, life isn't going to be dull with these two running amok." Marnie giggled and scooped up Dickens before Tater could roll him again. "C'mon, you ratbags! Let's see if Gram and Hannah will babysit for a few hours."

Tom kicked snow with his boot, squinted up at the rising sun, turned and watched Marnie go up the steps to the cabin.

"You think that she's okay to be wandering around town by herself? I just suddenly thought about her going out to my place alone to drop off groceries."

Danny agreed. "Yeah. I was thinking about that, too. Maybe Carl should keep an eye on her. If he's going to the parade meeting, maybe he can bump into her at the grocery store and… Nah. That's not going to work. He wouldn't have a reason to go to your place, and if she sees his car following her, well, that's going to piss her off. Let's take the direct approach."

Marnie came down the steps, ready to go into town.

"What's the plan?" Tom asked.

"Watch and learn." Danny shot Tom a wry smile.

"Gram and Hannah are going to keep an eye on Tater and Dickens. I'll be back before 1:00. Are you two taking off soon?" Marnie asked.

Danny brushed snow off Marnie's side mirror. "Yeah. I've got that meeting at Drake's."

Tom nodded. "I'm heading to the office first and then to the hospital. I have to check in on Reuben and Captain Sterling."

"Be careful, please." Marnie frowned. "I'm concerned after everything that's happened this week. Gram and Hannah are safe and sound in the cabin, but you two are running around chasing after…Well, that's the problem, isn't it? We don't know who we're chasing after."

Danny jumped on the opportunity. "Perfect segue, Marnie. We're not comfortable with you going out to Tom's on your own to drop off groceries. Do you think that you could ask Carl to go with you?"

"Sure. If he doesn't have things to do. It is Saturday," Marnie replied.

"Great! If he can't go with you, call me. I don't want you going out to Tom's alone. If someone is following you…Well, we don't know who we're looking for, right?"

"Okay." Marnie opened her car door, climbed in and set her bag on the passenger seat. She turned the car on to warm it up and got out again. "Maybe we could all check in with each other every hour or so. A phone call. Not a text. Maybe we should turn on our GPS trackers like we did when we went hiking the day after Thanksgiving."

Tom agreed. "That's a good idea. Danny, how about if we check in with you every hour?"

"That sounds good to me. Marnie, you call on the hour. Tom, you call on the half-hour."

Marnie checked her watch. "Okay, first check is 10:00 AM. I gotta go, guys. Chat in a bit!"

Marnie opened the car door and climbed in. She turned at the knock on her window. Danny stood there, head tipped to the side, grinning. She rolled down the window. "Yes?"

Danny leaned into the car and kissed her. "See ya later, and be safe."

"You, too." Marnie rolled her window back up, turned her car around and accelerated slowly down the driveway. She held up a hand and waved to Danny and Tom.

Tom pushed snow with his boot toe again. "I've been sayin' it for days…"

"Something is rotten in the state of Denmark." Danny finished Tom's sentence.

"Yeah. Somethin's rotten all right," Tom whispered.

~~~~~~~~~~~~~~~~~~~~~~~~~~~

Marnie checked in with Danny at 10:00, and Tom checked in at 10:30. Marnie was on her way to caroling practice with the children who would be singing on the float on Sunday. Carl hadn't been at the parade meeting and wasn't answering his cell or home phone. Tom was on his way to the hospital to check in on Captain Sterling and to question Reuben. Danny was at Enlighten Crystals searching for Grace Wilmot.

As Tom left the station, the sergeant on duty, Sergeant Halpin, called Tom over to his desk.

"Hey, you might want to mention to Danny that Grace Wilmot was arrested last night, but made bail. I just saw an E-mail from Danny saying that she's a person of interest."

Tom scowled. "Danny sent that E-mail yesterday afternoon. Why are you just seein' it this morning?"

Sergeant Halpin held out his hands. "Hey, man. The system fell over right around 3:00 yesterday. Nobody realized it until 4:00 this morning, and by then, it was too late. We'd already cut her loose."

"Did anyone call Danny to tell him?" Tom asked.

"Nah. I just found out. Guys on the desk overnight don't know shit. They called the IT guy, but didn't report it. We gotta get better people in overnight. Beau and me, we've been tellin' the Captain that for years. He just shrugs it off and walks away," Halpin complained.

"Well, I'll let Danny know, but you might want to send a message out to all of the department heads. Danny is gonna be pissed!" Tom said, shaking his head in anger. "You got a current address for Grace Wilmot?"

"Yeah. I checked it out. It's a fake. It's a diner down on Railroad," Halpin said. "I'll talk to Danny. Maybe we should reach out to the chief. You know, he knows that Captain Sterling is in the hospital, and he hasn't reached out – the assistant chief hasn't reached out, either. It's like we're invisible over here. Ever since the superintendent retired… I don't know. Makes me wanna puke. How come they don't reach out? Protocol. Nobody follows protocol no more."

"Hey, Danny's doin' the best that he can. He's juggling Cap's load plus his own. He's reached out to the chief. Don't know what response he's received." Tom shrugged. "I gotta go. Headin' over to the hospital to check in on Cap and a suspect."

"Have a good one, Keller," Halpin replied with a wave.

~~~~~~~~~~~~~~~~~~~~~~~~

Danny entered Enlighten Crystals. It was pretty much what he had expected – shelves of crystals in every shape and color, pendulums, crystal balls and the overwhelming scent of incense.

Danny asked a young redheaded woman wearing a tiger-eye necklace his first question. "When is Grace Wilmot scheduled to work again?"

"I don't think that Grace has a set schedule. Customers call her for appointments. We don't make appointments for her."

"When was she here last?" Danny asked.

"I don't know. I don't work every day. You might want to ask Miranda. She's over there – see, the girl with the arm sleeve."

Danny approached Miranda. "I'm Detective Gregg from Creekwood PD. I'm looking for Grace Wilmot. Can you tell me when she worked last?"

"She was here for two or three hours yesterday, but I don't know when she'll be in again," Miranda replied.

"Do you know where she lives?" Danny asked.

Miranda shook her head.

"Do you have her phone number?"

Miranda shook her head.

"Do you have Grace's client list?" Danny asked.

"Oh, God, no! She doesn't let anyone near her clients! They make their appointments with her and only her! We're not even supposed to talk to them." Miranda practically shouted her response. Customers turned around to see what the commotion was about.

"Miranda, I need you to stay calm. Can you tell me who owns Enlighten Crystals?" Danny asked quietly.

"I don't know." Miranda answered with a head toss.

"Who hired you?" Danny asked.

"Um. I don't know. I sent my application in online, and I was told to report for work a few days later. I had a two-week probationary period. They liked me, and I stayed."

Danny rubbed his chin. "Does the store have a manager?"

"Cassie doesn't work Saturdays. She'll be here tomorrow at 10:00."

"Okay. Thanks, Miranda. You've been helpful. Listen, if Grace comes in, don't tell her that I was asking about her, okay?" Danny said sternly.

"Is she in trouble?" Miranda's eyes popped.

"Should she be?" Danny raised an eyebrow.

Miranda did a whole body shrug. "I don't know. She scares me and the rest of the girls here."

Danny frowned. "Why's that?"

Miranda leaned close to Danny and whispered. "She gets angry if we go anywhere near her 'consult room,' as she calls it, and she threatens to tell the owner if we do anything that she doesn't like."

"Is that right?" Danny remarked. "Well, let's see if I can fix that for you."

"Don't tell her that I said anything! God! She'll put a curse on me!" Miranda's facial expression could only be described as sheer terror.

"I'm not going to tell her anything. Don't worry," Danny reassured. "I'll speak to Cassie tomorrow."

Danny left and walked to Drake's Drugs. Before he entered, he called Marnie.

"Hi, Danny. I'm just finishing with the kids. I'm going to go check on Carl. I'm kind of worried that he's not well. It's not like him to not answer his phone."

"Can you wait about 45 minutes? I'm going into Drake's now. It shouldn't take long. I can meet you there."

"Um. Yeah. I can go grab some groceries for Tom and meet you at Carl's when I'm done," Marnie suggested.

"Perfect! I'll call you when I'm done here."

"Okay. I'll chat with you soon." Marnie hung up.

Danny entered Drake's through the side door closest to the pharmacy. The pharmacy door was closed, the lights were off and no one was around. There was a note on the counter.

"Due to a chemical spill, the pharmacy will be closed Saturday, December 12th. We will reopen Monday, December 14th at 8:00 AM. We apologize for the inconvenience.

Should you require immediate assistance, please call our Hudson store for support."

Danny sniffed the air, but couldn't detect anything. He went to the front of the store and spoke to Mrs. Walters. She had worked at Drake's for decades.

"Mrs. Walters, good morning!" Danny called out.

Mrs. Walters was a petite white-haired woman in her seventies. She wore a gray wool skirt, black tights, a white blouse covered with a pink cardigan and black orthopedic shoes. Her glasses hung around her neck on a silver chain.

"Good morning, Detective. What can I help you with?" Mrs. Walters smiled warmly.

"I had an appointment this morning with Mr. Drake and some of his staff. Nobody is here, and I'm wondering what happened. A chemical spill? What spilled exactly?"

"Oh, dear! Mr. Drake raced out of here at 9:30. The pharmacy smelled to high heaven! A case of formalin fell from a shelf and broke open. The fumes were overwhelming. No one could work in there today. We've turned on three or four fans and cracked a few windows a smidge."

"Is that right?" Danny turned to look back at the pharmacy counter with an unimpressed countenance on his face. "How'd the case of formalin fall? Wouldn't you have something like that on a lower shelf to avoid that kind of problem?"

"Well…" Mrs. Walters began. She turned to see who might be listening and motioned for Danny to move closer. She lowered her voice. "Mr. Drake mentioned that Erin Matthews stocked the shelves poorly. Apparently, she had everything in the wrong place. He had to let her go. He said that she was gossiping and bothering customers. I never noticed that about Erin. No one ever complained about her to me, and everyone complains about everyone to me. I think that she's a dear child. She was always polite and punctual, and she took pride in her work. It didn't matter what she was doing, she did it well – always with a smile."

"Thanks for your help, Mrs. Walters. I'll be back on Monday morning to speak to Mr. Drake. I hope you have a lovely day." Danny nodded and headed for the door.

Mrs. Walters cleared her throat. "Will you be at the parade tomorrow, Detective?"

Danny turned back. "I will."

"I'll see you there. We have a hot chocolate stand there, you know. It's a Drake's tradition. Hot chocolate and shortbread. Every year. Mr. Drake will be there, you know." Mrs. Walters winked.

Danny grinned. "Is that right? Well, you have a fabulous day, Mrs. Walters. I'll see you tomorrow." Danny gave her a tiny salute and walked out the door.

Back in the square, Danny scooted around the back of Drake's to check on the "cracked window" story. Three windows, behind iron bars, were indeed cracked. Danny stood on the edge of the brick foundation and sniffed the air. He didn't smell formalin.

"Well, it couldn't have been that bad," Danny said to himself.

Danny went back around to the square, looked left and then looked right. He couldn't remember the direction of the bookstore. There was a book that he wanted to get Marnie for Christmas. He remembered that the store was in the laneway at the back of Marnie's office. Danny walked just a bit further and turned the corner. Cobblestone Lane was the location of the bookstore. It was aptly named because it was, in fact, a cobblestone lane. It was in the oldest part of Creekwood, and many of the original buildings still stood proudly. Cobblestone Lane retailers included a cobbler, a butcher, a barber, a gift store owner and a florist on one side of the lane. The opposite side of the lane was home to Mrs. Backus's bookstore, a tea store, a framing shop, a jeweler's and a small art gallery that featured local artists. All of the shops had green and white-striped awnings above their doors and Christmas decorations on the front windows.

Tom called as Danny walked into the bookstore.

"Hey, what's happening?" Danny asked.

"Captain Sterling isn't doing too well. He's got pneumonia," Tom advised. "I told the hospital to keep me updated, and they said that they would. Is there family who we should be calling?"

"Damn! I don't know. Captain Sterling has always been a bit of an enigma. I'll call the chief again and see if he'll call me back. Maybe Cap's admin Stacey can help with that. She's back on Monday – I think."

"Yeah. She's back on Monday. I heard a couple of people talkin' about her yesterday. She doesn't know Cap's in the hospital yet," Tom replied.

"How'd your conversation go with Reuben?" Danny asked.

"He checked himself out this morning. He's in the wind, as they say on TV. The officer on the door went to the bathroom at 4:00 AM, came back and Reuben was gone. Don't worry. We've already discussed that his ass is yours on Monday. I've been to Reuben's apartment, and he's not there. How about your conversation with Mr. Drake and his staff?" Tom asked.

"Nada! Nobody there. The day's been a bust!" Danny rubbed the back of his neck. "I've gotta call Marnie. She's got your groceries, and she's heading to Carl's place. He's not answering his cell or home phone. She's pretty worried."

"How 'bout I meet you two there? I can get my groceries, take them home and then head out to your place. My folks called about an hour ago. They aren't going to be in until around 7:30. They're renting a car at the airport, so that puts them at my place at 8:30 or so."

"Sounds like a plan. See you soon." Danny hung up from Tom and called Marnie.

"Hi, Danny. I'm at checkout. I should be done in about 15 minutes."

"Okay. Tom and I are meeting you at Carl's. He'll get the groceries from you, and I can follow you home. I've got one stop to make. I'll see you at Carl's in about 20 minutes."

"Okay. The grocery store is crazy! I hate shopping on weekends, especially this time of year. See you soon." Marnie hung up.

Danny went into the bookstore, turned around and left. The register was 10 people deep, and the aisles were full of shoppers. He walked down the lane and looked in the shop windows. He made a mental note to come back on Monday or Tuesday during the day when shoppers were at work. He wandered back up to Town Square and browsed the food stalls. A bag of roasted chestnuts would hit the spot.

~~~~~~~~~~~~~~~~~~~~~~~~

Marnie parked outside of Carl's house. His car was in the driveway. It was covered with snow, and his steps and sidewalk hadn't been shoveled from last night's snowfall. She sat down, impatiently waiting for Danny or Tom. She turned on the radio and closed her eyes. Tom pulled in behind her a few minutes later, and Danny pulled in right behind him. Marnie heard a car door slam, turned the music off and got out of her car.

"His car's here," Tom said, pointing to Carl's car.

"Thanks for that, Captain Obvious." Marnie rolled her eyes.

Tom glared at her., "You got a key?"

Marnie shook her head. "No. When he and Michelle were together, she didn't like that I had a key to his house. He had to ask for it back."

Tom pulled a confused face. "He and Michelle aren't together? They were at Thanksgiving, right?"

Marnie nodded. "Yeah. She broke up with him shortly after. She's moved to Albany."

Danny stood on the front stoop waiting for Marnie and Tom. When they caught up, he opened the storm door and knocked.

Marnie stepped off the stoop and peered in the front window. She shook her head. "I don't see him in there. He hasn't been out. The only footprints are ours. Should I go around back?"

"Tom, you want to go around back? We'll stay here just in case he comes to the door," Danny suggested.

Tom went around through a side gate and went up onto the back porch. He peeked into the kitchen and didn't see any movement. He tried the back door. It was unlocked. Rather than walk all the way back around, he called Danny and told him that the door was unlocked.

"We'll be right there," Danny replied. "C'mon, Marnie. The back door is unlocked."

Marnie and Danny walked around to the back, and they all went in the house. They stood in the kitchen for a moment, then Marnie called out. "Carl! Carl are you home?"

Marnie sniffed. "I can smell pipe tobacco. He must have lit his pipe at some point this morning."

They heard a thump upstairs. She turned to Tom and Danny. Each had a hand on his pistol.

"You know, maybe he's not alone. Maybe he didn't answer his phones or the door 'cause he's busy. Know what I mean?" Tom proposed, raising his eyebrows suggestively.

Marnie and Danny exchanged glances.

"Makes sense," Marnie agreed.

"Yeah, but what if that's not it?" Danny asked. "What if he's hurt? What if he can't get to the phone? With all of the crazy stuff that's been going on, I don't know that we should risk his safety for the sake of not embarrassing him."

Tom pushed Marnie's shoulder. "You go upstairs. He'll be less embarrassed if it's you who catches him with pants down."

Marnie slapped his hand away. "He would be mortified! How would you feel if I walked in on you?"

Tom shrugged. "You have. Remember senior year…"

"Will you two knock it off! I'll go." Danny sighed. "Marnie isn't going up there. Geez, Tom! We're the police here. Where are the stairs?"

Marnie pointed him in the right direction.

"Carl! It's Danny! I'm coming upstairs!" Danny called out. He turned to Marnie and Tom and quietly said, "Please have your pants on."

Danny found Carl on the floor at the top of the stairs. Danny turned Carl on his side, checked his pulse and called downstairs. "He's up here. He's passed out in the hallway. Call 911."

Marnie raced up the stairs, and Tom called 911.

Danny looked up at Marnie. "His pulse is slow, but he's got one. Is he on any medication?"

"I don't know." Marnie searched her memory. "I think that he may take blood pressure pills, but I'm not sure. I'll check his bathroom."

Marnie ran out into the hallway a few seconds later and thrust a prescription bottle at Danny. "Here. It says to take four first thing in the morning."

Danny opened the bottle, looked at the tablets and clenched his jaw. "He didn't check these before taking them. This isn't blood pressure medication. These are sleeping pills. These are the pills that they gave me after Sarah died. If he took four as the prescription says… Stay with him. I need to make a call."

Marnie sat on the floor and spoke softly to Carl. "It's going to be okay, Carl. Danny and Tom are getting help. We're right here with you. Stay with us." Marnie bent down and kissed Carl's forehead.

Still on the phone, Tom came upstairs and put a hand on Marnie's shoulder. "Where's Danny?"

"He went to place a call. The bottle that should have had his blood pressure medication had sleeping pills instead. He took four. The dosage on the bottle said four." Marnie squeezed Tom's hand. "The prescription was filled at Drake's, Tom. I got Danny's prescription at Drake's."

Tom pursed his lips, and his eyes grew dark with anger. "Your folks talkin' to you yet? It would be a good time for them to start talkin'."

Tom stormed off down the hall. He spoke to the 911 operator as he walked. He explained that it was a possible accidental overdose of sleeping pills. He checked every room upstairs. His hand remained on his pistol the entire time. He stomped downstairs. Marnie heard the front door open and slam.

Marnie looked up and closed her eyes. "Mom? Dad? A bit of help would be appreciated!"

The ambulance arrived and administered a dose of flumazenil. Carl was awake within a few minutes – groggy, confused and nauseated.

One of the paramedics took Carl's blood pressure again. "Mr. Parkins, we think that you should come to the hospital. You need to get checked out by a doc."

Carl nodded slowly and glanced around. "Okay. Yeah. I… I don't know what happened."

"You took some sleeping pills, Mr. Parkins."

Carl swung his head around and scowled at the paramedic. "No, I… I took my blood pressure pills."

"Didn't you notice that they weren't your usual pills, Mr. Parkins?"

Carl stared at the paramedic. "No. My doctor changed my prescription. It was a new prescription. I took my blood pressure medication." Carl scratched the back of his head, a dazed look of bewilderment on his face. "I took my blood pressure medication," Carl repeated defiantly.

The paramedic patted Carl's shoulder. "Okay, Mr. Parkins. You're coming with us to the hospital. Let's go. Can you walk, or do want us to bring up the stretcher?"

Carl scowled. "I can walk. I'm fine. I took my damn blood pressure medication!"

Danny, Marnie and Tom were at the bottom of the stairs looking up. They could hear the conversation. Danny and Tom exchanged glances and both ran up the stairs.

Danny put a shoulder under Carl's shoulder, and Tom put his shoulder under Carl's opposite shoulder.

"C'mon, Carl. We're gonna get you to the hospital. We know that you thought that you were takin' your blood pressure meds. We know," Tom said quietly.

"We've got you, Carl. Marnie is right downstairs. We're going to follow the ambulance to the hospital," Danny said.

"I don't want to go to the hospital," Carl replied.

Marnie called up from the bottom of the stairs. "Carl, I think that you should go to the hospital. I'll come, too. I'll meet you there."

Carl perked up when he heard Marnie's voice. "Marnie, will you drive me? I don't want to go in the ambulance. Will you drive me?" Carl asked childishly.

"Yes, of course. I'll drive you, Carl," Marnie replied.

Danny turned to the paramedic. "That should be okay, huh?"

The paramedic nodded. "Yeah. If that's what it takes to get him there. We'll follow along. He should be fine. It would just be better to have him checked out."

"I'll take Carl to the hospital. Why don't you two head to the cabin and get ready for the meeting. I'll drive up as soon as we're done. I'll probably bring Carl with me if he's up to it. We'll just have to get him home afterwards."

"I'll drive him home after, Marnie," Tom agreed.

Danny and Tom helped Carl to Marnie's car, and once he was settled in, Marnie climbed behind the wheel. She rolled down her window.

"I'll see you guys in a bit," Marnie said with a wave.

Danny leaned into the car and kissed her.

"Keep us posted, huh?"

Marnie nodded and closed her window. Tom tapped the roof of the car and waved.

"What the hell is going on, Tommy?" They watched Marnie's car disappear from view.

"I'll throw another Shakespearian quote at you that Marnie loves. How about, 'Something wicked this way comes.' That sound about right?" Tom asked.

"It's not coming, Tommy. It's already here." Danny puffed out his cheeks and rubbed the back of his neck.

-CHAPTER FIFTY-SEVEN-

Marnie and Carl were in the car by 1:15 on the way to the cabin. Carl was hungry and couldn't wait to eat, so Marnie pulled into a Dairy Queen. Carl munched on a chili dog, onion rings and a vanilla malt on the drive. Marnie snacked on French fries.

Marnie gave Carl a sideways glance.

"You want to talk?"

"No," Carl replied through a mouth full of chili dog.

Marnie turned on the radio, and Carl sent a dirty look her way.

"What? You don't like music today?" Marnie asked, mildly irritated.

Carl took a sip of his malt. "Not Christmas music. I've had enough of Christmas!"

Marnie changed the station.

Carl pulled a face. "Country? Really?"

Marnie rolled her eyes. "You sure that you didn't take cranky whine-ass pills this morning? Geez!" She changed the station to classic rock. Carl settled back in his seat and ate.

They drove the rest of the way in silence, except when Wild Cherry's "Play That Funky Music" came on the radio.

The afternoon was overcast, and the clouds were low. Marnie glanced up when they got out of the car.

"Those look like snow clouds."

Carl glanced up and scowled.

"Hey, Mr. Cranky Pants, how about we take you inside and get you some coffee or tea?" Marnie teased. "You know, Danny and Tom were worried when I told them that you weren't answering your phone. It's good. I think that they trust you."

Carl furrowed his brow. "Fuck Danny, and fuck Tom! You know, I've been doing everything that I can to gain their trust. I never did anything to either of them. As a matter of fact, before Danny, Tom was always polite. He and I never had a problem until Danny came into your life."

Marnie rested her arms on the roof of her car and stared with mild astonishment at Carl – mild astonishment because she'd been waiting for this outburst for a few weeks. Carl had done everything possible to gain their trust, and Tom's behavior *had* changed toward Carl. She'd said this to both Tom and Danny. She'd told them repeatedly to cut Carl some slack. At the end of the day, she couldn't fight Carl's battles for him. He needed to stand up for himself.

"Carl, you're telling me something that I already know. How about you put on your big boy pants and tell them how you feel. I've been fighting this battle for you for weeks. Speak your mind. Tell them to fuck off and stop treating your poorly." Marnie pushed herself off the car and headed for the porch.

"I haven't because I didn't want to make problems for you. I didn't want it to mess up *our* relationship," Carl confessed, throwing his hands up in frustration.

"Make problems for me? Carl, you're my friend and closest confidant. We've been through a few wars together. We've battled each other from time to time. Nothing you could say to Danny or Tom is going to mess that up. I'm a big girl. I can take care of myself. If Danny and Tom get pissed about you sticking up for yourself, well, they'll need to put on *their* big boy pants and suck it up. Enough! Say what you need to say, and move on. I'd be willing to bet that they'd respect you if you did. Neither of them is afraid to speak their mind. You shouldn't be, either."

Carl thought about what Marnie said for a minute. "What about Andrea? I'm getting really sick of her treating me like scum."

"Well, I'll talk to her. She needs to understand that you and I are building the practice so that we all have jobs for many years to come. That one is on me, and I will handle it." Marnie thought back to last night – a conversation that she overheard between Danny and Andrea. "You know, last night, I did overhear Danny telling Andrea that you're a good guy. I was busy, so I didn't eavesdrop long, but I did hear that. That's something!"

Carl nodded. "Yeah. Hey, I'm cold. Let's go inside."

~~~~~~~~~~~~~~~~~~~~~~~~~~~

The cabin was warm and noisy. Danny, Tom, Jalnack and Rick were all talking at the same time.

"Hey! One at a time!" Marnie shouted from the front door.

Everybody turned to see Marnie and Carl standing at the door.

Danny walked across the room and put his hand out to Carl. "Hey, it's good to see you looking better. How are you feeling?"

"Did they pump your stomach? That's the worst! You look a lot better. Do you want a drink? We've got coffee made, and we've got ginger ale in the fridge." Tom asked.

342

Marnie nudged Carl gently with her elbow and threw an "I told you so" expression his way. Carl smiled and nodded.

"I'm feeling much better. Thanks for coming to the house with Marnie this morning. Tom, a ginger ale would be great, thanks."

"No problem, buddy." Danny patted him on the shoulder. "C'mon in and take a seat. I was telling everybody what you and I talked about yesterday. I was wondering if you've had other thoughts?"

Marnie disappeared into the kitchen. Gram and Hannah were sitting at the table. Dickens sat in Hannah's lap, and Tater had taken up guard at the window.

"Hi, there! Have you been banished to the kitchen, or was there too much testosterone in there?" Marnie giggled.

"Oh, no. We came out here a few minutes ago to have a chat," Gram replied. "How's Carl feelin', love?"

"He's okay, Gram. I'm going to run upstairs and change into warmer clothes so that I can take Tater for a run. Can Dickens hang out with you?" Marnie asked.

Hannah nodded. "He's happy here in my lap. Daniel took him out about 20 minutes ago. He should be fine."

"Thanks! I'll be back in a sec."

Marnie tried to sneak through the living room to the stairs, but didn't quite make it.

"Where are you goin'?" Tom asked.

"I'm going to change so that I can take Tater for a run," Marnie replied.

Tom frowned. "You're not going to sit in on this?"

Marnie laughed. "Once you have your hypothesis together, I'm here for you. Tater needs some exercise, and so do I." Marnie raced up the stairs before Tom could ask any more questions.

She went into her room; grabbed leggings, socks, her running boots and her big hooded sweatshirt; and took them down to Danny's room. She changed quickly and was just tying her running boots when Danny came in the door.

Danny leaned on the wall and tipped his head to the side. "Hey, everything okay?"

"Yeah. I have a theory, though. Remember the other night when Tom and I saw the spooks in the woods?"

"Yeah." Danny nodded.

"I'm pretty sure that was staged by Grace Wilmot. I think that she got some of her crew from The Collective to set up something out there."

"You were gonna go running around in the woods by yourself to prove your theory?" Danny sighed.

"Oh, c'mon, Danny! It's broad daylight. How much trouble can Tater and I get in walking through the woods during the day?" Marnie scrunched her nose up at him. "We'll be fine."

"Yeah, you'll be fine. I'm going with you," Danny said, kicking off his shoes and pulling a pair of fleece-lined track pants out of his dresser.

Marnie sat on the edge of the bed and waited for him to get changed. "This is silly. You should be downstairs in that meeting."

"No. I should be out traipsing through the woods with my crazy girlfriend. I should have been out there in the woods days ago checking it out," Danny replied.

Marnie shrugged. "Suit yourself. Tater and I would love the company."

Danny sat on the edge of the bed to pull on warmer socks. "Hey, did you ever take any of that mela… mela… Whatever the hell that was that Mr. Drake mentioned?"

"Melatonin?" Marnie asked.

"Yeah."

Marnie shook her head and pursed her lips. "Nope. You didn't take any of your prescription meds either, did you?"

"Nope."

"Hmm. I didn't think so, since we're both still standing. We should give the bottles to Rick."

"Good idea." Danny ducked into his bathroom and took the two bottles off the shelf.

"I'll grab mine. Be right back." Marnie raced up the hall to her room and grabbed the bottle out of the medicine cabinet. She raced back into the Danny's room. "I've got a theory," she said.

"Tell me about it on the walk," Danny pulled a fleece over his head and winced.

"Is that wound giving you trouble?" Marnie asked.

"Nah. It's fine."

"Let me take a look." Marnie lifted up the back of his fleece and removed the dressing. "It doesn't look terrible, but we should put some antibacterial salve on it tonight before bed. It's a bit red."

"It's itchy. It's been driving me crazy all day." Danny squirmed.

"We'll take care of it later. We'll give it a salt water bath and put salve on it. Later. C'mon. Let's go before it gets dark," Marnie said, heading toward the stairs.

"Did you say sponge bath?" Danny grinned, grabbed her around the waist and tickled her.

"C'mon! You're going to pop your stitches." Marnie giggled.

"Okay. Let's go play Scooby-Doo. You can be Velma, and I'll be Fred."

"Hey!" Marnie yelled.

Rick raised an eyebrow when he saw Marnie and Danny come down the stairs together. Danny shook his head at him as a warning not to make a big deal about it.

"We'll be back shortly. Marnie remembered something that we need to check in the woods." Danny turned to Tom. "Those ghosts and goblins from the other night – Marnie thinks that they were planted there."

Tom raised his eyebrows. "Interesting. So Marnie's Daphne and you're Shaggy?"

"Yeah. Sure. We'll be back in a few minutes." Danny pulled on his boots, went out on the porch and waited while Marnie clipped Tater's lead onto his collar.

"His sense of humor gone?" Tom teased.

"It wasn't that funny, Thomas." Marnie sighed. Then she laughed. "Actually, it was. He just called me Velma and himself Fred. Thanks! Back soon!"

Danny was on the pathway to the lake when Marnie came out onto the porch. He was looking down, following footprints. He looked up every so often and then back down at the path.

"Nobody has been out here today but me. I'm the only person who has walked down to the lake, yet there three are sets of boot prints."

"Tater and I walked down there this morning. Um... Hey, Danny, does that floodlight work down there near the dock? The one up on the pole? I've never seen it lit up before." Marnie pointed to the floodlight situated above the dock.

"Yeah. It's up there so that we can play hockey on the lake in the winter and so that I can get my boat docked in the summer. I guess that I should check the light, though. There is one more set of footprints than there should be, unless Tater was wearing boots." Danny studied Marnie. Her expression told him everything. "You think that I need to check that when we get back?"

"Tomorrow morning is fine." Marnie's eyes drifted to the woods behind them. "Let's go. I don't want to be out there at dusk." Marnie shivered.

Danny walked up behind her and gave her a hug. "C'mon. Let's get this done."

They walked up the driveway to the point where Marnie thought that the "black mass" had been looming.

Tater growled, and the hair on his scruff stood up as soon as they stepped off the driveway and into the brush.

Marnie glanced over her shoulder at Danny. "Didn't bring your gun, did you?"

Danny nodded and patted his pocket.

"I think it was right around here. I remember that bent reflector pole on the road," Marnie said, stepping carefully over felled trees and boulders. "Look! Danny! Look!"

Marnie pointed to a black bag a few yards ahead of them. They could see a piece of heavy twine hanging from a branch. As they got closer, Tater's growl grew louder.

"It's okay, Tater. Shush. It's okay." Marnie patted his neck firmly.

Danny bent and picked up a stick. He poked the bag gently and picked it up on the end of the stick. It was stuck on a bramble bush, but came loose when Danny gave it a good tug. "It's got some sort of light inside of it. Look at that!"

Marnie moved closer to the end of the stick and the bag. There was definitely a light inside of it. "I bet that it has a remote control or something." She walked around and gazed up at the twine. It was rigged into the tree with a small pulley system. It stretched about 30 feet between two large trees. "It looks like the bag got snagged on that bramble bush."

"Dammit! I didn't bring an evidence bag." Danny pulled an irritated face.

"I did!" Marnie did a little celebratory dance and pulled four garbage bags out of the front pouch of her sweatshirt.

Danny looked up at the pulley. "Hey, Marnie, how are you at climbing trees? There is no way that those branches will hold me."

They worked together to gather the evidence. Marnie climbed the first tree with no issue. The second tree was a bit harder, but she finally got down the pulley. She was covered with sticks and dead leaves and had a few scratches on her face, but the pulleys and twine were safely tucked away in an evidence bag.

"Okay. Where's the other location?" Danny asked.

"I think that we should get in the car for that one. It's right at the top of the driveway." Marnie pointed east.

"Let's go get the Jeep." Danny placed a hand in the middle of Marnie's back and guided her forward.

They tramped out of the woods and back onto the driveway. Danny looked up at the sky and then down at his watch.

"Maybe we should do the other one in the morning. It's 3:00. It's going to be dark soon."

Marnie nodded in agreement. "Yeah. I think that's a good idea. I don't want to run into Percy the bear in the dark. Tomorrow morning, we check the light and gather evidence."

"Marnie, why do you want me to check the light?" Danny asked.

Marnie shrugged. "Just a feeling."

"That's good enough for me." Danny took her hand, and they walked back to the cabin.

The woods crackle at dusk. Twigs snap. Deer run. Birds make their way home to their nests. Rabbits scurry to their burrows until sunrise, and owls hoot. A light snow began to fall as they stepped onto the porch. Marnie glanced up and watched the clouds rolling over.

"I think that we're going to get a good snowfall tonight."

"Perfect night for hot chocolate and peppermint schnapps." Danny smacked his lips and grinned.

"I was thinking that a glass of wine might be nice," Marnie replied.

Danny nudged her gently toward the cabin. "Wine *and* food. I'm starving!"

~~~~~~~~~~~~~~~~~~~~~~~~~~~~

Tom stood in front of the fireplace with a cup of coffee in his hand. Marnie knew by the expression on his face that he'd had a break that he hadn't yet shared. His jaw was a bit askew, his lips were pursed and his gaze focused on a sparkly Christmas ornament. She also knew that, in just a moment, Tom was going to announce his theory to everyone by beginning his statement with, "Now, I could be wrong, but…"

Rick stood next to him, adding another log to the fire. His mind was ticking, too. Marnie could tell by the way that he was biting the inside of his cheeks, looking up at the clock and counting his points on the fingers of one hand.

Jalnack sat on couch, his left leg on the coffee table and the other leg stretched under the coffee table. His chin rested on his chest, and his head bobbed slightly. Jalnack was ready to move on to other things. He was asleep.

Carl and Hannah leaned on the pool table. Carl's animated responses to Hannah's questions told Marnie that Carl had consumed far too much coffee today and not enough food.

"Anyone want to take a break and have something to eat?" Marnie asked.

The vote was unanimous. Marnie took off her boots and headed for the kitchen. Gram had already started to lay out a spread of warmed-up chili, Hannah's Irish stew, turkey club sandwiches, corn chips, potato chips and peanut butter cookies for dessert.

"Would it be bad to use paper plates and disposable bowls again?" Marnie asked Gram.

"Not at all, love," Gram replied. "I think that they're more concerned about the quality of the food than the crockery that we use."

"I agree!" Marnie giggled.

Gram went to the kitchen door and called out, "Soup's on!"

Over food, drink and cookies, theories were explained, debunked and added to a list. They all agreed that Grace Wilmot was blackmailing Mr. Drake. Danny handed Rick his prescription medication and Marnie's melatonin and asked if he could run tests. They also agreed that Danny's stabbing, Justin's death and William's death were all connected. They didn't believe that Grace Wilmot was the culprit.

"Now, I could be wrong, but that leaves us with Reuben," Tom said.

"Plus one," added Danny. "There was someone else in the garage that morning. I know that there were two people. What about William? His body had been moved. He wasn't a small guy. It would take two people to move him from the kill location to the tracks. How about Justin? There is no way that one person engineered that positioning. I still think that we have to consider Patrick."

Hannah, who had yet to speak, quietly added, "His demeanor when I caught him in Marnie's house was interesting. On the one hand, he was apologetic and unassuming. On the other hand, he was steely, confident and defiant."

Marnie remembered his response to Hannah asking him if he understood her. The way that he had said "crystal" had surprised her. Defiant was the word that Marnie had thought at the time, too. She heard Carl sigh and turned to him. "Carl, what do you think?"

"I just don't want to see it. Patrick was a soldier. His job was to serve and protect. He did several tours, helped a lot of people and saw horrible things. He *has* had a troubled life, but I just don't see Patrick killing someone. There is something about his character. He is fundamentally a good person. Let's remember that he remained calm when Marnie was trapped in the trunk. He was the one who got her out. He kept his cool."

"He was a soldier," Rick commented. "Surely, in that time, he took a life – maybe more than one. He's obviously capable of great things when he is under stress. He was a soldier, and that takes guts and calculating precision. Perhaps from time to time, his fundamental goodness lapses. Perhaps what he has seen has caused him to see an enemy where one doesn't exist. Is Patrick easily manipulated?"

Carl shook his head. "I don't see it. Maybe I don't want to see it."

"Well," Danny began, "I think that we've solved enough for one day. We'll follow up tomorrow. If anybody thinks of something to add, send a text. Send a text to everyone sitting here except Gram. Gram doesn't need to be woken up in the small hours of the morning."

Everybody nodded.

Tom touched Hannah's shoulder gently. "If you send your contact card to me, I will send it along to the guys, and I'll send you their information."

Hannah nodded. "Yes, of course. What's your number?"

Tom gave Hannah his cell number, and there were beeps throughout the living room for the next few minutes.

"Okay. We're all meeting at the station tomorrow at noon before the parade. We can spread out and see if we can find Reuben or Grace Wilmot. I'll go to Drake's stall." Danny turned to Rick. "Rick, do you think that you can have my prescriptions and Marnie's melatonin analyzed by then?"

"No problem. I'll drop it by the lab and get someone on it tonight," Rick replied.

"Gram? Carl? You're going with Marnie tomorrow, right?" Danny asked.

Gram wrapped an arm through Marnie's and nodded. Carl nodded, too.

Danny considered Carl for a moment. "Hey, Carl? Do you know how to fire a pistol?"

Carl was surprised by Danny's question. "Yes, of course. I went to university on a ROTC scholarship."

Tom choked back his surprise. "Really?"

Carl saluted. "Captain Carl Parkins at your service."

Danny asked, "Army?"

Carl nodded.

"You were in Afghanistan, too." Danny made the connection to Patrick.

"Yeah." Carl replied dryly.

"Okay, then." Danny clapped Carl on the shoulder. "Reuben has already harmed Marnie once. I'm thinking that may happen again. Hopefully, not at the parade, but who knows. There's a degree of erratic behavior – in my opinion." Danny considered their options. "You know, there's a law, Posse Comitatus, that may cover what I'm thinking, but I don't believe that the department can issue you a weapon, Carl."

Carl shrugged. "The department doesn't need to issue me a weapon. I have one and a concealed weapon permit."

Danny gulped. "How did you get that? It's nearly impossible!"

"I'm a psychotherapist. I practiced in New York City for three years. Any idea how many credible death threats have come my way in that time?" Carl smirked.

"Okay, then." Concerned, Danny turned to Marnie. "Do you get death threats?"

"Only from ex-lovers, brothers and childhood friends," Marnie quipped and winked at him.

Danny pointed a finger at her and frowned. "Not funny!"

Danny's phone rang. He held up a finger. "I gotta take this. I'll see everybody tomorrow."

"Hi, Dad," Danny answered. "Hannah? Yeah. She's here in Creekwood with me. She's staying through the new year. We want to talk to you about Christmas and a few other things."

~~~~~~~~~~~~~~~~~~~~~~~~

Tater and Dickens raced from the kitchen through the living room, around the pool table and then back around again. They slipped and slid across the hardwood floors and bunched up throw rugs as they flew through the rooms. Dickens nipped at Tater's legs, and Tater sat down on Dickens's head.

"We've got our own canine entertainment center right here!" Danny laughed.

"Life is interesting with two Border Collies, that's for sure." Marnie giggled.

Gram came downstairs and sat in one of the big comfy chairs. "I'll be headin' home before the snow becomes a worry. I've got work to do, and you know that bein' away from the diner drives me to distraction."

"Before you go, what are your thoughts on the discussions today?" Danny asked.

"Like I told Marnie, beware of a wolf in sheep's clothing," Gram replied vaguely.

"Gram, I have a question for you." Marnie sat forward on the couch and considered her words carefully. "I've had so many visions over the last few weeks that I'm not sure what's real, what's prophetic and what's nonsense. The vision that continues to bombard me is one of Grace and Kate sitting in front of a Ouija board. I know that one is accurate. I know that happened. I don't know how – I just do. There's a little voice in my head telling me that they didn't close the session properly. Would that create problems for people like you, me and even Danny? Would it tie up communication with the other side of the veil?"

"I suppose that it would depend on who they were talkin' to." Gram replied. "Who they were callin' in. Who can't you reach, love?"

"My parents. They're there, and I'm getting some information from them, but it's not clear. It could be my fault. When I tore the veil returning to all of you? I know that Danny told you about it," Marnie revealed.

"How do you know that I told Gram?" Danny asked, brow furrowed.

"Don't you tell her pretty much everything? Let's face it, when it comes to things like this, of course you spoke to Gram about it," Marnie replied. "I'm not upset. I figured that you would tell her. I was going to tell her."

"The veil is fragile, dear, but I reckon that the angels have repaired it by now. They're quite industrious, you know." Gram grinned and her eyes twinkled. "Now, if Grace and Kate were indeed communicatin' or callin' out to your parents, and if they left the session open, I suppose that it could be causin' a problem. Ouija boards are menacin' objects. It is beyond all order and all that is holy that one can be picked up in a department store or online. Menacin' things, they are."

"Gram, do you think that it's possible to close the session, um, remotely?" Marnie asked hopefully.

"I do believe that it is. It's simply a matter of moving the planchette to 'goodbye' and putting it away. I'll take care of it when I get home. Don't give another thought," Gram replied offhandedly.

"Gram?" Marnie raised her eyebrows. "How are you going to take care of it?"

"My darlin' girl, I've been dealin' with the likes of Grace Wilmot a lot longer than you've been alive. I'll conjure up an image of the board, I'll close out the session and then I'll go to sleep prayin' for the sweet angels of heaven to put it away in a safe place. Grace Wilmot has only the power that people give her. I tell ya, she'll have none of mine." Gram stood and put on her coat. "Fear is a feckin' waste of time. Remember that."

Marnie hid a smirk behind her teacup. Danny did the same by turning toward the front door.

"C'mon, Gram. I'll walk you out." Danny held out his arm and led Gram to her car.

Marnie's phone rang. She didn't recognize the number, but at least it wasn't a private number.

"Hello?"

"Marnie, it's Sam. Don't hang up!"

Marnie rolled her eyes and threw back her head onto the back of the couch. "What?! What do you want, Sam?"

"Kate hasn't been answering her phone. I spoke to her on Friday, and she wasn't feeling good. She said that she was going back to bed and that she would come see me today. She never turned up, and she isn't answering her phone."

"So! What do you want me to do about it? Maybe she doesn't want to speak to you, Sam. Did you think about that?" Marnie huffed.

"You listen to me, sister dear! She does want to speak to me! I'm telling you that something is wrong! Tell that piece of shit Tom Keller to go to her apartment. Now!" Sam shouted hysterically.

Marnie calmed down. Sam sounded scared – worried. Marnie softened her voice. "Sam, are you sure that she isn't just trying to avoid you? She did roll on you. Maybe she's afraid to face you."

"For fuck's sake, Marnie, she's… something is wrong! I can feel it! Something is fucking wrong! Are you going to help?"

Danny came back inside and plopped down on the couch next to Marnie. Marnie mouthed the word "Sam" and rolled her eyes. Danny's jaw clenched, and Marnie held up her hand.

"Sam, I really don't know what I can do to help. Kate's a big girl. She can take care of herself."

The shriek that came down the phone was horrifying. Marnie held the phone away from her ear and shivered. Danny took the phone away from her.

"Sam, this is Detective Gregg. Stop calling your sister! When I find out who's giving you phone access, they're…"

"Please help Kate! Something is wrong with Kate! Please help her!" Sam screamed down the phone.

"Sam, so help me God, if this is some type of setup…"

"It's not a fucking setup. Take a fucking SWAT team with you. I'm telling you that something is wrong! Something has happened to Kate!"

Danny rubbed his chin and then the back of his neck. "I'll take care of it." He hung up.

The drive into Creekwood was slow going. A whiteout kicked up as soon as Danny hit Lake Road. Danny hugged the yellow center line because he couldn't see the shoulder. He called Tom and apologized. "Hey, I know that your folks will be there soon; I'm sorry to bother you."

"My parents called about 15 minutes ago. They're spending the night at the airport inn. The roads are bad, and Dad doesn't want to drive all that way in a storm. What's up?"

Danny filled in Tom on the conversation that he and Marnie had with Sam Reilly.

"You think that it's a setup? You think that he's trying to get Marnie alone at the cabin, or do you think that we're going to get ambushed?" Tom questioned.

"Neither. I think that he was scared. If you'd heard him, you'd agree. Marnie thought so." Danny turned down his wipers and turned up the thermostat. "Hey, these roads are bad. Want me to pick you up, or do you want to take your truck?"

"Nah. I'll meet you there. Don't go out of your way. Who have you got meeting us there?" Tom said.

"We've got Connor, Jalnack and Tartello."

"Okay. I'll see you there in about 15." Tom hung up.

Officers Peter Connor, Sam Jalnack and Tony Tartello were standing on the sidewalk to the side of Kate Parish's apartment building when Danny arrived. Tom pulled up about 5 minutes behind Danny.

"What are we doin' if she doesn't answer the door?" Tom asked.

Danny held up a key. "Marnie gave it to me. She doesn't know if Kate changed the locks, but we can hope that she didn't. Tony, did you speak to Judge Lawrence?"

"Yeah. She's got a digital search warrant coming my way in a few minutes. I told her that we just needed to do a welfare check, but considering the circumstances, we thought that it would be better to have a warrant. I told her that Kate Parish is possibly conspiring with Grace Wilmot, a person of interest in two murders, and that we think that Parish may be harboring the suspect. The judge is good. She'll take care of us," Tony replied.

Danny laughed. "What a load of bullshit! You and Tom have the judge wrapped around your little fingers."

Tony smirked and shrugged. "Hey, when ya got what the judge wants, your life is easier."

The search warrant came through a few seconds later, and they walked up the steps into the building's foyer. Danny checked the call box outside.

"We're looking for apartment 5D. Where's the elevator?" Danny asked.

"There isn't one," Tom replied. "When Kate moved in here, Marnie and I hauled boxes up the damn stairs, and Kate instructed the furniture company where to put her new furniture. What a pain in the ass that day was."

They climbed the stairs, found apartment 5D and knocked hard. A neighbor stuck her head out her door and closed the door quickly when she saw the police.

"Kate! Kate Parish! It's Detective Gregg from Creekwood PD. Please open the door!"

Danny put the key in the lock and opened the door. He stepped inside and let out a long whistle. "What the hell! Somebody's been busy trashing this place."

Tom stepped through the door. "Kate! It's Tom Keller!"

Tom and Danny heard a noise toward the back of the apartment. Danny put a finger to his lips as Connor, Jalnack and Tartello came into the apartment. They stood in silence. Another muffled sound came from the same direction. They all pulled their weapons and crept through the living room. Danny turned back, motioned for Connor and Tartello to stay by the door and signaled for Jalnack to come with Tom and him. Tom whispered the layout – two bedrooms, a bathroom and a walk-in closet were all off the long hallway. Two doors stood open. Two doors stood closed. Tom pointed to the first door and mouthed the word "closet." He pointed to the other closed door and mouthed "Kate's bedroom." Danny took one side of the door, and Tom took the other. Jalnack stayed back, pressing himself against the wall. Tom jiggled the doorknob and threw open the door. Gun out in front of him, Danny entered the dark room. Tom leaned in with his Maglite and hit the wall switch. Kate Parish was curled up in a corner, arms covering her head. She rocked and sobbed. A pair of scissors lay on the floor near the door, and long tresses of Kate's raven hair had been cut off and flung about the room.

Danny and Tom exchanged confused glances. Tom crossed the room and put a hand gently on Kate's shaking shoulder. "Katie, what happened?" his voice soft and comforting.

Kate lifted her head slightly. Tom didn't hide his shock when he saw the brand of the Eye of Providence singed into her forehead. Her hair had been cut chaotically – nearly down to her scalp in some places with only a few of her long tresses remaining. The look of fear in her eyes chilled Tom to the bone. Kate jerked up suddenly, wrapping her arms around Tom's neck. She clung to him, and a sorrowful moan escaped her throat, followed by gut-wrenching sobs.

Tom gathered her up in his arms and carried her to the living room. He set her gently on the couch, checked her for broken bones and asked Jalnack to get her a glass of water. When Jalnack returned, he handed the water to Kate. Her hands shook uncontrollably. Tom gently held her hands in his and helped her drink the water.

"Katie, what happened? Who did this to you?" Tom coaxed.

"I don't know!" Kate cried, her mouth agape in fear and shock.

"Kate, help me find who did this. Tell me," Tom pushed.

Danny handed Tom a box of tissues from the bathroom. Tom handed the box to Kate. She ignored it. Tom stood, disappeared down the hall and returned with a wet washcloth. As he washed Kate's tears away, she began to calm down. She rested her head on Tom's shoulder and chewed on her bottom lip. Danny, Jalnack, Connor and Tartello moved to the background, hoping that Kate would talk to Tom. Tom put his index finger under Kate's chin and lifted her face. Her indigo eyes – dazed, dilated and terrified – gazed up at him. Her bottom lip pushed out in a quivering pout.

"Katie, who did this?" Tom asked one more time.

Tears welled up in Kate's eyes. "It was that horrid creature," Kate cried. "That horrid, masked, ninja creature!" Her mouth opened again; a long, horrified groan pushed out; and her agony filled the room.

"Okay, Kate. I think that we better get you to the hospital and have you checked out by a doctor."

"No! I don't want to go to the hospital! I don't want to go anywhere! I want Marnie!" Kate wailed. "I'm sorry! I'm so sorry! I'm sorry!" Kate collapsed into Tom's arms and cried.

Tom turned awkwardly, searching the room for Danny. "Danny, what's next?"

"The hospital. It has to be the hospital. We need to get a team over here. They need to go over this mess and find us a clue. Anything." Danny glanced around at the chaos and hoped against hope that there was a clue in the debris.

"Katie, c'mon. I'll drive you to the hospital. We'll get you checked out." Tom stood and held out his hand. "Kate! We need to go."

Kate stood, wobbled and reached out for Tom. Tom rolled his eyes.

"Kate, I'm not tryin' to be an asshole, but I've seen this act before. You've always cried damsel in distress. It's been your game since we were kids. I know that you've been through a lot tonight, but I'll be damned if I'm going to carry your sorry ass down five flights of stairs."

Kate leaned on Tom's arm and walked slowly to the door.

"I'll call you as soon as I know somethin'." Tom called over his shoulder.

"Same." Danny called back. He turned to Jalnack, Connor and Tartello. "Okay, let's get a team in here and see what we can find."

~~~~~~~~~~~~~~~~~~~~~~~~~~

Marnie and Hannah were on opposite ends of the couch reading. Dickens snored on the cushion between them. Tater rested quietly on the hearth with Danny's slipper. Both glanced up when they heard the car door slam. Tater popped up and rushed the door, then he sat and wagged his tail. Danny pushed through the door at 10:15, his face drawn and his hair ruffled from dragging his fingers through it repeatedly. He bent and scratched Tater's ears.

"Anything exciting happen around here tonight?" Danny asked with a weak smile.

"There was a tyrannosaurus in the front yard, but Tater and Dickens chased it away. Other than that, it's been quiet," Marnie teased. "How's Kate? Everything okay?" She set her book down on the coffee table and turned to look at Danny.

Danny glanced up at the ceiling. He'd gone over what he was going to share. He didn't want to upset Marnie with the gruesome details. "Give me a sec. I need to get a drink."

"I'll get the drinks," Hannah volunteered. She set her book down, shoved her feet into her slippers and disappeared into the kitchen. She returned a few minutes later with three glasses of whiskey. She handed one to Marnie and one to Danny. "Here you go, little brother, you look like you need to take the edge off."

Danny pulled off his coat, threw it across the back of a chair and plonked down in the chair closest to the fire. Marnie sat forward, elbows on her knees, waiting impatiently for Danny to update them. When Danny finally did share details of the evening, he decided to *not* leave out details. He wanted Marnie and Hannah to have a clear understanding of what or with whom they were dealing.

"Oh, my God! That's horrible! Have you gotten an update from Tom?" Eyes wide and jaw slack, Marnie stared into the fire, trying to make sense of the mayhem around them.

"Yeah. He called me when I was driving home. The doc gave Kate a once over and drew some blood at Tom's direction for testing. They cleaned her up, and they kicked her to the curb. Tom was sure that they would keep her overnight, but they didn't see a need." Danny took a long sip of his whiskey.

356

Hannah disappeared into the kitchen and returned with the bottle of whiskey. She topped off Danny's glass and offered more to Marnie. Marnie declined. Hannah set the bottle on the coffee table and sat back.

"Where is Kate now? Tom can't be taking her back to her apartment." Hannah asked.

Danny shook his head. "No. He's bringing her here." Danny grimaced and awaited an explosion from Marnie. When she remained quiet, he continued. "We don't have anyone to keep an eye on her overnight. We're tapped out, and I can't approve any more overtime. We need to have every officer out on the streets looking for Grace, Reuben and this ninja character – unless the ninja and Reuben are one in the same, which is possible." Danny kept his eyes focused on Hannah, his whiskey, Dickens, Tater –anywhere but on Marnie.

Marnie stood, picked up the poker and jabbed the logs in the fire. Sparks flickered up and disappeared. She set another log on the fire and pushed it around with the poker. She was trying to calm down. Kate Parish in Danny's home was beyond comprehension. An internal conflict between compassion and anger broke to the surface. "Kate Parish should not stay here, but if there is no other option and she must come here, I'm going home." Marnie put the poker down and went upstairs.

Hannah watched Marnie walk away, then leaned across the coffee table and smacked her brother on the leg. "Daniel Gregg, how could you? Grandmother told me everything that happened. How could you bring that woman here? I don't blame Marnie for being upset. Kate Parish sounds like a dreadful person!"

"Hannah, I don't have anyone to guard her. I don't have the resources." Danny frowned and shook his head. "I'm doing the best that I can. Kate can't stay at Tom's. He's alone, and who the hell knows if we can trust her. We don't need her hovering over Tom in the middle of the night with a knife. At least here, you and I are both capable law enforcement officers, and we can keep an eye on her."

"I think that you're crazy. This whole scenario is ridiculous. How did you think Marnie would react? Seriously, Daniel." Hannah's steely gray gaze met Danny's steely blue stare.

Danny threw his arms up. "I don't know! You know, Marnie is the most compassionate person I've ever met. I thought that she might be a bit ticked off at me and… I don't know!"

"Understand that you're stuck between a rock and a hard place?"

Danny spun around. A sheepish look on her face, Marnie stood at the bottom of the stairs.

They all turned to the low grumbling of Tater's growl. He sat in front of the door, ears flat to his head and the scruff of his neck standing on end. The crunch of tires in the driveway followed by footsteps on the porch told them that Tom had arrived with Kate Parish.

Danny put a protective arm around Marnie. She pulled away, called Tater and went into the kitchen. Hannah picked up Dickens and followed Marnie and Tater into the kitchen.

"I didn't have a choice!" Danny yelled.

Hannah stuck her head around the kitchen door. "You always have a choice, Daniel."

~~~~~~~~~~~~~~~~~~~~~~~~~~~~~~~

Tom came through the door first. Danny gave him a thumbs up. Tom shot him a look of disbelief. Danny shrugged. Tom pushed the door open for Kate. She walked into the cabin and glanced around casually.

"Where's Marnie?" she asked.

Danny answered. "She's in the kitchen. Have a seat, Kate."

"You're not going to tell me to make myself at home, Detective?" Kate collapsed into the chair next to the fire.

"No, Kate, that's the last thing that I want you to do. You're only here for three reasons." Danny frowned. "One, I'm a cop, and it's my duty to protect people. Two, we have a lot of questions for you, like where is Grace Wilmot. Three, I thought that it might be good closure for Marnie to beat the shit out of you in a safe environment."

Kate shot him a bored look. "Marnie Reilly would never hurt me. She's not wired that way. We all know that."

Tom glared down at Kate. "You! Sit there, and don't move. I've had about enough of you tonight." He grabbed Danny's arm and pulled him into the kitchen, walking backwards to keep an eye on Kate.

"What the hell are we doin'?" Tom asked in a loud whisper.

"We're gonna get some answers out of her, and Marnie is going to tell us if she's lying." Danny turned to Marnie. She nodded reluctantly. "We're going to stick her upstairs in a spare room, and we're gonna make sure that she stays in there," Danny replied.

Hannah grabbed Danny's arm. "Daniel, let me question her. She's used to *playing* men. I can see it on her face and in her body language."

"She's not going to play me, Hannah," Danny replied firmly.

"Yes, she will. She's already got you and Tom hot under the collar. Let Hannah take a crack at her. She won't be expecting that." Marnie suggested.

Tom and Danny both shrugged.

Hannah went back into the living room and sat on the couch opposite Kate.

"Who are you?" Kate asked dismissively.

"Special Agent Patterson of the DEA. Do you know what that stands for? Of course you don't. You're stupid. DEA stands for Drug Enforcement Agency." Hannah's condescending tone confused Kate.

"Why are you talking to me?" Kate wrinkled her forehead. She held her hand up and grimaced with pain. The brand of the Eye of Providence was red and weeping.

Hannah glared at her. "Three reasons. One, I don't find you even mildly charming or attractive. I think that you're a spoiled rotten princess who is used to manipulating men. I would have said cocktease, but that's rude and unprofessional. Two, I have no compassion for people like you. I don't feel sorry for you, and I want to see you in prison. Three, I'm goal oriented. I want to see you in prison, and I *will* put you there."

"My lawyer is very good, and I'd like to call him now," Kate replied smugly.

Hannah shook her head. "No. You've played too many games, Kate Parish. I want to know where Grace Wilmot is now, or Tom is going to drive you back to your apartment. When he's driving you back, he's going to announce to police dispatch on an open channel that you will be there all alone and that you've spilled every little secret that Grace Wilmot has."

Kate's eyes opened wide. "I don't know anything! I don't!"

"Where is she, Kate? Where's she hiding out?" Hannah asked.

~~~~~~~~~~~~~~~~~~~~~~~~~~

Tom and Danny were in the Jeep 30 minutes after Hannah finished with Kate. Tom called the station and asked Officer Tony Tartello to get paperwork ready for a search warrant for Silo 3 on Railway Street and to send it to Judge Lawrence. Tom then woke up Judge Lawrence with a phone call, asking her to please sign off on the warrant. The judge was more than happy to help. Tom called back Tartello and asked that he and his partner Connor meet him and Danny at the silo with a pair of bolt cutters, a new padlock, two Tasers, pepper spray and the warrant.

Danny and Tom sat in silence in the Jeep outside of Silo 3 watching snow fall for about 15 minutes. Danny turned and looked in the rearview mirrors every couple of seconds. Tom tapped his fingers on the dashboard until Danny glared at him one too many times.

Tartello and Connor screamed in beside them and jumped out with the warrant, bolt cutters and other items as requested.

They walked quickly up the tracks and huddled outside of the silo.

Danny set a few rules before going into the silo. "Okay. Don't fire your guns in there. We use only the Tasers or the pepper spray. We don't want bullets ricocheting off the walls and hitting one of us. Okay? Remember that Grace Wilmot has absolutely no powers. She can't hurt any of us, even if she sticks pins into a little doll. She's a fake. She's a charlatan. Don't turn your back on her, though. She's slippery."

Tom, Tartello and Connor all nodded in understanding. Tartello handed the bolt cutters to Tom, who cut the padlock off the hatch. Danny eased open the hatch and held his gun in front of him with his Maglite resting on top. If someone was on the other side of the hatch with a gun, Danny wouldn't miss that shot.

Danny entered and Tom followed, right hand extended with a Taser ready to fire. Tartello and Connor remained outside, standing on either side of the door. Danny holstered his gun and pulled out the second Taser. They shone their flashlights around the silo.

It was deathly quiet and freezing cold. Danny put a hand near one of the heaters. No warmth radiated from it. Danny blew out air and could see his breath. It was 22 degrees outside, and it felt nearly as cold inside.

"Tommy, I don't think that anybody's here. It's freezing. A person would freeze to death in here." Danny moved closer to an area set up like a dining area. Atop the dining table. he spotted the Ouija board that Marnie had seen in her visions. He shone the light onto the dusty board. The planchette pointed to "goodbye," and there was a clean track in the dust where the planchette had recently been moved. Danny smiled. Gram had kept her word.

"Hey, Danny! Somebody's home, and he looks scared stiff – literally!" Tom's flashlight shone on Reuben Wilmot's dead face, frozen in fear – literally.

"Dammit!" Danny shouted. He crossed the room in three big strides.

Pinned to Reuben's chest was a page ripped from a book with a poem by Robert Frost.

> *Some say the world will end in fire,*
> *Some say in ice.*
> *From what I've tasted of desire*
> *I hold with those who favor fire.*
> *But if it had to perish twice,*
> *I think I know enough of hate*
> *To say that for destruction ice*
> *Is also great*
> *And would suffice.*

Danny and Tom stared at the poem and at one another.

Danny turned away in anger. "Pfft. I was going to get Marnie a book by this guy for Christmas. Not a chance. No fucking way!"

-CHAPTER FIFTY-EIGHT-

Sunday, December 13th

The drive back to the cabin seemed longer than usual. It was one minute past midnight. Tom and Danny had waited for the coroner and forensics to finish with Reuben's corpse. They sealed the silo with the new padlock that Tartello and Connor had brought with them earlier. Danny texted Rick and asked that he get his team in as soon as possible on Sunday to give the silo another search. He told him that the key to the padlock would be in his top desk drawer where Tartello was instructed to place it.

"I don't get it. Why kill your own son? Why lock your child inside a silo and leave him to die?" Tom asked.

Danny sighed. "I think that Reuben was about to spill his guts. I think that he told his mother that he'd had enough, and I think that she killed him. She dosed him up with something and killed him. We need to get someone back into his apartment. Where was his computer when they searched it the first time? Did somebody steal it, or did Reuben hide it above the ceiling tiles or something?"

"Wasn't that Justin's computer?" Tom asked.

"We didn't find his then either, did we?" Danny ran his fingers through his hair and rubbed the back of his neck. He wrestled for a few minutes in silence. Tom interrupted.

"Hey, Hannah did great tonight," Tom said grinning, giving Danny's arm a light tap with his fist. "She did a great job getting Kate to talk."

Danny nodded. "Yeah, she did. She had a good plan, and it paid off. I don't think that Kate is going to give Hannah or Marnie any trouble. Hey, did you see Tater snarl at Kate? That's exactly how he was with Sam."

"Yeah. Tomorrow's going to be an interesting day. How are we going to draw Grace Wilmot out of her hidey-hole?"

"I don't think that we need to. I think that she's going to be at the parade. She won't be able to help herself. She loves to blend in and weave through a crowd. I think that she is pathological and that she needs to feel that she's getting one over on us." Danny grunted a laugh. "She has no idea that Gram will be there."

362

"What's that supposed to mean?" Tom asked, eyebrows raised.

"Nothing." Danny grinned and focused on the road.

Tom glanced sideways at his partner. He sometimes forgot that Danny shared the same keen "insight" as Marnie and Gram. Danny just didn't like to admit it or use it for that matter.

~~~~~~~~~~~~~~~~~~~~

Hannah and Marnie were in the kitchen drinking hot chocolate when Danny and Tom returned. Tater and Dickens were standing at the windows staring into the darkness.

"Where's Kate?" Danny asked.

"Upstairs. We put a chair under the doorknob. She can't get out. There's no way that she's going to climb out the window in just a T-shirt. We took her clothes and shoes away from her." Hannah grinned.

"How did you do? Find Grace?" Marnie asked.

"No, but we did find a blue Otter Pop," Tom quipped.

Marnie scrunched up her nose. "You found what?"

Danny scowled at Tom. "We found Reuben Wilmot. It appears that he was drugged and left to freeze to death in the silo."

Marnie considered that for a moment. "Is that possible? He was in the hospital last night and frozen to death tonight?"

"The coroner's assistant says yes. They'll do an autopsy in the morning." Danny stood behind Marnie's chair and rubbed her shoulders. "Hey, do you think that we can play 20 questions in the morning? I'm beat. If my head doesn't hit the pillow soon, I'm going to fall asleep standing up."

"Yup. I think that we all need to get some sleep. Big day tomorrow. We need to go check the spook at the top of the driveway, and we need to check that spotlight." Marnie pushed her chair out and stood.

"Do the knuckleheads need to go outside again?" Tom asked.

"No. They just came in a few minutes before you came home." Marnie advised. "Tom, if you're staying, you're in my room."

Tom nodded wearily. "Yeah, I'm staying. I'm not driving home tonight."

Danny picked up Dickens, and they all went upstairs. At the top, they could hear Kate sniveling in the spare room.

Danny rolled his head back. "Who wants to check on her?"

Hannah walked over and hit the door with her fist. "Go to sleep, Kate."

Kate wailed, "I need to use the bathroom!"

Hannah rolled her eyes. "Fine. You pull any of your shit, and I will drop you like a sack of potatoes."

Hannah moved the chair, opened the door and let Kate out of the room. Kate ran into the bathroom without looking at anyone. They all stood in the hall waiting. They heard the toilet flush, water running and the doorknob turn. Kate raced from the bathroom back into the bedroom and slammed the door. Hannah propped the chair under the doorknob and turned back around.

"There. She should be good until morning. I'll see you all in the morning." Hannah walked into her room and shut the door.

Tom, Marnie and Danny all echoed, "Good night!"

~~~~~~~~~~~~~~~~~~~~~~~~~~~~~~~~

Danny rolled onto his back and stared at the ceiling. He glanced at the clock. It was six o'clock. Marnie stirred next to him. She rolled over, draped an arm across his chest and snuggled closer.

"Can't sleep?" Marnie yawned and snuggled closer.

"Nope. My mind is racing through the last few weeks. I've been thinking about how quiet my life was before I met you." Danny laughed.

"Admit it, Detective Gregg, your life was pretty boring before you met me."

"My life was normal. I got called out to a homicide at your house and everything fell to…"

"Fell into place?" Marnie interrupted.

"Not what I was going to say, but yes. Everything fell into place just like you said." Danny laughed, adjusted his pillow and grimaced.

"Your back bothering you?" Marnie asked, sitting up.

"It's itchy. The stitches are just itchy." Danny squirmed and sat up.

Marnie turned on the bedside lamp and looked at the wound. "It still looks fine. Doesn't itchy mean that it's healing?"

"It does, but it's still annoying."

They both turned at the knock on the door.

"Yeah?" Danny said.

"Are you two naked?' Tom giggled on the other side of the door.

"Hang on!" Danny yelled. He got up and put on a pair of sweatpants. He grabbed Marnie's leggings and sweatshirt off a chair and tossed them to her. He waited for her to scramble into them and opened the door. "What?"

"You're grumpy! You need coffee." Tom walked in and sat on the foot of the bed. "Hey, I've heard Kate speaking to someone this morning. Did Hannah let her keep her phone?"

Marnie shook her head. "No. Hannah took her handbag and put it in the hall closet last night."

Tom stared at the door. "Huh. I know that I heard her voice. Maybe she was talking to herself. Crazy people do that, you know."

Dickens stirred in his kennel, and Tater jumped up on the bed. He turned in a circle and lay down with his head in Tom's lap. Tom scratched his ears. "I also don't know how to make coffee in the percolator. I need coffee, and I need someone to make it for me. Let's all go downstairs, I'll take the knuckleheads out and one of you can make me coffee."

Danny leaned on a dresser. "Are you serious? You interrupted our morning because you don't know how to make coffee?"

Tom stood up, opened Dickens kennel and took him out. "Yeah. I really want a cup of coffee. Kate *was* talking to someone. C'mon, Tater." Tom disappeared down the hall.

Danny scowled. "He is banned from overnights here until he learns how to make coffee."

Marnie laughed.

"I'm going to go out and check that light now while it's still dark. You'll make coffee?"

Marnie got up and nodded. "I will make the coffee and breakfast. Bacon and French toast sound good?"

"Perfect!" Danny wrapped her in a hug and kissed her. "Tom Keller ruined my plans for this morning."

"Tom Keller won't ruin my plans for tonight." Marnie winked at him and went into the bathroom.

~~~~~~~~~~~~~~~~~~~~~~~~~~

Marnie was busy cooking the French toast when Hannah and Kate came into the kitchen. Kate sat on a barstool. Hannah went behind the counter, got two coffee mugs from the cupboard and filled the mugs. Marnie put a sugar bowl, creamer jug and two spoons on the counter and poured milk into the creamer jug.

"Good morning, Marnie," Kate purred. "It bothers you that Detective Gregg invited me to stay, doesn't it?"

Marnie frowned at her. Hannah squeezed Marnie's arm and gave her small hug.

"No, Kate, it doesn't bother me. After all, he didn't invite you. He had nowhere else to take you, so he had Tom bring you here. There's a big difference between invite and duty of care – a big difference." Marnie peeked into the oven to check on the bacon and turned back around. "By the way, Kate, you look like shit! That little brand on your forehead is there forever, unless of course you can convince your daddy to pay for more plastic surgery."

Anger rose in Kate's face. "How dare you, Marnie Reilly! I was attacked last night! I could have been killed, and you're over there making fun of my face. How dare you be so cruel!"

Marnie shook her head and laughed with disbelief at Kate's anger. "You and Sam killed Ken Wilder. You and Sam killed Officers Web and Weaver. You and Sam almost killed Tom and Sam Jalnack. Do you really think that I am going to find any sympathy for you? You blamed everything on my brother when we both know that you manipulated him. How dare I? Fuck off, Kate. Just fuck off!"

Kate started to speak. Hannah reached across the counter and grabbed her arm.

"I'd suggest that you be quiet. Stop talking. If Marnie were to come around the counter and throttle you, I wouldn't stop her. My money would be on her. I think that she could kick your ass."

Hannah went around the counter and sat on a barstool next to Kate – to keep an eye on her.

Tom and Danny came into the kitchen. Tater and Dickens raced in behind them. Tom plopped onto a stool next to Hannah. Tater stood at Kate's back and growled. Marnie snapped her fingers and pointed. Tater and Dickens went to their dishes and ate kibble. Danny went behind the counter and gave Marnie a bear hug, lifting her off her feet and kissing her forehead.

"That's smells good. What can I do to help?"

"Not a thing. The table is set and ready. I'm waiting on the bacon," Marnie replied.

"Get me coffee!" Tom yelled with an impish grin.

Danny took two mugs out of the cupboard, poured the coffee and pushed one across the counter to Tom. Tom sat at the end of the counter next to Hannah. Danny turned to Kate.

"We've got a cell at the town lockup ready and waiting for you, Kate. We're busy today. You need to be protected, so into a holding cell you shall go. I spoke with the DA. He says that it's perfectly legal to hold you in protective custody. I spoke with your lawyer, and he understands our concern." Danny smirked.

Kate raised one eyebrow sharply. "When will I be out of protective custody?"

"As soon as we catch whoever it is running around town trying to kill you." Danny took a sip of his coffee and leaned on the counter. "Any information that you can give us would be helpful. It's up to you."

"Did you find Grace Wilmot?" Kate asked.

Tom spun around on his stool and poked his head around Hannah. "None of your business," he said to Kate.

"You're horrible, Tom Keller. You've always been horrible!" Kate wailed. She stuck out her bottom lip and clenched her hands into fists.

Tom laughed. "Yeah, and I have boy germs. Isn't that what she used to say, Marnie?"

Marnie shook her head. "No. Donald Harrison had boy germs. You had cooties."

Tom grinned. "That's right. Cooties." He stood and went to the windows. He peered out, watching the deer on the trail below. "You know, Kate. There are a few words that you could learn. Ever heard the word 'grateful?' How about 'thank you?' How about you just say, 'Thank you, Danny, Tom, Marnie and Hannah, for saving my ass. Thanks so much for letting me stay here last night.' Have you ever thought about that, Kate? How about, 'Sorry for trying to set you up, Marnie, and for trying to kill you, Tom.'" Tom turned around and glared at her. He shook his head. "Nah! I didn't think so. You never think about anyone – other than yourself."

Tom followed Danny into town. Danny lost the toss, and Kate had to go with him. He put her in the back seat on the passenger side and used the child safety locks on the doors and windows to keep Kate from running. They dropped off Kate at the lockup at nine o'clock, dropped by a café to pick up takeout coffee and then went to see Rick. He was at his desk, feet propped on an open drawer, glasses on the end of his nose and reading a report.

"What have you got for us?" Danny asked.

"Mornin'. Did you guys bring me a coffee? The price of knowledge is a cup of coffee," Rick said, peering at them over the top of his glasses.

Tom handed him a takeout coffee and sat on the edge of his desk. "What have you got?"

"Okay. Marnie's melatonin was laced with a hint of midazolam – probably wouldn't have hurt her, but still not good. She would have slept like a baby. Someone used a fine syringe to empty some of the melatonin from the gel caps and replaced it with midazolam. Danny," Rick looked over his glasses at Danny, "Your antibiotics were capsules. You obviously didn't take any because the capsules were contaminated with Thallium, also known as rat poison – the same thing that our friend Reuben Wilmot drank in his cranberry juice. You didn't get sick, so you must not have followed your doctor's orders. Naughty boy." Rick glanced up and back down again. "Your pain pills were pain pills. No contamination." Rick took off his glasses and set the report down on his desk.

"Someone wants to kill me and just wants to knock Marnie out?" Danny asked.

"That pretty much sums it up." Rick nodded.

Tom nudged Danny. "That realization is going to fester all day."

"Yeah." Danny rubbed his chin. "No fingerprints?"

"Just on the bottle. Mr. Drake's fingerprints are all over it," Rick replied. "We knew they would be."

"Did you find anything useful at Kate Parish's apartment?" Tom asked.

"Nothing," Rick replied.

"Your guys are over at Silo 3 this morning?" Danny asked.

"We're heading over there as soon as I finish my coffee. Dr. Markson is coming in to handle Reuben Wilmot's autopsy. Next of kin hasn't been notified yet?" Rick asked.

Danny shook his head. "We can't find his mother."

"I'll keep you posted. As soon as I know something, you'll know something." Rick swung his feet down off his desk drawer.

368

"Yeah. We'll do the same. See you a bit later. Thanks, Rick." Danny waved, and he and Tom left. They walked outside and headed to their vehicles.

"Where to now?" Tom asked.

"Let's go have a little chat with Alice Wells. She may be able to shine some light on Grace Wilmot's haunts," Danny suggested.

"I'm right behind you." Tom pulled his truck keys out of his pocket. "Hey, what were you doing down by the lake this morning?"

"I don't know. Marnie asked me to check that spotlight," Danny replied.

"Did she, now?" Tom frowned.

"Why?" Danny asked.

"Hmm. She knows something that we don't know," Tom replied.

"Is that so?" Danny asked. He stopped walking and put a hand out in front of Tom. "What makes you say that?"

"Call it a hunch," Tom responded and started walking again.

~~~~~~~~~~~~~~~~~~~~~~

Hannah knocked on Marnie's open bedroom door and stuck her head inside.

Marnie was checking her phone for messages and glanced up. "What's up?"

"Do you think that I could borrow your long, light-gray cable-knit V-neck?" Hannah asked.

"Yeah. It's in the third drawer," Marnie replied, pointing to the dresser.

Hannah pulled out the drawer and the sweater.

"Who are you dressing for? Tom or Carl?" Marnie asked, head tipped and eyebrows raised.

Hannah spun around, her face red. "What do you mean?"

Marnie tipped her head to the other side and pulled a "who are you trying to kid" face.

Hannah tossed the sweater up and threw her head back. "I like them both!" She looked down at the floor and back up again. "I know that William just…"

"Hannah, let's forget about that. I know that you and William weren't involved. It's okay."

"How did you know that?" Hannah asked, mouth open with shock.

"Gram and I have a lot in common. I know that you think it's hooey, but I know that you and William weren't a couple in the same way that I know that Tom is a bit sweet on you. You needed to say that you and William had a relationship so that you could get in to see him. You were looking for something, but you didn't find it. I know stuff." Marnie shrugged.

"Tom is sweet on me?" Hannah asked, forgetting all about William.

"Yup. I've been waiting for you to show up in his life for some time. I could see your face, but I never imagined that you were Danny's twin sister." Marnie stood, opened a drawer on the dresser and pulled out a long red V-neck. "Wear this with a black or white skivvy underneath. Tom loves red, and polish your boots. Tom notices things like that."

"Thank you, Marnie! You're right. William was a good friend. When he was assigned to Creekwood, he just left. No word. No goodbye. He was assigned a new partner from the Hudson field office and just disappeared overnight. He was my mentor, and I didn't want to be left out, but I was left out. I went to the morgue looking for clues. I didn't find any. Anyway, Tom and Danny have involved me, so that's good," Hannah explained.

Marnie pondered Hannah's answer for a moment. "You don't know who his partner is? You don't know who he was working with here in Creekwood?"

Shaking her head, Hannah responded, "I have no idea. I've never met any of the agents from the Hudson field office. There are a lot of agents in the field." Hannah twisted her mouth and shrugged. "Hey, I'm going to get dressed now." She smiled and considered what Marnie had told her about Tom. "Tom's sweet on me, huh? Thanks!" Hannah raced down the hall to her room.

Marnie shut her door and took a bag out of her closet. She dressed in layers because she knew that the day would be long. She also knew that, this time of year, she needed to be prepared for anything… because she knew things that the others didn't – except for Gram… and Danny on occasion.

~~~~~~~~~~~~~~~~~~~~~~~~~~

Danny called Marnie while she was on her way to Ellie's to drop off Tater and Dickens. She didn't want to leave them at the cabin alone.

"Hey, Danny!"

"Hi, everything okay?"

"Yes. Everything is fine. I'm just heading to Ellie's to drop off the knuckleheads. Everything okay with you?"

"Yeah. We just had an interesting visit with Alice Wells. She told us that she had the police come to her house on Friday night to remove Grace Wilmot. I read the report. Alice fired her pistol at Grace." Danny chuckled.

"Is Alice okay?" Marnie asked.

"She's doing remarkably well. She has all of those packages wrapped, tied and tagged."

"Wow! There were a lot of packages. That's amazing!"

"Yeah. She gave us a few leads where we might find Grace. We're going on a hunt. I'll see you at the station soon?"

"Yes, you will!" Marnie replied.

"Okay. Bye!" Danny hung up.

He drummed his fingers on the steering wheel. He had a niggling feeling – an uneasiness that he couldn't let go. He scanned the street in front of him. Creekwood was bustling with people this morning. Market stalls were set up in the square. The smell of pine, cinnamon and ginger floated on an unusually warm breeze for this time of year. Danny glanced at the temperature display on his dashboard. It was 38 degrees, and it was only eleven o'clock. The phrase 'something wicked this way comes' was stuck in his head. Maybe that was all there was to it – a stupid phrase and nothing else, but it *was* something else. Marnie knew it. Gram knew it, he knew it and Tom knew it.

They say bad things come in threes, Danny mused. W*ho 'they' are is anyone's guess.* Danny mentally counted out the events of the last week. One, William's murder; two, Marnie being locked in the trunk; and three, Alice nearly dying. One, Allen nearly dying; two, the garage stabbing; and three, Justin's murder. One, Carl and the sleeping pills; two, Reuben's murder; and three, Kate's attack. Danny thought for a moment. One, antibiotics contaminated; two, melatonin contaminated; and three… Danny thought and thought to come up with a third, but he couldn't. Then it hit him – Captain Sterling! That completed the cycle of three. That was it! It was over. The cycle of three was complete. No more bad news. That's it. Done!

Danny's phone rang. It was Tom. "Yeah!" Danny answered.

"Hey, I'm gonna have to leave you for a while. My folks just had a bit of fender bender this side of Hudson. A pickup truck rear-ended them at a stop sign. I gotta get over there. I won't be long. The car is drivable, but Mom is having a fit. I think that Dad might leave her at the side of the road. Sorry, man."

"Go!" Danny said and hung up. He hit the steering wheel with the palm of his hand and threw his head back against the headrest. "Shit! One, Tom's folks. Two more to go."

~~~~~~~~~~~~~~~~~~~~~~~~~~~~~

Danny parked, wandered through Town Square and stopped in front of Enlighten Crystals. Officer Tony Tartello had arranged a warrant to search Grace's consult room and the rest of Enlighten Crystals. There was a young woman standing near the door, and when she saw him, she flipped the sign quickly to closed. He held up his badge and the warrant. She backed away from the door.

"Open the door, or I *will* break it down!" Danny yelled.

She stepped back another few inches and shook her head. Danny turned around, spotted a garbage can, picked it up, stepped toward the door and threatened to break the glass. The girl ran to the door and unlocked it.

Danny pushed his foot into the opening. "Cassie, I presume?"

"You can't come in here. Miranda told me that you would be coming back. I can't tell you anything. I don't know anything," Cassie professed.

"I got news for you, Cassie. I can come in. I can search the premises. If you don't answer my questions, I will take you down to the station, and you can answer them there. Now, step back and let me in."

"You're going to ruin my business! I've been rushing customers all morning. I knew that you would be back, and I didn't want customers in the store when you did!" Cassie wailed.

"I can't cause your business any more damage than you have done yourself. Why did you associate yourself with Grace Wilmot?" Danny asked, his tone measured. "I know that you own the store, Cassie. I did a search, and there you were."

Cassie backed up to the register counter on the back wall. "Fine! Search for whatever you like!"

"I will, thanks," Danny replied. "First, why don't you tell be about why you're letting Grace Wilmot blackmail you? Why didn't you come to the police? Is it really that bad?"

People have "tells." It could be as simple as the expression on their face, a nervous tic, the way that they hold their head or the direction that their eyes look. Every detail told a good cop what the person in front of them was thinking or feeling. A good cop also knows when a person is hiding something, and Danny knew that Cassie was hiding something.

Shock and fear look pretty much the same with just small differences. With fear, eyebrows are pulled up and together, upper eyelids are pulled up and the mouth is stretched. With shock, the entire eyebrow is pulled up, eyelids are pulled up, the mouth hangs open and the pupils dilate. Cassie's expression showed a bit of both, but her mouth gave her away. She was afraid.

"Cassie, why don't you tell me what Grace Wilmot is holding over your head," Danny suggested. He continued to assess her; it was clear to him that she was to trying to figure out whether she would cooperate. He never took his eyes off her face because her face was giving her away.

"Okay. Anything that I find in Grace's consult room will be tied back to you. It's your business, so if there *is* anything questionable in there, that's on you." In three long strides, Danny stood in front of the locked room that Miranda had pointed out on Saturday.

Cassie grabbed his arm. "Wait!"

Danny stopped, waited and stared down at his watch. "I will – for about 2 more seconds."

"Okay! I think that Grace is running drugs out of her consult room. I was in juvy when I was a teenager. I was stupid and got busted a few times for selling dope and pills that I stole from my nana and pop. I saw how bad that life was. I went to college, worked hard and opened this store. I thought that I had put all of those awful days behind me. Grace remembered me as soon as she came back to Creekwood. She told me that she would tell everyone in town about my past – make things up if she had to if I didn't help her. I was protecting my reputation," Cassie confessed, hanging her head.

"You know what. If you'd come to the station and told an officer what was happening, someone would have looked into that for you. Blackmail is a pretty serious thing. It's a felony in New York state. You know that, right?" Danny studied her face.

Cassie shook her head. "I figured that, with my past, nobody would care."

Danny laughed. "Well, apparently, you don't know much about Grace Wilmot's past. If you had mentioned her name, there's not a cop in Creekwood who wouldn't have helped you. She's a bad seed, Cassie."

Grace's consult room was locked, and only she had a key. It took only seconds for Danny to pop the lock. Grace Wilmot had a tidy little operation going. He read through her notebook, checked under the drawers and found zipped bags of cocaine, ecstasy and several other things that he didn't recognize. He bagged up everything, took pictures, got a statement from Cassie and boxed up everything in Grace's room.

As Danny handed her the receipt for Grace's belongings, Cassie gulped when she realized that Danny was taking everything with him. "What am I going to tell Grace when she comes in and everything is gone?"

Danny stopped at the door and smirked. "How about you tell her that a ninja broke in and stole everything last night. Tell her that the ninja was caught on CCTV."

Cassie's jaw dropped. "A ninja?"

"Yeah. A ninja." Danny waved and headed back to his truck, chuckling as he went.

~~~~~~~~~~~~~~~~~~~~~~~~~~~

The noon meeting at the station was a quick-and-dirty half-hour breakdown of the task at hand: find Grace Wilmot. Danny passed around photos of Grace to the beat cops and gave them strict instructions to arrest her immediately for drug possession and trafficking.

"Get her in cuffs, guys. Don't take any chances. She's as slippery as they come," Danny advised.

Back out on the street, Danny asked Tom, Hannah and Marnie to accompany him to Station Hall, and he explained why.

"I've read through Grace's notebooks. Here's what I think was going on. Grace advertised to her network that The Collective holds events at Station Hall. She then let them know that she can supply them with the drug of their choice if they attend an event by booking online using the code ENLIGHTEN or book an appointment with her at Enlighten Crystals. The sales of the event include the price of the drugs. Justin managed the ticket prices and instructed customers which seats to choose based on the drugs that they wanted. It was all done through E-mail, and Reuben handled that for his mother. That's how Grace knew how much money to take out of The Collectives account after each event. We've got to find those laptops. I'm betting that both Reuben and Justin had hiding spots in their apartments or whoever killed them took their laptops. Either way, we have to search their apartments again."

"We're going back to Station Hall to check under *all* of the seats?" Tom asked. "That's where the drugs were placed before each event?"

"Yes," Danny confirmed. "Many people would have walked out without them on Monday, thinking that they would be caught by the cops."

"Do you think that Alice and Allen had any idea?" Marnie asked.

Danny shook his head. "Nah. I think that they were unwilling accomplices. I don't think that they knew anything."

Marnie nodded. "Good. I'm glad to hear that."

"Danny, do we need a warrant? Want me to call the judge?" Tom asked.

"Nah. Station Hall is owned by Creekwood – a warrant's not necessary," Danny replied with a wrinkle of his nose.

"Oh, wait, Tom! How are your parents? Daniel mentioned an accident," Hannah asked.

"Yeah. A little fender bender. They're fine. We dropped off their luggage at my house, and I dropped them off at the square. They'll stay for the parade," Tom replied.

"Glad that everything is good with your folks, Tommy. Don't mean to be insensitive, but we gotta keep moving. We can chat later." Danny put out his arms and herded everyone in the direction of their vehicles.

~~~~~~~~~~~~~~~~~~~~~~~~~

The field trip to Station Hall paid off. Zipped bags of assorted drugs were found – not *under* the seats. Small slits had been cut into the front of each seat cushion, and the drugs had been slipped *into* the seats. Danny called in a team to gather up the evidence and document the seat number where each zipped bag was located.

~~~~~~~~~~~~~~~~~~~~~~~~~

Main Street was packed with shoppers, parade-goers and people watchers. The day was warm, and people were out in droves. Danny, Tom, Hannah and eight Creekwood PD patrolman walked the streets, keeping an eye out for Grace Wilmot.

Marnie, Carl and Gram were busy herding up the eight children who had won a place on the float through essays about charity. The parade was set to start in 10 minutes. The float was rigged with a refrigeration unit beneath its undercarriage. The design had turned out better than Marnie had imagined. The bed of the float was a skating rink surrounded by Plexiglas, allowing parade-goers to watch the carolers skate, but also to ensure the carolers' safety. A cardboard log cabin that was, in fact, a painted refrigerator box; small Christmas trees; and large candy canes on either side were at the front of the 48-foot-long flatbed trailer. Styrofoam snowmen and snowwomen sat in the back two corners of the trailer with bales of hay stacked at the back of the float so that the skaters could sit if they became tired. 12 poles, each 7-feet high, were secured around the perimeter of the float. Sapphire blue cotton sheeting stretched over the poles, creating a canopy over the skaters. White battery-operated fairy lights were strung under the cotton sheeting between the poles, and the lights twinkled like stars in a sapphire sky above the skaters.

Carl removed a section of Plexiglas and helped Marnie lift the children onto the float. Marnie and Carl helped them into their new skates, thanks to the kindness of the local sporting goods shop. They had kindly given each child a brand-new pair of skates and skate guards. Carl double-checked the sound system, and Marnie stepped inside the cardboard log cabin at the front of the float. She had a first aid kit, two blankets, water and tissues ready and waiting. The cabin had a Dutch door cut into it at Marnie's request so that she so could see out and wouldn't suffer a claustrophobic panic attack.

Carl sat at the back on a hay bale with a basket of candy to throw out to the crowd. Gram chose to ride in the cab with the driver, a witty and burly truck driver named Earl. He'd known Gram for years and was happy to have her in the cab with him. He handed her a large sack of candy to throw out to the people along the route.

On his walkabout, Danny spotted Patrick in the crowd. He waved, and Patrick stopped for a quick chat. Tom saw Erin; she stopped to flirt. Hannah didn't see anyone whom she recognized; she was laser-focused on finding Grace Wilmot.

Officers Tony Tartello and Peter Connor dropped by Drake's Drugs and arrested Mr. Drake for the contaminated melatonin, pain pills, nicotine patches and asthma inhaler. They hauled him off in cuffs to the shrieks of his wife and a few of his employees – but not all.

Alice and Allen, who was out on bail, stood across the street and watched the float of skating carolers join the procession. They made their way to the Christmas tree at Town Square for the finale.

The lineup of songs that the carolers would sing were chosen through a survey listed on the Town of Creekwood's social media page. Marnie added in "O Christmas Tree" for them to sing when they arrived at Town Square and the location of the town's Christmas tree.

The singing carolers were having a wonderful time. The crowd cheered at "Rudolph the Red-Nosed Reindeer" and clapped for "Jingle Bells" as they went by. Marnie found herself getting a bit teary when they sang "Away in a Manger" and "We Three Kings" – these were family favorites. The magic of Christmas can do that sometimes.

Two blocks before Town Square, a clown on a unicycle took a tumble and knocked into his friend on a pair of stilts. They stopped the float, waited for the clowns to recover and then all carried on to Town Square.

Marnie could hear the crowd cheering as they approached Town Square. Carl gave her a nod, and she told the children to sing "O Christmas Tree." Carl moved slowly to the front of the trailer and asked Marnie quietly if she smelled smoke. Marnie sniffed the air and nodded. Carl craned his neck around the side of the Christmas trees, but he couldn't see any evidence of smoke. Marnie glanced up at the skaters and, to her horror, saw smoke billowing from the hay bales at the back of the float. She punched Carl's arm and whispered in his ear. "Look…"

"Do we have a fire extinguisher?" Carl asked.

"It's in the cab," Marnie whispered.

Carl grabbed a giant candy cane, herded the skaters to the front of the trailer and stood in front of them, pretending to direct the choir. Marnie called Gram's cell and asked her to have Earl stop the truck slowly and bring the fire extinguisher to her. As the float stopped moving, a burst of flames shot from the hay bales. The children turned from their conductor and began to cry out. Suddenly, Patrick appeared at the side of the float and ripped off a Plexiglas section. He climbed up and told Carl to get down.

"Get down! I'll hand the children to you," Patrick ordered.

Marnie threw the cardboard cabin over the Plexiglas, worrying that it would catch fire. She grabbed the two blankets and slid down to the end of the trailer. She put her arms out and held the blanket as high as she could to block the flames from the screaming children's heads. Next to the smoldering bales, the Plexiglas buckled as it heated and began to melt.

Marnie heard Danny yelling out to her. She glanced up and saw Tom and Danny pulling the Plexiglas off the back of the trailer. She shooed the children toward Patrick. Danny and Tom moved to the sides of the trailer and began removing more Plexiglas panels. Marnie slid to the hay bales and kicked them off the back of the trailer into the road. Earl ran around the side and extinguished the bales as they hit the road. Patrick handed the last child safely to Carl and turned to see if Marnie had gotten off the trailer.

"Marnie, get off the trailer!" Danny yelled.

Marnie looked up to see the canopy of sapphire blue sky and the fairy lights in flames falling toward her. Patrick looked up, sucked in a breath and dove across the ice rink. He grabbed Marnie around the waist and slid them both off the trailer to the asphalt below. The canopy fell, and a sizzling duet of the fire and ice filled the air.

~~~~~~~~~~~~~~~~~~~~~~~~~~~~~

Marnie got to her feet and put out her hand to help up Patrick. He took her hand and struggled to his feet.

"Patrick, are you okay? Thank you! Thank you for getting the children off the trailer, and thank you for saving me, too. Are you okay? I have to make sure that the kids are okay. Are you okay, Patrick?" Marnie searched Patrick's face.

Patrick nodded. "You've got some scratches, Ms. Reilly. I'm sorry about that."

"It's Marnie, and I don't care about scratches. I care that everyone is okay."

Danny and Tom raced around the end of the trailer.

Marnie grabbed Danny's arm. "Are all of the children okay? Is Carl safe?"

Danny nodded. "Everyone is safe. Everyone is okay. Let me look at you. You hit the asphalt pretty hard. Look at that road rash." Danny kissed her cheek and hugged her tight. "Patrick, I will never be able to thank you, man. Thank you so much for getting Marnie off the trailer. Thank you so much." Danny held out his hand to Patrick, Patrick took Danny's hand and Danny pulled him into a hug. "Thanks, man. I can't thank you enough."

Tom had Marnie off her feet, giving her a bear hug, when Marnie saw a familiar face running through the crowd. She shouted, "Hey, that's Grace Wilmot! She's just about to run by Gram!"

Danny and Tom ran around the side of the trailer, but before they could get to Grace, Gram had spotted her. Gram stuck out her arm and clotheslined Grace Wilmot. Grace fell to the ground with a dull thud. Gram turned around and winked. "Come get her, lads!"

They did.

-CHAPTER FIFTY-NINE-

Grace Wilmot and Mr. Drake sat and waited in separate interview rooms at Creekwood PD for the better part of 2 hours. Danny and Tom were quite happy to allow them to stew.

Marnie gave her statement to Officer Tartello in the coffee lounge, and Patrick gave his statement to Officer Connor in the bullpen. Carl, Earl and Gram would give statements as soon as an officer was free to speak to them. A counselor was made available for the children.

Danny walked into the interview room where Mr. Drake sat stewing. Mr. Drake had called his attorney. David Bennett nodded to Danny. Danny glanced down at the file in his hand and leaned back against a wall opposite Mr. Drake.

"Hi, David. You representing Mr. Drake isn't a conflict of interest? He did contaminate Marnie Reilly's melatonin. Isn't she your client? It may be good to note that he also contaminated my antibiotics with thallium, but then again, I'm *not* your client."

Mr. Drake's eyes grew wider, his shoulders shook and he dry-heaved into his handkerchief.

David drew in a breath. "I went to Mr. Drake's home and obtained this file and these audio tapes from his desk. He wants to cooperate fully with the police department. Grace Wilmot has been blackmailing Mr. Drake for years, and he would like to share every detail with you."

Danny smiled broadly and sat down at the table. "Let's make a deal."

~~~~~~~~~~~~~~~~~~~~~

Grace was shocked to see Tom Keller walk into the interview room. She had been expecting Detective Gregg, even hoping that it would be him. Grace had skulked and fretted, her visions abandoning her except to anticipate this conversation. He would have been the harder of the two to interview her. She was mildly disappointed. There was no challenge to look forward to now.

Tom tapped the edge of a folder on the interview table. "Grace Wilmot, my, my, my, you have a checkered past. What are you doing back in Creekwood?" Tom leaned against the wall and turned on a recorder. "I'm going to record this interview. It's Sunday, December 13th at 4:55 PM. I know that you've been read your rights by the officers. They tell me that you don't want legal counsel. Is there a reason for that?"

Grace sneered. "I don't need legal counsel. I have done nothing wrong." Grace pursed her lips and smirked.

Tom nodded. "You're waiving your right to have an attorney present during this interview. Is that correct?"

"Yes, of course. That's what I just said," Grace snapped.

"Great! Let's discuss why you've been blackmailing Philip Drake. No point in denying it, Grace. We have letters, E-mails, text messages and voice recordings from you to him. You were quite nasty in your communication. Nasty, nasty," Tom commented, his head down as he pretended to read through the file.

Grace's jaw dropped as she feigned shock. "I haven't been blackmailing... Who was it? What was the name? Drake?" Grace pretended to search her memory. "I don't appreciate you calling me Grace. It's Mrs. Wilmot."

Tom glanced up and frowned. "Yeah. Anyway, Grace, how about you take the twist out of your knickers and tell me why you had Mr. Drake contaminate medications? Marnie Reilly's melatonin and Detective Gregg's antibiotics, to name just a few. See here!" Tom held up pages of typed spreadsheets. "I have a whole list of people you tried to poison or make severely ill in your attempt to… What? Take over the world? We also have another dozen or so people we're interviewing who claim that they have proof that you blackmailed them. Oh, and you also sold drugs to them. Let's not forget that. You see, Grace, we're trying to figure out your motives. Why are you such a nasty piece of work?"

Grace suddenly shrieked and burst into tears behind her wrinkled and grubby handkerchief. "He killed my husband! He did it! The medication he gave my husband killed him and left little Reuben and me all alone!"

Tom rubbed his chin and pulled another piece of paper out of his file. "Is that right, Grace? Is that what you really believe? 'Cause that's not what your husband's autopsy notes and recent developments show. I reached out to a good friend who works in forensics and another good friend who works in pathology. It's amazing the things that we can find out these days. Did you know that your husband's case file was still in evidence? Yeah. We law enforcement people, we're pack rats. We hold onto things for years."

Grace stopped crying immediately and pulled the handkerchief to her mouth as she shrank back in her seat.

"Yeah. I sent one of our officers down to evidence to gather up everything. They took it over to the forensics lab. Top-notch lab. We've got some of the best. Anyway, long story short, they found traces of thallium on your husband's clothes where he had vomited on his shirt, pants and shoes the day that you took him to the ER. You know, there was still a blood sample kicking around. How lucky for us, huh? Funny thing is that you can find thallium if you know what you're looking for. Did you know that, Grace?" Tom raised his eyebrows at her over the top of the file.

"What do you mean? I didn't poison my husband! Philip Drake killed him! He gave him medication that killed him!" Grace argued.

Tom pulled a face. "Hmm. No. That's not how it went down. We've got a lot – I mean, *a lot* – of evidence that speaks differently to your claim. Did you know that you left boxes at Alice's house? Boxes that she gave to Justin. He stashed the boxes at his apartment. Did you know that? Yeah. Let me tell you, that was interesting reading. Our officers found the boxes after you killed Justin. We went back and collected everything. We've had a few of our guys goin' through all of it. Who helped you with that, Grace? Who helped you kill Justin?"

Grace gasped. "Justin is dead?!"

Tom thought her reaction was convincing. He decided to throw out another.

"Yeah. You know that he's dead, and we know that you killed him. Just like Reuben. How could you kill your own son, Grace?" Tom pursed his lips. "Hmm... then again, you did kill your husband." Tom reached into his folder and threw the photos of Justin's and Reuben's dead bodies down on the table in front of Grace.

Grace's hands and the filthy handkerchief went to her face. "No! No! Not my baby! Not Reuben!" Grace sobbed and sobbed and sobbed.

"I'll have one of the officers take you back to your cell. We can continue this interview tomorrow. Ending interview at 5:15 on Sunday, December 13th." Tom left the interview to get himself a coffee and to leave Grace with her thoughts. Tom heard her sobs mix with maniacal hoots and caws. He shivered – just a little.

-CHAPTER SIXTY-

Marnie sat on a barstool while Danny and Tom fussed over her cuts and bruises. Patrick sat next to her holding the gauze and salve, while Hannah and Gram fussed over him. Tater and Dickens were at the window eating each other's dinner. Tom's parents sat at the kitchen table drinking hot chocolate with peppermint schnapps. Marnie smiled at them, noting that Tom was the spitting image of his father – tall; lanky; stormy blue eyes; short, black hair; and a perfectly-shaped Roman nose. Marnie thought that, next to her own mother, Tom's mom was the second-most beautiful woman in the world. At 5'4", Mrs. Keller's height was the only thing average about her. Her auburn hair, emerald green eyes, porcelain complexion and sculpted cheekbones left most people staring. She hadn't changed much over the years, and Marnie thought that the laugh lines and the touch of silver in her hair made her look chic.

"Thomas, it's nice to see you and Marnie playing nicely after all these years," Declan Keller remarked with humor.

"It is nice to see that you two have grown up. When did we see you last, Marnie?" Abby Keller mused.

Marnie giggled. "Last Christmas."

"Well, you've both obviously matured in the last year," Abby laughed.

"That's my influence, Mrs. Keller," Danny quipped.

"It's Abby or Abigeal, Danny. Mrs. Keller is too formal for friends," Abby replied. "I'm not sure if it's your influence, but it's nice to see Tommy taking care of Marnie instead of dunking her face in mud."

"They were horrible children, weren't they? Horrible children." Declan smirked. "That's a rhetorical question. We know the answer, and there is no point in arguing."

Danny kissed Marnie's forehead. "There, I think that we've done our best."

Marnie stared up at him. A bruise was rising up on her right cheek under the road rash that stretched from her cheekbone to her chin. A small graze above her right eyebrow was beginning to show a bruise. The back of her right hand and the knuckles on her left hand were scraped and swollen.

Patrick apologized. "I'm sorry, Marnie. You took the brunt of the fall. I landed on you."

"That's okay, Patrick. Glad to be of service to a hero." Marnie laughed.

Tom checked his watch. "Hey, what time are those pizzas going to be here?"

"They said that they're busy. Probably another 40 minutes. Six-thirtyish or so. Why?" Danny replied.

"I'm going to run up to Jenkin's and get a couple of cartons of eggnog. Carl mentioned that someone had given him a bottle of brandy – not a very good bottle – and that he was going to bring it up if I could pick up some eggnog. "

"Ooo! Brandied eggnog." Marnie grinned and rolled her eyes. "I love brandied eggnog."

"Oh, God," Tom said, covering his eyes. "Are we going to have a replay of last New Year's Eve?"

"You shush, Tom Keller!" Marnie wrinkled her nose up at him.

"There they go!" Declan said with a laugh.

"I'm goin'. Anybody need anything?" Tom asked.

"Can I come with you?" Hannah jumped up for a barstool. "A drive would be nice."

"Sure. You can scare the goblins away." Tom winked.

"What?" Hannah scrunched her face.

Tom shook his head. "Nothin'. C'mon."

Marnie and Danny looked at each other. They'd forgotten to check on the second ghoul in the woods.

"We forgot." Danny hit his palm to his head.

"We did. We can go tomorrow." Marnie shrugged. "It's not a big deal now."

"I suppose not."

"Okay, folks. I am going to get changed, and I'll be right back," Marnie announced.

"Yeah. I better get going." Patrick checked the time on the wall clock and stood.

"Stay for dinner, Patrick. You're more than welcome," Danny coaxed.

"I-I-I've got plans, but thanks." Patrick pulled on his jacket.

"Okay, I'll walk you out. I've got to take the knuckleheads out anyway." Danny followed Patrick into the living room to the door. "C'mon, Tater! C'mon, Dickens!"

Carl banged the door open into the cabin just after six o'clock. "Where's Tom?"

Danny glanced up from the fire. "He and Hannah went to get eggnog. Why?"

"His truck is off the road near Jenkin's. I pulled over to see if he needed help, but he wasn't in it. He wasn't there." Carl stomped snow off his boots and pulled off his driving gloves.

"What?!" Abigeal shot up from the couch.

Danny tossed a log that he'd grabbed onto the fire and thought, *that's three – the cycle's complete.* "It's slippery out, and he probably spun out. Say, Carl, was his gun in the truck?"

Carl shook his head. "I didn't see it, but I didn't look all that closely."

"Were they coming back, or had they not gotten to Jenkin's?" Declan had been in the kitchen, but had heard enough to know that something was amiss. He crossed to put his arm around his wife.

Marnie came down the stairs in sweatpants, a long-sleeve T-shirt and slippers, holding her phone in her hand. "What's going on?"

"Tom's car is off the road near Jenkin's, and he and Hannah aren't there." Danny shot Marnie a "what the hell" look.

"I went into Jenkin's and asked if Tom had been in, and they said that no one had been in all evening," Carl added. "It doesn't make sense."

Suddenly, Hannah pushed through the front door, nearly knocking Carl off of his feet. She was covered in snow and fell into Carl's arms when he turned around.

"Oh. My. God!" Hannah tried to catch her breath. "Some psycho… in a… blue van… drove us off… the road." Hannah bent over and breathed in and out slowly. "This black ninja thing held a gun on us and motioned us to get into the van." She winced and struggled to speak.

Carl grabbed her around the waist and walked her to the sofa. Abby grabbed a soft blanket from the pile and tossed it over Hannah's shoulders.

Danny knelt down in front of Hannah. "Any idea who it was? Did you get the license plate?" Danny asked.

Hannah shook her head. "I don't know. I have no idea. Uh… No. There were no plates!"

"How tall?"

"Six foot, maybe," Hannah said. "Athletic. Face covered with a black balaclava. Black pants. Black shirt. Black gloves and black shoes." Hannah put her head between her knees.

Gram had dashed to the kitchen and now raced into the living room with a

384

glass of water. She handed it to Danny to give his sister. She glanced at Marnie. Marnie stared at her phone, then stared at Gram.

"We came to a turn, Tom opened the door and pushed me out! He pushed me out!" Hannah cried. "I shot at the tires, but they were too far away. I... I... he pushed me out! I ran all of the way back. I cut across the deer run."

Gram wedged onto the sofa between Hannah and Declan and comforted her granddaughter. She kept an eye on Marnie, who sank onto the ottoman.

Danny called the sheriff's office and made a call to Creekwood PD.

"Okay. We have an all-points bulletin out on a navy blue van. They won't get too far. Road blocks will be up, and they won't get through." Danny ran his hand through his hair.

A knock came at the door. Carl opened it. A young man stepped up to the door. "Pizza delivery." Marnie crossed to the door, took a five-dollar bill out of her bag, handed it to the pizza guy and took the pizzas. She set them on the coffee table.

Gram glanced up at Marnie. "Marnie, dear, why don't we go into the kitchen and make coffee and tea."

"Sure, Gram," Marnie agreed.

Gram turned on the water, filled the kettle and set it on the stove. Marnie filled the percolator with water.

Gram put a hand on Marnie's arm. "Marnie? What did the text message say, love? What have you been preparin' for all day?"

Marnie took a deep breath, opened the text message and showed it to Gram.

I've got TK. If you want to see him agn, mt me on the dock at 10 PM. ALONE! DG is next if you don't.

Hannah came into the kitchen. "Danny wanted me to get Tom's mother and father a whiskey. Am I interrupting something?"

Marnie shook her head. "No, but Hannah, I need your help."

~~~~~~~~~~~~~~~~~~~~~~~

Danny hung up his phone. "That was the sheriff's office. They have roadblocks up, and there hasn't been any sign of a blue van. I think that we need to start Plan B. Rick says that there are no prints in the truck that shouldn't be there. The tire tracks were filled with snow, and no one has seen a blue, black or dark-colored van in the area."

Marnie glanced down at her watch. "C'mon, Tater. C'mon, Dickens. Let's go out."

Hannah stood. "I'll come with you."

"Thanks, Hannah."

Gram sat in the chair closest to the fire with her rosary beads in hand. She nodded to Hannah and Marnie.

Danny called out, "Marnie, put your jacket on. It's not *that* warm."

Marnie took her jacket off the hook and carried it out the door with her. She handed it to Hannah when they stepped off the porch. Hannah pulled a pair of water shoes out of her jacket pocket and handed them to Marnie. Marnie took off her slippers and put on the water shoes.

"Okay. I'm going to send Tater back to you. He will be barking louder than you have ever heard him bark. As soon as he heads back, count to five and turn on the spotlight. Got it?"

"Got it," Hannah answered. "The wire is working just fine. I've heard everything that you've said the last few hours. Marnie, are you sure about this?"

"We're dealing with someone who thinks that they're a ninja, Hannah. I have training in kung Fu and karate. I know that I'm going to get my ass kicked, but if we don't do this, Tom and Danny... Hannah, I just couldn't imagine." Marnie's eyes filled up with tears.

Hannah took Marnie's hands and looked into her face. "We've got this. We've got this!"

Marnie nodded. "Remember, Tater's going to bark and run to you, and you hit the spotlight on the count of five. That few moments of chaos will buy us some time. If my visions are right – if what my parents are telling me is correct – there's a remote of some sort that will signal for Tom to be... oh, geez. I'm not saying it. Remember, you get Tater inside. I don't need him getting hurt. You keep everyone away from the lake no matter what."

"Keeping Danny up here is going to be impossible, and you know that." Hannah's face showed doubt that part of the plan would work.

"Yeah. I know, but tell him that I mentioned 'divine guidance,' and tell him that I told you that the torn veil has been repaired. Tell him that, and if that doesn't work, Gram will convince him," Marnie urged.

Hannah nodded. "Okay. I'll try. Do you know where Tom is?" Hannah asked.

"Not yet, but he is alive," Marnie replied.

"How can you be sure?" Hannah asked.

"Divine guidance. That's how I know." Marnie gave a curt nod. "Hey, I gotta go."

~~~~~~~~~~~~~~~~~~~~~~~~~

Marnie and Tater walked down to the lake. A figure stood motionless on the end of the long dock. Marnie stepped slowly onto the dock, holding tight to Tater's lead.

She whispered, "Place. Place. Good boy." Tater sat.

Hannah's description was correct. Dressed all in black, the figure walked toward her. The figure took several more steps, and Marnie recognized the build and the smell. It was definitely the walk that gave her away – not so much a walk, but a sashay.

"A wolf in sheep's clothing… Hello, Erin." Marnie shivered.

"Ha ha! Marnie! You've finally figured it out. All of these months and weeks, and you've finally figured it out. Your brother didn't give you credit. He said that you were the slow one in the family. Did you get the murder of crows that we sent you? He wasn't sure that you would remember or understand. The one that I threw at the window was my favorite. Unfortunately, his neck didn't break. I gave it a good try, though." Erin snickered and pulled the balaclava off her head, revealing wild eyes and a sinister sneer.

"Why are you doing this?" Marnie asked.

"Why? Let me see. You sent my boyfriend to prison. Yeah, that's right. Sam and I have been together for years. He was FBI, and I was an informant. He and I came to Creekwood to work with Grace and to get rid of you. He really hates you, Marnie. So does Grace… and Kate. Goodness, how one boring little person could create that much hate is beyond me. I don't hate you. You're just in my way. As for Grace, well, she's been useless. She's absolutely mad! She thinks that she's some kind of voodoo priestess or a mystic of black magic. Anyway, tonight, I'm taking over. I'll get rid of you, Tom and your boyfriend."

"Okay. Well, it sounds like you have a plan." Marnie shrugged one shoulder and tipped her head to the right. "What about Kate? I thought that Kate and Sam were together. I thought that they had a plan to kill Ken and me. What about Kate?" Marnie asked.

Erin rolled her eyes and spat. "Kate was a pawn. She was needed until she wasn't. Then you, your boyfriend and Keller had to get involved in William's murder. You could have stayed out of it. Sam, Grace Wilmot, Reuben, Justin and I had a good thing going until William got a good sniff of what we were doing. He and his partner fucked up everything!"

"Danny and Tom couldn't have stayed out of it. It's their job. What do you mean William's partner?" Marnie's mind raced. *Does she mean Hannah?*

"Oh, don't play coy, Marnie! You know exactly who I'm talking about. Your brother said that you do this. You play mind games with people. You try to throw them off!"

"I'm not playing a game, Erin. I have no idea who William's partner is." Marnie prepared herself to run if Erin had a gun.

"Liar!" Erin took two more steps toward Marnie.

"Why the tattoos, Erin? Why the Eye of Providence? Why kill William, Justin and Reuben, and why harm Kate?" Marnie asked.

"Don't be stupid! William played games. He pretended to be my friend. Justin was going to snitch. Reuben got cold feet after I stabbed your dreamy detective and was squeamish when I insisted that we do away with Justin. He wasn't going to help me. He got scared, and I knew that he was going to confess. I didn't have a choice. Oh, and let's not forget Captain Sterling. How could you have forgotten about him, Marnie? Hmm... I keep forgetting that you're stupid. Anyway, he was getting just a tad too close for comfort. He knew too much! Poking around. Asking questions. It's a shame, but I'm going to the hospital as soon as we're finished here. I love a good nurse's uniform. I get a bit bored with black." Erin struck a pose. "Don't you think that I would look good in... oh... purple hospital scrubs?"

Never breaking eye contact, Marnie tipped her head to the left and gave Erin what she wanted – a silent audience.

"Kate, well, she was annoying, whiny and needy." Frowning, Erin waved a dismissive hand and snickered. "As for the tattoo... I'm surprised that you didn't figure that out. Actually, I'm not surprised. As I keep mentioning, you are stupid."

Erin laughed wickedly, and her crazed eyes made Marnie wish that she had borrowed Hannah's gun.

Erin continued, "Your brother told me that your father had that tattooed on his forearm when he was in the service. The all-seeing eye. Sam hated it. I thought that you might have, too. I wanted you to know that *I* could see everything! I wanted you to know that you wouldn't get away with anything! Just like your father – he didn't let you get away with anything. He was cruel. Sam told me. Sam told me everything!"

"Pfft. First of all, my father wasn't cruel, and when we were kids, we got away with *a lot*. Second, that's not what the symbol means. It means protection. Providence – the divine protection of God – so while you may have used that tattoo on all of your victims to scare me, it didn't work. What you

388

actually did was ensure William's, Reuben's and Justin's entry into heaven. You protected them. Don't you see that? Oh, and I agree with you about Kate. She is whiny, needy and annoying, but you protected her, too." Marnie shrugged.

Marnie was bullshitting a bit and buying time. Erin hadn't revealed Tom's location, and she needed to keep her talking. Marnie's visions had been correct up to this point. She knew what was about to happen. She shivered at the thought. The lake was cold this time of year. Marnie was thankful for the thermal dive skin she wore under her clothes.

Erin took another step and another. She stood in the middle of the dock.

"Where's Tom?" Marnie asked, trying hard not to tremble.

"I don't think that I'll tell you." Erin sneered. "Then again, perhaps I should play fairly. Hmm… maybe just this once. A bit of a warning, though… You see this little device here around my neck? If anyone comes down to this dock – if anyone comes near us – I'll push this little button and BOOM!" Erin threw up her arms dramatically and snickered. "Tom goes bye-bye."

Marnie smiled, and her eyes lit up with smugness. "Oh, Erin, my brother obviously didn't tell you very much about me at all. You don't need to tell me where Tom is. You already let it slip. Your thoughts gave you away."

"What's that supposed to mean? No, I didn't! No, they didn't!"

Marnie didn't answer, but gave Tater a hand command to snarl.

"What does that mean?! I didn't let anything slip!" Erin demanded. "Get that dog out of here before I kill it! Sam told me that it bit him! Get it out of here! I'll kill it!"

Marnie turned back toward the cabin, and she whispered into the mic on her chest, "He's in the garage." Dropping Tater's lead, she whispered the commands, "Hannah! Scootchem!" Tater ran toward Hannah and the cabin, barking louder than she had ever heard him bark.

One Mississippi.

Two Mississippi.

Marnie turned back to Erin, continuing to count to five in her head. *Three Mississippi.*

"What are you doing?! What's wrong with you?!" Erin shouted, feeling for the remote dangling from its cord around her neck.

Four Mississippi.

Marnie whispered, "Five."

The spotlight shone into Erin's eyes. She lifted her hands to shield the blinding light. Marnie sprang forward, and Erin kicked out with her left leg. Marnie ducked and swept Erin's legs out from under her with her left arm and ripped the remote from Erin's neck with her right hand. She tossed the remote softly onto the ice, and it skipped gently into the frozen reeds. Erin got back to her feet and threw a punch at Marnie. Marnie weaved to the side, but not fast enough. Erin hit Marnie on her left cheekbone. Marnie fell back onto the dock and pushed herself back up as Erin came at her with a knife.

"A knife! Are you fucking kidding me?!" Marnie rolled her eyes. "A vision about that would have helped!" Marnie screamed to the sky.

Erin sneered.

A twig snapped at the edge of the lake. Erin whipped her head in the direction of the snap. In that brief moment of distraction, Marnie prayed for courage, kicked out with her right leg and struck Erin's arm. Erin dropped the knife and went over the side of the dock, but not before grabbing Marnie's shirt and pulling Marnie over the edge with her.

They both fell through a thin layer of ice into the freezing cold lake. Marnie tried to wriggle away, but Erin held tight to her shirt. Marnie struggled to free her arm. She fought her way to the surface and gasped for air just as Erin pulled her under again. Marnie got her head above water again and freed her arm from Erin's grasp. She felt her sweatshirt clinging to her tired arms, but she managed a couple of strokes. Erin surfaced, took a deep breath, grabbed Marnie's sweatpants leg and pulled her back under the water. Marnie squirmed out of her sweatpants and kicked hard.

Marnie looked up. She saw wavy bright light all around her. She kicked and kicked, swimming and searching until all that she saw was blackness. Her lungs felt ready to burst, and as she broke the surface, Erin grabbed her foot and pulled her under again. Marnie grabbed a dock post, pulled herself up and sucked in air. Erin wrapped an arm around Marnie's neck, dunked her under and pressed down on her shoulders. Marnie's feet touched the rocky bottom of the lake, and with all of her strength, she pushed up, catching Erin under the chin with the top of her head. The force was enough for Erin to release her.

Marnie surfaced again at the end of the dock, gasping and choking. She reached for the dock, but with her sodden clothes entangling her, she didn't have the strength to pull herself up.

Two big hands grabbed Marnie under the arms and pulled her up halfway onto the dock.

Erin surfaced, lunged forward and grabbed Marnie's left ankle. Marnie kicked out with her right foot, all the while being pulled to safety by someone wearing very large, black engineer boots. Marnie rolled over onto her back and crab-crawled up the dock.

Erin scrambled up onto the dock. She stood there dripping with water, trembling and gasping. Erin reached into the leg of her ninja suit and pulled out a tiny dart gun. Marnie shouted a warning as she was pulled to her feet, and something whizzed past her ear at the same time that a shot rang out from the woods. Marnie watched as Erin fell back into the water, disappeared beneath the surface and then drifted under the ice.

Marnie shivered and turned to see the man in the engineer boots standing a few feet behind her – the same man who had pulled her from the lake. He was much taller than she had expected.

"Hi, Mr. Gregg."

Chief Mac Gregg responded with a nod.

~~~~~~~~~~~~~~~~~~~~~~~~~~

Hannah raced to the end of the dock with a blanket and towels. Danny, Carl and Tater ran behind her. Gram stood on the porch holding Dickens.

"Marnie Reilly, what the hell were you thinking?! Have you got any idea how pissed off I am right now? My sister held a gun on me. She shot a hole in the floor in the cabin to keep me inside. I swear to God that she would have shot me!" Danny knelt down on the dock, toweled her off and wrapped her in a blanket.

"Damn straight! We needed to find Tom," Hannah retorted with a frown.

"Where's Tom? Is Tom safe?" Marnie pleaded for an answer.

"He's in the cabin. He's gonna be fine." Danny rubbed water from her hair with a towel.

"Daniel, you're going to rub that poor girl's hair right out of her head. We should get her inside. She's trembling, and her lips are blue."

Danny glanced up. "Yeah. Thanks for pulling her out of the lake, Dad."

Chief Gregg replied with a nod and a shrug. "I arrived and heard a commotion in the lake. I walked down to the dock and saw your young lady struggling. I gave her a hand, that's all."

Danny helped up Marnie, and they all headed up the path to the cabin.

Patrick walked out of the woods with a sniper rifle slung over his shoulder. "Uh, Detective Gregg, sorry to interrupt. My dive team is going to want to get in here in the morning to recover the body. I reckon that she's going to get stuck in the weeds over there in the bay."

They all stopped. Eyebrows raised. Jaws dropped. Shock – not fear.

Patrick pulled out his badge and held it up. "Special Agent Patrick Kowalski. DEA. William's partner."

Carl threw his head back and laughed. "I cannot believe that you were investigating me! Really, Patrick. Did you honestly think…"

Patrick cut him off and waggled his hand at him. "You wavered on the side of dodgy, Carl. Sorry. I did figure it out pretty quickly. I knew that you weren't involved, and I also knew that Alice and Allen hadn't a clue." Patrick grinned.

"Speaking of Allen… Patrick, were you the one who bailed him out?" Danny asked.

Patrick looked confused and shook his head.

"No, that was me," Marnie confessed, raising her hand.

"You?" Danny gulped.

"We knew that he hadn't done anything wrong *really*." Marnie shrugged a shoulder and winked.

"No, he didn't. I felt kind of bad for him," Danny replied. "Tom, maybe you can talk to Judge Lawrence for him."

"No problem. Then again, maybe we should send Tony Tartello over instead," Tom joked.

"Oh, and I do want to apologize for Sam bothering you, Marnie. He had access to a phone so that I could trace his calls and keep an eye on Erin and Kate. I really wasn't sure which one I needed to be more concerned about. I'm really sorry about that." Patrick stood, went to the fire and took a sip of beer from a bottle.

"That's okay, but when did you figure out it was Erin?" Marnie asked.

"At the same time you did. Out on the dock. She changed her voice every time she spoke to him. I never knew who he was speaking with, and he never called her by name. Today at the parade, I knew that something was going to happen, but I didn't know what. If I had known, I would have warned all of you. After the smoke cleared, I found a small detonator under the burning hay bales. It could have been much worse."

"'Fire and Ice'… That poem has never been a favorite." Marnie stared into the fire and shivered. She pushed herself up, tucked a leg beneath her and leaned forward. "It's a bit morbid, but I keep thinking about something. I find it strange that Erin tattooed William, Justin and Reuben with the Eye of Providence – a symbol of divine protection – and then killed them. Albeit, she didn't realize that it's a symbol of protection. Even so, how's that for irony?"

"Irony? I call it sick and twisted, Marn," Tom shot back with a visible tremble. "She had a gun on us when we got into the van. I don't know how she did it, but as soon as I shoved Hannah out the door, she jabbed me with a needle and knocked me out. She must have stopped along the way because, when we got here, there was tape over my mouth and my hands were zip-tied behind my back. She couldn't have given me much midazolam, though, because I was coming to by the time that we arrived at the garage. I tried to get away from her – I was just too groggy. Anyway, she zip-tied my ankles together when we got into the garage. I just keep thinkin' that she could have branded me, too. I'm really glad that she didn't, but she could have."

"We are so happy that she didn't burn your handsome face, Tom. We were worried sick about you. Your father and I… well, let's just say that we said a few prayers, and we are forever grateful that they were answered." Eyes teary, Abigeal Keller kissed her son gently on the cheek.

"I'm pleased that she didn't hurt you, too – only because I don't want to hear you complain for the next month," Marnie teased. "Be grateful that she was in a hurry. She needed to get down to the lake for her rendezvous with me." Marnie sipped her wine thoughtfully. "Does anyone else wonder how she got Justin up onto the garage door by herself? I don't see Reuben helping her with that. She said that he did. I don't know. I want to believe that he wasn't that bad. I guess that we'll never know." Marnie shrugged and took another sip of wine.

Carl and Danny exchanged glances. They knew that Reuben had helped, but Marnie could see Reuben's potential and just couldn't believe it.

"Hey, Marnie? Why was the spotlight so important? Why did you need me to check the light?" Danny asked.

"Because I knew that I was going to end up in the lake when all of this came down. I had a hunch. No! I *saw* that I was cold and wet. I didn't know how much ice was going to be on the lake, but I wanted to know that the light was working."

Danny pulled a face. "Why?"

"My dad taught me that, if I was to ever fall through the ice, I shouldn't swim to the light. He taught me to swim toward the darkness because that's the way out. The light fools you – it's where the ice is the brightest because it's reflecting the light. The darkness is where it's safe."

"Huh." Danny shrugged. "I didn't know that. I always think of the light as being good."

"It often is, but sometimes you have to swim through the darkness to get to the light." Marnie gazed off into the fire, a faraway look in her aquamarine eyes.

Tom leaned forward on the couch and tapped the toe of Patrick's boot with his knuckle. "I gotta tell you, Patrick. You had us all fooled. The act at Marnie's office, the cemetery, the stutter... It was perfect. We were all convinced."

"Okay, first of all, my friends call me Trick – for good reason. I'm the guy who is sent in to blend into the background – to trick everybody. The stutter is real. I've had it since I was a kid. It comes back when I don't know people or when I lie. It's a nervous stutter, and the backstory that Carl gave you is very much real. I didn't have everyone fooled, did I Marnie?" Patrick turned and winked at Marnie.

Mouth agape, Danny turned to Marnie. Anger flashed in his steely blue eyes.

"Hang on! I did have my suspicions when Hannah and I caught you in my house. I saw a bit of defiance in you that day, but I wasn't sure. It wasn't until you rolled me off the trailer that I knew. Carl said that you had been burned in a house fire as a child, but you went into the flames anyway to save me. I knew that there was something going on." Marnie smiled. "Plus, there's the fact that I'm clairvoyant, and I kept getting visions of you with a badge."

"Why didn't you tell me?" Danny asked, a spark of hurt in his voice.

"I tried. You told me that you didn't want to talk about my parents. Remember?" Marnie said, poking him gently with her toe.

Danny thought back and remembered that moment by the bathtub. "Yup. I remember."

"I knew! Not about Patrick, but the other stuff! Marnie told me everything!" Hannah stuck up her hand. "That's why I shot the hole in the floor. I wanted you to know that I was serious, Daniel. I would have done anything to keep you inside. I didn't want that psycho Erin to kill Tom."

"That's why I pushed you out of the truck," Tom said, nudging Hannah's hand with his own. "The thought of your pretty face being branded like Kate's..." Tom shivered.

"Pretty?" Hannah asked, a smile spreading across her face.

Tom nodded. "Yeah."

Danny, Marnie and Gram all exchanged glances and grins.

Tom cleared his throat. "Uh, Marnie, how did you know where I was?"

Hannah frowned and added, "Yeah. I didn't hear Erin mention where she was hiding Tom, and I could hear everything that both of you were saying."

Marnie grinned, and her eyes twinkled. "She didn't have to say it."

"She thought it, Hannah," Gram added.

"What?" Hannah replied. "Thought it? Oh, you two are going on about hoodoo voodoo stuff again, aren't you?"

"Hannah, I knew where Tom was the same way that I know that your mother used to sing you and Danny "Galway Bay" every night before you went to sleep. The same way that I know that you still hear that song when you have trouble sleeping. The same way that I know that Danny hears it and your father hears it. You hear it because she *is* singing it to you. You just have to listen, believe and trust. She's always right there beyond the veil."

~~~~~~~~~~~~~~~~~~~~~~~~~~

As Danny fell asleep that night with Marnie's head resting easy on his chest, he smiled. The cycle of three was complete. He closed his – but just for a second. He recounted the events of the last few hours. One, Tom's parents' fender bender; two, the incident on the float; three, Erin kidnapping Tom and Hannah. That was three, and a new cycle started. One, Erin attacking Marnie… *Shit!*

-CHAPTER SIXTY-ONE-

December 24th - Christmas Eve

Christmas Eve was Marnie's favorite night of the year. It always held a certain magic for her. She was busy in the kitchen baking meat pies and whipping up hard sauce for the plum pudding that Gram was bringing for dessert. She'd streamed Christmas music from her iPad to the speakers around the cabin and sang along with Perry Como. Tater and Dickens were out for a walk with Danny and his dad, and Hannah was upstairs choosing an outfit to impress Tom.

There would be twelve for dinner this Christmas Eve and twelve for Christmas Day. Allen and Alice were joining them tonight, and then the two would be having a quiet Christmas Day at Alice's. Aunt Janet and Uncle Giles had plans tonight, but would join them tomorrow for Christmas dinner. Marnie's excitement for everyone to arrive was becoming a bit too much.

Danny and his father returned with Tater and Dickens.

"Hey, Marnie! You got your wish! It's snowing!" Danny called out from the living room.

Marnie stepped to the windows at the back of the kitchen and hopped up and down.

"I love the snow, and it makes Christmas, well, Christmas."

Tater and Dickens raced into the kitchen and sat at the window. They watched a squirrel family race from pine tree to pine tree and run up the trunk of an old hickory. Danny and his father came into the kitchen and plopped down on barstools.

"Something smells great, Marnie. What are you baking?" Mr. Gregg asked.

"Meat pies. I hope that you like them," Marnie replied. "It's one of my favorite Christmas season dinners."

"If they have meat in them, I'll like them. Marnie, call me Mac. Mr. Gregg is too formal."

"Thanks, Mac. Well, it does have meat in it. Three kinds, in fact." Marnie grinned.

"What time is everyone arriving?" Danny asked.

"Um," Marnie said checking her watch, "Should be any minute. I told everyone three o'clock. Hannah and I covered the pool table, and there are munchies set out there. We've got mulled wine and cider steeping in the Crock-Pots. We also have a full bar and wine and eggnog in the fridge. We should be ready for an army." Marnie laughed.

"That's what I like to hear, Daniel – a woman who takes charge." Mac slapped his son on the back.

Danny winked at Marnie. "She's pretty bossy, too."

Hannah ran around the corner from the stairs and into the kitchen. "Okay, does this look good?" She twirled for inspection of a pair of black tights, long polished black boots and a knee-length, Christmas-red sweater dress. Her hair hung loose in waves around her pretty face.

"You look perfect, Hannah." Marnie nodded.

They heard a knock, and Tom called out. "Hey, the Kellers are here!"

"C'mon in!" Danny called back.

~~~~~~~~~~~~~~~~~~~~~~~~~

They gathered in the living room by the fire. Patrick and Carl arrived together, Alice and Allen followed. Gram arrived a little late because the diner was busier than usual.

"I'm sorry for being late, love," Gram said. Marnie took a basket and a stack of packages out of her arms, and Danny helped her out of her coat.

"Okay, everyone, have a seat, please. I have to give out a few presents now because, if I don't, there's going to be a problem. Everyone sit!" Marnie hopped around with excitement, and she turned and dashed upstairs.

"What is she up to?" Gram asked Danny.

He held up his hands and shrugged. "I have no idea."

Marnie appeared at the top of the stairs holding a puppy. Danny met her halfway and took the pup.

"Marnie, what are you doing?" Danny laughed.

Marnie giggled. "You take him. I'll be right back!" Marnie raced back up the stairs.

Danny stood at the bottom of the steps with a squirming terrier in his arms. Gram took the pup from Danny and cuddled him.

"Oh, aren't you a lovely wee lad," Gram said, turning the pup over to make sure that he was, in fact, a *he*.

Marnie returned, and at the top of the stairs, she called, "Come."

Three dogs raced down the hall and down the stairs. Tater and Dickens ran out from under the pool table, and they all rolled and tumbled across the floor.

Marnie knelt down on the rug and called a black Lab puppy to her. She picked it up and handed it to Tom.

"Merry Christmas, Tom!"

"You got me a puppy?" Tom's face lit up, and he jumped up off the couch. "What's his name?"

"Ellie called him Shadow, but you can call him whatever you like." Marnie twisted around.

"Good, Gram. You have your puppy. Ellie called him Jack. He's a Westie-Jack Russell cross."

"Oh, Marnie, he's lovely!" Gram beamed.

Hannah was on the floor, sitting next to Marnie and patting a large Belgian Shepherd puppy.

"You're beautiful," she said.

Marnie laughed. "I'm glad that you think so. She's yours. Ellie called her Sophie."

"Oh! Really!" Hannah threw her arms around Marnie and hugged her. "I've been wanting a dog ever since I saw you with Tater!"

Marnie turned around to see where Danny had gotten to. He was on the floor next to Hannah. A blue merle Australian Shepherd pup was in his lap.

"That's Maggie." Marnie beamed.

"She's for me, isn't she?" Danny asked, ruffling Maggie's fur.

"Yup! She's for you." Marnie sat on the floor and tossed a tennis ball for Tater. A cacophony of toenails clattered across the floor in pursuit of a lone tennis ball.

"Ellie has a few more rescue pups at her place who need homes. Everyone else gets a rescue puppy gift certificate to pick out their own. That's if you want one, of course. Except Declan and Abigeal. They travel a lot!" Marnie giggled.

Abigeal looked relieved. "I was worried there for a minute, Marnie."

Tom leaned across the coffee table. "Hey, Marnie. This was on the porch when we came in," Tom said handing Marnie a package.

"What a beautiful package!" Marnie said. "Should I open it?"

Danny nudged her and nodded. "Yeah. Go ahead."

Marnie unwrapped the package carefully, pulled away a piece of tissue paper and revealed the *Collected Poems of Robert Frost*. There was no card. She frowned and opened the book. Written on the flyleaf was a message.

"What's it say? Who's it from?" Danny asked, scooting closer to her. Marnie looked up. Her face gave it away – fear and shock.

"Danny, when are they transferring Sam to Bayview?" Marnie asked, eyebrows raised. She held the book out for everyone to read.

Merry Christmas, Marnie.
Enjoy it. It's the last one that you'll ever have.
Love, Sam

Danny stared at Marnie and counted two in his head. *One to go.*

-The End-

400

ACKNOWLEDGEMENTS

To Harper, I greatly appreciate your patience when I disappear into my office to write about murder and mayhem. Thank you for the cups of tea, for proofreading pages, for being my sounding board, for advising on mental health and veteran questions, and for being by side through this crazy adventure. I love you more than pizza.

To Dougal, Callee, Midget and Mags, thanks for the visits, cuddles and walks to keep your crazy dog mom sane.

To Jane Hackett Backus, Laurie Lashomb, Karen Harper-Peck and Wendy Flood for proofreading my first draft. Your insight, edits, questions and support help me be a better storyteller.

Karen Harper-Peck, thank you for your expert advice on ways to commit murder.

To Nicole Ballingal, your cover design rocks! Thank you for being the inspiration for Divine Guidance being put on paper, and for always being honest. Dr. Ellie Nikol is an homage to you.

To Jane Hackett Backus, thank for proofreading, giving development advice and copyediting my first draft. Your guidance is golden. I love that you are still my teacher after all of these years. Mrs. Backus's bookstore will be a much busier place in the future.

To Laurie Lashomb, thanks for being on the other end of Messenger to answer my incessant questions. You are my soul sister – even though you drink lolly water.

To Janet E. Adams, thank you for allowing me to borrow Eli, Barley, Chicken and Dewey.

To Russ Ceccola, thanks so much for editing Torn Veil. I literally hate "that" and commas.

To Mom (Gram), thank you for giving me the gift of books, for not bridling my wild imagination and for encouraging my love of writing and my thirst for knowledge. "Go get the dictionary" and "Go get the encyclopedia" are emblazoned on my brain forever!

To Dad, thank for the gift of story time with Uncle Zeke. You taught me to be a storyteller.

To Wendy and Lori, thank you for reading to me when we were little. *There's a Mouse in Our House* and *Inside, Outside, Upside Down* run through my memory often. Thanks also for our childhood games of make-believe - which no doubt have inspired a few passages.

To all of the dogs I've loved before, Tater and Dickens are for you.

Shari T. Mitchell grew up and was educated in Northern New York State. Shari's true passion is writing. Her 30+ years of strategic marketing have helped her put pen to paper and focus on her creative endeavors.

Shari loves creating multidimensional characters with whom her readers can relate. Crafting the mystery is her favorite bit – plotting the twists and turns of a murder mystery is addictive.

She shares her home in North Carolina with her partner in crime, Harper, and their crazy rescue dogs, Dougal, Callee, Midget and Mags.

Shari's favorite authors include Robert Frost, Agatha Christie, Mary Higgins Clark, Ruth Rendell, Michael Connelly, Jonathan Kellerman, David Baldacci, Louise Penny, Kathy Reichs, Patricia Cornwell and Michael Koryta.

She loves cooking, hiking, gardening, reading and writing.

Divine Guidance, the prequel to Torn Veil, was published in 2015, and is available on Amazon.

CPSIA information can be obtained
at www.ICGtesting.com
Printed in the USA
LVHW091159051120
670807LV00005B/261